In Good Company

In Good Company

A Novel

Matthew "Pete" Lester

Started 4 July 2021
Finished 19 April 2025

Burning Bulb
PUBLISHING

In Good Company
By **Matthew "Pete" Lester**

Burning Bulb Publishing
P.O. Box 4721
Bridgeport, WV 26330-4721
United States of America
www.BurningBulbPublishing.com

Cover designed by Gary Lee Vincent with additional artwork by Pete Lester.

First Edition.

Paperback Edition ISBN: 978-1-964172-39-2

Printed in the United States of America.

Dedication

Inspiration to write and reflect on my adventures came from my wonderful family, Debra Lester, Drew Lester, and Carson Lester. Special thanks to my parents, Donna Lester, and Larry Lester. This is for all of you. I love you and look forward to a lifetime of memories and laughs and more fishing. I would like to give special thanks to my brother-in-law Charlie Turner, a Marine, who married Angela, my terrific sister.

The memorable 2013 cross-country drive with my father, Larry Lester, became a time of reflection and added settings and places inside the story *In Good Company.* I am certain this novel would not exist without that trip and yet proves how reflection and recall adds more depth and width to life experiences as well as literature. We witnessed the backdrop of the Wasatch Mountains of northern Utah, then we trailed across scenic Highway 80 through Wyoming, crossed the Continental Divide, and took the southerly route through the Rockies of Colorado; and one memorable day in Raton, New Mexico, my father traded hats with a young kid at the state line for a photograph; still, we laugh about it. Next stop, the much-anticipated Cadillac Ranch, located in the Northern Panhandle of Texas, ten miles west of downtown Amarillo, Texas. Congratulations to my mother, Donna, for buying her first Cadillac. A big hug and much love for you all. Next, Dad and I satisfied our hunger and claimed mouth-watering steaks at the world-famous Big Texan Restaurant, located in Amarillo, Texas. We feasted in Texas on 4 July 2013, but rested that night in Elk City, Oklahoma. The following day, we headed to Oklahoma City, Oklahoma, Little Rock, Arkansas, and made it to Nashville, Tennessee, where we were lost near the airport. I called my wife, Debra, and we found our hotel. The following day, we beelined the Dodge truck to Troutman, North Carolina. Home. For me, the most memorable time of the trip was spent in awe of Amarillo, Texas, a true Texas restaurant and the major reason the city was included in this book.

Table of Contents

Foreword #1
by Holland Webb

The year was 1988, and I was 11 years old when I first heard a Vietnam veteran open up about his experiences at war. Although the men who had fought in Vietnam were still young when I was a kid, the subject was still either too painful or too controversial to merit a mention in polite conversation.

Even in fiction, Vietnam struggled for traction. Sylvester Stallone's *Rambo* franchise, Tom Selleck's *Magnum PI*, and a few dozen made-for-TV movies dominated the Vietnam narrative. Eventually, the war seemed to get skipped over in favor of World War II narratives and revivals of 1980s and 1990s family-life comedies.

Against this background, Pete Lester has created *In Good Company*, a story that takes readers from a POW camp in Vietnam through the mountains of West Virginia to Texas and even Europe in a sweeping search for friendship, healing, and significance.

Readers of Pete's other novels will meet old friends in the pages of this book, along with a whole new cast of characters, locations, and themes. Most importantly, however, they will glimpse inside the minds and hearts of the men who braved the conflict in Vietnam and rebuilt their lives — serving as bridges to a future of prosperity and challenge.

Army Specialist Steven Bailey (the Author's Father-in-Law).
Steven was the millionth soldier to process from Hawaii to Vietnam
and served from 1968-1969.

Foreword #2
by Solon Tsangaras

I read a lot. Not only because I enjoy reading, but I am also a proofreader, which has me reading outside my 'comfort zone.' I gravitate toward horror, mystery, and crime mostly, so when I was given Pete Lester's book *Sunday Rain*, a western novel, I was exploring a very different genre. By the end of that novel, I could not wait to read Mr. Lester's next novel, and I was not disappointed!

In Good Company, Pete Lester's novel about Vietnam POWs and their lives after being freed, was a flashback to the '60s for me. *Sunday Rain*, with its incredibly descriptive language and situations, had my imagination drawn into the Western world and life in the 1860s. I could 'feel' the atmosphere of the trek across the country, experiencing the hardships of the individual characters and eagerly looking forward to the next page and the next page! 'In Good Company' sparked memories of growing up in the time of the Vietnam War, watching Walter Cronkite on CBS news, and seeing actual protests against the war. As I mentioned earlier, I actually lived through the era of 'In Good Company', which was an incredible flashback of that time for me.

In Mr. Lester's latest novel, you are thrust into the cruel hardships of prisoners in a Vietnamese POW camp. The language used to describe their treatment by the guards, how they got to know each other, and subsequently, having their lives intertwined after being rescued from their confinement, makes the reader a part of the story, rather than just a casual observer. The reader is taken on a life's journey of how these brave men, who survived unimaginable brutality, dealt with life after war. The reader is drawn into their world, almost to the point where one would talk to the book and try to offer advice to the characters!

Pete Lester masterfully uses very descriptive language, precise dialogue for that generation, and situations that have the reader experiencing the characters' lives rather than just reading about them. Yes, there were some parts that a hard-nosed old man like myself actually got misty, and I'm not too proud to admit this.

I will not give away any plot points or be a hated spoiler, so let me just say that *In Good Company* is a great book with the possibility of a series of sequels. If Pete Lester ever decides to write a screenplay, it would make an incredible motion picture.

I am looking forward, once again, to another novel by Pete Lester.

To The Reader
by Michael J. Bisbano

Once again, as in all of your novels, I was drawn in by the first chapter and remained captive until the very end.

Your uncanny ability to expand the story and introduce characters amazes me!

Yes, there is a great surprise ending, but throughout the book, one encounters many surprises in the life of Beau.

I felt excitement, joy, sadness, and ambivalence for the characters, to mention a few emotions.

Congratulations on another job well done.

Yours truly,
Michael J. Bisbano, Sr.
Seabees, MCB-1
1972 - 1974

Acknowledgments

The creation of this fictional novel happened because of dedication and imagination, where ideas became a fine story for publication. This ancient craft of storytelling was expanded from campfires to all cultures, thoughts penned to pages, a simple method that held its ground in an evolving age of literature. Works by this author are found online and in person. Through connections in New York, Nashville, London, England, and Cody, Wyoming, Pete's novels have recently landed him in the Western Writers Hall of Fame.

I thank my sons, Drew Lester, and Carson Lester, for their support while I write. Special thanks to my loving wife, Dr. Debra Lester, for her encouragement while I write and research on weekends. I say a good hobby (painting and writing) is even better than television.

My great friend, and nationally known writer, Holland Webb, kept the manuscript leaning forward. Additionally, I'm grateful for the team at Burning Bulb Publishing. I tip my hat to CEO and Film Director, Gary Vincent, and editor, Solon Tsangaras, an outstanding team who promote and publish great books. Hugs and handshakes to my friends across the country and to those who offer encouragement in my writing and painting career. I give special thanks to the crew at Western Writers of America, in Nashville, Tennessee, and to the gang at the Buffalo Bill Center for the West McCracken Research

Library, in Cody, Wyoming, for the recent induction of *Saddles of Barringer* (a modern-day western novel under the pen Tennessee Gunns) and the induction of traditional western *Sunday Rain* into the Western Writers Hall of Fame. My journey has been incredibly blessed with lifelong friendships and a host of encouragement.

Inspiration

Amid the 2021 pandemic, Pete outlined *In Good Company* after listening to music from legendary artists from the 1970s: Joan Baez, Dave Loggins, Neil Young, James Taylor, and many others. After a visit to Richard's Coffee Shop, a well-known military museum located in Mooresville, North Carolina, the book was planned. Pete heard stories from Vietnam Veterans, like Specialist Steven "Beetle" Bailey (known as the One-Millionth soldier to process from Hawaii to Vietnam), who eagerly shared his experiences, of which, in part, sparked characters for this novel. Special thanks go to Allan Stiltner, President of the Wyoming County Board of Education, in Baileysville, West Virginia, who also served in a Mobile Riverine Force in Vietnam. Mixed with geography and drama, this story was meant to brand hearts about Vietnam, while better understanding how civil unrest impacted people, even today. This story is dedicated to those who served in Vietnam, from 1 November 1955 - 30 April 1975.

In part, Pete's cross-country trip with his father, Larry Lester, in July 2013, which began in Utah, and turned to the Colorado Rockies, then onto the Cadillac Ranch in Amarillo, Texas (on his father's 63rd birthday, 4 July), sparked ideas for Part II. On Independence Day at Grenville, New Mexico, the landscape was covered with a pure-white layer of hail from a hard storm. Later, Pete and his father stopped to paint cars at the famous Cadillac

Ranch, alongside Historic Route 66, outside Amarillo, Texas. The Cadillac Ranch art exhibit has been a major attraction for more than five decades. The automobile artwork was created by a group called the "Ant Farm" in 1974, and has been visited by millions of people.

Pete Lester has been known to use the pen name Tennessee Gunns. His work   implores multiple generations through the genre of Southern Fiction and Western novels. Pete's mission is to keep alive the dreams of explorers and "Soul Searchers" through good storytelling, challenging curious minds with humor and figurative imagery.

The idea for *In Good Company* was born to broaden journalism and express freedom in literature, pushing for more creativity from artists and novelists. This book hopes to inspire more talented writers to join the movement of uncapping expression through the revival of visual and liberal arts. His work has inspired the rise of past masters, new and old, and opened doors for more creativity, both in business, and in the art world. Pete coined the concept of "Emotional Intelligence within Literature," developing novels from the depth of human conditions and real-life experiences, living it, where actions and dialogue unlock memory banks. This idea employs writers to craft storytelling and figurative language, for the ages and for self-reflection.

In a post-modern world, readers drift in a time of crowded content, more so than ever before, and use social media to draw large crowds who appreciate the genius of storytelling and good entertainment. The use of descriptive language related to cultural themes rings true when connected to historic events; still, the reader can experience emotional recall and express dialogue, reflecting on timeless moments - of war, of love, and of special events. Exceptional novels ring the bell of literary expression and reflect the heart of the human condition.

In the novel *In Good Company,* the author reminds the reader of an unforgettable era in American history, crafting events with fictional characters. Here, the author lands his footprint in "Contemporary American Literature," by spinning audacious chapters and painting images through memorable dialogue. In 2017, Pete stepped into the world of Southern Fiction as a popular novelist and international painter. In 2022, a man from London called, and challenged Pete to write a Western Fiction novel. Known for his big imagination, he penned an exceptional story, *Sunday Rain.* People speak of his strong characters, hitting the hearts of readers, years later.

Here's a reminder of some strong characters from novels: From *The Tobacco Barn,* Mickey Starr, Nedra Starr, Volt Hendricks, and Tipp Starr; and from *Saddles of Barringer*, Ringo Bare, Clem Cline, and Doc Greenway. In *When Geese Fly South*, readers latch onto Weston Laramie, Sorano Tanaka, and Jason Laramie. In his traditional Western novel *Sunday Rain*, readers uncover unforgettable characters, like Chas Bellew, Jackie Ray Monroe, Sunshine Frenchie, and Atohi.

Within Pete Lester's novels, the juxtaposition of human condition and depth of emotion are admired by educators and authors; his ability to descend and ascend the underdog is a noteworthy trademark that few writers hit. His work harnesses the tug of war between characters, even from the beginning, especially when readers turn the pages in *The Tobacco Barn* and *Saddles of Barringer.*

For the purpose of teaching young writers, Pete Lester was the first to create the "Cast and Reel Model." His model is obviously a fishing term. However, in literature, Pete's "Cast and Reel Model" simplifies the art of story character advancement, by propelling the protagonist into a complex situation, a tight spot, so to speak. He naturally "Casts and Reels" the main character through the stages of Exposition, Rising Action, Climax, Rising Action, and Resolution. This Model builds the plot and storyline. In terms of writing, the "Cast and Reel Model" will soon simplify the overview of storytelling for students.

Soon educators and students will adopt Pete Lester's "Cast and Reel Model" for storytelling in the classroom. The apex of the "Cast" examines internal and external struggles, maturation, hope building hope, determination, while "Reeling" deals with Coping, Resolution, and Resilience - the keeper.

In part, the conviction in Neil Young's voice influenced this novel. In 2021 when Pete heard the song *Old Man* (released in 1972), the lyrics inspired him to write his fifth novel, *In Good Company*. His goal consisted of linking Vietnam with the brazen trail of the Cadillac Ranch in Amarillo, Texas, along with saluting the iconic New River Gorge Bridge, and to show how war, music, politics, and art transformed society. The super-decade of the 1970s remains as a giant footprint in social and cultural themes, still today, in composition, and with marking creativity.

From his first novel, readers have explored archetypal literary criticism, meant as a sacrament of "Threading Mentors and Morals" into an ever changing multi-cultural society, and where ethical behavior, such as the "Cast and Reel Model" was used in each book.

Like the influential spike of the Ant Farm with the Cadillac Ranch art exhibit, so did the musical expression exceed its mark at the Woodstock Music and Art Festival, building culture through entertainment and talented expression. The same brilliant themes and practices continue to seed music, art, and literature; still today, such as with this novel. Pete uses literature (liberal arts) and world events to reflect on a time period for good storytelling. This novel was spun from the most talked about generation of the 20th Century - the dynamic decade of the 1970s, and built on memorable and real-to-life characters, making the book an admirable novel in a post-modern society.

Much like real-life, Pete Lester's characters are driven by adventure. The "Cast and Reel Model" in this book throws the main character across geography and history, where the protagonist is propelled by socioeconomics, emotions, war, and relationships. This novel targets the idea of "Soul Searchers" and self-discovery, unraveling one's true-self through cultural changes. *In Good Company* was written as a celebration of expression, using pop-culture, love, and adventure. For example, the protagonist in this novel, Beau Le Mans, struggled with life, death, love, desire, social stressors, hope, preservation and influence.

Several towns in this book are actual places and names. Steven "Beetle" Bailey spent time in the U.S. Army (1968-1969) during Vietnam. Interviews were collected and with much curiosity: the good and bad of war were collected. Thousands of soldiers, sailors, and Marines did not return to tell their side of the story, in part, so this novel was written as a dedication to those who served and gave the ultimate sacrifice for their country.

Mainly, this book was written to pay tribute to the 58,220 soldiers lost in the Vietnam War, honoring their memory and service to America.

During Vietnam, social expression and iconic cultural themes unknowing impacted generations, and still films, novels, and books improve memory loss through emotional storytelling. For this reason, Pete Lester uses the phrase "Emotional History" in this acknowledgement. This book is meant to do the same, where art and music tap into human emotions and improve memory-thought processes, reflecting on a half century of transformation in America. The "Cast and Reel Model" brings untold stories to the printed page. The goal here is to construct a novel from actual perspectives, to keep alive untold stories, impact thought processes, and to teach the art of creative writing, using iconic moments in history.

Simple lyrics from Neil Young, such as "I'm a lot like you were" resonates the power of how past events improve memory loss, causing reflection and self-examination. Elements such as art and music have proven to stimulate the mind and spark conversations about past events while changing quality of life, so play *Old Man* again, Neil Young.

This book is a work of fiction. Names, characters, places, and incidents are products of the author's imagination or are used fictitiously. Any resemblance to actual events or locales or persons, living or dead, is entirely coincidental, but some could have happened.

Background

Amid Vietnam, Army photojournalist Beau Le Mans, is a far-wandering soldier, skin and bone, and held captive as a prisoner of war. He often imagines himself home again, climbing the majestic mountains of West Virginia, far away from war. For Beau, he knew himself best afoot, submitting to the grand vision of country roads, and standing atop the peaks of the Blue Ridge Mountains. The colors of autumn, coolness of streams, and family kept him motivated while absent from the mountains. Natural things, like faces, he saw in the bark of bamboo, perfectly curved faces, the way the wood held them landed his mind homeward. A handful of hopeful thoughts kept him going each day and he wanted to find that special someone. What would it take to bring him home again?

He wanted to climb the rocks in the Palo Duro Canyon, a state park in Texas, and in time, thoughts of writing became his mission. Beau battled amid the cruel chess world of war and he wanted to expose the reality of Vietnam in the *Army Times*.

In Good Company is a riveting fictional war story and a post-war adventure for a young man from war to love. Vietnam stories from "Boots on the Ground" soldiers, like Steven "Beetle" Bailey, Allan Stiltner, and others inspired this novel. Stories from veterans at coffee shops, church meetings, and at the Veteran's Hospital provided insights about post-war issues.

"In my mind, for me, the war never ends," said one soldier at the Veterans Hospital, in Hickory, North Carolina.

This fictional novel turns back the clock to a time of turmoil and brokenness in the world, where Americans marched and protested against the war. For some soldiers, a long life struggle of PTSD, alcoholism, and drug abuse followed. Some found the G.I. Bill to propel their careers, while evidence shows, some soldiers and sailors failed to recover from Vietnam.

This fictional story is packed with multilayered characters and crafted images, found here, matched with *Sunday Rain*, *Saddles of Barringer*, and *When Geese Fly South*, may be the most real-to-life masculine composite of Pete's literary works; for culture; for the ages and for classroom reflection. Written for generations to ponder, this story has a lasting impact; written for those who love the greatest era - the 1970s, and how people coped with war. Pete's "poetic rhythmic style" ascended his novels into the public eye about eight years ago, and his style compares to Charles Frazier, William Faulkner, and Louis L'Amour. His radio interviews during Covid were with Disc Jockeys from Toronto and New York City, and he was recruited by publishers in London, and Texas. Several public school systems in West Virginia, and North Carolina, have been known to use Pete's books in the classroom. Internationally, his work caught the eye of readers in Honduras, London, Canada, and South Africa. Pete's novels craft meaningful dialogue, adding readership through compelling narrative and drawing readership into the vital, yet subtle "Moral Thread" of literature. In a short span, his work has spun across various genres, from drama, adventure, and Western novels.

Pete has written four timeless novels in six years, from his initial stamp of a coastal romance in *The Tobacco Barn*, triumphs of fatherly love in *Saddles of Barringer*, and the projected classic Shenandoah Valley love story with *When Geese Fly South*. His second Western novel, *Sunday Rain*, made a splash in the Great West.

In 2023, Pete switched gears from Southern Fiction to Western novels, penning the winner, *Sunday Rain*, a post-Civil War odyssey, set in 1871. Here again, readers anticipate *In Good Company*, a dramatic wartime novel to land a lasting footprint in literature.

U.S. Navy Radarman Third Class Allan R. Stiltner, 1968,
The Mobile Riverine Force (MRF) in the Mekong Delta,
Don Tam, Vietnam.

Here Comes the Sun

Vietnam Poem
by
Pete Lester

. . . and I see the ones at war, the unsure faces, the strangers, the naive, the youth, men of every race, enlisted, from unknown towns and proud places, eagerly trained, and ready, for each one, here comes the sun.

. . . and I see the ships at war, the serious faces, close friends, the artful, the educated, men of every race, sailors from unknown towns and proud places, bags packed, minds ready, for each one, here comes the sun.

. . . and I see the planes at war, helicopters, too, goggles on faces, the driven, the proficient, the practiced, men of every race, pilots from unknown towns and proud places, cockpit and canopy, the flying aces, for each one, here comes the sun.

. . . and I see soldiers, sailors, Marines, painted faces, brothers in arms, the prideful, the motivated, men of every race, from unknown towns and proud places, inflight, marching, and adrift, for each one, here comes the sun.

. . . and I see the fighters at war, the crying faces, the brave, the seasoned, the carried, men and women of every race, Americans from little towns and wonderful places; standing for freedom and liberty, for each one, here comes the sun.

. . . and I see all of them, every brave face, served and died; for the sake of humanity, men and women of every race, color, and creed; those who served, now heard and known; for each one, here comes the sun.

. . . and I see the red, white, and blue; for those who lived; for those who died; the unsung heroes; a candle burns bright, for each one, here comes the sun.

—Written on 30 October 2022.

- This poem was published by the Western North Carolina Veteran's Art and Writing Festival, 1 September 2023.

PART I

CHAPTER ONE

↔

The Other Side of War

"All I wanted was a 1966 Chevelle. Instead, I joined the Army and carried away a lifetime of stories. The Lord above has a mysterious way about Him, and somehow, I found the open door from Vietnam."

—Beau Le Mans, 1969

↔

Le Mans marked 367 days as a POW.
"Henderson, get down, man, before you get us killed."

Flowery bamboo surrounded the smoky Vietnam camp and a gloomy canopy of evergreen blanketed the hazy land. Inside, a grand vision of escape became the only way of survival for Beau Le Mans, and he knew dodging guard dogs and the Viet-Cong was nearly impossible. Prisoners had soaked up the worst of life, the mud, the muck, beatings, and lived like soup sandwiches. As long as the sun shined, a flame of hope burned, and for Le Mans, the leader in the POW camp, was known to feel the warmth of tomorrow's freedom. Each night he shivered, flat atop a wooden-framed bunk, and thought of home. His only company was an army of ants beneath him, and beside him, a soldier from

Robin's Egg, Texas, Henderson, and two Vietnamese brothers, Cadeo, and Hien, arms deformed, and unable to fight for their own country.

"The other side of war, guys," said Le Mans smiling, "is freedom."

"Will we live to see the other side," Henderson asked, "or will we be caught in the crosshairs of this side?"

"I refuse to die an easy death, soldiers." Le Mans told them.

No one heard the low voice of Le Mans that night.

Unsure of the month or even the day of the week, his thoughts still pounded steadily with a desire to be somewhere else and tears rolled down his dusty cheeks with an infinite hope of returning to the mountains; Baileysville, West Virginia, his home. What was spoken of more than anything, thoughts of home, not just from Beau Le Mans, but from all his POW friends. He knew the year was 1969. The war played on, like a cruel chess match, back and forth, but who was winning? Did anyone know, or was it more about pride and the untold stories that lived behind enemy lines?

We've all lost something in this fight, thought Le Mans, something we can't get back or give away - we can't be ourselves anymore, who we were, who we are, down deep, and he knew the bite of being devoid of liberty. Or who God made him to be, he wasn't able to find his purpose, to find love and to settle down. Each POW spoke of being pushed into the rough corners of life.

"Does anyone know or even care about where we are or who we are? We've lost ourselves," said Le Mans, eyes half closed. "Will we find a way out, boys?"

During his time inside the small POW camp, images of country roads, daunting mountains, and rainbow trout turned a smile in a dusty world. He found beauty in the simple things of life. Freedom, and all the wavy grain that came with it, spread a thrill and beat in his journaling hands.

"Will I ever hold my family again?" Le Mans asked himself the same riveting question each night when he thought of his baby brother and how he was killed. "Only God knows." He answered the best way he knew how. Then, he prayed the Lord's Prayer. The words he'd known since he was seven, and they lowered him into bed.

At sunup, out of the corner of his eye, Le Mans saw a light shining in a Vietnamese hut. Three buildings stood, two for the Viet-Con, and one for prisoners of war. On the door hung a red lantern with a picture of a chicken.

"What's up with the chicken on the wall?" asked Le Mans, blue eyes anchored on Cadeo.

"In the Chinese zodiac, 1969, it is the Year of the Earth Rooster, the Vietnamese use fireworks, bang pots and pans to ward off evil spirits," said Cadeo, head nodding. "That's our custom. Strange, huh?"

"Yeah, really strange." Le Mans told him, learning about war and culture differences.

It happened the way Cadeo said. They saw the Vietnamese soldiers celebrate the Chinese New Year, a night of banging gongs, pounding drums, and all of them loved to drink too much. No different than Americans, Le Mans recalled.

"It's the Lunar New Year," said Hien, hand pointed. "A big feast for the first morning; for three weeks they'll party and celebrate, red-eyed. Men distracted."

"I have high hopes of something. Let's get out of here," said Beau Le Mans.

"We're all good friends, brothers even, pushed together by war," said Cadeo, dark eyes turned to the sky. "Yeah, yeah, yeah. Let's do something and go somewhere."

Mountains, rice fields, and a jungle of evergreen, all of it stood before them. Le Mans knew how to trek mountains better than he knew himself, rough, rugged terrain, and places he planned to see, a way out, was the open door of freedom. Le Mans imagined the crunch of fallen leaves in autumn in West Virginia, hunting the land, walking old logging roads, built by men who'd returned from WWII, and Korea. He lived for rushing rivers; rapids had cut seams into mountains, swift in the valley, rolling for thousands of years, and, a vast land settled by pioneers and mountaineers. Born and raised in the Appalachian Mountains of West Virginia, the easy life Le Mans once knew was far from bombs and firefights. Now, in Vietnam, he was beneath a canopy of giant leaves and amid terrors of a giant fiery war.

Slow rain trickled at night. The sound of water falling, a portrait of a new State Park in West Virginia, Twin Falls, a place he'd only seen once in high school while dating, covered his memory. He'd trade his big toe for freedom and the rush of cold mountain water across his face, and the thought of heavy snow made him miss Wyoming County. Raindrops trailed down large palm leaves, a little piece of heaven, and a good drop smacked his cracked lips.

The face of Beau Le Mans was rough, unshaven, and he was proud of the look of war, to serve, and to live, the claiming bite of survival. Heel-to-toe, cut legs, feet twitched, and he lived in discomfort. The rounded muscle he once carried on his frame from Army Basic, slowly faded away. He'd withered some, wondering if he'd ever write another story for the *Army Times*.

For days and nights, well, he'd counted several hundred stones, strategically placed by the fence, a daily ritual tilted toward a tight bamboo fence, and the stones pointed homeward.

"Beau Le Mans, are you alive?"

"Still kickin' and prayin' you'll stop snoring, Henderson," said Le Mans, flat on his back. He felt the warmth of the morning sun on his bare feet. His eyes popped open. Le Mans took a deep breath and readied himself for another day of punishment.

Guards had taken their boots, the part of war he hated, and they whipped to take their spirit and kill their soul. Le Mans knew he wouldn't last a day shoeless in the jungle. What he planned for each prisoner was to quickly wrap their feet in rags, if the door of freedom opened, and when the time came for an exit.

"If it's a prayer to Jesus, you can keep it," said Henderson, pulling on his chains. "It's year 2512, to me."

"Yeah, Buddhist Boy Caveman. Hate this piss-poor camp," declared Le Mans, neck popping from an awful night's sleep.

"Hey, happy birthday to you, happy birthday to you, happy birthday, Beau Le Mans, happy birthday to you," whispered Henderson, fighting the chains until he saw his friend's face.

"My birthday is in April?" said Le Mans.

"I'll celebrate it today. Buddhists think ahead. I may not be here in April. Hey, you got my rice lunch today, hillbilly. That's my gift to you."

"I appreciate you, Caveman. But the bad part is, you don't have enough food to share with a skinny ant. Eat your dang food, buddy, what little we get." Le Mans insisted.

"Dang, is that a smoke cloud!" said Henderson, lifting up. "Our boys must've found us."

"Yeah, baby, look at that cloud," said Le Mans. "The First Team found our camp."

"We'll see," said Henderson, arm toward the blaze. "Look at the fireworks. I feel lucky. Today, we might go home, boys."

"Where'd the bird go?" said Le Mans, who pounded the bed. "Come back, pilot."

"Don't count on it," said Henderson, chin on his chest.

"They'll be back with bagels and peanut butter," said Le Mans, chuckling. "I bet that plane had Texas steak on it."

"Shut up, man. You recite the freakin' menu every damn day!" yelled Henderson, "Stop that crap!"

Soldiers that starved spoke that way, talking about life, meals back home, and the way they left it, friends, family, and they wanted food and drinks on a silver lunch tray. They mimicked news reporters and spoke of what lies and stories Tricky Dick Nixon had printed. Le Mans thought of how his mother made chocolate cake, vanilla ice cream, and lit twisted candles on his eighteenth party. His father was the family prankster, but blew big blue balloons, balloons large enough to lift him out of the jungle and carry him home.

"It sucks, Henderson, not having ice cream," said Le Mans.

"Vanilla. I wish we had a truckload of Brenham Creamery," said Henderson. "The last time I had vanilla ice cream, um, 1967, something like two years ago, man. Now, look, Le Mans, you got me poppin' the dessert menu."

Early that morning a breeze rolled from a nearby hut, and the smell of breakfast broke through their nostrils, and the realization of cooked rice only a hundred feet away, was something else cruel to prisoners. Greed. Abuse. Hunger. They had the same routine every morning, tilting their heads toward the smell of hot rice cooking over an open fire. Le Mans grabbed his thin gut and covered his nose. Henderson moaned at daybreak. Less than a handful of food would be all the breakfast they'd taste each day, if any, a small gulp. The dog's bowl held triple of what a prisoner had in his hand.

"Gotta get out of here," said Henderson, relaxing his neck. "Back to Amarillo, Texas."

"We all need home, bud, right?" said Le Mans, laughing, head back. "Need to get back to Baileysville, my friend."

"We'll share a steak in Amarillo, Le Mans. I swear, buddy, I'm buyin' the first round, the day you get us out of here. I'll show you some fat Texas beef. Bigger than a truck tire."

"We'll get the best steak in Texas, I bet."

The door opened.

"Keep quiet! Shut up, stupid Americas!" yelled a Viet-Cong officer, spitting and lapsing into his own language. He walked away.

"Chin Vo," said Hien, lips in a mad pucker. "I hate him."

Time passed slowly, and through the eyes of war, faces wept and hearts broke for home. Le Mans had a vision to feel the coolness of a different place and be with a lovely lady. Not much had changed. Long days. Short nights. He remembered girls he'd dated and broken up with in high school. Memories. Hopes. Dreams. Being wounded, to him, started before the war with women. He was cut by barbed wire and his heart was beaten with his own cravings. Le Mans spoke less about his pain and more about his big dreams, to see France, visit his cousins, and hug people from the old country. Later, the only dry ground was home to a long tail feather, once held by a silver pheasant, one Le Mans called Chester, and had seen three times. To hold a feather might bring some luck to men who had not felt much fortune in a long while. Suddenly, Le Mans gasped for air, eyes dry as a cracked desert, now unwell and uneasily opened by stiff hands. The men depended on daydreams, the dreams of a creative Army writer, Le Mans.

"We need a big break, an open door out of here, Henderson, right?"

"Your Paul Newman eyes can't save us here, Le Mans. These aren't soiled doves."

"The Lord has enough power for us all."

"God missed my Christmas list, hillbilly. The Lord and Santa must not visit Amarillo or Vietnam." Henderson crossed his arms, a face borrowed a frown.

Le Mans had faith. However, the blood of Vietnam shot holes of doubt into the lives of thousands of good, godly men, men stationed "in-country." Henderson often drew the Dharma Wheel of Buddhism in the dirt, harboring not for the Earth Rooster, nor Jesus.

Henderson stretched his arms.

"I'm not sure where God is in Vietnam. Charley and his Communist company need a dose of a sharp bayonet." Henderson sat up. "My hippy life toward God, Le Mans, don't jive with your prayers to Mister Jesus."

"I don't see your Buddha daddy with a key and grilled steak, Caveman. How is Buddhism working for you, huh? You feel lucky today, Caveman, stuck in this Disney Land?" Le Mans whispered to him.

"Looks like Jesus has done as much for you as Buddha has for me, huh? Match that, Beau Le Mans, right? Jesus is still working on me," sang Henderson, marching and grinning.

The dry mouth of Le Mans watered for a pot of coffee, a dark roast, lip smacking good, the color of coal, the way his grandfather, Tippie, made it, dark. He imagined himself seated beside his grandmother, Pearl, who handed him golden flake biscuits, warm biscuits, the kind Jesus might have buttered at The Last Supper. Would the Lord serve biscuits at the breakfast table, he thought, biscuits covered in hot gravy, sided with fluffy scrambled eggs, covered with steamy homemade apples, and that's the way his imagination freely labored.

Months earlier, caked in earth, Le Mans saw the blood of "Victor-Charlie" and angry soldiers prodded him from the road to the jungle and onto a Vietnamese prison camp. Prisoners were tied to truck bumpers and thrown. They joked about being pushed into a new apartment, one flat cabin above a dirty town, made for out-of-towners.

"No talking!" yelled Chin Vo, armed.

"God, help us!" said Le Mans. "Water."

Then, they were beaten for begging and for having good conversations.

Out of the thousands of Americans in Vietnam, two men bent beside him, abused for deformities, not fighters, but imprisoned men, hardly thirty. Prisoners were tied, and stumbled between camps, joined by chains, and when one man fell, so did the rest.

"When we get to the next camp," said Le Mans, bleeding from a rifle butt to the mouth, "I'll get us free and find liberty."

Still, Beau Le Mans was uncertain of a good plan, all or nothing, just like Basic Training in Fort Jackson, South Carolina. Morning dew danced down the length of a giant palm leaf, the greenest tree he'd ever seen had made a canopy above his head, which became the most dependable natural funnel of fresh water during a rainstorm. Le Mans took his chances and hoped the God of clouds and water would pour coffee instead of water, a cup of Java Joe, or Grandpa's dark coal miner's coffee, just for him, but that wish world never happened.

Le Mans flipped his wrist to check the time. His arm hadn't seen a timepiece in a long while and he laughed aloud. The Viet-Cong took his watch when he was captured. That's when something told him the time was 2500 hours on a Thursday night and everything was going to be alright. He believed God was above the cloudy sky, amid the bamboo, walking in the wilderness, in prayer, and His spirit must have departed the camp, high above the green canopy. He truly believed the Lord watched him suffer and allowed him to feel slashes and ant bites and the discomfort of chains. Le Mans did not understand why.

When the morning sun eased up above the thickness of flopping palms, far distant mountains of Vietnam stood tall and abnormal from the likeness of the Blue Ridge Mountains, the ones he'd left behind. Small amounts of hope sprung through the greenery and warmed his face for a short moment, then like everything else, it disappeared with the birds.

He'd spotted the leader of the V-C walking by the camp.

"Is this guy a tunnel rat?" said Le Mans.

"He smells like a fat rat," Henderson said, still laughing, eyes closed from being beaten half to death by the welcoming party of the Viet-Cong soldiers.

Trained Viet-Cong fighters and tunnel rats crawled underground, making holes in the earth, a way to hide and kill more Americans. Some were more ruthless than others, but all were trained killers.

The V-C was known to disappear for weeks, living underground, maybe like the Earth Rooster. The Viet-Cong spoke with loud voices, shouting in their own language and mapped dirty grins toward Americans, as if they were President Nixon's right handed men.

"Smells like spring, Henderson," said Le Mans.

"Le Mans, buddy, we need to spring out of this dead rat hole," Henderson whispered, and grabbed his chin.

"When the time is right, we'll jump the wall, fly away, cowboy, high above it all, headed home on a one way carpet ride. No sounds of the U.S. Birds or booms in several days." Le Mans glanced at the darn sky, palm trees swaying, as the backdrop of thunder and lightning roared, and he thought of what hell on earth he'd signed up for. The war, fire fights, thunder and lighting, all of it, the useless battle hated by mankind. His mind weakened and body parts ticked slowly, hands first. What was left of a small bit of warmth, he rested and felt alive. Storms moved the broken sky and sunny days kept Le Mans hopeful for an open door.

Henderson opened his good-working eye, soaked up the milky-white clouds, gripped the bamboo wall and said, "Singing birds tell me it's springtime, hillbilly, better days are on the way."

"No. It must be the fall season," said Le Mans, resting his head against the bamboo.

"When luck gives us the green light, we'll roll out like a Fort Hood tank, and strike with double fists, man," said Le Mans, arm cocked at the V-C guards.

Weeks tumbled by like the humble house that held a broken black and white television. The flag waved at midnight on most stations. Hours seemed like a slow train on its way to anywhere else. Prayers said and lifted, but unanswered. They spoke of death, the dying, the sick, the wounded, and the last words soldiers said before they closed their eyes. No hurry or care was given to prisoners, it appeared, and hard times unfolded that way inside the jungle. Time was the enemy. The big war ticked on for both sides. Each side wanted to be somewhere else and with anyone else, doing something else, and reading the last chapter of *Farewell to Arms*. The war made men homesick.

Prisoners couldn't differentiate one sizzling summer day from the next and thunderstorms reminded Le Mans of the cry of a laboring mother. If storms weren't enough, mosquitoes carried deadly Malaria, Zika, and Dengue fever. Long periods of anxiety and meditation, and men battled the elements and the psychology of mind games, a cruel game played by foes. The worst part, self-infliction. All of them fought, and waited to live or die. Le Mans had a burning ember inside him, like a fire inside his grandfather's buck stone, to write something as a journalist, jot a spark of hope, a flicker for tomorrow's newspaper, and painted thoughts of a beautiful day, a day lost somewhere between a chain of prayers and unspoken daydreams.

To the Viet-Cong, American prisoners were no better than stray Chinese dogs, locked down tight and tied to the geography of Vietnam, even less humane than a ruthless wild boar. The sun and moon helped; one guiding light by day and by night another spark of hope lit the sky. Something to hope for during military unrest. Each dark day was as unsettling and rainy as the next. Dark nights were the worst. The cover of night was the darkest hour for prisoners, like an endless, wet coal mine, with no doors for the blue canary or the gentle smile of humanity was unknown.

Lips bruised. Eyes darkened by the V-C and a back once strong in the front leaning rest, now dripped in a cut crimson uniform. Le Mans never wanted to end himself, throw in the white towel, like most fighters after endless beatings by the V-C for grinning and laughing at them. Le Mans dropped his head and heard a familiar voice from the corner of the room:

"Beau, wake up, will ya?"

"Dad, is that you, Old Man? Pops?"

It sure sounded like his father's voice.

"Yeah, I'm right beside you, Beau. Hey, don't you give up on me. I'm right here beside you. They'll be better days, son, I promise you."

"I'll be home soon, Dad."

Time crawled by like an ancient turtle, Old Legs, wishing he had younger, running feet. That night Beau Le Mans slept without movement or worry; he rested in peace and serenity; his assurance was his father's words. Le Mans had held himself together the longest of any POW. Each man was caught amid the firefights of war, separated from their platoon, and some knew Vietnam was a one-way trip. New recruits. Fresh meat. Cherries off the boat! They heard it all when soldiers first arrived, shuffling, uneasy, and uneager to lace boots for death. As fighters, they stood strong, boots on the ground, and walked into the unknown, anyways, as Americans.

Less than a month in the Vietnam jungle, Le Mans was captured and beaten until he couldn't move his writing hand. He'd always thought about Moses, the Exile, an escape, so Le Mans created eye signals for soldiers, taught hand-to-hand combat and knew sign language. They practiced taps and knocked on wood until each POW was trained well and every man understood the signals and each one felt yoked to the plan. To get everyone out alive, that's what Le Mans instructed, crafting a swift formula of communication, so each soldier was taught to quickly overtake the V-C.

Stationed to the left of Le Mans in Sơn Tây, Richard "Caveman" Henderson, a true, hard-nosed Texan. To their advantage, two Vietnamese prisoners had fallen asleep early. Henderson and Le Mans spoke about their past, shared stories about women, and how they came to find themselves in a deadly warzone.

"Le Mans, hey, the same way you need to get back to West Virginia, is the same way I need to get to Robin's Egg, Texas. My wife, I mean, now ex-wife, Jeanette, the lady hates me as much as I hate Charlie, has her own nice place. Little Benny, my boy, still loves me, I guess."

"Where's Robin's Egg, Texas, Caveman?"

"It's a little ranch town, with horses, prize cattle, and just outside Amarillo."

"You'll see your family soon, Caveman Henderson."

"Admiral Stockdale thinks all the optimists die first, so what do you think, Le Mans?"

"I promise you, he's wrong. Stockdale has no control over what another man thinks in his heart, his faith, and what keeps him whole and positive inside the jungle." Le Mans studied the stars and the surprising glow of the moon, and he wept, too. It was normal to be broken. "I miss my younger brother, Wells. We used to hunt together, collect cars, and play baseball. We'll be home soon. Stockdale doesn't know my God."

"I didn't know you had a brother, Le Mans."

"He was killed last year." Tears broke the corners of his eyes. "Authorities have yet to find his killer."

"The world isn't safe anywhere. I'm sorry to hear about your brother. We've lost thousands of soldiers over here in this mudhole. I'll use a Claymore mine, 50 caliber machine gun and blow us a door out of here. Give me something to fight with. Le Mans, we need a big break."

"Ice cream, women, or artillery, we don't have anything, now what, Henderson?"

Le Mans sat on a bench.

"We need the guards to make one mistake," said Le Mans, "just one, and we're gone."

On most days, tied together, chest down, stomachs tight and flat, Le Mans fought the burning sunlight and blew flies from his face. Biting ants crawled on their legs and caused them to twitch and jerk. Unwanted insects ran into awkward places and crawled across their faces and darted into loose pants. They weren't the only people in the POW camp. Known as the unwanted brothers; weak men who couldn't fight and made embarrassing soldiers from the point of Viet-Cong soldiers, huddled together. War created more hatred toward different men, men with slow legs. Ants did not crawl on the brothers, Cadeo, and Hien, and the smaller man, Cadeo, arm deformed at birth, was the older brother. Hien, the bigger man, kept himself hidden and covered his deformed arm with his sleeves.

When the gentle breeze shook the green canopy, the two Americans, Le Mans and Henderson, stood amid a muddy camp. Their part of the mud camp was a hog pen, built just for prisoners; upon force; upon being called the worst; held among the missing in action. Fifteen meters away, tall, stout bamboo poles, cut and nailed, wired and roped, which made up the sides of the POW camp. Hundreds of bamboo made up the camp and sloppily positioned barbed wire found nailed and twisted around crooked posts. Doors were bolted and hinged, the only entrance for V-C guards to attack, stood uneasy at the front of the building. Only two patches of grass grew on the camp and peed on by the Earth Rooster, perhaps. Nothing else was green or had vibrant color inside the bulky walls. Perhaps the land was cursed, like Golgotha, with an unfavorable history; muddy and nasty, a land of nothingness. Did it have potable water or editable plants or fresh fruits, at least not within arm's reach? Beyond camp, fresh fruit grew wildly and naturally in the jungle, a place off limits and a dreamland for prisoners.

The most admired among the prisoners, the trusted man, far from country roads in West Virginia, who stayed alert and stayed alive, was Le Mans, a man trained to hunt in high mountains. The Viet-Cong guards kept an eye on his craftiness and capabilities, by the way he carried himself and led the pack. Le Mans and Henderson refused to sign their names as Communist sympathizers, refusing to join Victor-Charlie, and turn against their own country. They spoke how they would die a hard death first. Le Mans became popular for nicknaming guards, men who lived to torture him because he held a hopeful face. When guards walked inside the camp, Le Mans sang Sgt. Pepper and the V-C hated his face and voice. They had no idea about good music, The Beatles, but Le Mans was beaten for his glorious smirk and good singing voice.

Camp dogs liked Le Mans. They befriended him through the fence after rainstorms and meals. On dry days, guards unlocked prisoners and cursed them for soaking up the morning sunlight of Vietnam. They were chained and yanked and whipped in muddy flats, like recess for guards. On Christian holidays, prisoners were pushed into stagnant swamps because they followed Christ, but not one guard believed Henderson was a true Buddhist. No way. That's when the red-eyed guards left for breakfast. Finally, they walked on dry land, and that was when POW soldiers were flogged for pure entertainment. A small crowd had gathered and jumped and cheered. Everyone joked about abuse. The smell of burning wood meant it was time for rice and scrambled eggs. They spoke of the cruelty to claim only a pitch from a giant pot of food; enough food was cooked for villagers to take part. Prisoners raged in anger and shook the bamboo and steel bars, begging in starvation mode. No one spoke to the guards at breakfast. Prisoners closed their eyes in silence. Le Mans and others agreed to talk less about meals they'd eaten at home.

"God?" said Le Mans. "Lord, if you exist, you are real, all powerful and a living God, then keep us alive and let us find the door to freedom."

Le Mans remembered the last time he threw a baseball with his younger brother. He chewed his lower lip and spoke to God about Wells. He felt the time was near, it was time to leave. He thought God had heard him and prepared the hedges for an open door.

"What have I done wrong, God?" he asked.

"You killed a man. More than one." Le Mans told himself. "Can I not escape my own mistakes, Lord? Will I die here for my dirty deeds? King David committed murder and paid for it, confessing."

God never answered him.

Henderson opened one eye, face dusted, unshaven and licked droplets of water, and said, "Look! Who is that man in uniform?"

Le Mans stopped his lips. The man stood and looked across the landscape.

"Is that a new soldier?" asked Le Mans. "One of us."

The new man had thick shoulders and sported a mop of dark hair. Le Mans noticed the newcomer's clean face in the back of a truck. Sharp. The V-C yanked the soldier's arm, feet landed, and he was prodded inside like a calf into a barn. The door was immediately locked. The guards left.

"Name's Samuel Lawrence, U.S. Army," said the new prisoner. "Separated from my unit, knocked out cold with the butt of a rifle. I saw countless stars."

"How's the war treating you, Sammy?" asked Henderson.

Now... the camp had three Americans. Two Vietnamese prisoners stood at the door.

"Sam Law, huh?" said Le Mans. "Welcome aboard, Sam Law. Where are you from?"

"Winchester, Virginia," said Lawrence, who saw his new home, raw earth. Unbeknownst to him, Lawrence met decent men. The new soldier turned his head to the ceiling, warm daylight closed his eyes. Much less than any man expected, at least, his face found a friendly smile.

"I'm Beau Le Mans from West "By God" Virginia;" Pointing as he said each man's name, and introduced the other prisoners to Lawrence.

"Ben Henderson, Amarillo, Texas."

"See you've found the Ritz Hotel, Lawrence," said Le Mans, walking close to the new guy, hand out. "I see we couldn't keep this place a secret, follow GI."

"Motel 8 was booked," said Lawrence, laughing. "I'm a short timer, guys."

Henderson jerked his head, holding Lawrence's shoulder.

"You got wings under that uniform, Lawrence?"

"All of us are short timers," said Le Mans, flashing his famous smile. "The sauna is broken. The shop has our motorcycles. But, hey, Sam Law, the open-air thunderstorms are superb fireworks, like the 4th of July in Winchester. Oil massages happen after supper."

"You'll find steak and ale served by the Dallas Cowboys' cheerleaders," said Henderson.

"Ain't this the Heavenly Ritz, boys?" said Lawrence. "Look, look, look! Hot lady cooking at three o'clock."

She stood, full-figured, long black hair to her hips.

"Good eyes. You mean, Polly," said Le Mans. "She's better than a Donut Dolly, Sam Law. Make a man daydream, but she's a good lady out of our reach."

"But we have Cadeo and Hien, two fine Vietnamese brothers, to cook our morning coffee. They know the language when we need to speak to Polly," said Henderson, slapping the shoulders of each man. "She's been here about a week, I guess."

"Polly knows your language," said Cadeo, grinning.

"Here, Hien and Cadeo are the best of the bunch. Our brothers, too," said Le Mans, hands on the shoulder of each man.

"Same-same," said Cadeo. "Same-same, brothers." His teeth were few.

"Good to meet you, Sam Law," said Hien, hand out.

Cadeo and Hien accepted him as an equal, but waited to see if he was a man of trust or a talking traitor. For the rest of the day, soldiers whispered about sports and cars and drive-in movies. They hoped to make the next dinner on the ground at church and planned to find old friends.

Occasional movements of three Vietnamese guards gathered for meals around the bamboo, caught the eye of Le Mans, and gave Americans something to talk about. Loud voices meant men of rank and power had arrived; still, Americans watched the guards pace twenty meters away at a larger building, some drunk. Guards huddled and made their way behind bamboo trees to smoke, traded what they had in their pockets, and told dirty jokes.

Thirty meters away, Polly, cooked over an open fire. The most beautiful lady Beau Le Mans had ever seen, Polly, stood medium height, coal black hair, and had a small, oval-shaped face, a face that lingered in his dreams. Her laugh was contagious as she cooked meals, poured water into buckets, and labored. The soldiers watched her at sunup. Food tasted better when she served, having a lady made the difference and like an angel from heaven, Polly was the best part of the week. Rice and eggs, halved among the guards. Second, dogs got a good bowl. Hungry villagers served. Vietnamese prisoners ate if they were lucky men. Then, V-C guards fed pinches of rice to the camp parrots, and fed themselves again. Polly scooped the last few bites, if any food was left, American soldiers got a small parcel in a bowl.

With eyes needing a friend, Hien tilted his head, and Cadeo followed. When one of them spoke to Polly first, a bit of cultural compassion was extended and kindness could not be resisted on her part; two young men from her same region, caged and starving. However, Polly caught the welcoming grin of the pale Army journalist, Le Mans, the man with sharp blue eyes and the only man able to hold her attention while she cooked, just minding her own business. She saw Le Mans first. Polly slowed her labor and paced around the camp, winked, and suddenly fed the man from Baileysville much more than he'd expected. She'd cared for him with tenderness and a cheerful laugh. Their eyes met. Not like strangers at a train station, or a grocery store clerk, but something was exchanged, warm and unspoken. Le Mans was a generous man and quickly shared his extra scoops of food with his friends, especially Hien and Cadeo, who he hugged during meals. He depended on Hien and Cadeo to communicate with Polly. The two brothers did as much as they could for Le Mans who protected and cared for them. Le Mans took the attention off of the brothers, yelling and stomping, when the guards got close enough to pound Cadeo and Hien.

Polly shared extra food when she could get away with generosity. Rice was flipped in a stir-fry wok and topped with eggs, and raked into a round, wooden bowl for prisoners. Four good bits of food were split between prisoners and the idea was to keep the prisoners as weak as possible. Americans knew how the game was played. All of them knew the circle of hatred that came with the punishment of war.

Cadeo and Hien stood beside Le Mans.

"Polly overheard how the guards wanted to fight you," whispering, "fist fight you," said Hien. "They want to knock on you."

"Me?" said Le Mans. "Why?"

"Yeah, Le Mans, you." Hien nodded. "You American. They want to hit your face."

The Americans caught the eyes of each other and laughed.

"Chin Vo ain't no Rocky Marciano, buddy!" said Henderson, slapping Le Mans several times on the arm.

One of the new guards, name well known, unlocked the door, and stood in the fighting position.

"Here comes the Fighting Irish," said Sam Law, hands over his mouth.

"Let's dance," said Le Mans. "Do me the honors, Chin Vo, will ya?"

Most Vietnamese guards kicked like Bruce Lee, feet and hands, blocking punches, and round house, spinning their body toward the enemy. Everyone stepped out. The guards held the rifle of Chin Vo, pushing Le Mans, and yelled in their own language, mimicking the hits and grunts of each man. When Le Mans was belted, the guards were unable to stand still.

"You dead, American!" yelled Duc Vo.

Chin Vo kicked Le Mans between the eyes and landed flat. Le Mans fell in the dirt.

"One, two, three, get up, Le Mans!" yelled Sam Law.

"Count to a hundred, Sam Law. He ain't gettin' up, buddy," said Henderson. "He's too malnourished to fight. We're not strong enough fighters to go one round. The V-C has starved us, man," fists up, "and slapped us into the ring, Sam Law."

They carried Le Mans to his bed and dropped him. Cadeo poured water on his cut lips and pushed him.

Well, boxing, fighting, whatever you call it, the knockout punch, happened once a week in the jungle. The Americans lost. Winners slammed a rifle butt against the losers. After black eyes and bruises, the soldiers agreed nothing more was to be spoken about fighting, for their own protection and to keep themselves healthy for an escape. They humbled themselves in each other's blood, hands locked. One man doctored the wounds of the next, like a small hospital of brothers. No one felt alone or unfriendly after that day. Henderson was the last one to befriend anyone, even the ones he knew. They learned how to cope with their situation and survive on what little they had to live on, mostly laughs and feeding off of good humor. V-C guards continued to fatten hungry dogs before Americans.

"I was raised around German Shepherds all my life," said Sam Law, who watched the dog circle. "The short-haired dog deserves his share of food." Sam Law chewed on a long stick when he was nervous and pointed at the guard dogs. "He'll attack us for food if he gets a notion. I've seen it among wild dogs in the Shenandoah Mountains."

Le Mans educated Sam Law when he had the chance and taught camp customs, what the guards expected, and things he needed to do and say, just to stay alive. It was for his own good, a man who needed to keep his mouth shut and follow orders.

"Mad dogs attack slow men," said Cadeo, nodding. "Knock down little children for food. Sad thing. Bad thing. Sadness happens in Vietnam."

"Yeah, in America, too," said Sam Law.

Le Mans could not look at the dogs; he found Polly walking across the way.

In other circumstances, perhaps better days, more suitable places, Le Mans would have dated Polly and married her, too.

How sweet it would be to ride Polly around in my shiny blue 1966 Chevelle. She would be a doll, hair flying on a warm summer day, Elvis on the radio, and arm around my girl.

"She's a peach and a half," said Le Mans, and their eyes caught. "Polly deserves more than this rotten war life. It would be nice to see her walking around again, hiking the trails and playing tennis at Twin Falls State Park. I'd show Polly off to my family."

"O' man, she's a ripe peachy-peach, built to be loved. I'd like to take her Two-Stepping Texas style on a sawdust floor in

Amarillo," said Henderson, hand on his shoulder. "Polly is sweet as sugar cane, boys. I'd be her number-one GI. A little dancing and some boogie time, boys, and, uh, I know Polly wants a Texas cracker, Le Mans."

"She's a good woman, Henderson, and one to be left alone." said Le Mans, eyes locked, scoping downrange at her. "She's teasing us with her legs and grin. The lady knows how pretty she is, too. Watch her look and sway to the music."

"Bet she's a good kisser," said Sam Law, who held a toothpick inside his lips.

"I'd like to dance with her," said Henderson, rubbing his mustache and watching her walk around the camp.

With tilted heads and steady eyes, the soldiers examined her hourglass shape and seductive sweet style. Polly walked away loosely, head up, swaying in freedom. To see her was the best prescription for a man's broken heart, a lovely sight to mightily enjoy, especially to confined men. Natural thoughts rolled through the mind of Le Mans, and if, by some strange miracle, they'd meet after the war, things would be much different. He imagined civil thoughts at dinner and a warm twisted candle between them, words of sincerity, and plans of the future, perhaps.

Sadly, for Le Mans, that world did not exist. Another battle he'd lost with time and more days ticked away that year, like a big turtle headed uphill. Le Mans had not seen Polly for twelve weeks, so stones were placed along the fence in her absence. More beautiful than ever, Polly returned, yellow dress on, and eager to see Le Mans in the spring of 1970. Her hair was trimmed, earrings dangled, skin darker, and her eyes and face had makeup. Cadeo rose up against the building and waited and watched, like a student in a college classroom, just listening and observing her voice as she spoke to the guards. Hien's vision was poor and he acted like he was half asleep beside Cadeo, but he overheard conversations when people spoke in his native tongue. He was a man who was well aware.

Cadeo and Hien spoke short sentences in Vietnamese and faced Le Mans.

"Are we friends, Le Mans?" asked Cadeo, head tilted, eyes down.

"Yes sir, for sure, Cadeo." Le Mans sat up. "What's up?"

No one had ever called Hien or Cadeo "sir" before in their lives. The twins respected him for the value he'd placed in their lives.

"No good news," said Cadeo, head down. "No good news, Le Mans."

"What does no good news mean?" asked Le Mans, eyes on their sincere faces.

"What my brother is trying to say," said Hien, eyes nearly closed, "Polly married Chin Vo." His hands extended slowly. "She said it in our language. Loud enough so we'd hear her and tell you, I bet."

"No. Not the guard? No. No. No. What the heck?" said Le Mans, hands on his face. "Are you sure she's married to that fool?"

"I know the language of my people," said Hien, arms crossed. "I'm sorry to say that to you, Le Mans. No good. No good news. I see how you like her and she likes you."

"She can't love him. No good for all of us. He will be jealous and beat us endlessly for being men who look at Polly. He will abuse us if we scope his wife. The worst news I've ever heard, buddy," said Le Mans, sliding his hand down his throat to his chest.

"Le Mans, she might leave here forever soon." Hien told him. "It's her tradition to be a mother and wife. One day she will have a child with him. Her days are few with us."

Hien stood beside Le Mans. His small figure, arm on his tall friend's shoulder and Hien cried and sat.

"We kissed through the fence every day in May when Chin Vo was with his tunnel rats," said Le Mans. "She said she loved me."

"Didn't see a dang kiss, Le Mans!" said Henderson. "You lied, hillbilly."

"I kiss who I want, Caveman."

Cadeo walked between Le Mans and Henderson.

"You're not my friend, Caveman," said Hien, hands up to fight.

"You can't unscramble eggs, boy," said Henderson, yanking his shirt.

"Stop, Henderson!" said Le Mans, unlocking their hands. "Can't you see his white face, Caveman? The boy is sick."

"Yeah, let him go," said Sam Law, who held his forehead. "He's sick as a dog, man."

"Sick enough to sleep, Caveman." Hien told him. The man fixed his brother's shirt.

"Go away, Caveman," said Cadeo. "Bad sick. I need rest."

Henderson departed the crew. Cadeo pulled Le Mans aside.

"The marriage is true, Le Mans," said Cadeo, body shaking nervously when he spoke. "Waited for the right time to tell you, but there's no good time for bad news. I overheard them talking yesterday about a small, private wedding. We're all sad. My brother could not hold the bad news another day. We know you love Polly, so we had to speak the truth to you. Are we still friends, sir?"

"Always. Thank you for being honest. I'm stuck in prison. I want more for her than to marry Chin Vo. As long as I'm stuck in this rathole, there's nothing I can do," said Le Mans, who saw her from a distance and lifted his friendly hand. Le Mans leaned on the post and shook the fence. "If I was in her world, things would be different."

Cadeo pointed and said, "His brother is Duc Vo. Dead in his heart. They will take revenge against you, fight you, and maybe kill you this time, right? Guards talked of killing more Americans. Chin Vo wants to kill the next man who looks at Polly. They shoot beautiful birds for fun and it pisses me off. Be careful, Le Mans. No more chasing the lady."

With the two Viet-Cong Vo brothers, darting around camp, pacing became a habitually uneasy task for Le Mans. Several days had crawled by in pain for the mountaineer.

He remembered his talk with Cadeo: "Chin Vo is an evil man. He lives to punish and kill," said Cadeo, head tilted. He chewed a stick like Sam Law.

Le Mans pulled the wood from his hands and threw it down.

"Chin Vo and Duc Vo, men born amid the flames of hell and reborn with the devil. I hate them," mumbled Hien. "He will show rage. I know my people. He can't resist playing the big man and shaming Americans to submit."

Birds stopped singing and dark smoke rolled over the POW camp when Duc Vo and his guards commanded prisoners to move when the sun moved. Beatings repeatedly happened, just as Hien and Cadeo predicted.

"God help us!" yelled Le Mans. Blood rolled down his back and face."

Prisoners were tied, spread eagle, struck every five days or so. The rage of Chin Vo and Duc Vo happened, adding lashes when they were drunk and acting crazy around villagers. The ground became an amusement park of crimson. The purpose, to stomp out the lives of Americans, and break them into submission and cut out thoughts of finding the open door. After the beatings, the arms and legs of prisoners had deep wounds, especially Cadeo and Hien, the smallest two men in the camp. The twins were made examples of, showing how evil still existed, and how Communism could not be defeated, not even by Americans. The V-C must have thought less of the twins than they did the skinny dog that circled the camp for food.

By the fall 1970, prisoners staggered through rough terrain trekking to another POW camp called Briarpatch, Xom Ap Lo ("The Hanoi Hilton"), located about 35 miles west of Hanoi. The camp had no electricity. Duc Vo, Chin Vo, Polly, and three more armed guards prodded them like cattle, traveling over trails, miles and miles, and stumbled through the animal infested jungle. They'd crossed unstable bridges, slowly pacing and suffering from malnutrition. Cadeo, Hien, Le Mans, Henderson, and Lawrence held each other in shackles, being roped together like puppets. Right before dark, the prisoners loaded up into a truck, and by sundown, they'd reached their destination. Briarpatch was less of a hog pen than Sơn Tây, tucked away somewhere in the Hao Lo jungle.

The first morning in Briarpatch was the day of initiation, a rite of passage; for entertainment and for tradition, the chess match was one sided.

"Le Mans, here they come, sir," said Hien.

"How many?" said Le Mans.

"Ten," said Hien. "They will whack our backs."

"My soul is prepared," said Le Mans.

"My soul is," said Sam Law, hand on his chin, "but my back is not."

"I pick your Jesus, Le Mans," said Hien, as his round cheeks bent a fat smile. "Brother man and hillbilly."

"You're my brother, Hien," said Le Mans, hand lifted to his friend.

The prisoners found small cracks to watch for guards who approached the door.

"Ain't no difference than what my daddy did," said Henderson, grunting.

"Hate them all," said Cadeo.

"They must've heard my whistle at Polly this morning," said Le Mans, witnessing a half-dozen eyes.

"You idiot!" yelled Sam Law, jumping at Le Mans.

"Lock it up, Sam Law," said Le Mans, halting his friend.

"You a selfish prick, Le Mans," said Sam Law, pushing him away.

"I'm sorry, man!" said Le Mans, hands up. "I'm human."

"We're dead, bud," said Sam Law, walking away, "that's what we are, Le Mans."

V-C guards moved in, and made a game of torturing prisoners. The more villagers that cheered, the more belligerent the V-C acted, keeping prisoners poor in spirit, legs limping and to snap out every drop of courage. Typically, prisoners were gagged, held under water, gasping for life in a small, round well.

"Hope that whistle was worth it, Le Mans," said Henderson.

"She's a heck of a beauty," said Le Mans, blood on his lips.

CHAPTER TWO

Men By the Well

Chin Vo and Duc Vo stood beside each other and disagreed about how they wanted each man to die. The food supply was slow and they needed one prisoner gone. They used psychological games to scare Americans. However, at war, games got backed with a dozen real punches into the gut and head.

"Don't take my brother to the well!" yelled Cadeo, arms roped.

"No, no, no!" yelled Hien. No one was headed to rescue them and no one was en route to protect him, either. "Help me! Cadeo! Le Mans!"

Le Mans saw Hien struggling and gasping for air down amid the well, then he shouted, "Take him out! Put me in the damn well! Pull him out, Chin Vo!"

"Shut up! Shut that soldier up! Break his teeth!" yelled Duc Vo. "Restrain the American. Beat the Yankee!"

Guards roped and pulled Le Mans to the nearest tree. Tears rolled down the face of Le Mans, who caused them to take a beating with a selfish whistle. Sam Law and Henderson yelled and were hooked to different trees. Cadeo saw his brother's desperate eyes.

"Hien is in big trouble," said Henderson, looking at the red face of Le Mans.

Hien's eyes bulged, head jerked, and the man's adrenaline pumped, and he cried in angst.

"Pull him out!" yelled Cadeo. "Help him!"

"He's had enough!" said Sam Law, jerking his arms.

"I say when to stop the fight." said Chin Vo, fist curled, smashing the forehead of Sam Law.

The eyes and strength of Hien faded slowly. Cadeo knew other men who'd died in water wells. Sam Law watched Hien keep his head above water. Hien was without air. The guards smoked and finished their tiger beer. Guards entertained villagers with punishment, even chanting in their own language and cheered when Chin Vo placed his foot atop of Hien's head. The worse torture a man could withstand became a big joke between Chin Vo and Duc Vo.

"Let him go!" shouted Henderson. "That's enough!"

Four Viet-Cong men pulled Hien's soaked body, clothes full of water, dragging his arms, and dropped him flat. Hien was dead. Water filled his lungs.

"This is what you get when you mess with me," said Chin Vo, who kicked Hien's side. He never flinched from the boot kick.

"He's dead!" shouted Cadeo. "You killed my brother!"

"We pick who dies," said Chin Vo, "not you and not you and not you. Not yet." His hand landed on prisoners when he wanted others to see him.

Cadeo was heartbroken. He would've taken his brother's place if he could. Crimes of war had no rules predicated on fairness. Polly screamed and ran into a nearby building, hiding under the bed. Their good friend, a brother, Hien, eyes red, was beaten for laughing at Chin Vo when Le Mans whistled at Polly. He had not killed anyone until that day. Cadeo was numb to the world. Some things, family things, and broken things couldn't be persuaded by orders or by the warrant of more wounds and woes. The world lost a good man and a good friend was gone. Le Mans discovered how a wounded man healed with medicine, but the heart had a memory that medicine and time couldn't mend. Hien was a man who found the open door. Inside his shirt pocket was the silver pheasant feather given to him by Le Mans, both bird and man flew freely.

Le Mans remembered Hien's words on the whistling day: "All my life I was abused, Le Mans, but never by you, sir. If you can make me free, to run again, and help Cadeo, too, please. Because of the worry you have for your mother and father, and you are here, in this dirty place, and I know you loved your brother, Wells, I want to find my family, care for them, and share your Jesus story with them."

"As brave as you are, I promise you, Hien," said Le Mans, "you will lead us out and be the hero."

"I will lead us, Le Mans. Our friendship is special. You good man."

Hien was known to the three Americans as a good friend: the man's round face carried sincere smiles and everyone loved him. Cadeo wept for many days. Hien and Cadeo were best friends and brothers who could not be divided inside the camp even by death. After they killed Hien, prisoners watched the V-C guards more closely. Le Mans remembered his happy eyes, cheerful face, bravery, and wept at his own selfishness. Le Mans felt ashamed that the death of a friend was his fault. Hien was the kindest man he ever knew.

The V-C smoked and celebrated his death late into the night. "Victor-Charlie is no better than a dirty pig," said Le Mans.

"They are dirty men," said Sam Law, face cut and dried blood on his head.

At sunup, four V-C guards slammed Le Mans to the ground and beat him until blood spattered on the faces of the three other prisoners. Hands tied, Le Mans spent the next two nights barely breathing, head bobbing in the same well water that had taken Hien. To be beaten was a common occurrence among rejects in Vietnam, and to face punishment for being different or deformed, was worse than war for Le Mans. Not far from the well was a large bird cage that swung inside a small village of ten people. Prisoners were tied and caged, swaying for days, and slowly twisted by the tug of a long twenty foot rope, high off the ground.

Cadeo wept hard, wiping tears and blood into torn sleeves. He had felt more pain than most men and cried more tears than a small hospital of wounded people. Things worked that way in Vietnam, amid war, out of order, for more men than just Cadeo and Hien; the V-C made everyone hurt and bleed. The exposition of war stung. One day Cadeo cleaned his muddy face and combed his thick hair with tree branches. He stood with courage again, ready to fight, and spoke with clarity and walked beside Le Mans. Cadeo had one possession, a lucky stone, one he'd found in the dirt. He'd accepted his loneliness and dealt with grief, a fight he was brave enough to endure and planned his revenge against the V-C. After he'd lost Hien, Cadeo forgave Le Mans and thanked him for his stories of faith, and loved his jokes that forced him to laugh aloud again. Sam Law was the next soldier to be stuffed inside the birdcage for five days and he nearly lost his mind, whistled, and flapped his arms like a wild bird to amuse villagers. Followed by Henderson, who spent seven days inside the birdcage for his anger and sharp tongue. For his generosity, Cadeo raised his hands in the cage, sporting only a few crooked teeth by 1970, a beloved man of thirty-one years.

Cadeo walked toward Le Mans and shook his hand.

"I might be the next man in the well, Le Mans, so before it happens, I want to thank you. You are my best friend in this world. Hien would say the same if he was here. You should know this from us."

"I'm not sure why God sent me to Vietnam, but if it was to meet two good people, I've met the best two men this country has to offer. I'm your brother until you see Hien in Heaven. How about that, Cadeo? I am truly sorry for provoking the guards."

"You are forgiven. I know why we met, Le Mans."

"Why?"

"Because the Lord knows that I need to watch after you." His grin broke free.

"We watch each other, Cadeo, sir."

"No one calls me, Sir. I like it, Beau Le Mans."

"Don't worry for you brother anymore." Le Mans held his thin mustache.

"I am a good man who worries too much." Cadeo moved his feet, and said, "Why do you say that?"

"Because he's eating a big stir-fry lunch with Peter, James, and Jesus."

"You crazy, Le Mans, yeah, yeah, you crazy America. Your brother and my brother are both gone, now we are good brothers. Cool?"

"Cool. We make a good team." Le Mans held out his hand.

At Briarpatch, prisoners were given small portions of congee, a wooden spoon full of rice porridge, and small amounts of leftovers after celebrations. Polly slipped them more food. Village harlots or call girls, girls from a town away, caused V-C officers to become reckless and wild. On many occasions the V-C found themselves celebrating at night and became forgetful, darting into the wrong direction and felt too comfortable in a warzone. When the Viet-Cong staggered drunk and fell, Polly had eaten all she wanted, and offered prisoners leftover chicken and plates of warm rice and eggs. And for a short time, and regarded as pigs, Americans were hated and placed alongside rejects from Laos and other places in Vietnam, but they were only there for less than a week. Cadeo was the only man who remembered their names. No one had replaced the smile of Hien, like they'd expected to happen. Some villagers were punished for being deformed and slow to speech. Each man had his own failure to speak about, mostly failures from their youth and Henderson and Sam Law felt like orphans. Hare lipped men were abused and jailed.

The soldier with cracked glasses, Sam Law tapped his shirt for a cigarette, but his pockets had holes and smoke had not filled his lungs in months. The nervous POW from Virginia, Sam Law, would have sucked down two packs, if he'd had a smokey Joe Camel menthol handy, or a thin pipe to load. Even a pinch of tobacco for his lips would've tamed his nerves and settled his hands.

Without food, prisoners lost lean muscle mass, faced malnutrition, and begged for food from Polly, with their eyes and hands. They were whacked in the head by the V-C when food was spoken of, a cold task that happened often. It was common to be roped by the neck, jailed high in bamboo cages, even drugged, smacked with rifles, gagged, and beaten until the prisoner was unconscious.

"The worst part," said Le Mans, "being a man who wants to live, but feeling dead on the inside. Doesn't matter to the Viet-Cong who lives or who dies."

"Dead Americans are the best part of my day," said Chin Vo. Cadeo had overheard his words.

Humanity was at war, internal and external fighting; for pleasure; for leverage and for control. The V-C intended to forward the march of Communism. Americans planned to stomp it out. The chess match continued. Prisoners spoke of being fools, being captured, and for what good cause, but to die for their own country? Cars. Women. Family. Sports. Money. Nothing cool or popular was forgotten at times of war. Yeah, and freedom and their youth were the most talked about points of conversation.

Le Mans had his moments and held nothing back after the death of Hien. He spoke freely about protests being held by countercultural crowds, things worth noting, the unorganized legions who had no clue of the crimes against humanity that existed behind enemy lines and he couldn't wait to fire up his typewriter again. Torture was no longer a sin in a Communist nation; upon the start of the war, it was part of their military duty.

"Henderson?" said Le Mans, who waved.
"Yeah, hillbilly."

"Those camera-toting political activists we read about before we signed on, so let 'em walk in our boots for a week," said Le Mans, eyes closed. "I'll trade places with them anytime."

"I can't believe our journalists fall for the sympathy of Communism," said Henderson who sat, knees under his chin. "I hate war as much as the next person. They said American journalists rode inside Vietnamese tanks. How could they do such a twisted act?"

"They kill their own deformed villagers," said Le Mans, flat on his back. "I don't think they'd like to surrender to Communism inside a birdcage for a minute, witness death down inside a well or make peace talks with Charlie, while hanging in a thunderstorm above villagers, huh?"

Sam Law sat beside Le Mans.

"Nope. Is this what a year in Saigon is like without the ladies?" chuckled Sam Law.

"What year is it, anyway, Henderson?" said Le Mans, sighing. "Did the monsoon season miss us this year? It's hot as heck in Vietnam, boys." Le Mans scanned the camp. "God has forgotten about us Christians, my friends! Did we miss Christmas in 1970?"

"Le Mans?" said Sam Law abruptly, "Henderson ain't never seen the inside of a church," laughing, and falling backwards.

Henderson sat up tall and lifted his hands against Sam Law's nose.

"I was married inside a dang Amarillo Baptist church before I became a devout Buddhist!" said Henderson, yelling.

"What the heck does a "devout" Buddhist do anyway, Henderson?" said Le Mans, rubbing his chin, eyes raised. "Educate us, please, will you, Caveman?"

"We believe in Nirvana," said Henderson, widening his face with a proud smile.

"Nirvana?" said Le Mans. "What the heck is Nirvana?"

"The suffering of human life, spiritual growth, hard labor and meditation to the teacher, The Buddha," said Henderson, proudly.

"Jesus walked on water," said Le Mans, bobbing his head. "The Buddha can't top the miracles of Christ with Nirvana, can he?"

"You boys can carry-on all you like about The Buddha," said Henderson, walking away. "But karma is coming your way. Got to find the latrine, good soldiers."

Henderson ran to a tree.

"That man stays in the trunk of a tree more than anyone," said Sam Law, grinning.

"Guess that's part of his spiritual release," said Le Mans, leaning forward.

"I heard that," said Henderson, dropping his pants and making a moon.

"Shake your Buddha, Henderson," said Sam Law, pointing.

"Counting 1500 times, I've whizzed under this tree since we've been prisoners," said Henderson. "Fat rain hangs over my head and I need a good drink."

"Sounds like you got something to prove, Ted Williams," said Le Mans. "Swinging that baseball bat around in this God-forsaken jungle."

"Boy, I miss baseball," Henderson said, watering the ground. "Love to watch Mickey Mantle hit 'em out of the park."

"Speaking of baseball," said Le Mans, eyes closed and the sun warmed his sweating neck, "I saw Pete Rose play in Cincinnati; I believe it was in 1966."

"Don't you kid me, man," said Sam Law. "The new guy, Pete Rose, huh?"

"Yeah. They called him Charlie Hustle. He'll win a Gold Glove for the Reds next season. I'll bet you that much," said Le Mans, waving his hand. "He's that good."

"Texas Rangers, now that's my team, boys," said Henderson.

Moaning and groaning, "Gotta be a way past Charlie in this dang jungle," whispered Sam Law. He used both hands to test the strength of the fence. "Found a weak place, Le Mans. There's a shadow area inside the camp; I just know it. Few places where they can't find us in this hell camp. We'll get out of here soon." Sam Law struck the old bamboo fence and checked each pole. "Le Mans, it's been well over a year now, think they're still searching for three country boys like us?"

"The Air Cav won't leave us with these Communist pukes," said Le Mans, gripping his hands around the fat part of the wood poles and witnessing blocks, twisted wire and tied bamboo. Daylight broke a line between narrow bamboo poles, the only creak of light between being a prisoner and freedom.

"I've found the open door," said Le Mans, head low.

"You got an open door, huh, buddy?" said Henderson, shaking the bamboo fence in a strong rage. "Keep searching and you'll find us dead, Uncle Sammy."

"Listen to that pretty bird, hear it, huh?" said Le Mans, head canted.

"Don't hear anything," said Henderson, head angled to the green canopy.

"I hear it," said Sam Law, ear to the bamboo.

"He's tapping Morse Code," Le Mans said, eyes glued to the bird.

"You're a dang nutcase, Le Mans," said Henderson, pushing his arm.

Similar to Morse Code, tapping birds reminded Le Mans of something cool, something he'd taught himself in school. His dirty hands repeated the bird's pecking. Le Mans remembered communication without words, a little something he was well-trained in, which became a perfect system to adopt among prisoners. Le Mans coached Henderson, Cadeo, and Sam Law until sundown on how to effectively communicate Morse Code; for practice; for preparation, while scouting for the enemy.

Each day Le Mans trained the others. Prisoners softly tapped on hollow bamboo, high-valued communication, meant for short range talks, private places and a good ear was understood by adept Army soldiers. That week redefined prisoners, curling new faces of hope and practicing their craft of communication, individually coached and huddled in a small group. Le Mans trained Sam Law in Morse Code, who became an expert in a short while. Henderson nodded and ignored what was going on in the camp.

The prisoners laughed as if they'd conquered the V-C guards with their covert operation. Each prisoner knew how to communicate enough to signal with their eyes closed and effectively tap. They tapped and understood how sounds became crucial messages and soldiers planned to stay alive with their new secret. No one in a Communist country could decode their style of communication or had a clue how to understand Morse Code.

Le Mans tapped: "I will hide rice for an escape." Next, he rolled rice, golf ball sized pieces of rice and mentioned eating lizards and earthworms for protein when they needed more food for energy — something they hated to talk about, raw fish and snakes.

"Jerky would be a cool trip," said Le Mans. "Beef or venison, but this ain't no Charleston Shoney's, boys."

"Chicken, too," said Sam Law. "Pig-pork sandwiches. Fried eggs, man."

"Le Mans, I need to tell you something important," said Cadeo, hands crossed.

"What?" said Le Mans, eyes the look of a lobster. "Tell me, man, fast."

"Men will be coming for you soon."

"Me?"

"To kill you, my friend."

"You need to free us, like the birds. Think fast."

Within a week, Le Mans had collected rice and planned their big escape from Briarpatch. Four men needed one small pod of rice, worms, lizards, and slices of protein; real meat, but hopeful beef, was not dropped from the clouds. Something they could count on: Rats. Snakes. Lizards. Frogs. Fish. This type of real meat would not work inside slender bamboo poles, but Le Mans packed food he'd collected, bites of body fuel, for a mad exodus. Sam Law volunteered to be the brave point man, fighting the V-C guards when the time came to distract the dogs, and whack the opposition, and he'd do it nervously, too.

"Sam Law, step aside," said Henderson, armed crossed. "You're a little nutty in my book."

"I'm not the one who is crazy, here, Mr. Buddha," said Sam Law, up in his grill.

Big Henderson pushed Sam Law, but he caught himself.

"I'll be the hero on this great escape," said Henderson, flexing his arms. "You couldn't stick your finger up your...."

That's when Sam Law leveled Caveman. The Texan was flat on the ground.

"I'll stick my dirty foot up your Nirvana, Caveman." Sam Law pointed.

Le Mans saw what happened and ran between his friends.

"Stop it!" Le Mans fired back, face flushed, and he held each man back.

The three soldiers stood, arms out; Le Mans was the peacekeeper.

"You look like Raggedy Ann Lawrence," said Henderson.

"See if I ever save your life, Henderson!" said Sam Law, nose to nose.

"Hey, back off, guys! Lock it up!" sounded Le Mans, who pushed each man backwards, pressing his hands against puffed up chests. "Bad Haircut Charlie is our enemy, soldiers. We've got enough people trying to kill us. We don't kill each other. They want us to fight and cut each other."

"Let's fight to the death," said Henderson, shoulders back. "Gonna die anyway."

"Time to go," said Le Mans, watching the gate. "The time is now, to leave this pig pit, get gone, brothers. I'll tell Cadeo what's going on and when we need to exit Disneyland. I'm headed home to West "By God" Virginia. My hometown is overdue to see me. Had too much fun at Disney. Ready to build a boat, boys, like Noah."

"When we get back to the First Team, you're mine, Sam Law, boxing gloves."

"Be my best day in Vietnam, Henderson, was knocking you flatback."

"Save it!" said Le Mans. "Let's fight Charlie."

Broken mountain fog, steep terrain climbed into the sky, the height of a grand backdrop sheltered them. No machine ticked or no motorized Birds soared above them, and no Airborne Daddy dropped a rope to the riverbank. Tigers and snakes made up the worst of the jungle and other things would ease a man into a slumber for good, and all of it stood in the open doorway. Thousands of vines and trees blocked the way where a foot soldier had imagined an exit plan, hundreds of days earlier. Above them stretched an unwelcoming green canopy of fat trees that no man or animals had touched in decades. The valley floor of Vietnam was more deadly than any place in the world. Little time to debate the route, or flag a cabby, or build a yellow brick road.

"Our goal is," said Le Mans, looking over his shoulder for the V-C, "to find the rapids, float, make our way to the coast, signal a Bird, hunt Captain Hook, and go home." Le Mans carried a serious face and told each man the grand plan. "We need to rejoin the Cav Team and the time is now; it's here, soldiers. Let's go home or die trying. I feel it."

"I've prayed for this moment. My father wants me at Holy Cross College," said Sam Law, a big grin unfolded across his face. "I'll make it home to Virginia. Can't wait to catch a bus to South Bend, Indiana. My uncle lives there."

"Heck of a place, I bet, huh, buddy?" Le Mans told him.

"Yeah. Heck of a place, that's right, hillbilly. Holy Cross College is beside the Notre Dame Fighting Irish campus," said Sam Law, hands shaking nervously about his side.

"I'm the only true Irish fighter in this group, " said Henderson, fist on his chest.

Cadeo stepped up close to Le Mans and Sam Law.

"I saw a big waterfall when we first arrived, a mile away, plummeting a hundred feet or more. A long way to jump. Water points to the coast, I'm sure of it," said Cadeo. The man stood beside Le Mans, voice low, head up, and his smile told everyone how confident he was to make a run for freedom, like a silver pheasant flyer.

Henderson had his arms crossed, lip turned into a frown, head nodded.

"Good eyes, Cadeo. Flat and open land," said Le Mans, bent low. "That's a perfect spot to call in a Cobra helicopter, and hook a winged Bird. Remember the map and if we get separated, the rally point is one mile away, down at the waterfall. You'll hear the loud waterfall rushing before you see it. We're ready to fly out of here, men."

Soldiers agreed to draw a map in the dirt. They coached each other a half dozen days before it happened. In the rainy season, dry streams dwarfed into rushing rapids, and trickling waterfalls turned into roaring deep valleys that became impassable, descending across rugged land. It was predestined land, and Sam Law spoke of it being shaped and carved by God's hand, but time would tell if they could find a natural pathway, slip downstream into the valley without being shot.

"Where are we headed, Le Mans?" asked Lawrence. "What river?"

"Mekong River Delta," said Le Mans, armed crossed. He stood in what was left of his green uniform, once pressed tight to his body, now faded and torn into filthy rags. The sleeves were cut and pulled like strings of a mop head on his left arm.

"We need shoes, foot wrap," said Sam Law. "Giày ống."

"Good words," said Cadeo.

"I'm not Santa Claus, boys. I left my good shoes on the front porch in Wyoming County. Hey, boys, God will provide something, though. Keep the faith," said Le Mans, who dropped his head inside his cold, muddy hands. God was right beside them; he hoped. "Just counted my ribs. Skin and bones, soldiers. I need a Charleston Shoney's Big Boy burger." He gripped the flat, narrow bones, hips to his knees and counted them again. "What I'd give for a pot of my grandma Pearl's pinto beans and a slice of crunchy cornbread and some green tomatoes."

"Gotta try one of your Cherokee Purple tomatoes," said Sam Law, licking his lips. "I'll take my mother one when I get back home. She loves tomato and mayo sandwiches."

"My grandma Pearl's fried chicken will fatten you boys up in a week," said Le Mans, remembering how she grabbed his cheeks and filled his plate, seconds and thirds.

"Boy, my grandmother June could cook the best pork chop sandwiches in the world," said Sam Law. "I can count on you, hillbilly. Take us home to a pot of brown beans and golden cornbread, brother."

Sam Law held his hawk eyes on one of the best photojournalists in the Army, Beau Le Mans, a man ready to attempt the most deadly escape in his life and write his own headlines. He was born to explore the world afoot. What stood in his way? Charlie. How could each man live and tell his own story, the way it happened, he wondered? It was a dangerous move without weapons and no backup plan, and no leather boots.

"You were raised in the mountains, hillbilly, get us out of this dang rat hole, can you?" said Henderson, slapping his arm. "Or ... do you only write stories for the *Army Times* and play on a little pink typewriter, like the good Remington Raider, keeping your hands clean, huh? Did you ever really shoot a rifle at Fort Jackson? Or do you let the infantry boys do all the grunt work, so you'd have something to write about, Le Mans?"

"Nope. I'll show you grunt work!" said Le Mans, and the soldiers collided; two men rolled in the dirt and mud, slamming each other against the bamboo fence and landed on the ground.

In his Texas accent, Henderson shouted, "Just pulling your chain, man. Get off me, Le Mans! Grow your own tree, boy."

Sam Law and Cadeo laughed and weren't strong enough to break up two fighters in the mud, so they left them alone, fighting. Le Mans was the smaller fighter and seemed to have dry ground under his feet for several good punches and kicks.

"Now they'll kill us," said Henderson. "Look at that broken bamboo."

"Wait. Hold up!" said Le Mans, as he dropped Henderson and held broken pieces. He pulled his friend to his feet and tossed the pieces. "Listen," said Le Mans, whispering. "Stop what you're doing and get away from the fence." He pointed, head down, breathing heavily. "Walk back to the table, get away," said Le Mans, pacing. "Follow me, gotta a big-time plan brewing, soldiers. Let's go."

The prisoners followed Le Mans. Henderson had dirt in his hair and walked beside Le Mans, both men spitting mud and dirt.

"Sorry about roughing you up back there, Henderson," said Le Mans, dusting his hands, hair disheveled.

"Jackass, hillbilly!" said Henderson, rubbing the cut on his face. "Can't you take a stupid joke?" He brushed off his clothes. "Our roads will cross again, bud, in time. We'll settle this bout in boxing gloves. I love the sport."

"Oh, yeah, we'll have a rematch. I'll let you live today, Henderson."

"I'm sure we'll find the time."

"It's nothing, guys, drop it," said Sam Law, walking behind Le Mans. "Let's go at dark. You're one tough catbird, Le Mans. What's the idea?"

"Cadeo, sir?" waved Le Mans, who paced toward the Vietnamese prisoner.

"hillbilly," said Cadeo, "They are here. The V-C plans to kill at sunup."

They stopped.

"Not if they can't find me, Cadeo."

The small man's eyes lifted when Le Mans spoke and his English language was slow, but trustworthy. Cadeo respected Le Mans as much as his brother. They spoke for a moment about the plan; of Cadeo's part and how quick he needed to be ready to fight and exit the grounds. Sam Law and Henderson walked by Cadeo and Le Mans, and sat atop the table.

"One more thing, Cadeo, I need a favor from you, friend," said Le Mans, eyes popping with confidence and he nodded and rubbed his chin.

"Yeah. Favor? I can do it," said Cadeo, nodding, who knew just enough English to become dangerous. The Vietnamese POW was nervous, but he wanted out.

CHAPTER THREE

Night of Celebration

When private celebrations and traditions happened in North Vietnam, be it a birthday or holiday, not everyone knew about them. For the sake of war, Americans held no rights to any gatherings or celebrations in Vietnam, nor would they ever be honored guests. However, word spread inside the small POW camp, and Cadeo knew his culture and traditions as well as any Viet-Cong guard.

Polly was announced as the cook.

Cadeo overheard the details of the V-C guards who planned a big party and to kill him. That day became the most important week the prisoners had faced together, memorizing sounds, hand signals, learning the value of trust and soaking up Morse Code. They all feared death and spoke of life after death.

Would the plan work? thought Le Mans

The evening was meant to be remembered; fresh food, wine and beer were transported by a small truck from the villagers and handed out in celebration to the guards. Cadeo saw fear on Polly's face; she was dark haired and dressed in a bright floral outfit; for the pleasure of the Vietnamese celebration.

Two more ladies arrived, but not to help Polly in the kitchen. Tears rolled down Polly's face, because she knew what ladies of that type did for a living in the dark. They had other plans with men. More women showed up. Legs smooth, and sexy women dressed in expensive rented clothing. V-C guards pulled them from the vehicle and escorted the ladies to small rooms. Ladies kissed the guards like they'd been gone for many years.

A total of four Vietnamese women showed up, broken hearted, Polly, made five, all in their early twenties, hair pinned up, eyes outlined in dark lash, and red blush padded atop pale faces. They appeared as though they'd walked out of a cluster of puffy Angel clouds, or staged at the entrance of a theater in Hollywood. Le Mans stopped Henderson from whistling and held his shoulders.

"Don't draw attention our way." Le Mans convinced him to stop.

According to Cadeo, the ladies had been warned about having conversations with Americans. Women glowed with wide smiles, hips turned, walking past Henderson, Sam Law, Le Mans, and Cadeo, who wanted to jump and dance, eyes held to dolls of delight, fresh from hot romance films.

Gloom had passed, and the camp became an amusement park for a few short hours in the bright evening sun, and the setting became the most interesting day in Vietnam for Le Mans. About sundown, V-C guards exchanged beer for kisses with the ladies and paraded them around, making them dance and sing and turn. Only one of them had a voice worth recording and the others only howled. Men and women were intoxicated in an hour.

Polly had not touched a single bottle. Le Mans dozed off. Cadeo slapped his shoulder. Through the open window, Le Mans and Cadeo watched as Polly cried and held her face over the sink because her husband, Chin Vo, had taken one of the ladies to his room, locking the door.

In contempt, Polly ran to the door and waved for Cadeo, still crying.

"Le Mans, hey, Polly wants to see you after the guards pass out," said Cadeo, hands moving back and forth. "This is the time." He told Le Mans about her.

"Unsure. Afraid," said Polly, eyes wet. "They plan to kill Le Mans in the morning after the ladies leave." Polly looked at the hut where her husband was, and said, "Yes. Tell Le Mans, I will see him."

"Good," said Cadeo. "Go back to the party. We will meet you later."

One more thing was whispered to Polly.

Cadeo swiftly told Polly how Le Mans needed to say something important, words in private. The man whispered to her in confidence, low and brief, and both spoke in Vietnamese, touching hands. Polly had agreed to talk to him when the time was right. She had seen Le Mans several times over the past year and knew he was a good hearted man from the way he looked after Hien and Cadeo. Their hands met through the fence a few times, but Le Mans had only daydreamed longingly about kissing her. Le Mans cared for all the prisoners, especially Cadeo, taking him under his wing for nearly a year after Hien was killed. He felt Polly was the gatekeeper and might take a chance, open the door, and help them without getting everyone killed.

Duc Vo, Chin Vo, and three new guards, escorted the ladies in silk, stumbled into bed with them after they'd partied on snake wine and tiger beer. Then, the five guards passed out, alongside four women who were undressed. Le Mans had no idea how it would happen.

At that moment Polly rose from her bed, opened the door to her husband's room, and found a nude lady draped atop Chin Vo's naked body. The room was filled with smoke, and eyes were closed. No guards or ladies had made any movement in more than an hour. Le Mans signaled with a soft whistle. Polly dashed to where he stood, still emotional, but she unlocked the door. Le Mans reached for her, hands free for the first time. Polly fell into his arms and he turned her in a circle.

"Thought you had forgotten about me," said Le Mans.

"No, no, no. I went away."

"You were missed."

Words of affection, the truth, something original, and overdue happened. They kissed for the first time.

"No one has ever treated me with respect, Le Mans," said Polly, eyes wet and sniffing. "Not my father, not Chin Vo; for as long as I can remember, no one, but you, Le Mans."

Her hands were soft, frame thin, and her skin was perfumed like roses; for the first time she'd finally held him. They pressed each other under the shadow of large palms and what they'd planned, the big escape, slipped their minds for a brief moment.

"You combed your hair, Le Mans," said Polly, who turned a big smile.

"Yes; for you. Wish we'd met in better times, suit and tie times, and other places."

"Far from war," Polly said in a low voice. "I wish for the same."

Cadeo ran to Le Mans.

"Hurry, Beau Le Mans!" Cadeo pulled his shirt. "Good to see you free, Polly. The open door, Le Mans." The twin brother stood at the doorway and waited. "We are free from chains, hurry, go, Le Mans. Let's go, go, go, hillbilly." They both grinned.

"We are short on time," said Le Mans, holding her hand. "I've waited a long time to hold you, Polly, and feel you." Le Mans slipped on the shoes she'd handed him. "I'll come back for you."

"Can I go with you?" asked Polly, eyes sincere. "Take me with you." She begged and whispered in his ear. "Please, sir. Let's go far away together, take me to America."

"Beer and smoke worked like a charm, Le Mans. Good job, Polly," said Henderson. "Guards are knocked out, man. We'll meet you at the rocks." Henderson stepped outside the POW cage in a smaller man's shoes for the first time, rushing by Le Mans.

"Let's go to the cave," said Polly.

"The cave?" asked Le Mans.

For a time, they'd been shoeless, but that time had ended. Sam Law, Henderson, and Le Mans were laced up.

"We need to run, Romeo," said Sam Law, who stepped between them and pulled the shoulder of Le Mans. "Don't miss the bus, hillbilly. Get your ticket punched."

"You need a bath, Sam Law," said Polly. "What's a hillbilly, Le Mans?"

"A man from the mountains." Le Mans held her hand. "Let's go to the cave."

Down a narrow footpath, Polly pointed her flashlight into the mouth of the cave and faced Le Mans. Both of them forgot about war and punishment for a brief moment. They disappeared. No one was around. No dogs. No owls. No one followed them. They were finally alone.

"Now what, Beau Le Mans?"

"We made it this far."

The sun edged out the night. In nervousness they stood next to a pool of water, dripping above them was a steady stream of water. Without hesitation, they found each other. That special moment was for Polly and Beau, searching; then, few words were spoken, caught in a language they both knew. Walking out of the cave, Polly kissed and hugged him and neither one wanted to let go of the other one.

"I promise, Polly, I'll be back for you."

"I'll be waiting. I love you, Beau Le Mans."

"I've always loved you, Polly. Now, go hide. I'll find your camp."

Halfway down the pathway, tears trailed down her face and she waved to Le Mans as the sun shined on her pretty face. Neither one said farewell in any language. Next, when Le Mans looked back to check on his new love, the lady had disappeared into the dense jungle.

Le Mans prayed someone hadn't spotted her betrayal, an act of certain death. The buoyancy of hope, a spark of sunlight; of morning light, lifted his face before the absence of her and gloom hijacked what little optimism he had for her and any jolt of spirit was frozen on his stifling journey, which he knew would lead him far from cages and bars.

"I'll be back for her." Le Mans said in a low voice.

The shortest prisoner, Cadeo, the man who still held the keys to their escape, found Le Mans on the narrow path at sunup, being lifted off the ground, and said, "Let's go, hillbilly."

"You can't go with us," said Le Mans, holding his shoulder.

Cadeo's face which held hope had melted away his words.

"You lied to me, Le Mans. You said brothers, best friends, and now you lied."

"I will come back for you, Cadeo."

"No good. You lied." Cadeo pushed him. "Did you lie to Hien, the two of us?"

"No."

"I trusted you, man. Take me with you, Le Mans. I'm a strong fighter. I'm brave."

Cadeo extended his deformed arm for the first time toward Le Mans, for his courage and bravery, but most of all his close friendship and his small hand. Cadeo saluted him in perfect form.

"You are a strong fighter. Trust me, this is your land," said Le Mans, returning his salute. "Please stay with Polly and fight for her. I'll be back for you and her, if I make it to the coast."

With slurred speech, stuttering, Cadeo said, "This is no land for anyone, Le Mans. No one can enjoy a good life here. I am free, like the birds. I found the open door."

Cadeo's face dropped and he took a few steps down the same path where Polly had disappeared and stopped. Cadeo turned around, and said, "I am a good fighter. I deserve freedom, too, same as you do. Me and Polly will be no trouble to you. I beg you, sir." He offered his fists. "Take us to your country, Le Mans. We are good brothers. You love her, man. Take her. Don't lie to us."

"Please forgive me. I'll send soldiers, Cadeo. Helicopters will help you and Polly get out of here. Go keep her safe," said Le Mans, arms extended, waving , "Go, go, go, run free."

Cadeo crossed his heart and said, "God be with you, brother."

Cadeo took one step and turned.

"You come back for me and Polly, right, okay?" he said seriously. Cadeo lifted his deformed arm out to his friend in admiration. "Best friends, Le Mans. Love you, brother."

Le Mans nodded, and tucked a lump in his throat, and ran into the woods, so he felt, masking dishonor and induced by the thought of freedom, he kept to the path to the river. While Polly and Le Mans stood inside the cave, Cadeo had spoken with Sam Law, talking about a safe journey. Henderson ran into the jungle, resting until Le Mans joined them. Next, Sam Law followed with shoes he'd stolen from Chin Vo's porch, who was buck naked; immoral, improper, and now, shoeless Charlie, too.

Cadeo retreated with Polly and hid inside a deep rock cliff, far away from the Viet-Cong guards, who soon would be irate and hunt for three Americans, and a small Vietnamese prisoner. Le Mans was proud of the way Cadeo protected himself and felt confident he was with Polly. Two guns, one held with concern in Polly's hands, the other for Cadeo. Their exile to the rock cliffs was only temporary. The realization that Le Mans was gone frightened her. Being found made her sick and she vomited.

"It's okay, Polly," said Cadeo. "He's a good man; be back soon."

"Hope so." She wept.

Le Mans promised himself he'd return for Polly. A hundred times he'd dreamed of helping her to freedom, but he couldn't take her away as he first planned. She was someone he thought would be his wife. Reality, being free, and he hoped to one day rescue her from oppression and give her a decent life, a far better home, too. As Le Mans chopped his way through the jungle, her face had fallen into his memory, as if they held each other again inside the cavern, imagining music, candles and more suitable times. He heard her voice in the jungle and saw her face inside the leaves of the canopy and then, the morning sun was a warm feeling they'd be together.

Maybe God is with me, he thought.

Her words felt no different to him than a song or a poem: "If we'd only known each other in your country, Beau Le Mans, sharing our lives would mean more than Nirvana."

"If you've ever known love, say it now, Polly, right?"

"Right now, this is our moment, Beau. There's no tomorrow, no wedding bells, only right now, and it's something good you can tell others, though."

Le Mans remembered her shiny hair and placid smile; her sweet darling way; her contagious sense of wonderment and elegance, and the unfair situation he'd left her in, things that haunted him, was the heartbreaking reality he lived in - the war. Then, Le Mans ducked into the thick jungle and their lives were separated and over before they'd even started. He'd forgotten to mention how courageous she was for releasing three POWs, the way she risked her life for him: a statement of truth, the way she felt. He thought about how he'd ever find her again.

The further away Le Mans traveled from Polly, the louder the violin sounded inside his head: better brief and warm, than a man's cold regret, he thought. Music echoed in his mind that way, humming to the slow violin made his aching heart anxious to see her again.

The Americans disappeared down a dark, shapeless trail, one that narrowed and slowed their pace more and more as they left behind the most horrible part of their lives. Good friends. Le Mans hoped to see them again, part of him was left behind and they meant the world to him. To turn around, to help them; he'd be killed. Above all, the secret love Polly had given him, sparked an ember inside him, even as he distanced himself into the plight of the jungle. Hope fueled his steps, and still, two hearts caught between love and war.

I should turn back, he told himself a hundred times. *I hate myself for selfishly escaping, not returning for her and Cadeo; for both of them; with all her beauty, she still belonged to someone else.*

In an intentional act of trust and faith, the right thing for Polly to do was to release the three Americans and save her own life, if she could; Polly and Cadeo had given them the open door to freedom and they ran. No one could blame them. The men had made only a small amount of progress through the jungle, the land hindered by their uncomfortable shoes and flourishing vines that had woven and spread into thicket after endless thicket. No pathway had existed here for a thousand years.

"Where's the rice, Le Mans, I'm hungry as a wolf?" said Henderson, eyes rolling.

"Left the food inside the dark cave."

"All that planning was bull crap," said Sam Law, head bent back.

"Romeo, you're no hero in the jungle," said Henderson.

In a little while, the mighty roar of rushing water sounded in a deep valley, heightening spirits and they held and grinned at each other, as if they'd made it home: Baileysville, Amarillo, Winchester. The boys were headed home.

By the time they'd reached the riverbank, sometime at midday, resting and exhausted, blisters had formed on the hands of each man and the sun had baked their skin. Those final hours, the beginning of their first evening of freedom, had cost them time and energy. Escape happened with every swift swing and the coolness of the valley waterway was an unplanned reward of flat, algae covered rocks and a pond full of fish. Still, they were only a mile from where they'd left Polly and Cadeo.

"POW!"

Le Mans jumped.

"Gunshot?" asked Sam Law, splashing water on his face.

"POW!" All three men halted their process.

The second sound confirmed their questions. Henderson jumped and turned, legs nervous, and his hand pointed at the Briarpatch POW Camp. He said nothing. The Americans stopped stabbing for fish. Le Mans feared the worst had happened. Each man turned slowly to see the small, broken trail they'd cut; two shots had taken their hope away, as they considered the jeopardy of close friends.

"Let's keep going," said Le Mans, head down. "Nothing we can do for them now."

"He's right," said Sam Law. "They'd love to kill us for escaping."

"Jesus!" said Le Mans, who propped himself up with a long stick. "Did you think the shots were aimed to kill Polly and Cadeo?" He leaned against a tree and pounded his fist.

Walking past Le Mans with a fat fish on a stick, Henderson grabbed his shoulder, face tight, and said, "I'm not going back to find out. Forward march. They'll be fine. They'll live. Let's eat meat while we can."

"I've lost my appetite," said Le Mans, vomiting.

"Two dogs didn't bite the bullet, I bet you that much," said Sam Law, who followed behind Henderson. "Keep moving, buddy." He told Le Mans, face puckered and sour. "Charlie could've shot two chickens for breakfast, right?"

"Not likely," said Le Mans, head turned up toward the sky in prayer.

Le Mans thought of a dozen things he'd give her as he walked the riverbank, if he ever had the chance to treat her like a queen. New yellow dress. Flowers to match. New hat for dancing and dinner and pictures, and she'll need lots of framed pictures on the wall. Big birthday celebration. What was her favorite color? He'd spend the rest of his life asking himself the same questions, not to have the answers about Polly, was something of a tragedy, more or less the same for both of them. Her favorite color was obvious, it was the color of her clothes, yellow and blue, he thought. He imagined she answered him back with her favorite food and favorite place to eat in Wyoming County.

But Le Mans had remembered something, all the days she'd worn different shades of yellow and blue, the bright colors of flowers: a tall thought of certainty, happiness, the elongated notion of the same colors she preferred. Things like that captured his imagination of her life, from first glance, he noticed and thought of them living in America: until a day unlike the rest, he saw her soul through her sweet smile and honest eyes. They both lived and loved, and in that moment, a friendship was born. Goodness and love was anticipated. He hoped God planned for them to have dinner in a more civilized setting.

"Sad truth," Sam Law said. "Henderson is finally right about something."

"What am I right about?" said Henderson, leading the way.

"There's no mercy in Buddhism," said Sam Law. "I fear Polly and Cadeo suffered just like you said. No mercy exists in Buddhism. Christianity is much different, boys. There's grace and peace and mercy. My Catholic religion tells me so."

"Maybe they are doing just fine," said Le Mans, nodding and walking. He chewed his own catch, a small fish. "They could've shot Duc Vo and Chin Vo, and finally finished it, huh?"

"We'll never know," said Sam Law.

Three sweaty soldiers kept pace, and the realization of lost friends, the lack of humanity left a nasty taste of war in their mouths and in their memories. Le Mans knew they were being hunted. Soon they'd have followers, and, no doubt, more well fed V-C fighters on their trail. Predators and prey, he thought. Others would follow them. More and more V-C would gladly join the hunt for three slow Americans.

"We need guns," said Le Mans.

"I'll order guns from Montgomery Wards, hero," said Sam Law, laughing.

"Yeah. They'll be here in 7 to 10 business days, soldiers," said Henderson, chuckling.

Le Mans felt a blanket of uncertainty slowing him down and he battled the heat and vines of the thick jungle, belly full, now cutting a new pathway to freedom. Though destined to press on, homeward bound, Le Mans picked up the pace en route to the unknown. Finally free, only to broaden the gap between him and the fearless fighters of Ho Chi Min. Heavily burdened with the worst thoughts of mankind, he traversed, and became less compassionate and amped his warm blood toward his enemy. Moreover, Le Mans was the only soldier who glanced back, pondering his loss of friends, Polly, the past, and it was tough to turn toward the future and to leave behind his friendship with Cadeo and the good heart of Polly.

"Need a doctor, Le Mans." Sam Law showed his foot.

"Dang it, you're bleeding," said Le Mans. "Did you cut yourself?"

Lawrence sank to the ground and removed a shoe made for a different foot. Each man stuck to the soft earth for a moment, leaving footsteps, feet jammed into smaller Vietnamese shoes: one more disadvantage in a meandering cross stitch of nature and unable to take the roadway or find a Good Samaritan from Scripture, when they needed care. A thorn had embedded itself inside the foot of Sam Law.

"Can you make it until dark, Sam?" Le Mans examined his foot.

"Yeah, I believe so," said Lawrence, moaning. "Let's march on."

"Wait!" said Le Mans, dropping to his knees. "Don't move! I'll cut it out or cut it off."

"Please. Cut it out, hillbilly, use that nail you swiped at camp."

Henderson scouted for enemies while his friend operated.

"It's cut deep," said Le Mans, hands on the thorn.

"O' take it easy, man." Sam Law blurted out. "Bleeding like a cut pig."

"Got it," said Le Mans, uncovering a thin thorn the size of a toothpick.

"You ain't no writer, man, you're a doctor," said Sam Law, who wiggled his foot.

"Loosen those laces," said Le Mans. "Let's go, Winchester."

Nodding, "Better than nothing," said Sam Law, tall and confident.

Le Mans held his lucky machete knife, a comfortable fit to his open door, building rhythm and speed over his comrades, even taking the lead when Sam Law and Henderson rested, sweating in the shade, sucking down three bananas each. Staring at the hillside, overgrown and thick, hundreds of trees and vines twisted and crooked into a thousand different directions. Labor that made Le Mans angry at President Nixon and his boys.

Green vegetation climbed from the earth to the sky, like hundreds of giant beanstalks planted by Jack himself. The three men, bent and tired but made progress, hour by hour, swing by swing. The more they'd distanced themselves from Briarpatch POW Camp, the worse Le Mans became sick to his stomach about what might have happened to his friends. He closed his eyes, saddened by the unknown, but to return to his Vietnamese friends was immediate execution: an Army failure; and Sam Law and Henderson, carried on without him, sprawled under the tall palms and soaked in discouragement. All concurred about certain death and staying far away from Briarpatch.

"We put Polly and Cadeo in a world of danger," said Le Mans, voice low and tired.

"Forget about her, man, it's over, dang it!" said Henderson, head back. "We had no other choice. No compromise. She was the open door, the key to freedom. She's done her job, let her go, man."

"He's right. She was our exit," said Sam Law, who used bamboo as a cane. "She's not able to be on our team. How we left them was the best way: after you forget about her, you'll realize we're still at war. No one can win, not even love, especially when she's the wife of a Communist leader. She's a Commie lover, dude."

"Napalm can be your fireworks and bullets can be confetti, Romeo. You need to give up on that charade, Le Mans, it's over between you and her," said Henderson, out of breath. "You got what you wanted, didn't you, Lover Boy?"

"Shut your mouth, Caveman!" Le Mans fired back. "She's a fine lady."

"Bet she was silky clean," said Henderson, fingers in a circle.

"You two don't know a good woman from a bad one," said Le Mans, stepping in front of them. "Get out of the way."

Le Mans knew his Vietnamese friends were dead, so he took command of his troops.

"Are there any good people left in the world?" asked Le Mans.

"Not this side of the world," said Sam Law, eyes raised at Le Mans. "It's a sick culture of killers and rapists, the evil of Communism at work."

The man from Texas bent over, gagging and emptied his stomach.

"Henderson is sick, Sam Law," said Le Mans, watching his friend clear his stomach.

"You gotta get us out of this killer jungle," said Sam Law, waiting for Henderson to wipe his wet eyes. "Le Mans, you can do it."

"Had too much to eat. We'll see what kind of soldier he is, and time will tell if he gets us out of this jungle and down the river," said Henderson, face red. "I feel better, boys."

"Wish I was hiking the Shenandoah River in Woodstock, Virginia," said Sam Law, hand on his bamboo pole. "The Baileysville boy is a trooper. God will show him the jungle door."

Le Mans staggered, broken on the inside, and his face was as pale as a country biscuit. Nothing stopped him from swinging his machete in anger, cutting and chopping, the only way out of the jungle. The best part, the V-C would never find their narrow trail at the riverbank, thinking they'd hopped into a rice paddy or stayed on the easy, open road.

Morning rose and the world was the same. No Birds. No taxi cabs. Across the continent, no continental breakfast existed, or room service for peanut butter and bagels. The mind made the stomach suffer at meal time. Three Americans were exhausted. Politics and weapons and propaganda caused men and women to die in Vietnam and it's hard to say how many innocent lives were taken each day for trying to exit corruption. Thoughts like that crossed the mind of Le Mans. Polly and Cadeo were caught in the middle of a nasty war, a war watered by dirty politics. Le Mans felt a freight train of heavy guilt for befriending Polly, lying to Cadeo, and spoke less than the others the further they traveled from the POW camp. Two wonderful people were in harm's way because of his escape plan, he thought. As a foot soldier, swinging like a well-oiled machine.

Off the ground and away from the elements, the second day was no different than the first for Le Mans, and his friends. Downrange was an abandoned building, a village of days gone by. Homes were constructed in Vietnam after the Great Depression hit, which became the nickname of soldiers, "Disneyland of the Far East."

"Here's a good hideout," said Le Mans. "Let's do our laundry."

"Heck of a bunk, mates," said Henderson, speaking in an Australian accent.

All three men stayed hungry. Eventually, exhaustion defeated hunger and they slept.

They opened their eyes when Vietnamese voices sounded from villagers, twenty feet away. Breaking his cover, fully exposed, Sam Law stepped into a clear roadway to scout the area for more villagers.

"POW!"

A sniper, thought Le Mans.

The shot to the chest of Private Samuel Lawrence was fatal. He turned to Le Mans, eyes closed, chest of crimson and the man fell, not knowing what hit him. Another meaningless life taken, unarmed, too, but to a Vietnamese sniper, it mattered none. Le Mans saw his face in slow motion, the terms of war became evident again, parceled out before his very eyes and death hit home again and broke his heart. The sum of his days, hopes to be in South Bend, had ended in a foreign land.

"Get down, Henderson," whispered Le Mans, dropping low to the ground. He grabbed Henderson's leg before his friend stepped into the scope of another sniper.

"Was that the Cobra Sniper?" said Henderson. "We need Carlos Hathcock to back us up, the best sniper in America."

"Sam Law is dead," said Le Mans, dropping behind a canopy of vegetation. "Gone."

Henderson saw the body of Sam Law collapse, lifeless and helpless; still, there was nothing Le Mans or Henderson could have done to help him. That was war. They ducked into heavy cover and listened to V-C soldiers talking and laughing at the dead American. Le Mans wanted a machine gun, a knife, and an eye for an eye. One chance for redemption, just one rifle and forty rounds to pour firepower on the man who pulled the trigger.

The sniper's position was unknown. Le Mans and Henderson backed inside the thickness of heavy brush and leaves, and across the way, perched atop of rocks, scoping for more Americans, the confirmation of deadly Viet-Cong fighters. After the shot sounded, the hillside exposed too many V-C to count, hundreds of them fired at the abandoned building.

"Uninvited company," said Le Mans, eyeing the hillside. "Good thing we didn't do our laundry."

"They haven't spotted us yet. I gotta go to the latrine."

"What?" Le Mans whispered, face behind body-size leaves. "Hold it tight."

"They don't need to see the whites of our eyes or smell us, hillbilly."

"They'll be down here soon, double checking. I hope you have to whizz."

After a short rain, heavy fog blanketed the open landscape. Le Mans and Henderson had slipped deeper into the thickness of overgrown roots and tall grass. Both men stayed hunkered down until the Viet-Cong crossed the swampy trail. Faces covered in mud, Le Mans saw dark glasses, men in wait and ready to kill again. He also saw the sniper on the hillside. Like statues inside the jungle, two American soldiers blended into the bulk of nature and observed their enemies on the prowl.

Two trucks pulled beside the body of Sam Law, and soldiers jumped out.

In a heated rush, the driver yelled in the face of Sam Law. He blasted an automatic weapon into the air, yanking his weapon downward into the lifeless body of Samuel Lawrence, and a loud, lanky Viet-Cong soldier scouted for more Americans to kill. The man walked over narrow trails, pushing leaves, and shouting. Unknowingly, he'd stepped on foot of Beau Le Mans, and scanned the field beside the road where Sam Law was killed. The V-C had no idea that he'd crossed the ankle of an unarmed American soldier. The smell of cigarette smoke crossed the nose of Le Mans, and loud voices spoke until twilight. Two Viet-Cong soldiers pulled the bloody body of Sam Law to a tree and roped him several times. One man threw his Dog Tags into the brush. Two men struck lighters: one man burned his body while the other man cheered and shot into the high flames that burned into the night.

Birds on the roost were flushed into a nearby hillside when the crazy eyes of the V-C commander emptied forty rounds into the flaming orange body of Sam Law, charred and consumed. The rapid fire was the most doleful moment Le Mans had ever witnessed. After a radio transmission, two more truckloads of V-C arrived to scout the area. They observed the smoke-filled sky; men of levity and sickness loaded up their comrades and drove away.

"Thank God Sam Law wasn't burned alive," said Henderson, who whispered and rolled onto the flat of his back. "To torch his body was a hell of a statement to us."

"Thousands more will die in this same type of fiery hell. The only resolution would be to drop more big bombs, wipe out Communism, and change the hearts of men," said Le Mans. He shivered in anger, gripping mud and grass. In his mouth, he crunched the bark of a branch.

"Do you really change hearts by killing more of their brothers and sisters, huh, Le Mans?" Henderson held his face. "These people are as good as we are, man."

"Hearts have to be changed to press out Communism, Caveman."

"Regardless, we'll get out of here tomorrow," whispered Henderson. "Float to the ocean and find our way home."

"I believe to my soul, it's time to go home," said Le Mans, eyes filled with confidence.

Le Mans and Henderson had witnessed too many soldiers killed in action; for the cause; and had grown repelled with the scope of political leadership toward soldiers and the innocence of being caught amid the Big War. But who was to look after the innocent, women and children, Le Mans thought. Then, he rested for the night.

For their own safety, they watched Sam Law burn until the flames faded; skin charred black, clothes and another man's shoes melted to his body. From underneath the brush and vines, they were hidden and motionless until morning. They felt it was the best time to see the body, relocate and rally to the riverbank. They planned to advance a great distance on the third day.

Neither Uncle Sam nor Jesus had, by 1970, returned for the soldiers despite silent prayers for a visit from either one. Still, the moonlit sky was blocked with black smoke which sent a nasty message to all American soldiers. Nothing was left to do, but to advance their position and remain hidden. Le Mans and Henderson reclined in the cavity of a riverbank until it was time to close the gap on the body of Sam Law.

"Found his dog tags," said Le Mans, saying a prayer. They didn't spend much time at the body and made their way to the river, unwrapping their bloody feet in the water.

"Good deed, buddy. I was asleep. Back in Robin's Egg, Texas, I saw a friend burn to death, when I was a kid," said Henderson, eyes flashing restlessly and his face was disguised. "My best friend was twelve. The sight of Sam Law burning will never leave your mind. He deserved better."

At sunup, Henderson woke and stood up first, ready to advance to the abandoned building and collect any remains left behind by Sam Law, such as metal buttons, or any part of his uniform that could be given to his family. Something.

"Do you know if Sam Law was married?" said Henderson, who studied his friend's face.

"Never heard talk about a wife," said Le Mans, scouting the area.

"He may have a gold ring inside his pocket," said Henderson.

Le Mans grabbed Henderson and stopped him from pacing into the road where Sam Law was killed. The hillbilly had superb hearing and waved Henderson to the ground again. Four Viet-Cong soldiers popped out of the jungle and searched for more Americans, especially searching for three prisoners who escaped from Briarpatch POW Camp.

After ten minutes of scouting, the V-C patrolled where Sam Law was burned. Their base camp was most likely less than two miles or so away from where Sam Law was torched. They searched for more soldiers to burn, but found no one lurking.

"You want to fight us, Americans!" shouted the leader of the V-C. "Come out and fight!" He knew English better than most American immigrants, firing his weapon multiple times into the abandoned building, one Le Mans had not explored.

Later, Le Mans found a match and struck in the dry grass; high flames turned the sky black again and became their approach to drawing a helicopter into a dogfight. Le Mans raged on the inside from the horrific death of his friend, but he knew to remain hidden for as long as possible, was his safety ticket.

Was it the ticket to survival or death? Wishing he was at the Detroit Auto Rama, or somewhere else, anywhere else, rock climbing, or driving in the mountains of West Virginia, so Le Mans prayed often. However, Le Mans was amid hell on earth, missing in action, or killed in action, a man who had been missing for over a year. He was assumed to be dead by his company commander. Nothing to do but to reserve energy and think about his next plan.

"Let's steal a Jeep or make a US flag while we wait." said Le Mans.

"It's time to call President Nixon, make it collect to Tricky Dickie, dude."

Seated in front of crape myrtles, Le Mans watched Henderson remove thorns from his hands and legs, the same thing Sam Law had done, days earlier. In a pool of water, the time was right to clean up. The endless days of monsoons had dropped gallons of rain across Vietnam. Later, inside the mouth of a rock cliff, head dropping, half asleep, Le Mans held one eye lurking through a finger hole he'd cut in the broadside of a leaf and steadied his post, scouting. The soldier from West Virginia was hidden behind roots, lost in an endless jungle, far from civilization.

Suddenly, just after sunup four Viet-Cong soldiers occupied the roadway and blocked their open door. Ducking into the dry hillside, the two men had made it impossible for Le Mans and Henderson to advance their position. For the second time, they were stuck. Thick roots blocked Le Mans and the natural curve of mangrove trees cast long shadows over two lonely, homesick men and by sundown they'd spotted three Asia palm civets and one Pygmy slow loris.

Taught to hide in green moss and shallow water, Le Mans and Henderson itched from hundreds of bug bites. Both soldiers slipped into an overwhelming shock, and fell asleep from toxic insect bites. Henderson went first. Then, in a low tone, Le Mans mumbled unrecognizable words and blacked out. The two of them twitched sporadically for hours.

In another world of dreams, Le Mans pictured dinner with candlelight and wine, and he saw himself seated atop high autumnal mountains, spoke to strange images, seaward-moving pirates, pale faces, fiery spirits, even more animals were beneath him than in other dreams, and all the world was afoot. His dreams revealed eerie howling coyotes fighting in packs, people screaming in pits, strange lights and horses snouted and stood in the smoky haze of a mountain trail, a warning to the people, he thought. Henderson twitched and clawed his legs until blood ran, and he slapped the arm of Le Mans, who never finished his dream.

It happened again in a dream, hard confessions in Holy Cross chapel, but no one was there to listen to Le Mans. The soldier missed loved ones, some dead, some alive, missing them all. Within the next hour, Le Mans slipped into another dream, a door opened, and he stumbled across the afterlife of war, a place less civilized than before.

"Polly?"

He carried her to a door, a hundred yards away stood a hospital, one window, one door, and one single bed was in the room. The nurse was delightful. In her southern manner, she told how Polly was doing just fine.

While Polly slept, Le Mans reached for the window blinds, and tried to see the mountains of West Virginia, perhaps.

"I'm Eileen, sir." The nurse said and stopped his hand. "Please beware of the outside," she continued. "That was George's garden. Sir, he left you a letter. Here."

"What? Left me a letter?" Le Mans saw an envelope but left it on the table and refused to open it. "First, can I look out the window, see the wonderful world? I will read it later."

"I can't stop you, soldier."

Le Mans nodded, held the string in his hand and hesitated. The man pulled the white blinds, rolling upward, and opened the hospital curtains as wide as he could.

"I warned you, didn't I, soldier, huh?" Eileen left the room.

Greenery and golden mountains were gone, tops of trees burnt, leaves absent, just a few things stood, a man, a woman, hand-in-hand, walking and pushing a stroller. The barren land didn't bother them, yet fading into the distance, beyond the garden, where a flower garden once bloomed, they walked. To the left, wavy golden plains had faded into dust. Seeds were all around, unable to unfold. Wild animals and livestock were lifeless in the field, and some less graceful. Fires burned, and the air was dusty and smoky and breathing labored the lungs. He coughed and hacked against the glass, so he closed the window and blinds before the ashes covered Polly's white blanket.

The nurse knocked, and within a dozen steps, Eileen stood beside Le Mans.

"Life slowly disappeared, all at once," Eileen said. "The preacher warned us. You and Polly are the first patients I've had since the garden faded and the preacher went away. The hospital lasted, but, for most of them, they spent their last days together, not side-by-side in hospital beds, but worse." No one spoke for a brief moment. Each one examined the aftermath of war. "The ones with money tried to buy health, and the doctor died in his own grief, and tried to save his own family first, the wealthy ones, but the poor had nothing to lose or live for. That's who you see, the ones reading Scripture waiting on the Lord, still singing hymns and living a humble life."

"Whose jar of money is inside the window?" asked Le Mans, handing it to her.

"That man, Wells Le Mans, left the mason jar for the hospital. Said you'd be here and would need it soon."

"Wells? My brother. Where's my brother, Eileen?"

"Yeah. He is here. Out there."

"That's my brother, Wells, his wife, Elly, and their new baby!"

"Shut the window, Beau Le Mans!" The nurse grabbed his hands. "Wells can't hear you, Sir! You are alive and so is Polly. What you see is the afterlife."

"The afterlife? Why? What happened?" asked Le Mans.

"Talk to God, Beau Le Mans, just talk to the Lord." Eileen stood in the doorway. "Rules are made by Him, the Man upstairs. No one else makes the rules."

Three days had passed; Polly was still asleep. Le Mans divided his time between the three rooms. He saw the strangest things, carpenters working on a new church and building a maternity ward, off to the north. Le Mans helped the carpenters, and asked around, with the motive to find Wells Le Mans. No one knew his brother. One day Wells walked by the window and knocked and smiled, hair parted perfectly and joy filled his eyes. Head against the glass, Beau Le Mans, still in his green Army fatigues, and he jumped out the window when he saw the happy face of Wells.

"Wells?" hugging his brother at ground level.

"Beau, I'm fine, brother. I love you. Hey, we named our son after you."

"You didn't have to do that, Wells. Congratulations. I love you, brother. God, I miss you. Man, we had some good times growing up in Baileysville, didn't we?"

"Yeah, Wells, we did. We had the best of times. I'll see you around, Beau, okay? This place is wonderful. We are planting fresh flowers and spreading the Good News. Here's bread."

Beau stood and held a loaf of bread, still smiling.

"Yeah, take care of Elly and Little Beau, Wells. I love you, brother."

"Headed home, Beau, man, it's good to talk. See you in Eden on Sunday."

"What place is this?"

Beau Le Mans had spent the better part of a week in the afterlife, not knowing if it was Heaven or hell, but maybe it was something in between purgatory and paradise, something Sam Law spoke of in the POW camp. He had no clue what happened in the dream, but he was out of Vietnam, home, and Polly was alive. He'd asked around but no one knew about Cadeo or Hien, or if they'd made it. He didn't see either man. Le Mans knew the men were somewhere in Eden, throwing football with strong arms. Le Mans had his own thoughts.

Eileen sat beside the window and Beau Le Mans read stories aloud to Polly. He caught himself looking outward at the world, Eden: "People shared food and water, but more than that, people spoke of religion, and now God is all they hoped to find," said Eileen. "Churches are being built: that means God is with us, Emmanuel."

"Churches?" Le Mans pressed his hands. "Where are the trees, sawmills and lumber yards?"

"Every morning, God adds a new wilderness to Eden. Look at the trees tomorrow and you'll find thousands more trees and leaves in the forest than yesterday."

"This place is somewhere else, not heaven or hell, but something else."

"We are having fish for lunch. Will you be joining us for dinner on the ground, Beau Le Mans?"

"I'd be delighted." Le Mans stopped. "Can I go outside?"

"The war is over," said Eileen, grinning. "We are rebuilding the town; lives are changing because you have given us hope again, Beau Le Mans."

Fishermen caught trout in a nearby stream and potatoes were served. Others had fresh vegetables and drank cold, pure mountain water. Folks, hundreds of people showed up for dinner. Lilies and figs and berries started to sprout, and then, a lady walked behind Beau.

"Guess who?" a sweet voice sounded in Vietnamese.

"Polly! You are awake," he exclaimed, spinning her off the ground. "I love you, Polly."

"Where are we, Beau? I love you. It's good to be in another place and another time."

"Eden!" He held her face and kissed her.

A lady walked up to them.

"The Garden of Eden," said Eileen. "We are starting our first garden."

"Can I talk to God?" asked Le Mans.

Everyone looked at Beau Le Mans and Polly, and then laughed.

"God is all around, Beau," said Eileen. "Here, have some fish and bread."

Wells found Beau and Polly fishing together. The following day something very special happened in Eden, as a hundred and fourteen people witnessed it. Beau had on new Army fatigues and Polly wore her favorite dress, not yellow ...but in Eden, it was pearl white, and Eileen cried when Polly spun around.

"Do you Polly, take Beau to be your lawful wedded husband?" asked Wells.

"I do," said Polly, tears crowding her brown eyes.

Beau said the same. They were in love. Married.

Polly and Beau spent the evening outside, walking, far from war, and far away from Vietnam and America. Their time was spent with each other. Beau closed the door to their new home, a home built by carpenters, the first honeymoon home of Eden.

The next day was still dark, long before Le Mans usually woke up. On the desk the carpenters had built for him, was a thick book, Hemingway, *Farewell to Arms*, and beneath it was Fitzgerald, *The Other side of Paradise*. Then, to the side, a letter, the one Eileen wanted him to open from the beginning, penned tight to the window seal, two pages eluded him until a gust of wind blew the paper into his hands, and he opened it, words that read:

"I write to the followers, the next generation, a story: *The Fading: Babes to the Old and the Last Paperboy*," unsigned.

Maybe Orwell? Could it be Hemingway? Le Mans thought and hesitated, opening the seal, he read it aloud:

"Beauty merged into the twilight of the world, ashes covered the greens and the grays, bubbling to the dust of the soil, cone geysers, fiery strikes scorched the land, trees barren and life sparse, gloominess and smoke, far as the eye could see, the world had turned cold, the fading, babes to the old."

Le Mans held his face in fear, ashes in the window seal, the truth, he sighed and wondered why he was there in the first place, and, for him, what the letter meant - *Babes to the Old*. He turned the page, and read it again in silence.

Ashes buried the blooms of spring, the last lilies beneath this window seal, you will see. The black ocean was calm for three days, the garden faded in a week, and no one walked the roadways of a dark countryside. The last paperboy shook his head: if he was telling them about the rapids and high tides, broken jetties, and collapsed dams and fierce floods. Then, it was Wall Street. Beaches eroded and good times of yesterday and the goods of tomorrow are gone. The season to pray for the American Dream has faded away. No more time for sowing, sweet faces, pretty faces, life aged, and in a sudden reaping of fortunes, the fading. Some cried to God, their only hope, but it was too late. People were fading, babes to the old; the paperboy had the news, all of it was written. However, few outlasted the storms, the good ones, the good of the earth, some in their youth, huddled together. You will see them and the one who is in the mirror, that's you.

The world is fading, too long gone, neglected by the mature, the acts of mankind, over generations, hardened hearts, the ladder to the top, the glass ceiling, greed eclipsing God's right hand and too many social injustices to count across the country. No more loose windows or open doors, less knocking, the fading; for both, the rich and the poor, together no different than before. This is the last of the fading, one window, one door, but you are the "Babes to the Old, hope for the young."

No more was written on the letter. In the next window, Le Mans found a Mason jar, a bundle of cash, coins, things once valued, and tempted to be induced by the same vanity and cycle, but denied the riches to start afresh. He grinned, picked up a feather pen, in his own words, entitled his read: *Hopeful, Not Fading*, and penned his poem over the letter, closing the window, closing the open door—"Hopeful, Not Fading!" signed by Beau Le Mans, Eden, The Other Side of War.

"And that was my dream, Henderson." He told his heavy dream to his friend.

"Dang, man. What did Eileen, the nurse, what did she look like, tell me?" Henderson leaned and ready to listen. "I have a picture of that young Babe in my mind. Blonde."

"She was the sweetest face in Eden, that's all. You're missing the point of the message, Caveman. Stop being a sleaze bag, man! I met my brother, Wells, though. Polly was alive and became my wife. God was with us in Eden. The world was on the other side of war."

"You need to get your eyes checked, hillbilly."

"The best part of the dream, hey, I saw the future in the spring. The world will change in 1988," said Le Mans, adjusting his shirt. "Eden had a decorated table, celebrating dishes from around the world. Wells, Eden's preacher, blessed food from different cultures, rich and poor, in a world where humanity of commonality was the same - loving the afterlife. Bountiful tables and each person had more than enough to eat and share with others."

"No judgments or prejudices existed, huh?" asked Henderson, head tilted. "And all people groups were peaceful, eating in one room, huh, Vietnamese and Americans? Peace is the other side of war, Le Mans. It's the peace of God. Nirvana."

"No. Heaven. The Prince of Peace was in Eden," said Le Mans, nodding and grinning. All women and men were the same and everyone shared a time of peace with Christ."

"Eden, huh?" said Henderson, closing his eyes. "Did Fitzgerald or Hemingway write the letter in the envelope? I bet it was that nut Wadsworth."

"The author was my younger brother, Wells Le Mans, the preacher."

"Dang, Le Mans. Is your brother a genius, huh?"

"Yeah. My brother was top of his Rough Rider class in school."

"My dream was wild, for sure. Something crazy. I saw myself living here," said Henderson, head dropped low, face tight and serious. "My wife had long black hair and was a happy Vietnamese chic. Two sons and one girl lived with us and the youngest one, the seven-year-old girl, was an orphan. I had boats on the water as a merchant and was a good sailor, trading silk in a giant warehouse and selling sugar on the river, too. In my dream, my wife and I managed a hundred flat river boats, several trucks, two dozen small outpost warehouses of sugar, and our company was called, get this, "The King of Soda Pop.""

"Sounds cool, man," said Le Mans. "Like to have a bottle of soda pop about now."

Bug bites had filled their heads with craziness and dreams and images were spoken of when they could, like some type of drug had been absorbed into their veins. They'd spoken for hours about the details of each dream, beautiful faces, the people, the taste of good food and shiny colors of blooming plants: with exception, Henderson was not for godly things, and the man spoke less about angels and thoughts of the afterlife drained him. Henderson planned to work with a Buddhist, the Dalai Lama, who was born in the Wood-Pig Year, of 1935. The idea of Nirvana fascinated him.

"In another dream," said Le Mans, head back, "I saw myself with Polly, washing my body under a rushing waterfall at Twin Falls, a state park in Wyoming County," said Le Mans. "And living happy and free in the mountains of West Virginia."

"Sweet dreams, I bet. Dreams, that's all we got in this crap jungle." Henderson rubbed his chest.

"Polly had a necklace, long and it draped on her breast, and a wet yellow feather was pinned inside her hair. We walked to a two-story log cabin, had a good corral of horses, a hundred and seven Quarter horses thundered across a long, green stretch of a field, and we fed each other grapes and apples. That's what I dreamed, man."

"Tell me about your love life, Le Mans," said Henderson, falling on his back, hands behind his head, and he rested under a tree. Need more pictures in my head, so I can dream a little dream of my own. What happened under the waterfall?"

"Maybe later." Le Mans grinned and closed his eyes.

"You got two arms. Did you have more than one lady at Twin Falls?" said Henderson, who brightened his smile when he laughed. "Sounds like a place for twins. Babes for Beau."

"One lady is enough for any man, and enough... is one lady, for any man," said Le Mans, relaxing, legs crossed. "Get some rest, Caveman."

Blinking his eyes, Le Mans raked his legs with his fingernails and scrubbed bug bites with tree bark until he faded out from hallucinations again. Bugs continued to chew and bite his legs, riddled with endless irritation, and medicine was nowhere to be found. No remedy was in the jungle. No Eden Hospital nurse with a sweet face to treat injuries and care for bites.

Henderson woke up an hour after Le Mans, and made an effort to wash mud and bugs from his bloody legs and feet. Before sunup they whispered and scouted for any Viet- Cong who most likely hunted for them inside caves, under bridges, and on the roadway.

"Heard a thousand voices last night, echoing voices," said Henderson, who moved close to Le Mans, seated alongside the riverbank. "Strange voices stretched across the land, and popping in the sky was a giant Texas flag, heavy and free in the background. People were screaming and howling late at night, too. Something like a horror film, "Creatures from the Haunted Sea" at the drive-in. Le Mans, I laughed in the face of the big creature and chopped his head off with my machete. That stone-aged blade wouldn't cut hot butter, buddy."

"Same, same," said Le Mans. "Might be a good luck creature for us."

"Yeah," said Henderson, seated on a rock. "Same, same. The Texas flag waved until I made it home, man. Not sure I'm a true patriot for volunteering to serve my country. I'll be decorated for this bloody war in my battle dress uniform, proud, head-to-toe, and pinned in medals, I bet. None of that will ever happen. I'm just trying to survive, man. That's all."

"Your red eyes are dancing, Henderson, are you alright, Caveman?"

"Shuddered and shook all night."

"Hallucinations. Dizziness."

"Yeah. My life is whipped in the head, broken like a house in Tornado Alley. My stomach is empty. My butt is tired, but my heart is back in Texas," said Henderson, eyes and head bobbing. He popped up. "Enough of my misery, how'd you sleep?"

"Peaceful." Le Mans slapped his knees. "Need to stand and flex my legs."

"Wished I was eating pulled-pork barbecue and spicy baked beans back in Amarillo about now," said Henderson. "My stomach is flat as an ironing board. Wish my ex-wife could see me now. She hates me, though. My boy loves me. Dreamed about a stampede of wild horses, buddy."

"You make me crazy with this food talk. We're gonna die if we don't get a meal and shelter soon," said Le Mans, standing on tall rocks. "I gotta save us."

"Dreams beat this reality, bud. Been that way all my life," said Henderson, feet flat and sat up tall. "I'm a man who loves to be in another world."

"You're out of your head, man."

"I was flying across the Palo Duro Canyon, man, rocks so tall you could climb to the sky. Le Mans, I dreamed you were standing on top, yelling across the canyon at an eagle."

"What was I yelling about?"

"You stood on the famous Lighthouse Rock, arms out, yelling at a Bald Eagle. That bird was soaring and you dared the eagle to fight you."

"Sounds like me, right, huh?"

"Yeah." Henderson held a serious face. "Dude, you were yelling at another world. I believe the eagle's name was Uncle Sam. You sounded off at the government because they left us behind, here, in this trashing place. Sam Law is dead, man. He badly wanted to be at Holy Cross College. That leaves us to fight it out."

"The world lost a good man."

"Being a soldier is my own damn fault, I guess," said Henderson, who hit a tree with his fist. "Did this crap to ourselves. We failed. Starvation. Bugs. Snakes. It's not someone else's mistake, man. Look at us, Le Mans, it's us being hunted by the system. Uncle Sam put a target on our backs."

"Forget about it, Caveman. We have an open door, wide open."

"The glass is busted and the door is broken. It's a broken world. The government sucks out the life of good men. Uncle Sam kills the good parts of us. War is forever."

"They're trying to sell young men rainbows and ponies about fighting."

"Yeah. The recruiter said: 'You can be a hero, Ben Henderson. You are our next hero.' He sold a one-way ticket to Eden, Le Mans. If we want out, we gotta punch our own ticket to the other side of the war and get home."

"Why was I yelling at the world?" Le Mans double tied his shoes.

"It was about your writing."

"What about my papers?'

"You're the journalist, say something in the papers," said Henderson, head dropped, cutting bamboo. "Memories of war, I guess. Tell the truth and don't dance for Tricky Dick. Tell the world about your love for Polly, huh?"

"I gotta go to the bathroom tree."

"Don't leave me alone, man, and run off because you are mad."

"I'm not mad or afraid of Uncle Sam, Caveman."

"I'm doing my part to get us out," said Le Mans, who stood beside a bamboo tree. "It's my fault... It's my problem if we don't get out of this God forsaken part of the world."

Le Mans returned from the tree and sat.

"In my dream," said Le Mans, smiling, "our buddy, Sam Law, made it to heaven."

"Cool Catholic from Winchester got into Heaven by his grace, huh?"

"Yeah, the good man made it out. He had a white Labrador Retriever, fed the pup on the pitcher's mound at Wrigley Field," said Le Mans, body rocking. "He had a hot blonde with him when he walked to home plate."

"Sam Law ain't no lady's man."

"She was all over him. They sang 'Take me out to the ballpark, buy me some peanuts and crackerjacks, I don't care if we ever get back' and that's when Sam Law smiled and waved."

"Who was the hot lady?" Henderson leaned forward. "Tell me, man. I need an image."

"Cybil Shepherd. I miss the world we left. We might never see baseball again," said Le Mans, scanning for fruit.

"Cybil Shepherd is one cracker jack at Wrigley Field," said Henderson, slapping his leg.

"Sam Law loved the Cubs. Did you know that boy joined the Army because Ernie Banks served in the Army? Banks was the first black guy to play with the Cubs organization."

"That's cool. That man is fast to second base."

"That's the crazy part, and Sam Law invited us to meet him at home plate," said Le Mans, face long and eyes gazing into the woods.

"I'll take Cybil home after the game." Henderson chuckled.

"Glad he made it home. Now, it's our turn," said Le Mans, smiling. "Crazy dreams, my friend. Wild hallucinations are caused by bug bites. Toxic and heavy, though, man."

They spoke of the first time they killed a deer and how different it was than stopping the heart of a man. Henderson spoke about his wife and boy. They stayed in the riverbank until dark, slowly making progress to the ocean, part of their original plan to advance downstream, and see the sea.

"Still can't get over those hallucinations, man," said Le Mans. The moon glared on his pale face and his voice was tired. "I bet Saw Law handed his Purple Heart to Cybil Shepherd."

"Did he kiss Cybil?" Henderson tugged on his shirt.

"Yeah. She loved Sam Law. Cybil Shepherd is rockin' hot," said Le Mans, rubbing his chin.

"Jesus, hillbilly," said Henderson, chewing on a long piece of grass, laughing and grinning. "Cybil Shepherd is one hot Memphis tamale."

Le Mans held up his hand and cold rain fell gently across his face and he caught rain in the palms of his hands and held out his tongue as he stood. More rain fell through the night and they collected water and made a funnel with fresh cut leaves and bamboo until sunup. The river had risen and they'd hiked to a rock cliff for shelter at first light.

Le Mans shivered and waved Henderson to follow him downstream. They found a dry cavity inside the earth and waited under a ledge along the riverbank which became a good-sized, high shelter. The cave was lined in straw and grass covered from animals and the ground made a good bed sometime in the past, perhaps when he was in Wyoming County playing football with Wells. Le Mans and Henderson were hidden and slept.

The churn of Henderson's stomach reminded them of the dinner they did not have on bamboo plates, either. No words were spoken. Each man unwrapped his own feet, Le Mans first, and then Henderson followed, but they were dry and red. As if by some miracle, their restless legs halted from the painful itching. Hallucinations subsided. The two men slept in peace for hours. Upon awakening, Le Mans stood in the mouth of the dusty cavern, hand on the entrance, and a colorful rainbow arched in the blue distance. He saw bright red birds dotting a pearl blue sky and he thought about his mother's bird feeder. The dense fog couldn't shield the sunlight from his face and he witnessed colorful birds, one, two, three and a dozen crossed the sky. Henderson woke when he heard the birds whistling and agreed to hike behind Le Mans after the red birds flew away and the sun lifted over the high mountain tops.

"Caveman, I saw flashing faces in my dreams," said Le Mans, seated atop the roots of a mangrove tree, warm feet dangling and swaying at the mouth of a smaller, second cavern. "Dark fiery images of Sam Law, who spoke of Polly; she was alive in the dream."

"You know they killed Cadeo and Polly, don't you?"

"No way."

"They're gone, Le Mans. Dead. Put her on the belt and say goodbye."

"That's not what I saw and it's nothing I believe. Let's go. They both are alive."

Le Mans wasn't about to admit they'd been executed. Both men hiked silently, making their way downstream, jumping, flat rock to the sand. Etched in the head of Le Mans, a sense of peace, deep in his heart, he knew Polly and Cadeo may have found trouble but he felt they were still alive. He pictured it that way, believing they had escaped and lived in peace - and were not in Eden yet. They would grow old as neighbors for the rest of their lives, hair gray, legs weak, and one taking care of the other, just friends, sharing noodles and remembering each other's birthday. Le Mans hoped they'd remember him for what they sacrificed to free prisoners and themselves.

"What else did you see in that crazy dream, Le Mans? Amuse me."

"You mean, the dream I had about Cybil Shepherd?" said Le Mans, with a sparkle in his eyes, laughing. "It was heavy and romantic, dude."

"Yeah, I bet it was," said Henderson. "Speak up, tell me. Talk low. I gotta know Cybil."

"One of those good nights, Caveman."

"Not a day goes by that I don't think of home and how I need to be there and not here, fighting to stay alive. It doesn't make much sense to miss my son and ex-wife so much, does it?" Henderson wept a few times from pain, but that was one Le Mans let him have in peace.

"Nope. Makes no sense to be here. We have lost our fight."

When they first landed in Vietnam, soldiers called their enemies Viet-Cong, which was shortened in the military alphabet to Victor Charlie or V-C, and later became known as "Charlie," the most common of the military alphabet. They had not seen or heard from Charlie in days. When they weren't speaking of Cybil Shepherd, Le Mans and Henderson spoke of how they'd stay out of sight from Charlie and his anti-angels.

Henderson checked the trail leading outside the cave for Charlie and company, and scanned for movement in a long nearby field where villagers lived and worked. No one was close to them. Birds continued to sing and the day was warm on their faces when the dark clouds moved away.

"The rainbow colors made me hungry for senoritas and Tex-Mex food, Le Mans."

"Speckled corn and Mountaineer half runner green beans and a warm pan of golden cornbread, that'd be the ticket."

"We need to stop the talk about food," said Caveman. "Keep us hopeful, though."

"If heaven don't have steak, I don't want to go," said Le Mans, slapping his back.

They continued to grin and whisper stories, lowering their voices as they crossed fallen trees jammed between boulders from high water. The two men dropped under a bridge, out of the sunlight and rested.

"Sam Law disappeared with Cybil Shepherd into a dense stack of angel clouds," said Henderson, rubbing sweat from his forehead. "And, well, that Labrador pup followed them. They sat and kissed in the outfield bleachers of Wrigley Field."

"He's a lucky man in Eden."

"Yeah. What fighting Irish luck for Sam Law? The guy caught a homer from Ernie Banks with one hand. The greatest Cub on the field."

"Bet my image and your image of Cybil Shepherd ain't the same, hillbilly." Henderson shook his hand fast.

"Oh, I bet it's close, Caveman. Let's keep moving. I'll get Cybil popcorn and soda pop at the cave."

Two miles or so south of the cave, Le Mans watched Henderson doze off from exhaustion at a large bridge. Neither man felt hallucinations or saw Cybil Shepherd. Smoke swam across the sky, three miles away or so.

The eyes of Henderson popped open, brightly, the lobster look of a man covered his face and crawled to where Le Mans sat.

"I could go for a Shiner ale, couldn't you, Le Mans?"

"What is a Shiner?" Le Mans replied, eyes closed, head back, resting.

"I'll buy you a Shiner Bock and a giant steak when we leave this Disneyland vacation," said Henderson, pointing his thumb.

"Deal." Eyes half-cocked, Le Mans said, "I'd like to see Texas someday."

"That's good earth, hillbilly." Henderson assured him, whispering.

Le Mans whispered low to Henderson and from that point onward, it was normal to talk low, men at close range, hiding, taking cover in the creek bank watched each other's backs. Henderson killed a lizard with one swift chop.

"Sam Law needed a proper burial, though," said Le Mans. "We were the last men to see him alive. Last two men he spoke to about religion, tomatoes, college, or anything else."

"That college boy will have a proper burial, that is, if we can find this place again after the war." Henderson clutched his head. "We must get out of here. Got to be a sign from our boys. Need to stop Communist and halt unnecessary killing of innocent women and children. What a great loss of life, huh?"

"Yeah." said Le Mans, hand inside his shirt. "It's a heck of a way to live on this good earth, you said it."

"And we know abuse happens and the men who do it, stomp them out."

***

"Henderson? Look." said Le Mans, filling his mouth with a yellow fruit. "This must be Eden, Caveman. Pack your pockets with bananas."

"Bananas look different. What are they called?"

"Pomelo bananas." Le Mans opened each pocket and held fruit in both hands. "Pure fruity-heaven, my friend. Eat up. Good stuff," he said, juice down his chin.

Each man filled his battle uniform and stuffed his stomach with banana after banana. Their bellies popped full of fruit, tight as a football, and stood satisfied.

"One prayer answered," said Le Mans, as juice dripped on his shirt.

"This fruit saved our lives, hillbilly." He chomped as fast as he could eat one.

"Tastes good, Caveman. Better than popcorn and soda pop."

"Thank you, Jesus."

The thin face of Le Mans was covered in dark mud, battle-ready after the stop for Pomelo bananas, and a smile of hope ran across his face and eyes, stomach stuffed and leaning forward to fight. He knew he was alive and ready to travel again. They rested on their backs, half dozen bananas stuffed inside their pockets and a slow spring.

"Coast is clear," said Le Mans, who pointed his machete to where he thought his fellow troops were stationed as the sound of gunfire alerted their eyes and steps. They fell on their faces.

"Home free." Now, with the spirit and energy, Le Mans eased away from the fruit trees and led the way. "Henderson, let's take one last look from this tall hill, see if we can spot Charlie scouting our heads."

"Le Mans?" said Henderson, who chewed on a long banana. "When I rotate back, I'll tell Sam Law's Catholic family in Virginia, how he was a warrior, especially a God-fearing man. Good man, just like yourself."

"You'd better let me tell them. Winchester, Virginia, it's just a few hours away from West Virginia, plus his dog tags are in my pocket."

Le Mans dropped his head and closed his eyes and fell in a position of prayer and thankfulness for good food, just like "Old Blue Eyes" actor, Paul Newman, in Cool Hand Luke. He popped up, banana in hand.

"I'll tell them how he died a senseless death, too," said Le Mans, tugging on his green sleeves, and his feet kept pace. His pockets overflowed with fresh fruit, mind full, and heart broken. "Stay down before Charlie sees us, and burns us alive."

"Head down," said Le Mans. "Stay off pathways and trails, keep low." He dropped to one knee, breathed in fresh mountain air and waved his weapon. "Let's take the river, drop down into the trenches during the day and move with the moonlight later. We need to low-crawl, the way of the lizard."

"Yeah. No time to be brave."

He sat beside Henderson, scouting and alert, hidden in the shadows of trees and tall vegetation, and they waited for the right moment. For the next two days Le Mans and Henderson low-crawled, and stayed hunkered down behind grass, and had faces painted with mud and moss atop their heads. They lived on bananas, fought bug bites, and shared raw snakes; one reptile unknown to them became a meal of dislike.

The next couple of days blended together. Evening light cast a shadow onto a small seasonal village, even made movement and scouting risky. About midday two chickens walked into their trap. Food snatched. They had been free for seven days and celebrated, like campers and poppers. They'd hidden inside a shallow river cave and had stolen village fowl and vegetables. After a long week, Le Mans and Henderson had traveled from the mountains to the valley, hiking through miles and miles of unforgiving vines and heavy brush and spear thorns, and rested, just as the Letter in Eden read, the fading would happen. They'd dodged danger and battled nature for as long as they could and became homesick and restless. Meandering through deep streams and edged rice paddies that didn't resemble Texas, West Virginia, or anything else in America. They kept low and hoped for familiar colors on a flag, stars and stripes, and they waded in water, of names they could not pronounce, searching for the Home Team. The plan was to stay low to the earth, be careful in deep valleys, soaking up grand views of more and more green mountains and long valleys until Uncle Sam decided to fly a Bird overhead.

Into the second week of freedom, Le Mans spoke of Polly, Cadeo, and Sam Law, but Henderson focused on their drastic situation and avoided the past for Buddha's new path. And for the first time since Briarpatch, things changed.

"What the heck is that creepy howling noise, Le Mans?" He plugged his ears and sat on the roots of a fat tree, face curled in anger.

"Sounds like our boys are blasting out Charlie, playing eerie voices from large speakers, doesn't it?" said Le Mans, who covered his ears. No one felt comfortable until they saw American faces up close and personal.

Cupping his ears at sundown, Le Mans leaned against a wide, bent tree and heard familiar words, English words, being played through large speakers: "Daddy, Daddy, Daddy, Daddy." Le Mans scouted at sundown and then returned to report what he'd found.

"I can see the speakers, Caveman."

"Speakers?" He held a strange face.

"High and fat speakers. Yeah. The largest speakers in the military, I bet." Le Mans caught his breath, holding Henderson's shoulder. "Our boys are broadcasting voices through large speakers from a nearby post. I read about "Operation Wandering Soul" the week before I was captured. The Home Team is broadcasting eerie sounds, loud sounds and sickening noises meant to make Charlie irate."

"What for?" said Henderson, chin held. "That's the dumbest thing I've ever heard."

"Psychological warfare. Mind games," said Le Mans, waving his arm toward the speakers. "In Vietnamese culture, if the dead aren't traditionally buried, then the soul of the deceased wanders the earth, like a ghost or some strange spirit."

"That's a strange approach to war, Le Mans. Did you make that up, man?"

"No way. It's not the dead that bothers men, Henderson, but the living, V-C soldiers, like a sniper named Cobra or Charlie," said Le Mans, lurking under a banana tree.

The two men crawled to where they could see a tall row of palm trees and heard the loud mounted speakers. Smiles broke across each man's face. Henderson punched Le Mans in the arm, like when something good happened in high school hallways between friends.

"Do you think the words —'Daddy, Daddy, Daddy'—will help us win the war? Sounds foolish, doesn't it, Henderson?"

"Has it been done before?" asked Henderson, who crawled beside Le Mans. "Does President Nixon think he's our Daddy now?" chuckling. "Daddy Nixon, Daddy Nixon, Daddy Nixon. Sounds good, doesn't it?"

"No, not at all. Daddy Nixon needs to take better care of his sons in Vietnam?" Le Mans told him.

"No, Le Mans. I ain't no senator's son. Nobody is looking for us. Let's take off, find our way out of this hellhole," said Henderson, who had made his way inside the trunk of a fat tree. "Time's up, soldier. You need to see your hillbilly family. Let's go home."

"We'll be shot. Dead to right. Our boys shoot better than they see. It's not time yet." They sat for a few minutes, thinking about their situation. "I could eat mashed potatoes and roast beef in the chow line about now," said Le Mans. "But I never cared for the runny scrambled eggs, though. Not like momma makes at home in Baileysville."

Le Mans heard movement and slid down the small embankment, covering his friend's mouth with his hand and pointed between the ghostly voices, and said, "If our troops are playing "The Wandering Soul" voices, that means the North Vietnamese are at least three hundred meters away, camping in our front yard."

"True. Yeah," said Henderson, nodding. "Tucked away like tunnel rats. Now what?"

Henderson dropped down amid the trailing slope of the riverbank and closed his eyes and relied on Buddhism for help.

Le Mans called on Jesus. Next, they crawled through the edge of flat rice paddies by the light of the moon and held their heads above the waterline, advancing their position in a pool of water, even closer to home. Hidden under heavy palm leaves and branches about two hundred meters from an unknown American camp; two soldiers locked amid war, like chess pieces caught somewhere between Charlie and Uncle Sam. If a bush vibrated in a field, being pulled into a soldier's scope, either side would fire at them.

Ironically, a bird sounded, "Re-Up, Re-Up, Re-Up."

"No way, bird," said Henderson, voice low. "Re-Up, you're crazy."

The question was discussed, "Do we hide from Charlie, or run to Uncle Sam? Any wrong movement could stem a red hot attack of napalm, or endless rapid fire, not counting grenades, Claymore mines, and the slightest wrong movement meant grave diggers.

"If we had a comic book, I'd take off in the morning and find the CP," said Le Mans, watching fish surface in the shallows of a flat stream.

"Yeah, but we'll have the Viet-Cong on our backs and our boys scoping down range with M-16s and M-14s." Henderson objected. "We can't win now. Dang it, lost again."

"We can't signal to the home team that we're Americans, but if Charlie sees us first, we're dead meat, Caveman." Le Mans cleaned his hands and face.

"We're in no man's land," said Le Mans, face bent angst. "We're screwed, man, just two screwed soldiers with no open door, and caught with smelly cheese inside a deadly mouse trap of psycho-warfare."

Le Mans planted himself under the heavy roots of a mangrove tree and had no idea how he'd get the attention of the U.S. Infantry without being gunned down by his own sniper or alert Charlie, who'd unload fire, without compromise or mercy. Twisting and turning, the hillbilly rested on his left side, covered with leaves, but hidden from the enemy.

"How many days, we been on the run, Le Mans?"

"Ten days. Maybe eleven. Lost count while we cracked on hallucinations."

They'd concealed themselves beneath vegetation, soaked in rice paddies and floated downstream, for God knows how many days without being spotted. Lucky. Blessed. Each man had his own word and religion to be thankful for in the jungle. At twilight, the warmth of golden sunlight vanished, Henderson whispered about how dry Texas was in the fall of the year and how there were no armadillos in Vietnam. Then, two hours later his battle buddy became rattled and impatient, scouting the movements of Viet-Cong, who jabbered on the hillside, causing a tide of eagerness to roll inside Henderson's gut. After nearly two weeks in the jungle, Henderson knew the American flag waved only two hundred meters away. They'd made it close enough to wind food and smell truck diesel at sunup. Then, they turned back, in fear of being shot. Food was the only factor that made Henderson's legs twitch in the mud and river until waves and bubbles broke the surface of still water.

"To make it home would mean the world to me," said Henderson, propping his restless leg up against the roots of a tree after he'd returned from scouting the area. "First thing I'll do..." rubbing his neck, "is chill with a cold one, call President Nixon, and put a stop to this endless dogfight in Vietnam."

"When we get out of here," said Le Mans, who sighed, closing his eyes, "for me, the first thing I'll do is buy you a steak in Amarillo, I promise you that much, brother."

"Man, I'd love to see you make it to Texas, Le Mans."

"We need to get out of here, though," unbuttoning his shirt. "You can bet on it, bud. Got too many plans in the mountains, far away from here to give up now."

"When you make it out, my friend," said Henderson, scooting along the riverbank.

"When we make out, Caveman," said Le Mans, interrupting his friend.

"Yeah, man, I'll take you to meet the Dancehall Dolls of Amarillo. Some of the most beautiful women in the world live in West Texas. Jeanette, my ex-wife is one of them."

"Is she a dancer?" whispering, stepping out of the river to see if anyone was around. "You miss her, I bet?"

"Yeah. Good dancer. I'd rather watch her dance than eat steak. She practices Country and Western on weekends. Her style, the way she spins, drives me crazy. Sweet as sugar, too. She's got heartbreaking Amarillo brown eyes. Cool happy lady, that's what I call her. Honey blonde hair in the summer sun and a bit darker around Christmas. To me, she's the most beautiful lady alive."

"How old is she?"

"Turned twenty-one the month I shipped out. Missed two of her crazy birthday parties, I bet, by now," He cleared his eyes. "Hard to believe."

"Early twenties, huh?" He stayed low, "How old is that boy of yours?"

"Little Benny was born five years ago, May of 1965."

Le Mans heard movement from the Viet-Cong, more voices and chatter, less than a hundred meters away. He ducked, bent low, motioning Henderson to drop his voice and get down, who seemed to forget he was inside a warzone when he told stories. Loud. Careless. Le Mans warned him that he wasn't at a tailgate party at a Texas Tech football game. His barrel voice echoed off the water when he mentioned his ex-wife, the more he spoke of her, the closer they got to being captured, or even killed.

The sun dropped lower, and thank God the chatter disappeared. Henderson closed his lips. Talking about women was the only way to keep their sanity and encouragement for better days, the promise of tomorrow.

"Is Jeanette a Buddhist, like you?"

"No. Baptist, just like you, hillbilly. Drives a black truck, burns the wheels on old Route 66. Other times, she wears glasses and looks like some Ivy League librarian when she walks into a record store."

"Did you meet her in a record store?" Le Mans found a low growing banana tree.

"Yeah," said Henderson, looking through the fat palm leaves. "We dated after I brought her The Who t-shirt and kissed her."

"You should've bought her The Who shirt and the album," said Le Mans, grinning.

"Not all folks got black diamond coal money, bud. Do you have a radio in the hills of West Virginia?"

"I got Buffalo Springfield, The Doors, The Kinks, but The Who are just average in my book," said Le Mans, raising his hand. "There's uninvited guests to the right of the river, Caveman."

Le Mans gently raised his finger to his lips. They watched their reflections dance atop clear water. For the first time in a long while, Le Mans caught a glimpse of his thin face in the flat water and didn't recognize himself. Ears and eyes opened for the enemy. They sat in the shadows, mud tall on their pant legs, covered in leaves and grass. Henderson guarded the base of the mountain, crawling and checking for snakes and the ultimate tunnel rat, Charlie. After an hour, the seven V-C soldiers moved out, two villagers floated down the river on a sampan boat, and two ladies picked baskets of fruit about fifty meters away. Henderson and Le Mans were not spotted, but had bad company.

"Where's this Twin Falls State Park, you keep talking about, Le Mans?"

"Wyoming County, West "By God" Virginia."

Henderson was fading fast. He'd stopped eating and started dozing off at odd times and became sick and dizzy. Le Mans saw his friend asleep again and dropped down beside him and ducked behind the waterfall. He needed to keep his mind focused on the mission or he'd have no chance of making it by Charlie alone.

"Jeanette Henderson, huh?" said Le Mans, making an attempt to shake Henderson out of his fading slumber. "What's your father's name?"

"Bad Ben Henderson, meanest man alive, strong as a bear, too." Eyes half-cocked, Henderson flexed his bicep. "Hangs from the barn like a spider monkey, too. What about you, hillbilly, what woman did you leave behind in the hills? Got any kids running around?"

"No wedding plans. No kids," said Le Mans. "Look!" He waved. "Planes. Get down. Hot zone."

The ground lit up in a blaze of thunder and fire. Napalm and fire blanketed the valley. Machine gun fire came from the hillside and planes popped and cracked from Charlie and Uncle Sam, locked amid a heated battle. The earth was on fire across the deep gorge, but their position at the water was safe, far from the firefight and the spread of napalm and a 50 caliber, they watched in amazement. They knew the position of the enemy, hundreds of them positioned on the next hillside and another fifty V-C hidden in rice paddies across the long bottomland village. No way out. Some were killed in the firefight.

Tunnel rats could be to their left, downrange, it was unknown how much traffic they had in a two-mile radius.

"Listen," said Le Mans, eyes alerted. "Caveman, we need to get out of here and now. We got company at three o' clock. They're moving in on us, like John Wayne and his big cattle drive."

They agreed to leave the safety of the small waterfall and hunker down like two mud turtles in a long trench between the U.S. Army camp and a hundred Viet-Cong, hidden in tunnels; two days crawled by until Le Mans hatched a new plan. They survived on fresh water and two fish. He had talked Henderson down a dozen times from blowing their cover and meeting their fate. The big Texan was bent on raising cane against President Nixon and slapping the boys in Washington around. Moaning and groaning, Henderson was one step closer to being in the crosshairs of Charlie.

Henderson draped his body over the roots of a mangrove tree and became restless as a sinner on the front row of a Billy Graham Crusade. On the other hand, hidden in the pocket of a mudbank, Le Mans kept him from being the next casualty in Vietnam.

"Tomorrow, Caveman, we'll get out of this damn jungle," said Le Mans. "Live or die, we won't stay one more night in the mud. We'll sleep on white sheets and soon we'll be ragged by the First Sergeant for being overweight, my friend. Homeward bound."

"How can you say such a ridiculous thing, hillbilly?" said Henderson, eyes red with anger. "You are stupid, man. We are stuck in Vietnam until the war is over."

"God will be with us," answered Le Mans, pulling his necklace from his collar. "Here, take it. My cross necklace is yours now."

"What do I need with a cross necklace, huh? I don't need a piece of wood."

"That cross will keep you alive. Take it. That's my promise to you, Caveman. Your dancing Baptist ex-wife might have a cross on her neck on Sunday. Are you afraid to wear a cross?"

"You don't know my ex-wife. I'll wear the dang cross when I'm a crispy critter, you'll get it back, okay?" said Henderson, holding a funny smile. He latched the cross around his neck and loosened his shirt. "Hope or fear, I'll hold neither one of much value. Let's fight the V-C until somebody dies."

"The cross will bring you hope," said Le Mans, tapping his heart.

"What do you say, we run for it right now, man, right now?" said Henderson, arm stretched out. "Since I have the cross and some hope, hillbilly. We're too close to Disneyland to crawl with the snakes in this jungle."

Suddenly, a fighter jet dropped a half dozen bombs, popping just a mile from their position. That's when Henderson stumbled from the top of the riverbank and fell, sliding and tumbling from his position, landing on jagged rocks. He didn't say a word in fear of being found wounded, but grunted and jerked his bloody legs.

Le Mans wondered how anyone could survive a fall from that distance.

"God, my left leg is busted up," Henderson grunted, biting a stick to keep from screaming in a world he hated.

"Hey, you alright?"

"I'm alive and busted."

"You fell thirty-five feet down a rock cliff, my friend." Le Mans scanned the trail he made through the rocks and mud to get to his friend. "Should be dead. The vines grabbed you, saved you, or was it the cross, brother Henderson?"

"It wasn't the cross, man. My left leg is in two pieces." Henderson held his wound. "I'm screwed."

He tried to stand, limp by limp, but he fell several times and caught himself.

"Whoa, hey, you're not going anywhere, Caveman." Even bracing his broken leg with two bamboo sticks and long, knotted vines, and he wasn't going far. Le Mans squatted down. "It's broken smack dab into, bud. No lie. It's bad."

"Can't dance with a broken leg, hillbilly," said Henderson, grinning in pain.

Gripping Henderson's hand, Le Mans relocated his friend down a long trench and propped him up beneath a low-growing palm tree. The man needed medicine and water. The worry of infection and disease crossed his mind, but the worst part, Henderson did not have faith, and the cross was just wooden and not a rescue helicopter.

"Got to sound-off if my leg doesn't stop hurting, hillbilly. I got us in a hell of a mess."

"I need to crawl out for help."

"Hey, you better not leave me, Beau Le Mans."

"Do my best, soldier." Le Mans told him, racking his hand through his hair.

Henderson struck the ground; leg throbbing and he pounded the tree until it shook in anger. "Man, I'm tired of Charlie messing with my head. I need painkillers."

Twenty-three days had passed since they'd escaped the POW camp, and freedom seemed as far as America for either one of them.

"It's time to flag a pilot."

"They can come get us both, right here." Henderson moaned.

"Man, you need to lock it up before you get us killed." Le Mans bit his lip and pointed at the injured man.

His hand set lightly on his friend's busted leg. Le Mans used his friend's shirt for bandages and pulled the vines snug. Suddenly, two loud voices sounded upstream. Le Mans covered Henderson with leaves and retreated, sinking into the cold river, and floated under a stack of fat Mangrove roots.

More voices echoed across the river valley; one V-C soldier was alone, smoking, fifteen meters, and cigarette smoke carried into their nostrils. To smell him was the closest anyone had been since Briarpatch POW Camp, weeks earlier. Le Mans slid deeper behind thick vegetation, dark eyes hidden and the only air he had was through the end of a bamboo stick, a trick he'd learned in a John Wayne film.

His head slowly broke the surface, emerging cautiously amid the shadowy parts of the water, popping up under the broadness of shiny, green leaves. He scouted for the enemy once more. Henderson blended in with the bark and moss of nature, but not enough.

One man yelled and walked straight to Henderson's face, half asleep, head hanging on his chest, still in great pain, legs tied with his shirt and some bamboo poles.

"Yankee! G.I. Henderson!" yelled the V-C soldier. "My favorite American."

"Kill me now. I'm not going back to Briarpatch!" said Henderson. "Shoot me, right here. Kill me, Chin Vo!"

"You are no better than a dead dog!" said Chin Vo, holding a gun to Henderson's head.

Chin Vo eased the hammer on the gun.

"Click."

His gun jammed. Le Mans eased out of the water, arm lunged, back and forth.

Le Mans pulled his machete from Chin Vo's back, lancing him in and out, and piercing his heart. His surprised face saw Caveman Henderson, back arched and the gun fell from the hand of Chin Vo, and landed on the chest of Caveman. The American man he hated, had won.

"You got him, Le Mans," Henderson said, pushing Chin Vo into the water. "He's graveyard dead, buddy. You saved my life. I owe you one."

Le Mans cleaned the blade in the river water. Henderson checked the weapon. One bullet was inside the chamber and the clip was full.

"Miracle. One down," said Le Mans, head bobbing and his eyes spoke of something that was long overdue. Long awaited, he felt even.

"Leave him for the snakes and rats," said Henderson, examining his weapon.

"More company," said Le Mans, checking the pockets of Chin Vo. "That rat had my watch on his wrist. Here's a picture of Polly in a yellow dress. Nothing goes back to the way it should be."

"She's a widow, Le Mans, and beautiful," Henderson said, tucking their former captor's pistol inside his pants. "Duc Vo will come looking for his brother. He will hunt for us, but it's a big hairy jungle."

Hand signals were shared, nodding for hours. They waited until the enemy moved away from the roadway and left the area. No more Viet-Cong attachments joined them. Le Mans planned a new mission, unsettled, and nervous in the cold river, the red stained body of Chin Vo began to stink by the next day. Le Mans helped Caveman to higher ground, and assisted him downstream. Both men found a position one step closer to the U.S Military, nicknamed Disneyland of the Far East.

"This jungle is for the birds, Caveman," said Le Mans, raking mud and leaves from his cracked feet. "Paradise would be grabbing a fat greasy funnel cake, watching Little Jimmy Dickens sing at the West Virginia State Fair this year. Hold onto your hat, Henderson, I'll fishhook you out on a whirlybird. If I'm guessing right, the 1st Cavalry Division might be closer than we think. We're going home." A giant smile broke across his face.

"Soldiers of the First Team, huh?" said Caveman, eyes brightened. "Our boys from Fort Hood, Texas. We might know a few bad boys from Texas."

About the time their eyes closed, the eerie howling speakers played again. They plugged their ears with their fingers, just to grab some shuteye. Le Mans counted the twenty-fifth night of freedom and carved wooden ear plugs out of bamboo with the good knife he'd taken from Chin Vo's pocket. He handed

Henderson two sticks to plug his ears, and the men made faces at each other, just to keep their wits about them. Henderson propped himself up close to Le Mans, resting in great pain. Each one leaned against trees to sleep. One eye was open for Charlie. Both waited for Uncle Sam and some room service.

"What is all this howling crap, man, anyway?"

"Our guys are trying to persuade the V-C to get out, go home with all the howling voices and recorded conversations," said Le Mans, opening his eyes.

"They ain't afraid of Daddy Nixon."

"Nope. Recorded voices won't scare them, but Viet-Cong guerillas are scared of the afterlife."

"Ghosts?" Henderson asked, turning a skeptical face, as if he was joking.

Le Mans wiped sleep from his misty eyes.

"Our guys are playing howling voices again to exploit the Buddhist belief, your people, not mine, Caveman," said Le Mans, holding his wooden ear plugs. "Once a V-C soldier dies, their body must be buried in the family plot or their soul wanders aimlessly in the jungle, restless and without peace for eternity. I'm surprised you didn't know that about your own religion."

"No. Didn't know that," said Henderson. "I don't care anymore about religion or my country who left me to die."

Taking the prone position at sunup on the riverbank beside Le Mans, Henderson crawled, felt stronger and scouted the enemy for two hours. No movement happened.

"What's your plan to get us the hell out of here, Le Mans? Big guy, wake up, huh?"

"You'll be back in Amarillo before you know it, making love to Jeanette and holding a Shiner Bock. And five minutes later, you'll be throwing the ball with Little Benny."

"Five minutes," chuckling. "In my dreams, for sure," lips tight. "She loved being in bed when the rain pounded on the wide tin roof. The birds would be there after the rain. That's when Jeanette and her political father named our town, Robin's Egg."

Le Mans rolled over on his back, spoke of a painted orange and blue sky, imagined flat land, red and brown soil, sweet tea in a toast of tumblers and more horses and Robins than a man could shake a stick while reading the *Saturday Evening Post*.

"Where's your Robin's Egg ranch?"

"Little place, just outside Amarillo, the nickname of our small ranch. It's a cool ranch her parents bought in 1950." Henderson wept.

"In West Virginia, leaves turn before it rains, and animals and birds grab the last bite of food off the trails and hide inside the trees. The wind is moist, 'fore the bottom drops out of the sky and it floods the valleys." Le Mans tried to keep him amused.

Le Mans nervously stepped twenty feet away.

"So, where are you going, Le Mans?"

"Walk across the water like Jesus and play John Wayne. Stroll down Jungle Brick Road to Disneyland Far East until I see an American flag."

The vast land was soaked and mud covered each man. Le Mans cracked his lips like a rodeo clown, and moved close to his Texas friend, and said, "Wish it was that easy." He pointed downstream. "We're gonna ride these logs until we hit the ocean, find a clearing, and get out of here. That's the only way out."

"Then, man," grabbing the shoulder of Le Mans, "we'll rip off our shirts, walk up the beach, find our brothers in arms and get outta Dodge City. Don't want to die outside Xo Ap Lo, or in some rathole camp in the Mekong Delta. Make sure you bury me in Texas, hillbilly."

"You're not gonna die, man. Here's my idea," said Le Mans. "I'll pop up on the bank behind us, see how many Viet-Cong rats are roaming the rice paddies, and then make a break for our post." Pointing to the flat lands, he said, "If I make it, you follow later and maybe one of us will make it home, huh?"

"Nope. It's an order that you stay here. This broken leg is not going anywhere. We stay here, and wait for the Cavalry," said Henderson. "Scout for the count," sighing. "Wait until the edge of the sun falls low."

"You will die without medical attention on that broken leg."

"You're right. Just make it to camp without a bullet in my back, Le Mans."

"Agreed. Okay. Wait here, Caveman. I'll have a cold one ready for you, brother," said Le Mans, cupping the hands of his friend.

"Wait. Hey, Le Mans? Take this picture of my wife when you rotate back to the States. Tell 'em," sniffling, "just tell her I did my best and I love her and Benny."

"So that's Benny and the honey blonde, Jeanette, huh? You can tell them."

"Take the damn picture in case I don't make it, Beau Le Mans."

"Beautiful family, Caveman, see you soon." Unbuttoning what was left of his uniform pocket, Le Mans tucked the photo down and buttoned back his shirt. "I'll get it to Little Benny, if you don't beat me home. Here's a picture of my '66 Chevelle, my baby."

Birds flushed out of a nearby tree, were flying overhead, and Le Mans slowly raised his hand as if someone spooked him. They didn't move for ten minutes. Le Mans said, "Time to fly the coop."

The sun broke through the dark clouds, blinding the hillbilly. The man moved behind a big rock, and Le Mans, eyes blinking, and fist flexing, didn't want to leave him wounded.

"You got other pictures?" asked Henderson. "Girls, perhaps?"

"Heck no. Can't afford no dang camera," said Le Mans. "Went out with a girl from Pineville, but, the truth, she broke it off. Said she was too young to be a war widow. Her mother told her that much."

"Yeah. My ex-wife divorced my butt a few months before I shipped out." He rubbed his chin. "Told me the same thing, buddy. I feel you, dog. I think she had another guy."

"Why?" Le Mans asked him. "She had to have a better reason, man, you were already married."

"The truth. Women love a man for trust, good looks," said Henderson, laughing. "And a big, big bank account. You know what I mean."

"Come on, bud. Must be more than that. What did you do wrong, send all your money to the television preacher who was dating the horse track owner in Dallas, and break your trust and in one failed bet, you lost it all, huh? Or was it a show pony woman?"

"I lied, Le Mans," said Henderson, head down, eyes honest. "My life was troubled from the start. She saw right through me in less than a year, man. Unfaithful dirty dog. She walked out. Caught my butt in bed with another woman. Three times."

"You dog, you. Three ladies, huh?"

"Check. Yeah, yeah. I blew it. That was my third strike," grunting and biting his lip. "One bad divorce," said Henderson, sniffing. "Don't break your trust with a woman. It's the worst kind of gambling. And, Le Mans, don't lie to a lady. A woman remembers every word a man says."

"You cheated on her, huh, Caveman?" He saw the truth in his friend's misty eyes.

"Yeah. She said, 'You're no good for me, Ben Henderson.' I struck out, man. She would not let up on me and left my butt. That's when I happily volunteered for Uncle Sam's Army. Joined up to be a warhorse."

"You volunteered for this, huh? Same as I did. Signed up to be a fighter, but for the most part, I've been fighting myself, who I am. Rebelling, that's what my mother calls it. Hell of a way to find out about yourself. To rebel, to regret, and there's no way to be a hero. I'd rather be on the other side of the war, out of here."

"Our emotions will lie to us. We should counter our emotions with the truth," said Henderson, leaning, and face puckered at Le Mans.

"Did your father tell you that?" He crossed his arms.

"My Dad drove us to see Billy Graham preach in El Paso, back in 1962. Looks like our sin and selfishness got us both in Vietnam, hillbilly. Same, same."

"The truth about a hard-boiled egg, you have to heat it and crack it 'fore you taste the best part. The inside is where you will find yourself, the truth is your heart, and sometimes it happens when you're alone. It's a shame we had to be shipped to Vietnam to find ourselves," said Le Mans. "That's my truth for you, soldier."

Finally, they understood each other. Henderson and Le Mans told the truth after a year and a half of being friends and enemies inside a POW camp. Henderson told the truth about why Jeanette had left him. Listening for an hour or more, Le Mans saw him breakdown and cry again. He'd opened up and told his story without all the barn aroma and lies that accompanied most of his stories.

"If you ever find the right lady, treat her like a queen and from the start, be true to that woman, Beau Le Mans."

"Yeah, it's the best way," said Le Mans. "Someday. When you get back home, make it right, get Jeanette back and tell it the way you told me. She'll take you back, buddy."

They whispered in close quarters for most of the night and heard the howling voices that kept them up until morning, talking about home and close friends and dreams. Henderson told him about Robin's Egg, Texas, and what made Jeanette fall in love with him from the start. Henderson spoke about Buddhism, the truth, and Le Mans countered him with Christianity. They disagreed when it came to the best players in baseball and football.

"Keep the gun. I'll check this field and be back in a jiffy," said Le Mans, holding his machete in one hand and a banana in the other.

"Watch your back, bud." Henderson warned.

"Do the same," said Le Mans. "Hey, I'll be back in a few. I'd like to hear more about the baseball field at Robin's Egg, Texas. Your eyes closed last night before you finished your story."

"Cool. You bet," said Henderson, eyes wide open. "Hurry back, my friend."

Le Mans nodded, slapped hands with Henderson, and wished him well.

"Go soldier at high speed, grunt on, Caveman, grunt on," said Le Mans.

"Be the hero from West Virginia," Henderson told him, laughing.

"When we get out of here, we'll have lots of candy and beer," said Le Mans, nodding. "See you in an hour or so."

That next morning, the sun found a gap between gray clouds, breaking the curtain of darkness and fog. The wide door of the jungle had opened under the sky, courage ran inside his veins, and Le Mans stayed low, and faced a long, narrow pathway alone. Noise echoed, men screamed, the battle raged in the distance, and he heard most of the fighting, as black smoke rolled into a towering mushroom cloud.

Battered and partially washed out, the river was low for easy access and connected the land to the high terrain. Beyond his sightline was a long open field where the howling voices played each night. After Le Mans left, Henderson stood, leg wrapped, and hopped in the opposite direction. To his far left was fresh flowing water, and he stayed in a small swampy area.

Le Mans scouted and returned for Henderson, positioning himself, a man trapped for two days beneath the bridge, where he saw fish swimming in a deep hole of water, frogs chirping in the mud, and colorful birds nested high in the tops of flowery trees. Henderson had vanished and didn't keep to his part of the agreement. In that length of time, streams and rivers emptied from the mountain rain, making his feet like a soup sandwich again. Two hundred yards away, Le Mans vacated the bridge area and found berries and would've taken the life of a green frog, but he needed fire to cook the creature, so the frog's life was spared. The frog became his friend and stayed beside him until dark, and it was a moment he'd never forget. Buddies.

He drank from a gentle spring, cool and refreshing and the water reminded him of Wyoming County, homeward bound. His father took him to the Grand Park Opening of Twin Falls; prayed he'd never have to serve in Vietnam, and that's where he saw his first waterfall. Then, not far, the second waterfall, Twin Falls.

After three days apart from Henderson, Le Mans heard gunfire on a nearby hill, but Henderson had not returned to the rally point. Le Mans watched two Viet-Cong soldiers operate weapons on a narrow rock cliff. The morning that followed was a fat tangerine sun that reflected off the slow flowing water, low in a deep valley of wild flowers. Le Mans was hungry and waded up to his knees through the jungle to where the rice paddies spread about the land, like corn did in the Mountain State. He became delirious, but alert and killed two Viet-Cong soldiers in hand-to-hand combat; Wounded and praying; he passed out an hour before a rotor head pilot spotted him face down in the water beside two dead Viet-Cong guerillas.

In his dream, he heard Henderson, waving his arms, and yelling, "We're going home, hillbilly!" He woke up, but Henderson was not inside the helicopter and not hooked to the line. Le Mans laughed aloud and was no longer a prisoner or missing in action. He'd made it to safety on the twenty-eighth day from Briarpatch POW Camp, some seven miles from where he'd last seen Polly and Cadeo.

Three days later, Le Mans met with the CO, Commander of the 1st Cavalry Division and explained how Henderson slid into a deep trench, broken leg, and waited by a bridge. Like a ghost, he'd disappeared.

Using the etched map, U.S. Army Warrant Officers found Briarpatch POW Camp, the exact place Le Mans had described the camp, and the place was an abandoned post. The first night back at Headquarters Company, codename Disneyland Far East, Beau Le Mans celebrated with cooked food and a half-dozen cold soda pops. That night, he saw armed villagers in a dream: one stood smoking in a straw hat beside two Viet-Cong soldiers, who had a dozen questions about Henderson. He didn't answer the first question. Later, Viet-Cong guerillas left the area, but the dream revealed Henderson, a man still alive and kicking with a broken left leg. The man eased into the brush and stayed beyond the rice paddies and disappeared.

Henderson must have crawled and edged himself through the water, Le Mans pondered. Then, suddenly Caveman peered into a mirror of water at the end of the rice paddies and stood in his dress blues and walked through the jungle in a pressed uniform. Bizarre dreams happened to Le Mans after the bug bites marked him.

"That's where I saw you, Le Mans," said the Warrant Officer, "with the sun burning a hole in your back. I could have seen you from Space."

"Thank God for freedom."

"You were face down amid rice patties, and I took you to Cuchi on a stretcher and it looks like you've recouped."

"I owe you my life, WO."

"I heard you were getting a Purple Head," the officer slapped his good arm, "Headed home. Shot in the shoulder."

Le Mans exercised his muscles slowly and became a comfortable recluse. He drew pictures and wrote stories and spoke less about his time as a POW. One soldier came in on a stretcher, a second soldier was spotted alive, and a third soldier failed to move after multiple wounds. None of them were Henderson. The medic told Le Mans he'd died a hard death, like Sam Law or even worse.

"He's in God's hands now." The CO told Le Mans.

Aircraft moved about for ten days after Le Mans returned to his unit. There was still no sign of Henderson. No one had seen any moment where he was last positioned in the jungle and a Recon unit confirmed the bridge area patrol. When Le Mans was lifted out, he remembered the faces of the gunner and the Warrant Officer pilot, and wrote about what they said to him. Le Mans organized one last Recon effort with the WO, but no one was found and Sam Law's body had been taken by the V-C.

"Is this the bridge, Le Mans?" asked the Warrant Officer.

"We were in the trench for several days. That's where I killed Chin Vo."

"There's no soldier in the trench, Le Mans."

"He's here somewhere. I know him too well."

Then, the jungle got hot when the V-C fired from the hillside. The gunner bagged two bandits and nailed two more armed villagers in straw hats. Le Mans and the Warrant Officer disagreed about where they thought Henderson had been taken. The enemy who had blocked their open door for weeks, one-by-one, had slowly been defeated. Le Mans saw the body of Henderson in a dream, the way it happened, the way he woke up inside the helicopter beside the WO, when he was discovered.

Still, he worried for Henderson who had been moved from the list of POW to MIA. Ten more days had passed, and nightmares and hallucinations stirred inside of Le Mans. Henderson had not yet resurfaced. Was he KIA?

The war played on and a hundred more names had been announced since Henderson, who was rarely mentioned other than in the ranks of the Missing In Action. Le Mans printed his story two weeks later and became famous for his news columns about his life as a POW.

PART II

CHAPTER FOUR

↔

The Sunchaser, 1974

Trout broke the surface in the shallows of the New River beneath Beau Le Mans, who had come home to the Mountain State to teach rock climbing. He'd rafted rivers and hiked the highest peaks in West Virginia. His writing had slowed and he'd worked freelance after his Purple Heart. The breeze in Fayetteville reminded him of the breath of peppermint from a candy store he'd visited in downtown Beckley.

When he returned home, the first thing Beau did was buy a 1974 civilian Jeep, off the showroom floor in Beckley, West Virginia, and that's where he'd found some good flavored candy in an old general store. As soon as he got home, his father gave him his grandfather's property, and the two war veterans walked the land and had lunch in the kitchen. An eagle he'd seen while driving the Jeep, soaring several days in a row, had nested in the deep valley and made a home of the New River Gorge, same as he did. Surrounded by the rugged mountains again, the landscape bent and rolled and stood tall, far as the eye could see, mountains in each direction. He loved it.

Beau had longed for home, rocks, rivers, and family. To him, the mountains were the other side of the war he'd written about. Beau loved the mountains and deep valley floor of Fayette

County in the early morning fog, and he was known as the only photo journaling rock climber in the county. As he looked eye-to-eye with the eagle, he was hooked to the rocky cliffs of the New River Gorge and thought of Henderson. His new profession was only a few miles from his father's new restaurant. His mother and father had relocated from Wyoming County to Fayette County while he was in Vietnam, leaving behind his friends and old family farm in Baileysville. Tragically, Wells, his young brother, was killed the first week in Fayetteville.

Not a day went by that he didn't think about his Army buddies, Ben "Caveman" Henderson, and Sam Law; and Beau, heartbroken, lost sleep, and felt guilty for leaving Caveman behind with a broken leg. He knew Little Benny would miss his father and his ex-wife loved him at least once. Someone in the jungle knew something about Henderson and whatever happened, it was undeserved and unresolved. The government claimed Benjamin Henderson was Missing in Action (MIA).

Beau's father recommended his son speak to the local minister about his nightmares and flashbacks. The broken parts of Beau's life were real, and he'd brought all of his past home from Vietnam. He refused to seek any type of professional counsel, but his father and friends at the diner encouraged him to explore his thoughts like he did the mountains. His father felt his son needed to condition his emotions as much as his muscles.

Beau listened and followed his father's ideas for the first time in ages. Beau noticed things on the forest floor, and he respected nature more than he did before the war, but to talk about war and writing, it was something personal and private. Something in the woods always reminded him of Vietnam.

By the cool spring of 1974, blooms burst through the good earth of West Virginia and a blanket of snow had melted away. The smell of the mountains was something he'd almost forgotten, and Beau could no longer ignore a kaleidoscope of stunning colors and silken folds along the trails of the valley floor. Later, he stretched out at night on his green Jeep, and like some old storybook, he was still mesmerized by dancing stars and the glitter of the wide, yet peaceful New River Gorge skyline. Owls and 18 wheelers made the only noise, and who could forget the hound dogs? He watched as God showed off His power and amazement to the world, a rare treat on a clear night. Thankful he'd made it home in one piece, Beau was finally at home.

His family eagerly opened a chain of diners from Fayetteville to Sutton, stretching along Highway 19, and each one was packed with travelers and truckers. The vast landscape through West Virginia, dotted with white and pink dogwood trees, and in May, trees had bloomed in the high country of the New River Gorge. It was the home he'd found again. The rugged Blue Ridge Mountains span into the distance like an endless tapestry of high mountain terrain, but no matter how majestic, Beau still fought with the images of being buckled to the geography of Vietnam. Not even his pastor could pray away what had happened to him across the world, four years earlier.

In mid-May, Beau was perched on the cliffs, sandwich in hand, and clothed in his camo shorts, and his feet dangling over mighty cliffs of the gorge. He wore his coveted Rough Rider shirt from high school, a school named after Teddy Roosevelt and the Rough Riders, a hard-nosed team well-known beyond Wyoming County. To his left, the remnants of Native American dwelling places gained his attention, and he thought of the people who had walked the mountains long before the first white man cut his way through the deep gorge, like he had to do when he escaped the POW camp. On that morning, he was the only rock climber in the New River Gorge valley. Far from war and guerilla forces, he heart was relieved to be in wild and wonderful Fayette County.

He'd written a few articles for the local newspaper and started life over. Beau was brokenhearted for the families of MIA and KIA soldiers and how he'd grown callous to war stories and kind of lost touch with his typewriter. Beau was grief stricken. Uneasy and rattled, he'd accepted signs of PTSD. He coped while fishing and hiking which brought comfort when he spoke to God and memorized Scripture. Aside from his normal Sunday services, rock cliffs were his sanctuary and radio sermons from Billy Graham echoed across the majesty valley.

He loved the idea of being near the New River, one of oldest in the world, and could not figure out how God made a river meander north, but He did. The sun burst through the milky clouds, elements of the deep valley drew people to the depth and beauty of the stunning gorge. Thus, work on the New River Gorge Bridge had commenced, causing dust clouds to take flight across the gorge. Beau soaked up the sun, where Father Time offered his benediction from a snowy winter and birds returned and fish teased him when they broke the surface of the river.

Beau bathed nude in a cold, shallow part of the river, and lathered himself in a splash of cherry shampoo to celebrate a good day of rock climbing. Leaves sprouted, like a painted picture of dogwoods and daffodils, complementing the valley floor in an array of tender pastels. A car stopped next to his Jeep.

"Do I have an audience?" said Beau, half submerged.

"Do you want company, Beau Le Mans?" said a tall lady, pulling her cinnamon colored hair underneath her chin. Her eyes lingered on the sharp contours of his chest and wavy abs. "Nice eagle tattoo on your shoulder, Le Mans."

Inside his mind, Beau had seen an angel, flashing red nails. He sat in a pool of water, heard bubble gum popping, and a lady walked up beside him.

"How'd you know my name, Lady?"

"I know a few things about you, Beau. It's Naomi, not "Lady" or anything else, got it?"

Beau nodded, still dazzled. "Nice car."

Another lady stepped out of a blue 1970 Monte Carlo Super Sport.

"Is this double trouble, Naomi?" said Beau, head tilted.

She nosed around the camp, picked up his notebook, read it, and walked around the sandy riverbank. His fire burned low. Beau was curious about the two beautiful ladies and scratched his head. He leaned back, arms spread open, and thought they must be rookie cub reporters from Beckley.

"I don't need any Girl Scout cookies today," said Beau, hand on his chin. "I make my own peanut butter snap cookies."

"Aren't you just Johnny Carson, or what, Chef?" said Naomi, sunglasses in her hand. "The man at the coffee shop told us where we could find POW Beau Le Mans." She blocked the sun with her hand while she checked him out, bending her knees.

"You didn't speak to my father, did you?" asked Beau, face turned. "Dang it."

"Nicest man we've ever met," said Naomi, blowing a bubble. "And your mom is a precious lady."

"There goes my secret hiding place," said Beau, Army hat over his midsection.

"Here's a towel, Beau," said Naomi, dangling the towel out of his reach.

"Did he tell you; I was the best Chef in the hills?" He laughed.

"I didn't hear the word "Best" from him. He said you cooked a mean Chicken Masala for Bigfoot, though. That's when two nosy ladies from Morgantown couldn't resist meeting a nude chef and a war hero."

"No war hero. But these hands do cook a mean masala, ladies." Beau lathered his blonde hair, washed his face and shoulders before he eased toward the towel she tossed into the branches of a shrub.

"Why did the newspaper call you "Man of War?" said Naomi, hands on her hips.

He toweled his face, said, "Man of War, yeah? They didn't say that, did they?"

"Last month."

"What newspaper?" He wrapped his waist. The ladies dropped their heads and watched him.

"The Fayette Tribune," said Naomi, grinning.

"I was nearly a casualty of war," said Beau, dropping his head. "Prisoner of War, that's all. No Yeti and war hero lives here. Your friend doesn't say much, Naomi, what's up?" The natural beauty of the driver caught his eye.

"Anna Katsen." She poured water on the fire. "Good to meet you."

"Hey, my fire." said Beau, "I'm freezing."

"I can tell by the lack of wood," said Anna, giggling beside Naomi. "Name's Anna."

"Kinda salty, aren't we, Beach Bunny Anna."

"You need to grow your own tree, guy," said Naomi, hands over her face.

Beau admired the view of smooth, long legs while he dried his hair. She walked over to the Monte Carlo, grabbed a camera, and snapped a photo of Beau Le Mans, half nude, and draped in a long towel.

"Yeah, I'm salty. But this Beach Bunny found you," said Anna, still peering through the camera lens.

"I didn't know I was lost. Me and Jesus got that part all worked out in Vietnam." Beau rubbed his shoulder. "That part about me cooking for Bigfoot, that's true, by the way. Don't print that, Cub Writer."

"Looks much smaller in a lens, though," said Anna, camera in one hand and Naomi's shoulder in the other. She waved her pinky finger and winked her darling blue eyes.

"My heart is bigger than you think," said Beau, breaking a big smile.

"I've read about you," said Anna, pointing her camera.

"Me?"

"Yeah, the infamous Man of War. That's a cool trade name, Beau. I heard how the newspapers wanted to snatch you up, put you to work as a Rat Writer; write and interview soldiers for war stories," said Naomi, hands splashing the river. She removed her dark sunglasses and studied the scar left behind by a bullet in Vietnam.

"Are you a couple reporters from Morgantown?" asked Beau, slipping on his sandals. "I'm not interested in talking to the newspaper, ladies. Please respect my nude privacy."

"No way!" said Anna, grinning at her friend, and giggling. "We just graduated from West Virginia, doing some traveling and taking cool pictures of interesting people."

"We photograph the best subjects, though." Naomi said. "Small things that seem larger than life."

"Larger than life, huh?" He studied their faces. "WVU has a top tier communication program. We can be friends, if you don't let that picture leak, like Watergate."

The man pondered why two lovely ladies interrupted his river bath for twenty questions, but his father taught him to count his blessings and be friendly to all females, beautiful or not.

Naomi had all the questions. Anna was cool; a lady with painted blue eyes caught his attention.

"I don't shake hands, Anna," said Beau, checking out both ladies. "We hug in Fayette County. I'm a wartime hugger."

Anna touched the book he was reading and held his clothes.

"Are you cold, Beau?" asked Anna.

"I'm fine," he told her, walking to his Jeep. "I love May in the mountains."

Naomi followed him as if they were best friends.

"I'll hug you," said Naomi. She held him with a firm grip. "Great to finally meet you, Beau Le Mans. I've never met an Army journalist before."

Anna loosened his towel and stepped on the piece closest to the ground.

"Oscar Meyer does have a first name, doesn't he?" said Anna, hand touching her lips. "Nice buns, Beau."

"He's very fine, Anna," whispered Naomi. "I'm taking him, girl, half clothed and totally handsome."

"Good meeting you ladies, but I've got to do some work at home," said Beau, tucking his shirt inside his shorts and taking a deep breath. "Blue cold."

Anna flipped her bandana to him. Next, she handed him his hat.

"Some hot soup at the diner might warm his blue butt up," said Anna, pacing over to Beau's Jeep. "He might be the first tour guide of the New River Gorge."

The ladies stood beside his Jeep.

"Your father said you'd show us around town," said Naomi, making a figure eight on the Jeep hood, "unless you're too busy with your girlfriend, huh?"

"Ex-girlfriend. She was a berry." Beau jumped in his Jeep, combed his hair, slipped on his sunglasses. What were these girls up to? "Yeah. I can skip work for a few hours."

Anna plucked leaves from a holly tree, and said, "Maybe you haven't met the right berry yet, Mister Beau." She flipped the leaves at his chest and grinned.

"Not all berries are good for you," said Beau, eyes on Anna.

"Hard to believe that no lady has roped the Man of War to a wedding chapel, the famous Army hero and journalist, huh?" said Anna. "He might not be able to commit himself, Naomi."

"I pick my berries very carefully. Some are poisonous."

"Let's go, Anna," said Naomi. "Hot soup and crackers sound good. He can't hang with two sorority sisters from Morgantown, anyways. We're taking up this man's precious afternoon."

"I could tell you weren't from the Carmelite Monastery." He lifted his head and crossed his arms.

"We are just as holy as you are, I bet?" said Anna.

Three things Beau didn't argue about: War, religion, and good company. So, he remained wise in his ways and said nothing more about God or nuns or war and wasn't about to turn down soup and crackers with two pretty ladies. He was smarter than that.

Anna pulled the Jeep keys from his camouflage shorts and looped them on her fingers. "Looking for these?"

"Sure."

"My grandfather had a Jeep when I was growing up in Pittsburgh. I learned to drive a three-speed CJ-5 when I was sixteen," she said. "There's no standard manual transmission I can't handle. Move over, man. Hope it will go in gear, Beau."

"Can a sorority-berry handle a real standard shift?" said Beau, slapping his Jeep gear shift. "Takes a bit of coordination with good hands and hips to make it work in rhythm."

"To me, it's not much bigger than a golf cart. Couldn't be that hard." Anna buckled up in the driver's seat. "Do you mind?"

"Go ahead."

"Where do I put the quarter to start this thing?" said Anna, touching the dash.

"Quarter! This ride is better than the State fair," said Beau, watching her try to start the Jeep. "Don't forget, you have to pull the choke, warm it up first."

"She held his knee. Like this, Beau, right?" said Anna. Then, she pulled the choke and found first gear. Working her feet and pressing the gas pedal and clutch. "Is this how to warm up the engine, Beau?"

"Yeah. Make sure you ..." Beau listened as the Jeep stalled out. "Is this your first time with a stick, a real three speed?" He saw her eyes behind glasses, and she didn't answer him. "I can see that you're not used to being in the front seat."

"Nope," said Naomi, blurting out loud. "Second home."

"Shut up." Anna told her, sticking out her tongue. "He's a clever one."

"Yeah. Johnny Carson says, "make a girl laugh and you can wake up with her.""

"But, you're not funny, dude." Anna blew long hair out of her face.

Beau held her hand on the stick shift and pulled her leg off the gas pedal. "This way, just turn the key. I believe it's warmed up and purring. Now try it again. Choke. Clutch. Shift. Easy. Smooth shift it. Or you'll have to start over."

"I trust ya. Don't make me cry. Make me laugh." Her hand turned the key, the engine fired up and she held a curious grin. Her eyes rounded in surprise. The engine stopped.

Beau could tell she was a rookie driver, but a brave one. What she had done to impress him seemed to be working and, in a short time, he wouldn't mind being her teacher.

"I'm not careless. Push the choke back in, pop the clutch, smoothly pull down, down more and put it into first gear," suggested Beau, snapping his seatbelt and relaxing. "Remember, the Jeep, it's a three speed, Doll."

The engine fired, and she said, "How's that?"

She popped the clutch and found first gear and pushed her glasses on her nose. Anna pulled the park brake and the Jeep smoothly rolled into first gear.

"Why, Anna, huh, I've found a berry that can drive a Jeep."

"I haven't picked one yet, Beau."

In time and through the hillside turns, Anna Katsen changed gears like a pro. Beau saw the opportunity to make a new friend, and she was as good of a friend as he'd made in years. Somehow

Anna and Beau were like two puzzle pieces who had found each other and made the perfect picture and framework for association. All good friendships started that way.

"Just because you warmed the engine and made it run, don't get your hopes up for another hug or a hookup, Man of War," said Anna, pulling her long hair over her ear.

"Hope, it's all I got," said Beau, holding on and letting her drive.

The Jeep was open to the elements. Beau waved at everyone he knew along the roadway, from farmers to bridge workers, and even the mailman. The Monte Carlo that Naomi drove followed closely behind them, a super-sport that had no trouble keeping up.

"Where are we going?" shouted Naomi, leaning out the window at a stop sign.

Anna stood in the Jeep, held the steering wheel and shouted, "Follow me!"

Beau held the handle and pointed.

"Follow you?" said Naomi, talking to herself. "I'm hungry."

"Beau, where are you taking us?" asked Anna.

"A little mystery is good for the soul, Anna," said Beau, arm holding him up. "Do you like surprises?"

"No one likes surprises," said Anna, downshifting at a stop sign and stirring at him, holding her eyes for as long as she could, but he caught her a handful of times.

"Seeing you was a big surprise today," said Beau. "I like surprises now. Wow! Watch the curves." He sat up tall and told her who lived at each farm. "Take a right at the top of the hill and you'll see my house."

"You live alone, right?"

"Alone."

He stopped to get the mail and suddenly she pulled back her long hair and covered her head with a straw sun-chaser hat. At that moment, Anna reminded him of Gunilla Lindblad, a Covergirl model for *Vogue*, who was spotted often wearing a straw sun-chaser hat like the one Anna adjusted over dark glasses.

"What are all the workers doing?" asked Anna.

"Construction workers," said Beau, flashing a peace sign. "Here from all over the country to build the New River Gorge Bridge. Some are steel workers from Ohio, some engineers from Georgia, and others drive big trucks from three countries wide. All of them eat like bears each evening at Cafe Le Mans and have dad's famous roast beef sandwich."

"That's why we couldn't find a hotel in this town, huh?" said Anna, shifting gears. "Everything is booked for weeks. Hope you don't mind us staying at your place, Beau."

"Yeah. All booked up. Lucky for you, you've made a friend with a Jeep and a five bedroom farmhouse," he told her. "I rarely see the place for rock climbing and being the top chef at the restaurant."

"We are friends, aren't we?" said Anna, eagerly. "Friends, with the writer Beau Le Mans, a prisoner of war and voice of the soldiers. Good to know you."

"My pleasure. I hope we have a chance to see more of each other."

"Me too."

"My home is not too far from here. There's a small cost involved for staying with me, though," said Beau rubbing his chin.

"Cost?"

"Well, it's more of a trade than anything else."

"Trade, huh, Beau? We might as well stop right now. If you have that on your mind." She slammed the brakes. "Forget it."

"Relax."

"What pray tell might it cost me or what's up with a trade?" she asked, squinting her eyes at him, grinning.

"It's simple, one dance," said Beau, grinning. "One dance for every night you stay."

"How about a nice thank-you card instead?" she told him at the end of a long driveway. "I don't often dance. Naomi is a great dancer, though. She'll boogie down."

"Okay. I'll dance with Naomi each night," Beau said, leaning on her shoulder.

"Your father has already given up permission to stay as long as we like, smarty pants."

"O', I see, you've charmed another man. Magical, huh?"

"We thanked him for his kindness and the meal was free," said Anna, placing her hat atop his head. "You can get a dance or a hug from Naomi, for the sake of mankind."

Beau signaled his hand to park beside the barn.

"Bet my father said 'stay the summer,' didn't he? I can stay at my parent's home and give you and Naomi some privacy. They live about ten miles from here," said Beau, jumping out of the Jeep.

"No. You stay, cook chicken masala, Chef Beau Le Mans," said Anna, with a sincere face. "But he also said you'd offer your home for a trade."

Beau heard his dad: "A hundred records, lava lamp, and you two ladies will love falling asleep in his giant bean bag chairs, but he'll trade you."

"I'd be uncomfortable without you as our tour guide and chaperone," said Anna, watching the Monte Carlo pull into the driveway. The Jeep started to roll.

"Whoa. Whoa! Push the park brake, Anna," shouted Beau, hand on the gear shift.

"Close one, Beau. But, I got you, Babe," said Anna, pulling her sun-chaser hat low on her head and blushing behind dark glasses.

"I have a little request for you, Anna," asked Beau, catching the keys.

"A request of me, huh? Speak?" She jumped outside of the Jeep and followed him to his front porch.

"We can talk later inside." Beau walked around the front of the vehicle and was searching for something. "Lost my lucky leather belt at the river, I guess. Dang it. How will my pants stay up? I loved that belt."

She lifted up her shirt and unsnapped his belt from her waistline. "Maybe your good nature will provide, soldier?" said Anna, looping the belt around his neck.

"Maybe nature will." He took a deep breath and knew his father had the right idea about letting them stay at his place. "Let me clean up the house really quick, while you take pictures of the mountains."

A few steps and Beau stood inside.

"What's up, Anna?" asked Naomi, leaning on her friend. "He is so hot, girl."

"He wants a favor." Anna hugged her sorority sister.

"Yeah. Already. Are you?"

"It's not that kind of a favor, girl."

Naomi ran up to the front porch.

"Ummm, somebody is already swapping favors, I guess." said Naomi, giggling and kicking in the swing. "Did you ask him for our little favor, lady? We need him."

"Not yet."

"Do you think he'll let you write an article about him for grad school or for the newspaper?" asked Naomi.

"Girl, after I'm through with him, he'll type it for me." She held up her little pinky.

They kicked their legs high and swung wide across the wide farmhouse porch.

"Shhhh," said Naomi. "Beau is at the glass doors."

He opened the door that led into a large living area and a curious smirk ran across his face. He'd changed into his favorite bowling-style shirt and sandals.

They walked inside the great room and made their way to the refrigerator. The home was spotless, as if no one lived inside the farmhouse. Not a speck of dust was on the furniture, it was clean and neat, like a military barracks, but farmhouse furniture.

"Please pardon the mess, my mother and father decorated the place while I was in Dallas last summer, but ... I think you'll like the paisley country sofa just the same."

"Dallas, huh?" said Anna. "What were you doing in Texas?"

"I attended Southern Methodist University for three months. My religious father thought college would get my mind off the war. I agreed and spent the summer in Dallas, Texas, studying theology and broadening my mind about the Lone Star State and the Lord."

"Are you a Methodist?"

"I was a Baptist from Wyoming County. My Dog Tags tell me, I'm a Baptist. Dad likes the Methodist church now. When you own a cafe in Fayette County, everyone invites you to their church. We've attended Sunday services at a Presbyterian church, a Baptist church, and occasionally we hear the Roman Catholics sing. We've seen everyone but Jesus in our cafe."

"Well, theology man, huh?" said Anna. "You calling on the Great I Am."

"Yeah. I guess so. Texas is a beautiful place to study." Beau held out a platter of crackers and cheese, both Wisconsin and Pennsylvanian-made varieties, for each lady to sample. "The crackers, well, they were made by the mother's hand," whispering, "a little experiment with wheat, flour, water, fennel seeds, olive oil, salt, sugar, and poppy seeds."

Beau had a contagious and gentle face, pulling his ten day old beard and his thoughts of Anna in sunglasses and a wide hat had appealed to him. He saw her spinning in style and Southern dignity, soaking up sunshine on the beach in the Outer Banks and maybe even in Key West with him. When an honest man like Beau saw Anna in real life, he imagined himself with her, going places, and walking around the Big Mango Marketplace in Dallas, and catching up on everything he'd missed while at war.

As sure handed as he was in high school, Beau locked onto Anna's hand and led her upstairs, a little tour of the place was his pleasure. Suddenly she tossed her hat at him in a playful way. The hat spun high and Beau caught the brim before the straw slid across the hardwood floor. He held his pants and placed the hat atop her cinnamon hair and pulled it tight.

With a big grin, Beau was impressed with Anna, a lady who laughed and wasn't afraid to spill the beans on likes and dislikes about his home, either. Only a few women in his lifetime had caused Beau to stutter and stammer and lose his grip on words, but he finally found his composure and a sweet berry. He tightened his belt and leaned against the wall and tried to be cool. She knew what he was up to and ignored him.

And from that moment on, Anna had his attention, giggling and joking with him as they surveyed each enormous bedroom and he told stories about the decorations and how his mother carefully painted each color. She was way ahead of him on home design and decorations, clever and more worldly in comments and comebacks than he'd first predicted. After some crackers and a few glasses of wine, Anna opened up a little more with each sip and they sat across from each other at the table. Naomi listened to them with one ear and watched television while they spoke about Texas, told stories about the war, and how he was invited to Washington D.C. to meet the Commander and Chief.

"You met President Ford, Beau?" said Anna.

"Yeah. Met Ford, Nixon, and LBJ, but I'd given my Purple Heart back to have had the opportunity to have Maine lobster and ale with JFK and Jackie."

"That would have been the berry, man," said Anna, crunching crackers.

"Ford invited the Prisoners of War to the White House. It was last year and we had dinner with him, good discussions, and a few others showed up. Took a grand tour of the place and enjoyed my stay, but I'll never go back."

"That must have been something else," said Naomi.

"I recommended we have a National Day of Recognition for POW and MIA soldiers. I'm sure it will happen soon," said Beau, toasting the ladies.

Beau left the room and slipped off his shoes.

"He may need help," said Naomi.

"I hope so. It gets dark in Fayette County."

Naomi sat beside Anna, and whispered, "Would you, you know, after just one day with him, girl?"

"Naomi. I've wanted him since I read his first article in college."

"Keep your pants buckled. Promise you won't fall on your back so fast."

"I don't make promises."

The warm sun faded, Anna stood in the grandness of the great room window and looked at the darkness of night, relaxing and speaking of interviewing him for an article in the newspaper. At that point, he wasn't about to make her hitch a Greyhound bus or sleep outside in the barn for her lack of personality or failure to be amiable. Beau had pondered the interview, but he couldn't decide. Lifting her eyes and head when he spoke piqued her curiosity and postponed questions about the war and the interview she needed dearly for her personal interest, so she could land her first big job in journalism. To her, big interviews meant big pay and a good career move. Blushing were Anna's cheeks from the wine, casually joking, face partially hidden, and behind her hat, the ladies spoke in private. Her friend grabbed her hand before she fell and was taken aback about how bad Anna wanted to kiss him.

Eagerness ran through his veins and he had a sincere attraction to Anna from the very start. His Vietnamese sweetheart, well, she was too far away, if she was alive. He was curious about Anna's thoughts and why she'd stopped in Fayetteville to see him, and where she was headed after Fayette County. Had to be more than just a grad school interview, he thought. It was a simple friendship, not like all the rest and just plain conversations, something natural and fresh rolled from their tongues, a new friendship happened. The sight of the two was something unexpected that morning before they met. Beau didn't know yet what to do with his warm thoughts about Anna, and it was way too early to invite her to stay the summer. He said to himself, "Where does she plan to travel, though, all their luggage and a typewriter?"

To Beau, something inexpressibly different ran through his mind, a spirit of expression and flirting resonated so easily from her personality at dinner, too, where she'd done most of the storytelling. She held her part of the conversation about college and her desire to see the countryside, especially Texas. Beau fell into a moment of wonderment and he didn't mind answering questions about his own life and the hardship he'd faced in the Army as a prisoner. For sure, he had his share of questions about food and sports and likes and dislikes and less about materialism and wealth and more about art and nature and places she'd like to see. More emanation and purpose rang from her conversation than other ladies he'd spent time with in Wyoming County. She was impressed with the way he'd described his Barringer Stew, and aside from the carrots, she said he'd make a good chef.

Anna held up his favorite instrument.

"Do you mind if I play the guitar?" asked Anna.

"Please do." He told her, arms crossed.

Then, she dusted off his guitar, the one he'd played only a handful of times since coming home from Vietnam. She sang John Denver, some Joan Baez and knew some of the "Old Man" by Neil Young, and she adored the style of Joni Mitchell and Carole King. That part of her was sewn into his soul, and he complimented her after each song, clapping and cheering. Naomi was drifting off during the slow songs and ready to call it a night.

Beau brought in all their luggage and the heavy typewriter.

"I think it is past my bedtime," said Naomi, waving and climbing the stairs to her room. "See you two night owls in the morning." She winked at Anna, leaving them alone for the first time.

Beau filled Anna's glass and brought out more pepper jack cheese and crackers.

"You have an excellent voice."

She stopped playing and sat beside him.

"Thank you. I've sang all my life, brightening the rooms, songs in coffee shops and opening up for a few no-name bands in Morgantown and Fairmont. I don't see myself on stage, taking in the lights as a career or packing up a van for some cross-country tour. Not me. I love to investigate and research current topics."

"Don't know how it is for a woman, but I've often thought about how a man has two close passions inside his heart. For me, I finally decided one passion was a hobby and wondered what would have happened if I pursued the other one. I've gotten away from music and write a little and jot down ideas about books and songs. I have a hundred ideas about books and articles."

"Let's hear it, Elvis, huh?" she asked, crossing her legs, guitar by her side. She was close to his face and sniffed his French citrus cologne.

"No. Not yet. I do write a few ideas, though." Beau pointed to a cedar chest that sat beside the bookcase and under a painting of derby horses. "Some are in the chest and others are folded, tucked inside books, and packed away somewhere. I usually add to the stories when something needs to be noted. They are dreams, some songs, some old ideas about more stories and what

I felt and saw in Vietnam. I collect names of soldiers, the ones I've lost."

"Oh," touching his cheek, and jumping to his cedar chest, "I'd love to see them, put the words to music and make melodies, finish your thoughts. I'll help you with stories from Vietnam. They are worth printing, Beau. We know about writer's block and doubt our own, don't we?"

"Yeah. Sweet of you."

"Look at all these untold stories, Beau."

"While in Vietnam, I was a journalist for the Army Times, writing and taking photos during the war. Stories took me to the frontlines. Maybe writing was the reason I was captured, got too close to the fire, inside the action with the infantry might have cost America too much pain."

She sipped her wine, and said, "To be honest, I used to read your articles on microfilm at the Wise Library on campus. That's why I wanted to become a journalist or a war correspondent. I wasn't sure back then. My scrapbook is full of your heartfelt stories and articles."

"What? No way? That's cool, Anna. Yeah, grow your own tree, girl."

"I love it. I wasn't the only student. One of our professors made us research the progress of the Vietnam War and we pretended to be war journalists covering the fighting. Being a West Virginian, your stories were stacked at the front of the library, some were on microfilm and others made the front page of the newspaper. You have a few articles that made national headlines, as well."

"Brought the truth back to America," raising his glass, "the way it happened. Pissed the president and Cabinet members off, I heard. They're still mad about my lack of candor. Remember this, if you learn anything from Beau Le Mans, write stories from the front lines and people will respect your snap, Anna, and follow the truth."

"I imagined what life was like for you, trying to type stories during the war, with bombs and fire fights, the cries of wounded, and more casualties than the day before. How did you keep your sanity, Beau?"

Beau's face squinted and his hand pressed his neck.

"PTSD." His head twisted. "Sorry. I write for the ones left behind, like Sam Law and Henderson, Hien, Cadeo, and Polly."

"I didn't mean to break your peace, man." She held his arm.

"I'm fine. Don't feel sorry for me."

She leaned in and held a pillow.

"Relax, Beau."

He walked around the room.

"Before I was captured, my days were spent writing, alongside other journalists and nosey authors from *Stars and Stripes*. My Sundays were spent with the chaplain and mostly in prayer with the guys who cared to memorize Scripture verses. We chased God."

"I rarely pray," said Anna. "Lost as apple sauce."

"Stopped the church scene, huh? I will call on the Man Upstairs for help."

"I'm not sure I understand the whole concept of God and Divinity," said Anna, crossing her arms. "Where do your prayers go, Beau? I mean really, come on, dude? It's like talking to yourself. No one speaks back, right?"

He flipped the pages.

"God speaks to me. It's simple," said Beau, with the Bible open. "Our Father who art in Heaven, hallowed be Thy name, and that means Holy is His name." Beau told her about the meaning of the Lord's Prayer and how Jesus taught the disciples how to pray. "Our platoon would've lost our marbles if it wasn't for the Lord's Prayer. I became the leader and a better person for praying. I wrote dozens of articles after I escaped the POW camp and mentioned how prayer was pivotal in my escape and helped soldiers cope with the war," lifting his head. "I'm not afraid to say, this soldier spoke to God in Vietnam. I heard His voice. Prayed a landmine didn't blow off my leg or blow me into a thousand pieces. Said my prayers at chow time and at bedtime. God had a plan to bring me home. I'm a believer."

Anna shifted her legs nervously and was a bit uncomfortable, chewing cheese and chasing her bite with more wine. Her legs were cold and Beau grabbed her a warm blanket as the night cooled down atop the mountains.

"I didn't realize you were a religious man. Maybe a preacher, sort of, huh?"

"No ditch digger. Not preaching, just handfuls of faith. Cross my heart each day," he said, grinning. "Start and end in prayer."

"You're one cool cat. What did you talk to God about? Did the Lord answer your prayers?"

"Not all of them, but I'm here, aren't I?"

"The night is still young for me, Pope Le Mans."

"Pope? I want to be a college professor, Anna, and forget about being a pastor or a monk, or whatever my father has in his Sunday School teacher head." He walked around the room and told his desire to be in the college atmosphere as an instructor.

"I don't think so, Beau."

"Why not?"

"You must finish a Bachelor's degree first, sweetheart. To be honest, I don't see it ever happening. You're too busy, doing some of everything. College is a discipline, Dear."

"The Army trained me well enough to carry my thoughts before I carried a pen. Thank you very much. Looks like I did it in reverse, huh?"

"Nope." Anna walked to where he stood. "We pick our own paths. My path fits my life, what I do, living for the headlines, as an educated writer, with a degree on the wall. Sheepskin."

So pretty, yet fought for her right to challenge him against what she knew and what he knew about being a professor, and this greatly reddened the necks of each one, and they appreciated the honesty of worldview and the other's perspective. Beau had his style of training, juxtaposition, or at least he thought he knew, without being on a college campus, the style and type of mentor and professor he desired.

"And that's one thing I prayed for in Vietnam, well, to stand as a college professor." Beau mimicked a teacher, book in each hand, waving and parading, pretending he had his own journalism class in front of him.

She crossed her legs and arms, face as curious as an investigative reporter. "Do your parents know you want to walk away from the restaurant business, forget about Southern Methodist University, and pursue academia?"

"Nope." He placed his books on the table. "They would be against it, much like you are right now and say I have a long way to go for an education."

"You little spill as a teacher didn't convince me, but each to his own, dude."

"My Pops is immersed in the cafe world and teaches cooking on weekends. Something like that. Dad wants me in the pulpit, drawing my sermons from people skipping out on the bill, acting like they're going to the restroom and never coming back. He'd want sermons on intolerance and what causes sin to spread like a wildfire. Why do people commit murder for fun and rob handbags from old ladies?"

Anna held a pillow over her chest and walked across the room to rest on the large bean bag his father said she'd like to fall asleep in for a nap.

"Why won't you be straight up with your folks?" she asked, curling her arms around the pillow. "Tell them what you want to do with your life, huh?"

"Yeah. I will. I will. I'll get to it."

"What are you afraid of?"

"I'm not afraid of anything!" He lifted his voice. "Got it? I lost my brother. My job since he died has been to take over his part of Cafe Le Mans and help with the kitchen duties, supplies, deliveries, and a hundred other things that spin my wheels."

She raised hands and leaned back. "Okay. Okay. I didn't mean to rattle you."

"What I learned from the Army, Anna, is do what you have to do to survive and to keep the operation going or you fail. No one likes to be a failure, right? That's good discipline."

She ignored him for a short minute.

"I was accepted to grad school," said Anna.

"Hey, good news. My father said if I stayed in college, he'd pay my ways to graduate school and beyond, if Uncle Sam dropped the ball on the G. I. Bill. I haven't gotten very far, though. Who can trust the government with giving money away for something good?"

Beau dropped into his own bean bag, facing Anna.

"Umm, why can you get your sheep skins, Miss Anna, but I can't, huh? Don't women fight for equal rights and equal pay and equal amounts of coffee in their cup at the cafe, huh? Isn't it a social thing, a peaceful thing, and aren't we to pull an oxen out of a hole when he's down, right?"

"Fair is fair. Equal rights for every man, woman, and child, Beau. But it does not happen that way, in society, of course, in real life. Sounds good on paper."

"No. No, no." He held a football. "You're not jumping ship on me, little lady. Give me that gusto speech, the words you spoke on campus to motivate students to be the best Mountaineer on the planet, go walk on the moon, catch shooting stars, and all that bull crap."

Anna sat up tall, pulled the football from his hand, and raised the ball above her head. She stood and stiff-armed him, and spun the ball on the floor.

"Like Army recruiters do, you mean?"

"Let me get my famous football coach's voice ready. 'Mean men, you want to be great at what you do, right? You want to win, don't you?"

"Yeah, Coach Beau!" She jumped.

"Okay, team." She smiled at him. "Your greatness starts today, not tomorrow. If you want to be worth something, be worth something right now. You want to win? Put your heart on line, be a winner, and be the tough man that no one expected, men."

Anna opened a glass case. Then, she punched his arm and donned on a pair of boxing gloves.

"Losers make plans, and keep making plans, but give up the fight. That's a loser in my book. You're a quitter, Beau. That's what I see. Talkers. Talkers. Beau, I think you're a talker. Until you prove it, here, you're a loser in my boxing ring until I've seen you win. My next guy won't quit."

"We've known each other for less than a day, Anna," sniffing, and slowly he strapped her boxing gloves and slapped them together. "And, well, somehow you already think that I'm a loser."

She danced around, feet chopping like George Foreman, half sober, punching.

"I think a winner collects wins, like boxers, stays on track, trains, has discipline, and knows he will hold the trophy, Beau, and sees himself with his hands raised high. From what I've read, you don't stick with anything long enough to win and have a winning track record. You make jabs about the war, and don't finish the fight."

"You don't know me, Anna. You don't know me at all. To survive in a POW camp without giving in and breaking into a thousand pieces. This guy didn't quit to fight as a Communist sympathizer, just to get hot meals, a warm shampoo on my head and new clothes. By God, it took bravery and courage, and a stone champion to walk out of the POW camp."

"Beau, from what I see and what I've heard, you're a guy who jumps around from girl to girl, job to job, with a good line, being smooth talker," hand on his face, "and makes it seem like it's all the girl's fault or you ain't digging it, Cool Daddy. That's a loser, Beau. A talker and a man who gives excuses, that type of guy, dude, is a loser in my book."

"If you really think I'm a big loser, hit me, give it your best shot. Knock me out and make me the loser you think I already am."

Anna punched his face.

"Okay. I'm a champion. I clocked you."

He rolled his eyes, head whacked.

"Take off the gloves, give it a rest. We both have our own opinions on life. Make up your own opinion. Don't recite what your daddy or some professor thinks is a loser, or a winner. You haven't lived outside of Pittsburgh long enough to see the face of a mother's loss or a soldier who fought with every breath and died. See, life is unfair. We will see who makes it, won't we? Give me twenty years or so, and we'll see who teaches college and who becomes the loser or winner."

Anna left for the restroom and returned.

"I'm sorry we don't agree. You are right, I am limited in my travels and experiences. But, for me, I have a road map and I'll travel and see things, fight to see hurt faces and help them."

"I know you will."

She shuffled through pictures in silent mode. He cooled off, just the same. She left Beau's idea of being a college professor inside in hands and head. Or, was it just talk?

"Here's a book with a hundred Polaroids in it, Beau. My God, what's this?"

"My important stuff."

Beau effortlessly flipped through his pictures and poems and told her about his family portraits; spoke about hardships in the coal mines in Wyoming County, and what it took to make a living inside the coalfields of Southern West Virginia. Pictures of his ancestors, some from America, others from France, held the first few pages.

"Here, my great-grandmother once smoked a Hobbit bent long stem pipe. She lived out Proverbs 31 in her life. Stitched quilts, mean bean soup and kept Rhode Island Red chickens and fried eggs for anyone who needed a meal in Baileysville. The women made covers and pillows, just in case someone fell on hard times or lost their job. I loved her chicken and dumplings. She didn't name her chickens," holding a famous grin, "she fried 'em up in a pan."

"She was a saint, Beau, I bet." Anna held pictures, reading the names and years.

"Here's a picture of my grandparents." Old family pictures rested inside her hands.

"Cute couple."

"Neither one had a college education, barely passed eighth grade, but they made it through the Great Depression, and the Spanish Influenza, and lost half their brothers and sisters in the war. Would that make them losers? You know enough about them to make a judgment call, right?"

"That's not fair, Beau."

"Your perception of what a winner is, one from the coalfields, one from the war, compared to business suits, doctors, and lawyers from Pittsburgh, like your father, right? What has your family taught you about "these kinds" of people, the working class, the lower socioeconomic working class, I'd like to know, Anna? Does education make you better than a coal miner or a truck driver or cafe owner? Tradesmen make a solid living building the New River Gorge Bridge, so your father, a well-dressed man who travels the coalfields representing criminals, losers, sporting a good life as a Criminal Attorney."

"I didn't mean it like that, Beau."

"You did mean it that way. In Vietnam, I took lots of unnecessary crap from so-called educated journalists. I'll write again one day and I've picked up a few things in my life. I change my own oil and raise hundreds of vegetables so the poor and the wealthy can eat."

"Education has its perks and opens doors to society." She held up the pictures in better light. "Some doors are closed to you because of your lack of..."

"Could you educate me? Could you let me know what you expected when you met my working class family at Cafe Le Mans, who cooks over a hundred meals a day for this community and feeds the homeless and needy, not just on Christmas Eve when folks in larger communities volunteer their precious time one day per year for two hours at a soup kitchen. My family works every day in the kitchen. We feed the rich and the poor alike... without judgment about suits, truckers, or those having a rough year because the lumber yard cut back their budget thirty percent and fifty-four families faced unemployment in the Mountain State because the "Big Man" can purchase forestry products overseas for a fraction of the cost of West Virginia hardwoods. What did you think when your college class, future grad students read my military articles, and now you rest inside my family's farmhouse? Are we classified as losers when it comes to how professors and politicians rank voters in rural and suburban areas, like the coalfields?"

Tears began to fall from Anna's face. He handed her a tissue from the table.

"I see your point, Beau. Colleges and those who teach high ed identify the working class by the textbook standards. Unemployed. Jobless. Lost time working because of an accident, it's all inside the text."

She cleaned her face.

"Does that make them losers?" asked Beau, arms crossed.

"Let me finish, please. And, well, um, those who lose a job or the unemployable, and those the human resources department pins the unemployable, that's how they're defined or classified. We have to define people in this country."

"In your father's line of work, would that make them losers? Is he that type of man?"

"Yeah. He is. It's sad to say, but he would define some of them as losers, in his book."

"A perfect work history does not make anyone better than anyone else. This only means they've been fortunate not to face unemployment or cutbacks with a company. I'm sorry your family feels misfortune, makes a person a loser."

"We have differences, Beau. Our differences have been ingrained in our upbringing and may always make us have the wrong judgment about others we meet before we get to know them."

"You should refrain from defining losers and winners, Coach Anna. We all play a vital role in this so-called melting pot of America. That truck driver will be laid off when this bridge is finished, and next year, that same man, with a CDL, might drive your little girl to school each day. Imagine that, because change happens."

After their debate ended, they'd discovered great differences existed about careers and education. They spoke about hiking Coopers Rock State Park, feet cold, and snow falling over Thanksgiving break. Thousands of people roamed the mountains, couples even, finding out in the same poetic way, the way Beau and Anna met, and lived in the gap of differences and knew about harsh injustices.

"I grew up under a Baptist deacon, found God on my fourteenth birthday or at least I felt close to God as a teen until I saw blood spattered across Vietnam. Then and now, deep down, I'm not so sure the Lord was ever there. He must've forgotten about us, because we lost thousands of good soldiers. But I dodged bullets and bombs. Here, I am."

"God was there. The Lord brought you home, didn't he?"

"Yeah. Am I the lucky one though, Anna?"

"Yeah."

"Men the same age as me, size and background, hobbies, fought as hard as I did and didn't make it back. Why?"

"The war broke us all."

"Just recalling how we lived and died would break any man's soul. My mother said I was a gifted writer. I lived off of words, memories, not touch. But the work I did in journalism was some of the best work to be printed from the war. Being in a situation that seems lost, isn't terminal for a soldier or a sailor. Not every day is Disneyland and Dairy Queen at war."

He clutched his hands behind his head and felt he had won the debate.

"You know what college doesn't teach, Anna?"

"What?"

"What college doesn't teach you, is what you feel when an experience happens?"

She mirrored his pose, arms behind her head, eyes on the ceiling.

"What do you mean?"

"Your college books tell of job loss, the injured worker, and how to complete the proper paperwork. However, what do you say to your wife and kids when their vacation is canceled because he loses his job at the mill or she's fired because the company is having a down year in the real estate business?"

She blinked and nodded.

"I see what you are saying. It's a long list of the situations. Colleges need to prepare students for how to handle a situation when it hits their own household. You're making me more aware of the thoughts and feelings of workers and how colleges need to prepare for the management side. They make us think we'll be in a better position with a degree."

Beau rolled over on his side, looked longingly at her flawless skin, and became hopeful. To debate, pick apart a situation, was for her. For Beau, he was reserved, the outdoorsman type, the loner, and enjoyed himself that way.

In her car were newspapers and notes from her journalism classes. She ran to her car and returned with several binders, pictures of Beau Le Mans in his uniform. He had not seen every photograph taken in his Army uniform.

"My professor said First Team Le Mans is a literary warrior, a roaring lion in a fiery jungle of lambs. Other writers can only speculate what you had to endure as a soldier and a writer, keeping your mind sharp as a wordsmith."

"These were taken before I was a prisoner. Here's one after I was rescued. Skinny."

"You look fine." She held his hand.

Anna knew more about Beau Le Mans than his own mother did. He had discussed his work to students at SMU, especially the columns written after his time caged in a POW camp. Inspired by his work, she aimed her own style of writing and learned, picking his brain about concepts and capturing emotions, things left aside in most articles. She noted elements of journalism and showed him a few articles, some recent, that she was motivated to print.

Beau Le Mans, a gifted journalist and an exemplary leader within his field was impressed by university professors, the level he wanted to achieve, though enough of his work to cover the material in higher education. That's where Anna found his writing to be vivid and relevant, a man with a memory so tight and true, she'd predicted Beau had a treasure chest of untold stories reserved for times less war-torn and jovial. Stories so graphic and detailed in his mind, the war, the talk in hospitals, and yet the horrific days he'd spent beaten and flattened in spirit, and arched days worked on his confidence as a writer. She wanted them and wanted to study the culture of Vietnam, having real discussions in her quiver of stories would propel her education and add value at WVU. To keep Beau to herself meant the world to her, moving in transition from undergrad speculation to first person narrative as in graduate school. Her father would be proud and so would a legion of professors.

"I've actually read your work over and over. One article captured my attention."

"Find it. I will tell you the background. Much of what people don't realize about writing is the backstory, the framework of what soldiers endured," tearing up, "in Vietnam. Real war. Real pain. I hope you understand what I am "not" saying."

"I think so. Do you mean when a soldier caps their story, what they were feeling, and so the story never made it to press because of the pain, real pain?"

"Anna, you have the potential to be a journalist. A great one."

"I have one for you. It's the question my professor could not answer about you when I asked."

"Shoot." He poured soda and made a midnight snack of mayo sandwiches. No meat.

"How did a guy, and don't bite my head off for asking, man, or get me wrong, here," she said, holding her hair. "My professor asked the question, using you as a prime example, 'How does a guy, a guy from Wyoming County, high school diploma, from the coalfields, learn to write at a high level for the Army Times?' and that no one could answer in the class. He had no idea."

She tapped her notebook, soda in the other hand, and waited.

"I won't bite off your head. Out of respect, I'll say it." He chewed his sandwich and swallowed before finishing his thought. "But Hemingway's last formal education was high school, not WVU, like Don Knotts or like Billy Graham's degree from Wheaton College. Experience is what college students lack. You can learn technique and style, but to get that Monte Carlo of yours rolling at top speed, a blue collar mechanic, much like my brother was, has to fix it. Wells was a good garage mechanic. He felt life, like my job as a journalist, Anna, and that's how you become a good writer. You have to try on the shoes of the other person."

The eyes of Anna rolled, face bent in giggling, and then laughter bubbled.

"I know you are good, but Beau Le Mans, country boy, is comparing himself to Ernest Miller Hemingway, are you? You're still a big hillbilly?"

"You don't get it. Geography and region don't define a person, Anna." His face flushed red. "Once you can get past your aloof "Pittsburgh" self, you'll understand much more about life and people and how hard it is to make it. Most people would not write about the dribble on the face of a child during her first birthday, or how a young man felt when his prom date backs out an hour before the big event. What about a man who loses his wife of fifty years? Is he allowed to cry and be alone in a mountain cabin? Would the newspaper call him a recluse and label him? Perhaps the educated or the undereducated share something, rather than the sharp knife of typecasting or stereotyping someone because of where their ancestors decided to settle down and start a family.

"I see."

"You see, but you don't feel it, way down in the heart. One of the reasons I joined the Army - brothers. To write from the heart. You can't teach compassion for humanity. I have compassion when I see a family broken-hearted when their son does not return from war."

Her eyes popped round.

"I didn't mean to get you started again."

"Yes, you did. When you said, 'A guy like you, from Wyoming County, the coalfields,' and I believe those words are exactly how you profiled my life and stomped on my style, my upbringing. Let me tell you something, while you were having hamburgers and fries your freshman year, this guy, the one from Wyoming County, West Virginia, not Pittsburgh, was fighting 24/7 to stay alive. When the discussion about my home county and lack of education was taking place, this infantry journalist was amid bloodshed, death tolls mounting, and wrote about my brothers in arms and what they faced each day. Let me add, I would've loved to have been in Morgantown, turtleneck too loose, eating popcorn, watching the Mountaineers beat the pants off the Pitt Panthers in 1969, but I was a little bloody, and busy fighting the Viet-Cong."

"We have different lives, Beau, and our roads and past, hometowns, are way different roads. We can learn from each other and travel some."

"Tell your professor to accept talents and differences from the coalfields of West Virginia, just the same as he does his Pitt Panther colleagues on Homecoming Weekend, okay?"

Beau was pissed.

"Here, read this article," said Anna, hand out. "This is the one cool article that brought tears to my eyes and broke my heart. That was the moment I was sold on your writing."

"Which one?"

"*Christmas in Chains.*"

He sat in the rocking chair, working his legs in a steady rhythm, eyes vacant, and his head rested inside worn hands, clutching himself in a miserable lean.

"Should've died that day."

"You almost died?"

"All of my stories demanded the birth of truth, this is, if I had to hand-crank the equipment myself. Was there another article that caught your attention?"

"My professor loved "*The Last POW at Briarpatch Camp.*"

Beau stopped rocking his chair.

"I mean, what article pressed your journalism button? I want to hear about you. Don't recite from the faculty; use your own thoughts and ideas."

"Okay. It wasn't an article. A photo caught my eye. One man was dangling from a helicopter, just pulled from the rice paddies."

"That's me. I'd finally made it. Skin and bones and barely alive when the gunner of the helicopter pulled me inside the aircraft and landed at the Infantry camp. That was the most emotional page of my life. The camp took that photo when they found out I was not KIA or MIA, but a POW."

"Amazing photograph."

"The pain feels like it happened yesterday. I remember the bug bites, howling voices and the last time I saw the pale, crying faces of my friends, especially Sam Law and Henderson. The last time you see someone, you don't always know it's the last time, but you feel something, on the inside, something special, even years later. Goodbyes are worse than broken legs." Beau held his face, massaging his temples, and looked at the calendar. "And sometimes it ... it won't let go of me, and I can't leave it behind, especially when I'm alone. For me, nighttime is the worst time. It's hard for others to understand what happens to a man inside a POW camp."

"The difference between us is, your pain, the war you left behind, it's like a ghost."

His eyes closed, breathing deeply, sighing and suddenly he sat up, hands on his knees and thighs. He was back inside the bamboo POW camp.

"I see soldiers, close as brothers, like my real brother Wells. Men I'd spent time with in prison, like Henderson, Sam Law, Hien, Cadeo. Men half-dead. Beaten. Then, she was with me."

The sofa was less than a few feet away, and Beau sat beside Anna.

"A lady?"

"Polly," he said, gasping for air.

"My cousin had PTSD after the war. Rest."

"Sometimes I lose control of myself."

She held him and rocked back and forth.

"I'm here, Beau. Calm down, will you? Who's Polly?"

"The only family I had for a Vietnamese Christmas was Polly, Sam Law, Hien, and Cadeo. They'd taken all of our personal items, but they couldn't take one thing from us."

"What was that?"

"Polly's song. Oh, the V-C tried, but Communists couldn't stomp her song or face from my memory. I hope she's alive. It's good to be friends with you, Anna."

"Beau?"

He nodded.

"Who was Polly? Was she your love affair or some one-night stand?"

"Love affair? Nope." He wasn't saying. "We were a beautiful unpainted canvas, the two of us. The VA doctor said I'd have frequent flashbacks. Nights would be the most uncomfortable. It happens so often I've become used to my life in some rewind fashion, a form of expectancy has redefined my enjoyment. Sunsets don't excite me that much anymore. I hate being alone, Anna," he said, rocking back and forth. "I need something to drink."

"Here's water."

"I can't take the discomfort and not being able to control myself. I'm sorry."

After his drink, Beau fell back into a large stack of cushions on the sofa.

"Darkness is my enemy. Memories hit hard when the dark, high mountains and the night sky meet in a lonely way. I don't know how to stop anxiety attacks, though."

"Does talking about Polly cause the attacks to subside?"

"Yeah."

"Who was she?" She made circles on his legs.

"I count her as a wonderful soul."

"What did she do to make you think that?"

"She didn't have to do anything, but be nearby."

He leaned up, elbows on his knees and he finished his water. She sketched a face on a piece of paper.

"Was she pretty?"

"To me, Polly was…. She was with me. Hair and dark eyes and the way her face dropped and turned when she laughed, and her hair hung low, and touched her eyebrows. Polly held a long smile in a respectful way, as friends, not of arrogance. She was married."

Anna had questions as if she was jealous of Polly, a lady who held Beau's attention, yet still. She asked about the women of his past, some were unspoken. He never talked about her old flames. It wasn't that she wanted to meet Polly, but she wanted the same desire for herself, to be in love again. Anna pulled her long hair into a ponytail, put on pink pajamas, and made herself comfortable with buttery popcorn.

"What did you think about Polly, Beau?"

He opened the sliding doors.

"I thought of us having dinner together." The cool mountains had them boarded in for the night. "Gets cold in Fayette County, don't you think?" She nodded to him. "Tell me more about Polly."

"My greatest concern for Polly, is she alive or dead? Is Cadeo alive?"

Anna sat the notebooks down and faced him.

"Let's talk about you. I want you to feel welcomed and comfortable beside me. You have treated us like queens, Beau."

"No one in their right mind would let two beautiful women in a Chevy stay the summer in this home. This creepy farmhouse might have ghosts from The Battle of Fayetteville, Anna."

They laughed like there were more people in the room.

She saw pictures of Beau with his Army platoon in Vietnam. Every other question was about Polly, not his other friends inside the camp.

"If it bothers you, I'll stop asking questions about Polly. It seems she kept you alive."

"In a way, she did." He leaned way into her lap. "My hope was to get back home, far from war and I hated to leave my friends."

"If you believe in God, then, this meeting between us was meant to happen, Beau."

She sat, held her glass, and said, "To good friends."

"May we always be close."

He enjoyed Anna's company and they laughed and felt something strong, something more and unresolved, a certain closeness and one he wanted to develop with a good woman. His prayers after Vietnam concerned finding a good lady were answered. The clock on the wall became one-fifty. Then three. Then half past four.

He told her every story he knew in Vietnam.

"What happened to Polly, Beau?"

"Don't know." His memory drifted back to the last time he saw her. "She was my best friend and something super, to me, and an angel who treated me different from other prisoners. Polly disappeared into the jungle. Her life was in danger because of our close relationship. Any relationship with an American meant trouble or death from the V-C, that is, if they caught you."

At five in the morning, she said something sweet.

"You can relax and forget about Polly. I got you from here on out. Let's fall asleep together tonight."

He whispered something.

"No," she said. "I don't think that is sleeping."

She caressed his hands.

"Why did you stop writing? People who follow your work, good people from Army bases to universities and even at the White House and Pentagon, saw eyes eager to read your columns."

He was close enough to kiss her, Beau held back his face. Then, he took a deep breath and walked across the room and sat at the bar. His back was to her.

"I'm a big fan of your stories, Beau, and have been for years."

He spun around on the bar stool and looked into his drink.

"I don't write anymore or do interviews, Anna," turning away again. "Gave it all up, along with smoking and late-night bourbon. Leaders in Washington don't want to hear about their own debacle; Make another ghastly memory of the war, the way it happened in Saigon when 19 guerrilla fighters crawled through a hole to kill a team of journalists. I've tried to put images of the war away. Won't be typing for the Army Times or anyone else."

"The truth needs to be heard. Why stop now?"

"Time I turned in my pen. Gotta get up early."

She stopped at the bottom of the stairs, and said, "Does your typewriter, the one in your room, need some company? Forget I said that. See you in the morning, Beau."

She shut the door.

CHAPTER FIVE

↔

Straight Shooters

At mid-morning, Beau took his motorcycle to Cafe Le Mans. Half asleep from a late night of chatting with Anna, he had black coffee and his normal plate of scrambled eggs and gravy. His father knew something was up with his son, as he hardly spoke about anything. Not even a word about two beautiful ladies who stayed the night. Beau was busy at work cooking, but thought about Anna as he made bacon and biscuits for bridge workers.

"Dad, I'd like to cut off early today?"

Mr. Le Mans steadied his eyes and face, and saw himself at his son's age.

"You just got here. What's clammed up your pipes, anyways?"

"Need to check on Anna and Naomi."

"Ladies, huh? You've been struck by lightning, son?"

"I'm fine."

Well, the old man cleaned his glasses and knew Beau was either crazy from PTSD or couldn't wait to see why two young ladies from Morgantown had tracked him down by name in Fayetteville, even telling his father they had collected newspaper clippings of Beau Le Mans from his Army days.

"We have fifty orders for the bridge workers, Beau."

"Sherman Le Mans!" said his mother. "You know he has guests, pretty ones too."

Sherman looked at his wife and threw a towel over his shoulder, frowning. Then, a giant grin spread under his mustache. His father knew.

"Yeah. Yeah, BettyAnne," said Sherman, marching over beside his son. "Beau, take your guests a couple bacon sandwiches. I'm working on spaghetti lunches and big Texas toast for the bridge workers."

"What if the ladies don't like bacon, Dad?" said Beau.

"Do you want to be the first man to be thrown off the New River Gorge Bridge? Everyone from here to Rome likes Sherman's bacon, Beau," said his mother. "Go, get, get, be gone, and feed those Mountaineer ladies. You have company, tend to them, and your father and I can handle it, right, Sherman?"

"Don't let him off the hook so easily, BettyAnne! Make him sweat a little and at least act like you were going to have him cook all day."

"He'll be fine, Sherman, leave the boy alone," his mother defended him. "Go fishing or hiking, but don't get too close to the ladies. I know what Sherman meant by "lightning strikes," you know. I don't want to hear about thunder and lightning from you two in the morning, got it? Don't be practicing anything romantic, either."

Sherman grinned at Beau, pushing him out the door.

"See ya, Zeus." Sherman told him as he cranked up his motorcycle.

Anna and Naomi loved Beau's country house, long views of the mountains in the evening, big and cozy, of the grand style, nestled on a hilltop in Fayette County. Beau told the ladies how the home was a modern-day mansion, indeed. Beau's grandfather, Norman Le Mans, built the towering three-story Edwardian home after WWII. Not too far away stood the old barn, which overlooked the flower garden, fish pond, and the farm home was amid fifty-four acres. Vegetables were grown for soups and salads and carrot cake. His grandfather's Cafe Le Mans had been in the family since President Truman's first year in Washington. Though Beau missed Twin Falls and Wyoming County, his second home was the pure countryside of Fayetteville, a raw river town, where spirited folks lived, folks who needed a good meal and their restaurant was located amid travelers. That's why Naomi and Anna stopped for lunch. Parting with his real estate, Norman Le Mans gave his son, Sherman Le Mans, a busy forty-four seat diner to lure him from the coal mines of Wyoming County to be a chef. He was introduced to a new career in the food industry. Norman didn't forget Beau when he died, three days after Kennedy was shot, and that cold November day was an unforgettable time in 1963. Beau didn't take over the land until his post-war days.

For good reason, the Edwardian home was left to his grandson, Beau, just for him, not Wells, and that's why they left Wyoming County after Norman died. His grandmother died a decade before Norman. Beau enlisted in the Army and his father called him "Man of War," and Beau served in the Army before he made his way to Fayette County. And, sadly, his brother, Wells, was buried in Fayette County.

Other than a few days of shifting rain, May of 1974 held a warm breeze much like April did and cotton clouds drifted steadily across the blue skies, which forced the bridge workers to hang around Cafe Le Mans and crack jokes about Beau

"Zeus" Le Mans. Nearly every day Naomi and Anna jumped in the Jeep with Beau, exchanging stories from sorority days and how the Mountaineer football team had dropped seven under Coach Bowden.

The cold, blue river was something they tried, but couldn't dip for long. Somewhere along the high, rocky cliffs of the Blue Ridge Mountains, Anna craved more hot cooking from Chef Beau, who packed bacon sandwiches on trips across Fayette County. Naomi loved the crunch as much as Anna and they fought for the last slice. The two ladies mailed off letters to their mothers about being in good company and loved Cafe Le Mans in Fayetteville, West Virginia. Sometime about sundown each day, tired after hiking trails and bouncing about the road construction, Beau cooked chili beans, paired with cornbread for dinner. They'd talked about Mountaineer football and how Coach Bowden would handle the Pitt Panthers in October. Some debates turned toward muscle cars, Chevy versus Ford, and a decade of music on the radio, the country's fading leadership in Washington, and why they wanted to see the Cadillac Ranch in Amarillo, Texas.

Sometimes they agreed to be peaceful about politics, religion, and cars, even formed a civil pact to not discuss them over supper, in fear of indigestion or sin of language, whichever came first. Beau laughed, hands clutched, lost in admiration as his lively friends sat on the long front porch and debated whether the hound that barked across the mountain was a Bluetick hound or a Black and Tan coonhound, which became a Memorial Weekend game, of sorts, as they listened and echoed sounds across the New River Gorge.

Beau told the ladies about the cool day he met a host of renowned journalists, who had respected courage without compromise when he was with the *Army Times.* They were writers from *The New York Times, The Washington Post,* and *The Kansas City Star.* Le Mans made friends with a few delicate war hands, all men, huddled inside the U.S. Embassy in Saigon. One wet himself, afraid of the war. They spoke about war on the frontlines, where the dry pocketed journalist stood and listened, even copied, what Le Mans had fired across his own pages. He shook hands with Collins, Calloway, Cronkite, Safer, Adams, and Lowell, and all of them debated for an hour over dinner about the foment surrounding the Tet Offensive. Other aspiring journalists joined them, cub rookies, a lineup of names, curious writers and all of them could not be recalled, but Le Mans knew their faces in the newspapers and on television when they mirrored his frontline work. Then, bravely, journalists went on their own way chasing the war, and some landed in Laos, Vietnam, Cambodia, and others penned the truth and flew pages under the "edited copy flag" by the time it hit the press. No one wanted to be chopped, when the truth needed to be heard in England, Saigon, and the Americas. Some articles, the truth, on some occasions, became handled and o' lost.

Beau discovered later how some journalists disgraced the military field of journalism, penned and labored and learned. However, indeed, and in a brief stay, mercy was cried while "in country" and "boots on the grounds" journalists knew the names of weapons, outposts, pricks and party animals, and gave directions to new "warned" writers who could have spoon fed goats with their articles. No matter the act of inducement, deep compassion was felt for American soldiers and innocent Vietnamese, and how they both lived and died in a warzone. Eager writers swiftly became the very insiders they'd studied about in college, having heard about Ho Chi Minh's letter to President Truman, Richard Nixon's visit to South Vietnam, and American's task force to Vietnam. Beau educated Anna and Naomi on the backstory of the volcano-like progression that had evolved between America and Vietnam, some they had not heard of, like who observed President Eisenhower's treaty, whereas, "North Vietnam aggression means an attack and they "South Vietnam" should maintain their own independence, thus, America will act accordingly." Articles and letters linked to world powers, or the powers that be rushed to sign the line to continue conflict.

Beau whispered to Anna, "I've seen letters like these supporting their intentions and other covert operational messages and pages from the Pentagon, as far back as President Eisenhower's words and President Kennedy's statement," using his hands, "armed attack against North Vietnam would threaten the peace and security of the American people."

By the early 1960s, reporters slowly mouthed dust and chewed the bamboo of Battle and War, day by day, until they fetched the wounded and counted the fatally wounded. Several were soldiers they'd interviewed and hugged, days earlier. For the first time the world saw the war through the camera lens of photojournalism, writers and camera crews and a host of flooded eyes of people back home who coped with cracked hearts, the rest were broken and healed unintentionally.

"Journalists came to Vietnam fishing for leads, like bargain shoppers in a small village marketplace," said Beau, who had taken up smoking and drinking again with his guests while at his home, learning to write like a soldier did, after three weeks with his new friends in the farmhouse. In those days, Anna and Naomi smoked and drank, grew their hair long, and dressed in pink clothing. Peace symbols hung from the rearview mirror of the Monte Carlo and the Jeep.

And later, Beau taught them how war-torn journalists left the U.S. Embassy, beaten down, shell-shocked, less spoken, and more was written about Vietnam than books of Abraham Lincoln. They lived in the days of shock and awe photography, like the "Napalm Lady" photographed. He coached them about how journalists spread the truth of iniquity about bloodshed, carried by both sides, and hundreds of cities were pounded, caught in the heart of Charlie's Communism and Sam's patriotism. Some called it democracy. Who knew, years ago?

"What was the verdict, your thoughts, Beau?" asked Anna.

"The verdict of the Vietnam War was controversial. Was it worth the battle, the loss of men and women, and the absence of sons and daughters, fathers and mothers? Thousands of people are gone. To lose an uneducated man or woman, Anna, would your lawyer father say they were "less and lost" at war?"

"Not fair. I hope not."

"Don't look at the eyes of a person and judge one, or think you know their brutal pain because of their worn shoes. What about a sweet baby or someone blind, what do you think?" said Beau, fingers tapping his chin. "Make sure you let them be who they are, talented humans, brave men and women, and hope they are good for humanity."

Beau wasn't afraid to stomp out racism, misjudgments, and lack of compassion toward others, not just in his home, but wherever he went.

"Did journalists get more of a broken civilization than what they had bargained for in Vietnam?" asked Anna.

"Journalists?" said Beau, removing his glasses. "Yeah, I believe they lost their bravado. Several writers died."

"What happened, Beau?" asked Naomi, eyes steady on his face. "Were journalists threatened by Mr. President, and other top military generals, or was the candle of journalism stomped on by a chain of Feds?"

Naomi stopped peeling potatoes for dinner, and said, "Something happened to you, didn't it, Beau?" asked Anna. "Were you made an example of or struck down?"

"Yeah, something big happened to me. I want to hide on the rocky cliffs in West Texas. More than one woman warned me and more than a dozen men threatened my life, countered by papers, if I printed what I knew. Some brought dogs and threatened my life. One man said, 'I'll put more than a horse head in your bed, try snakes, Le Mans,' and that was spoken to me with sober eyes."

"Dogs," said Beau, lips tight. "Venomous snakes, too. They wanted my hurt and cuts to look accidental, of course."

"Good grief. You printed the truth and retaliation was lectured at you, huh?" said Naomi, pouring oil into the pan. "I just don't get it. Why? Politics can make you sick and twisted. Why can't we print the truth, Beau, in the field of journalism?"

"I'm sure you have some inclination of how powerful men work inside America, don't you? Position and money move the masses." said Beau, crushing ice from his lemonade glass.

"They really threatened your life?" said Anna, chopping hamburger meat. "Sick."

Beau had made cornbread in a cast iron skillet, just like his gifted mother and grandmother had taught him to do by the time he was a teenager. His idea was to make a second batch for later on, where he planned to crumble bread into a bowl with fresh milk for breakfast. Anna and Naomi, mouths watering, waited for the crusty, crunch cornbread to be finished and sliced.

"What about relationships? Dating? You're not that naive, are you, ladies?" said Beau, facing the dark window, the one he'd depended on for reflection and answers after he'd returned home from the Army.

"Ladies, ummm, well, I have been in love. Is that your question?"

"Men, ummm? We're well versed in men." Anna told him. "Let's forget our relationship and get back to journalism, Beau."

He gazed through the glossiness of the glass, recalling past reflections in water, and that's where he met the war again, face-to-face with his yesterdays, and planned his tomorrows. "There was a time when good stories were chased and collected, some even made stories up and rarely printed the real-to-life happenings. However, cameras caught the truth, but the same way, the Feds tried to view the footage first, but not always."

"The Boxer Rebellion was caused by fake news from four reporters," said Anna, slicing a Cherokee Purple tomato in a large plate, leaning the slices against the cornbread and lifting the plate. "Tomatoes are sliced."

"That's right! Lies caused American missionaries serving in China to die," said Naomi. "You can explore the concept of persuasion and candor in journalism courses." Salting the tomatoes, Naomi sat at the kitchen table. "No professor ever spoke of how the Feds threatened reporters and journalists. We didn't hear about this in the classroom."

"Some reporters mislead the public. Others build up controversy at the newsstand, drawing a crowd and persuading voters at election time. This type of persuasion gets folks talking, gets people killed, just as North Vietnamese forces did at the Tet Offensive in 1968. We lost 262 American lives when the Tet Offensive was over, weakening the support for the war by Americans - with real-time television witnesses back at home, too."

"Americans found out the truth, didn't they?" said Naomi, fork pointed. "The hard way."

"Right." Beau told them "You know the feed made it out, good photojournalism, and Americans felt for soldiers amid bombs and firefights."

"Wow!" said Anna. "I had a cousin who was killed during the Tet Offensive."

"Good journalism doesn't butter a pan and coat the public with fat, offering a bunch of lard, like I just did with the cast iron skillet, ladies."

"I'm sure it's like a good relationship," said Naomi.

"How so?" said Beau, walking close.

"You have to warm it up, turn up the heat, right?" said Naomi. "Draw a sincere interest. Match hearts."

Anna held her jealousy on Naomi. She changed the subject.

"Some people want to jade the public with half the story today, add some tomorrow, and a bit more with Cronkite on Sunday." Anna told them.

"Don't write your columns that way." Beau told her. "Give the whole story in one big bite. Never share bits and pieces of the story, especially war stories." Beau dropped his head, mouth full of food. "It looks like deception, not suspense." Perhaps his mind was locked in a handful of remembrance and pain.

"Vietnam was called "The Big Living-Room War" and the media brought the horror of war directly into our living room, didn't they?" said Anna.

"And bed rooms, didn't they?" said Naomi, flirting with Beau.

"Dorm room, Lady, not bedroom," said Anna.

"It's hard to predict how many journalists were bullied over the past twenty years. Sometimes the entire story a journalist had worked on for a week was burned and stomped in front of their very eyes. Film was pulled and exposed from cameras," said Beau, taking a big drink.

"What happened to journalists who spoke the truth about Vietnam?" asked Anna, turning, and facing Beau, waiting to hear the expected and honest truth from her friend.

" Just say it, will you?" said Naomi.

"I was leaned on, they called it. Threatened. I remember films, parts of history, pieces of war, some destroyed and stripped from the hands of photographers. Camera crushed. It wasn't unusual for pages to be stuffed in their faces. Frontline reporters, good reporters, too, were pushed and held from writing their stories. The more you realized these things about the government, the more you were talked down to as a writer or cameraman," said Beau, sighing. "Men in black suits were trained to dare a reporter to print stories. See what happens."

Beau crushed his cigarette into a tray he'd brought after a journalism conference in Washington, the year he left the Army.

"Or else, huh?" said Naomi, nodding. "Is this what we should expect to happen as journalists?"

"You should expect to be blocked and monitored. People love the truth in doses," said Beau, grinning, "but the war poured it on America and slapped politicians in the face for being in a war such as Vietnam. Kicked their butts."

"Why?" said Anna, standing at the sink.

"Bam! Boom!" yelled Beau, slapping Anna's behind.

"You scared me to death," said Anna, catching her breath.

"I wanna Bam and a Boom," said Naomi, flirting.

"Boom!" yelled Anna, who slapped her friend's tale. "There. That's all you get. No Bam for you."

"Bang, boom, pow!" said Beau. "They told the world we were winning! Reporters were told to print "Winning" in the newspapers, smiled at the cameras and told the world our soldiers had full control of the War in Vietnam." He slapped the table.

"Why do they want to hide the truth?" said Anna, raising her voice.

"Same as you do when you call your boyfriend and tell him you're at your good friend's home in Fayetteville, to conceal the truth, to not harm them, right, Anna?"

"Shut up, Naomi."

"You got a man, Anna?"

"No."

"Lies! Cover up. You'll make a great politician," said Beau, hand on his chin. "That's what leaders in Washington created, and people are dying without knowing the whole story about our soldiers, especially the time when Cronkite was in Hue, Vietnam, and after he left the Caravelle Hotel; perhaps he saw with his own eyes the truth and aimed to print it and was pressed. We don't know."

"Do you know Cronkite, Beau?" asked Naomi.

"My father knows Walter," said Anna, checking her nails.

"I know the truth when I see it." Beau walked close to Anna. "For sure, Uncle Walter became a good friend of mine," said Beau, eyes caught on Anna.

"How did you know that happened to Cronkite?" said Anna, taking a seat at the kitchen table.

"The whole story won't be known for fifty years, and they'll be heroes of old," said Naomi, flipping potatoes and dodging the grease popping out of the hot pan onto her blue and gold shirt. "That's the way the government hides things. Concealment. Bologna, that's what my father calls it."

"Until there's a big leak," said Anna, salting the potatoes and covering the vegetables with a big, round lid.

"You said it, Anna. Bingo!" Beau raised his hand. "America wants the war to walk away, sweep it under a giant magical rug of democracy and tape it a fancy color of red. To me, it's not going to fade away so fast. To politicians, Vietnam was President Johnson's blackeye, and a bloody spur for our troops, like me and others, who on the first week walked into a firefight on the frontlines. The worst thing in the world since Hitler terminated millions of good Jewish people in WWII."

"Do you think President Nixon will resign because of the cover-up in the Watergate scandal?" said Anna, stirring ice cubes into a glass of lemonade. "I think this will go on for years," she said, tasting the drink. "Who knows the truth?"

"Who knows if there's any truth in Washington?" said Naomi, twisting in a circle. "Everything is covert in Washington. We see lots of respect has been lost for the political leadership because of Vietnam, Watergate, and the heat they put on journalists during the war."

"The fact is, war messes with the election and leaders get embarrassed about it. They dodge the subject of how JFK was killed, and lied about how our boys were doing in Vietnam and the Watergate scandal, it was no different to Americans. As a journalist, I get sick just thinking about it," shaking his head and eating cornbread. "My articles embarrassed the dirty leadership. Oh, I was warned and pushed, and they said, "Shut your mouth, Le Mans!"

Anna walked to where Beau was eating at the bar, hooked her arm inside of his, smiling, and said, "I've got an idea."

"What?" he asked her.

"Hmmm. I'll be the writer," said Anna, sniffing his neck, holding his butt. "You tell the stories. How 'bout it, war hero? They would have no idea where the source came from, scratching their bald heads in Washington, and have no clue where I got the stories from." Anna tapped his nose with her fingernail and pointed to the cedar chest.

"I can write, Beau," said Naomi, who took his other arm.

"Hey," said Beau, "this pretty face has been struck a dozen times from what I know about Vietnam and have seen overseas. Look, they got pissed at Hemingway, pressed him, for what he knew about President Hoover, didn't they?"

"He was depressed and shot himself," said Naomi, frowning.

"Washington will always fight journalists and writers. They back us into a corner or take us to a medical examiner." Beau told them.

"There's talk about making Jimmy Hoffa disappear," said Naomi, glasses on her nose.

"We can be a team of writers," said Anna, kissing his cheek. "War stories are brewing because one writer, Beau Le Mans, the Man of War, with boots on the ground, can't and won't "shut his mouth" about Vietnam any longer." She leaned close to him and whispered, "I'll be your voice," curling a grin. "What do you think?"

"You have read my unpublished work, haven't you?" Beau held her shoulders.

"Some while you worked at the cafe," said Anna, looking at the ceiling.

"Don't be mad," said Naomi, stepping between them.

"That's okay. I have others, too," said Beau, moving Naomi out of the way.

"The *Army Times* printed twenty-six of your stories each year," said Anna, hand together. "I've studied all of them in Morgantown, and finally found you climbing rocks in Fayetteville. Did you know how hard it is to find a man from Wyoming County, hills and hollows, and you were never there?"

"You looked for me in Wyoming County?"

"I needed a firsthand story for a paper," said Anna, "but you had moved to Fayette County. To be honest, I had to meet you when I heard you moved north to Fayetteville."

"Anna had pictures of you on her wall," said Naomi, turning and laughing.

"That was for research purposes." Anna slammed her notebook.

"When we found out you were in Fayetteville, I thought it would be a professional touch to meet, talk to a real-life Army journalist, that's all. You're only a couple hours away from my dorm, anyway," said Anna, winking.

"Well, education and research, huh?" said Beau, twisting. "Is shacking up with a good-looking man for the summer part of your research for graduate school?"

"Nope. I-I-I don't think of it that way," said Anna, hand on her face, giggling. "We are not shacking up in sin, Beau. Our time is spent as writers, researching, creating a publication, and telling the truth about Vietnam or whatever we decide to do in 1974 and beyond. Let's call it a retreat by the river for writers."

"Yeah. We're just a couple of writers and Masala loving fools, Beau," said Naomi, rolling her eyes. "We're getting educated and shackled to typewriters in sin."

"We are in the same field. You can help jumpstart our careers, right?" said Anna, looking at Naomi for confirmation. "Right, sister."

"It could work, Beau, if you are willing to play ball," said Naomi.

"Ladies, I can dig how you connect journalism and war and sin, but I missed my family. My brother is dead. Investigate his unsolved story, huh? War stories don't make me happy. Love does. The world wants to get past Vietnam, move on, put war out of everyone's mind. Let's not think about what a great mistake it was for our leaders in Washington to dismiss my stories and skip on the truth. The war is not over yet. The CIA will kill me. I'm blacklisted. My stories have pissed people off. Mean people, ladies."

"Hmmm." Anna said, holding his shoulder. "You have material that needs to be published, huh? Let's call Uncle Walter and print your war stories in Pittsburgh. Dude, it would be so cool to interview you, take photographs, talk about serious projects. We could build something long term." Anna placed her hands on his hairy chest. "I'd see it as an honor to hear more about your experiences, starting from day one." She turned away and looked in the mirror. "You already have sororities, lots of them, humming and talking about you on the Mountaineer campus, Beau."

"What? On campus at West Virginia, huh? No way. Really?" said Beau, adjusting his collar. "I remember the baseball glove, it's over there on the shelf and we might play some hard ball."

"There it is. Yeah," said Anna, racing to grab it. "They saw your cool picture, the one without your shirt, just like you were by the river. Our sorority sisters passed the articles around during our March meeting. Right before we all had big plans to become writers and researchers and explorers of America."

Anna pressed her hand against his hand. Then, he fit the glove to her hand, and slapped the leather a few times. She stood, glove behind her back, like Sandy Koufax, and kicked her leg up, arm over her shoulder as if she was a pitcher in the majors.

"Catch, Beau. Hear me out about getting your articles published by Uncle Walt. I could stay with you this summer or we could travel, huh? Here we are. We could type them for you and submit the stories to Pittsburgh."

"We could stay the summer as a team of writers," said Naomi, posing steadily. "But, um, I want to see Amarillo and ride horses and drive to California."

"Right, Amarillo, Texas," said Anna, pointing at her friend. "I'm looking forward to seeing the stars over Texas. We could become close friends, show me Twin Falls State Park, and at the end of the summer, drive to Texas, right?"

"Drive Texas, huh?" said Beau, a grin stretched across his face. "Don't plan to write much this summer. Texas is on my bucket list, though. I can see the stars at night."

"Starting today, we might be more than friends," said Anna, pulling her long ponytail.

"Lovers, huh?" said Beau, eyes popped the size of homemade biscuits. "I'm game."

"We are writers." Naomi stood beside Anna, hand on her shoulder.

"Heck, we are more than writers, first class friends, and damn good ones, too." Anna's eyes observed her friends for an agreement. "Beau, you have wild stories, war stories that need female support and publicity, right? So we need good typewriters and a storyboard to build a timeline of characters about your life in Vietnam."

"I'll write his backstory!" said Naomi, hand up.

"Alright, heck yeah, I'll do it!" said Beau, hand out. "The world needs to hear what happened in Vietnam, and from someone who lived it. I won't promise anything with my PTSD... but..." tossing the ball from hand-to-hand. "Agreed. We'll recall my days chasing Charlie."

The team walked outside, slapping their gloves and Beau tugged on his hat.

Anna combed the ends of her long hair, tied her sandy blonde ponytail and dropped low, like Johnny Bench, the famous Reds baseball catcher. Her glove was wide, and she said, "Here, give me your best stuff, Beau Le Mans."

"You sure?" he said. "I have a wild arm."

"Yeah, for sure. Bring it on," said Anna. "Let's see what you got, Speedball Le Mans."

"I imagine we could play ball this summer and write," said Beau, standing in the stretch position. Anna's pretty eyes caught his attention. In the stretch, Beau saw himself with her in Texas and ideas flooded his mind, a little love struck puppy, and happy thoughts ticked inside his heart.

"I can shotgun your Jeep, and swim the New River," said Anna, eyes on him, ball in her hand.

"Lovers? Writers?" said Beau, ball in his hand. "What about you boyfriend? You can't have a Confederate lover and a Yankee lover. Your daddy ain't going to like that one, is he,

Scarlett?" He stood, a deep grin bent inside his glove. *What would she say and what would she do?*

Anna walked to Beau, grinned, and slammed the ball into his glove.

"Beau, I call the signs, got it?" said Anna, knees on the ground, and she raised up as tall as she could.

"Listen, I'll shake off any signs I don't like," said Beau, arm out. "That's teamwork."

"Yes, well, well, well," said Naomi, kicking dirt in a square she made beside Anna. "You're right, Beau, her big daddy would not like you, man?"

"Time out!" yelled Anna, who slammed her glove into the dirt. "I can forget about my ex-brother friend, if you can forget about your love in Wyoming County, Beau, huh?"

She kissed him. His eyes closed and he blinked several times after her lips pulled away.

"My boyfriend is history, how about your gal?" said Anna, holding his chin.

"Forgotten." He stepped toward home.

"No, no, no, Beau," said Naomi. "Don't press your luck." Anna walked back toward Naomi, hips twisting. "Daddy still won't like him," said Naomi, bat on her shoulder. "Will he?"

"Daddy doesn't need to know, right?" whispered Anna, winking at Naomi.

"Ummm, I got your back," said Naomi, high fiving her friend.

"We could play ball!" yelled Beau, body leaned toward home plate.

"Hope my PTSD doesn't get batty," said Beau, loud enough for the ladies to hear him.

"Here's the hot batty one," said Naomi, swinging her hips.

"Shut up, Naomi!" said Anna. "He's all mine."

"I bet," whispered Naomi, lips puckered and her eyes squinted toward Anna.

"For you, Beau, I'll do it. I'm game," said Anna, "Naomi is just being smart and jealous."

"I'm not jealous!" said Naomi, swinging her rounded hips at Beau. She smacked her gum and winked.

"Okay. I'll see what kind of game you can play!" yelled Beau, foot turning in the dirt. "I'll let you know about the peerage of life as an *Army Times* writer. Give me time to recall the events and turn the war in my head. I do have more good stories to share with you. Days hit me hard and I feel the need to write, but I don't want to relive the war. My doctor said, 'A soldier with PTSD, it would behoove you to leave the war behind and begin again.' Go to college and study fine arts or medicine or coach, Beau."

Beau cocked his arm and released. Naomi swung, but missed.

He walked over to Anna, dropped his glove and ball. She stood and he kissed her again.

"This is no game, okay? I'm not a player, and this is real-to life." said Beau. The man picked her up and spun her in a circle.

"That boy is in love, Anna," said Naomi, taking a seat on the porch. "Puppy love."

"But, Naomi, it's real to the puppy," said Beau.

"Good kiss," said Anna, voice low. "It'd be an honor to spend the summer with you and play ball, Beau." She stood, nose-to-nose, and hugged him. "Hope I can hold your attention as well as your ex-girlfriend did."

Naomi moved in, not wanting to be left out, and said, "Gonna be a hot summer."

Anna picked up the ball and mitt, fingers moving inside, and said, "But I still call the plays, Babe Ruth Le Mans."

Naomi watched and became jealous.

"When are we leaving for Texas, Anna? And, I have to get to San Diego," said Naomi. "I need some lemonade."

"Would you be a doll and make us a pitcher of lemonade, Naomi?" said Anna, hand swatting her away.

"I know when I'm not wanted." Naomi ran inside. "You need to be honest, Anna, tell him about our plans."

"Summer plans?" said Beau, head tilted in her direction.

Anna held the belt loops of Beau's pants.

"You're hooked, hillbilly. Forgot about the plans. It's the here and now."

"When are you driving to Texas, Anna? I heard her say San Diego."

"She's a dreamer. I don't know..." stuttering her words. "But, it's not every day a nice lady like myself meets a real-life war hero and falls in..." Anna turned away, "falls into a cool opportunity to learn something new about baseball in Fayetteville."

"When do you plan to leave for Texas? I want the truth."

"You mean, when can you hit a homerun... and then, what will happen?"

"No, I want to know how much of my heart to invest in this Puppy Love."

"Are you a gambler?" She grabbed his chin. "Look at those sweet cheeks. Are you afraid?"

"No." He rubbed her neckline. "A soldier likes to know the mission."

"The game of war and love are gambles, Beau. If you want, well, we can keep this game professional, I mean, writing... to ourselves." Anna said. She leaned against his chest.

"This game, I mean, writing and ball playing will be done at home, at night after work, and I'll be a happy man. Would you stay here and forget about Texas?" said Beau, who held her shoulders in each hand.

"I'll agree to write and play a little ball." She pressed his lips. "I'll keep it professional and sweet, of course. No promises."

"To write and play with the great "Man of War", is a true privilege." She took a deep breath.

"Did that convince you, war hero?"

"Almost Heaven," said Beau, grinning. "I don't grade a beginner that hard."

"Beginner?"

"Let's try it again."

That romantic moment was the true beginning of their life-long friendship.

The next night, Beau surprised Anna with a new fondue pot, cooking beef, cuts of rye and sourdough bread, melted cheese, and slices of melon and pineapple chunks lined the plate. Anna sang and Naomi played Beau's vintage Martin guitar, the one his father had bought for himself at a secondhand store after he came home from the Korean War.

For the next week, Beau and Anna were inseparable. Her vanilla perfume slapped his face and he was hooked under her spell. His father warned him about missing church and being a backslider. He'd depended on God, but morals and ethics faded with each sunset. The radiance of two ladies in his home was his slice of love, and it was one he'd dreamed about in Vietnam, and one the preacher did not approve of in town. He thought Anna was a peach in an apple orchard. They all grabbed the table when Beau had the white topping of Poke Cake on his face. Anna had a simple nature about her, and she lacked nothing in Beau's eyes, one elegant dash of goodness and kindness after another. After dinner, Naomi cuddled up in her bed and for the fourth week, she opened *The Great Gatsby* and fell asleep at two in the morning.

The nightly view on the porch became a ritual for Anna, kicking her legs under a summer blanket, and Beau decided to drag her back inside the old farmhouse to play Charlie Rich on the 8-Track player, but, in three notes, Anna surprised him when she knew every word.

"And, and, Beau, when we get behind closed doors, what do we do?" sang Anna and stood proudly inside his arms, resting on his shoulder each night when they danced.

"This is wonderful what you've done to treat us like queens. And no one knows what happens behind closed doors," said Beau, touching her nose.

"You forgot the words, Beau?" Anna whispered, hugging him firmly.

The door closed.

"I know what goes on behind closed doors," said Beau, chin on her shoulder. He walked across the room and turned down the stereo and the lights.

Changing tracks, Beau played Abbey Road, and no other song would've been more fitting for the moment. He didn't know what the song meant to her until he heard his father's voice: "You alright, Zeus?"

"Oh, Baby Anna," said Beau, "I'll never leave you." Zeus was struck by lightning.

"I've heard that somewhere before," she said. "Do you practice horrible lines in the mirror each morning?"

"No. Keep the nights hot and the days renowned," said Beau, hooking her jeans.

"Celebrated," said Anna, hand on his stomach. "Might be a night for your memory."

"Are you planning for a hot night?" said Beau, holding her waist. He lifted her up and gently put her feet on the floor.

They had fed each other lemon meringue pie. When her favorite track played, she kissed him. Oh, but the night was pleasant and dark, and the air was cool in Fayette County, especially for a home on a hill, and not far from the highway. They heard the loud freight train, loaded, full of coal, rolling through the turns of the long valley floor beneath the construction of the New River Gorge Bridge. Unknowingly, time had slipped away one Friday night and the glimmer of the stars was the only light at all.

"Here comes the sun, Beau."

"Pop! Pop! Pop!"

Beau hit the deck.

"It was just the mailman's car backfiring, Beau."

He sat on the floor and his face flushed the color of a tomato.

"Took me back to my days at war."

Anna made fresh coffee. Without hesitation, the first thing each morning, she played Abbey Road. Still lean, Beau stood, half dressed, and he plugged in the gift he'd bought for her birthday.

"Beau Le Mans, you shouldn't have done this," said Anna, kissing him. "I love it."

"It's a new instant brewing electric coffee maker; the one Joe DiMaggio recommends on television."

"That's really thoughtful, Beau. Will it get as hot as last night?"

"Nope. Brick House, Young Babe."

Naomi stayed in bed and didn't like early mornings.

Beau slowly danced and swung Anna in circles on her birthday. They sat at the bar and talked and kissed. The coffee was strong from a night of only a few hours of sleep.

"Was last night enough to keep you from jetting to Texas?" said Beau, one hand on her leg and the other on his coffee cup.

"Ummm, good coffee. We might dance tonight and see, "said Anna, lips tight, puckering.

Most of their private conversations were dealt with at breakfast while they have a room with a private view and no third-party company from Naomi.

"Why did they call you "Man of War" in The Dominion Post?"

Beau crunched veggies every morning.

"Tomatoes take me back to Vietnam. My father called me that, but I was called it for a different reason later on."

"What's the name from?"

"I saw a produce stand get blasted in the street and women and children .... Well, it was bad, really bad. It seems the higher ups and newspapers want to use my war stories to boost sales and draw attention to untold stories. They monitor and edit my stuff. There's more to say about what really happened in Vietnam," said Beau, hands in his pockets. He jumped up and paced around.

She waited for him.

"What happened?"

"Between Cambodia, Laos, and Vietnam, it's certain West Virginia counted ten prisoners of war, soldiers still missing in action, as of last year. They think I know more, saw more, heard more and will talk about more when the time comes and things settle down. I've been advised not to talk about the war. I'll keep my mouth shut, like the Feds and the Black Suits advised."

"You seem like the kind of man who wants to solve problems and find more prisoners of war, right? Write it down, Beau, will ya?"

"Yeah. I want 'em all out. Bring our fighters home."

She poured him more coffee.

"For me," said Beau, sipping the coffee, "to tell the world about the war would be a release of my soul and maybe pivot helicopters to POW camps."

"Please tell me how you escaped and made history. That's something worth telling. That's why I am here, to get inside your wild head, man." She reached for him.

"Okay. Yeah, we painfully escaped. Sam Law and Henderson, the three of us broke out of a POW camp. Cadeo was there. That's one hundred percent true. More soldiers have been left behind in Vietnam, I just know it. We escaped and beat the V-C system. Sam Law was fatally shot. Then, the body of Sam Law was intentionally burned. I have his dog tags hidden in my safe."

"Let me get a pen," said Anna, who sat across the bar from him. "Let's talk, Baby."

"Henderson, he was from Texas, a good man. The last time we saw each other, Henderson was under a bridge, leg broken, and his hand was open in my direction. I left him to fight alone, Anna. He was alone."

"You didn't leave him alone, Beau."

"Yes, I did. Henderson disappeared. I've hated myself for years. He's still missing in action. The newspapers think I know more about the V-C than I've said, and how they offer American soldiers a good deal to make a compromise, trading information for freedom and so does the Defense Department."

"Did they offer you a deal, Beau?"

His face was long, sat up and said, "Sure did."

"What type of deal?"

"The deal, huh, well, was to work for the Viet-Cong."

"To kill Americans."

"Yeah. To kill my cousins and brothers-in-arms," said Beau, holding his face.

"Did they let you go back to rescue Henderson?"

"Yeah. We circled by air a few times. He wasn't under the bridge when I returned, so he was declared missing in action. MIA. Henderson didn't make the 1973 Operation Homecoming. The DOD will not let me or any other journalists go back to Vietnam, ask questions, or try and track him down, for some strange reason."

He emptied the coffee and slammed the cup.

"You cannot fix the past, Beau."

"Yeah. Lots of deals. I'm not sure if they taught you that part in journalism school. The Vietnamese government had written contracts for American prisoners to sign."

"What?"

"It's true. Seven years ago Secretary of Defense McNamara said 89,000 Vietnamese soldiers had already been killed. That was the biggest lie Americans had ever heard. I was on the ground and several thousand V-C had died in dog fights, naturally. Napalm. Gunfire. Mines."

"Civilians burned in the streets, didn't they?"

"Some. Yeah. Men. Women. Children. I was advised not to publish my photos or write stories because of PTSD. They said my stories were unreliable because of my stress and my mind reprocessed what happened in Vietnam when I saw American films on television. They said what I witnessed on television was just being repeated inside my head, so I didn't write anymore.

The Big Feds said, 'Le Mans, you are confused. Your material has no credit and does not fit what really happened.' It fits, I told the guy. And two seconds later, three guys pulled my foot out of his fat butt."

"I would've paid money to see your foot kicking the hell out of the Feds."

"The Black Suits suck. The truth is, my part of the truth, they don't want me to remember more bits and pieces of the war, especially when the new PTSD medication kicks in. They see my stories as invalid, not first-hand material anymore."

"That's bologna!" Anna threw her pen across the room. "Do they really think you made those stories up or dubbed them from TV?"

"Yeah. I've got a box of film and good photographs to validate my stories. I back my own self up as a journalist. Pictures they've never seen before, hidden inside this house."

"In that old Army trunk and cedar chest?"

"Right there. That's my journals and treasures. They think I was using deception and being forgetful, not me. I can expose more about the truth and the genocide in Vietnam, as well. You don't forget certain things in life."

She held his hand and stood beside him.

"Can I see the photos, Beau?"

"Help yourself."

"Genocide, huh?" said Anna, who sat in front of the trunk. "Naomi! Naomi! Get down here."

"What? What is it?" said Naomi, who ran downstairs. "What's the problem?"

"Beau, are these photos part of the merciless killings by V-C soldiers?" asked Anna, hands on top of the trunk.

"Let me unlock it," said Beau, keys in his hands. "Go to it. Research."

Tears rolled down the face of Anna.

"This is making me..." said Naomi, who ran outside.

"She's sick," said Beau, who stood at the sink.

"No, no, no! I can't believe the unnecessary loss of life." said Anna, "We didn't study about genocide and information falsification, such as what we've seen at the Watergate Corruption. They've butchered the truth until no one knows what real stories are anymore. We did study Billy Graham, the moral law and ethical communication in journalism."

"I'm sorry, Beau. I cannot look at the blood and guts of dead people," said Naomi, eyes red.

"Here's some water," said Beau. "War is nothing easy."

"That's not war," said Naomi, hand of her mouth, coughing.

"Mr. Graham said the truth is a timeless message," said Anna, holding pictures in her hands. "Truth does not differ from one age to another, from one people group to another, from one geographical location to another, and the truth remains the same as when it was spoken."

"There you have it, Anna. Well, you can help me recall the facts and print the truth."

"I don't make promises, Beau." She held a shocked face. "But I will do my best to stick around for a while, be it a short or long while. Lovers to the end."

Beau sat beside her, rubbing her fair skin and long arms. Her eyes closed.

"I hope you stick around for a long, long time, Anna. I was handed a Purple Heart, told to leave Uncle Sam's war. They said, 'Le Mans, it's no longer any of your duty to report the war' and I was eager to do just what they said.

"How long have you been out?" asked Anna, breaking rubber bands from pictures.

"Five years. Every so often a man in a dark suit shows up at my home or at Cafe Le Mans to make sure I don't remember any part of the war. He hides behind dark glasses and offers his condolences for brother when he pays the bill, saying 'Keep your mouth shut, hillbilly' and the man leaves."

"Dark suit, huh?" said Naomi, cleaning her face. "The Big Feds."

"Yeah. Dark car. Dark suit. Dark glasses," said Beau, eyes looking outside.

That morning, Beau had made his way to the window, the one he'd found to be a friend, crossing his long arms where his mind faded back to his time as POW. He remembered his friends: Cadeo, Polly, and Henderson. None of their faces had surfaced. Beau still had one promise to the parents of Sam Law, a promise unmet.

After dinner, Beau's face was pale and slowly he touched the glass and said, "We'll talk another time about the war, Anna. I'm tired and rattled. Sometimes I see a man in a black suit standing in the yard at night, but I know no one is beyond this grass."

"Beau, that's creepy. Don't paint a Boogie Man in my head. No one is here at night." She divided her angel bangs. "When was the last time a man in black visited you?"

"The day before you arrived."

"I'm sorry, Beau. I understand. This heart is someone you can lean on, a good listener when you need one," hands around his belt, rubbing his stomach. "I know you'd like the past to vanish. We're such close friends now. You have friends in me and Naomi."

Beau turned around to kiss her.

"We're on the same baseball team, too. You're the pitcher."

"Teammates. Confidants. I mean, when you're ready, I'd love to hear your side about the POW camp, see your secret photographs of the war and take more notes."

He nodded and a giant smile ran across his eyes, kissing her head. She stood, arms atop his shoulders and kissed him and brushed his thin beard several times.

"When I'm ready, I'll talk," said Beau. "That may be a while, Anna."

Each night they watched a tangerine sun fade behind the shut in of the mountains and the melting blaze of the sun warmed his face, eyes closed, and for the last few minutes, Beau would not speak to anyone. While Anna freshened up in the mirror, Vietnam flashed inside his head and the burning jungle bent by a whipping wind across the high hills and caused him to pinpoint details and when she returned Beau was writing again. His mind was clear and ready to take on the Black Suits. Not much at first, but listing details, dates and months, and notebooks were labeled. He saw himself standing on a tall mountain overlooking a downward slope, one that led to rice paddies and tunnels, and overhead, endless clouds of napalm exploded across the landscape, one after the other, and then another cloud formed in the distance and the land burned and smoked.

"What is it, Beau?" she turned.

"Black clouds of smoke and fire."

The burning smell of the fondue pot made him stagger and the man grabbed the door frame, a bit of PTSD, just as the doctor predicted. Beau left the room and stood in front of the bathroom mirror and swiftly washed his face, eyes widened and he relaxed, counting to forty. He gasped for air, heart pounding, eyes yearning for calmness and peace. With a towel on his face, he became his old self again.

"To be normal again, just for one day," he told himself.

His face was long and pale. Haunting and howling voices worked on his weary mind, where memories and flashbacks repeatedly hit him, especially when the stars were absent from the sky. The worst episodes staggered him at night and he believed an evil spirit had trailed him to West Virginia, the same ruthless demon that had haunted him as a POW, a wavy spirit who triggered and made him check each room. He predicted freedom was far from his mind.

Beau made his way to the kitchen table before Anna returned and felt the heat from the fondue pot with both hands, hands steady. He saw the wild eyes of his First Sergeant inside the cooking pot.

"Boots on the ground, Le Mans! God be with you, son."

"Godspeed, First Sergeant."

"Le Mans?"

"Yeah."

"Go tell it on the mountain that Jesus Christ is born."

"Amen, First Sergeant! I will tell it on the mountain at home."

After five years of being in the mountains, it was thought Vietnam still lived inside him, echoing as if he was in the same closed war room. The smell of the tall, stainless pot and the heat of the fire, and felt warm, when he searched for Henderson and a voice in the mountains told him that he was still a prisoner of war.

"Go tell it on the mountain that Jesus Christ is born." Beau sat and mumbled.

"That's my favorite hymn," said Anna, stepping inside the doorway.

"Huh? Yeah, when I was down and out, the words of that hymn kept me alive in Vietnam, too." Beau turned away.

Images of war flashed. This time, his face reflected off the glossy window where he saw himself fighting again, and the battle raged in the depth of the glass. He was back "in-country" as if he'd never left Vietnam, a bit of PTSD battled, the rapids rushed across his feet and in the distance, high mountains burned and napalm exploded across the gorge.

"Did the doctor say you'd get better, Beau?"

"Better? I see images. As a journalist, Anna, I saw myself writing and photographing soldiers burning alive. I will not get better." Beau lit a cigar. "I still see them. I'll see them the rest of my life," pointing outside, "and especially at night between the street light and the moon."

"Do you see the V-C running through the ghostly fog?" said Anna, who opened the door, cool mountain air filled the room.

"Yeah. They're out there, still fighting. Somewhere." He took a deep breath. "I smell smoke, too. If you are going to be a writer, you must hold onto images and memories, Anna. Write about the brokenness of humanity as much as you write about homeward victories of sports and politics."

She unplugged the fondue pot.

"There. It's just the smell from cooking, Chef."

He stepped outside into heavy fog, still damp and cool on his face, breathing and relaxing and smoking in his cigar favorite chair on the porch. He blew smoke rings and rocked his legs and laughed.

"The mountains are beautiful, so cozy. Come and see. You have your world, Anna, and I have mine," he told her with an honest face.

"It's okay to have different roads as long as you're willing to go hand-in-hand together."

She sat outside under the glow of the porch light and observed him. Propping her feet onto the table, mimicking him, she lit her own cigar and then reached for his hand.

"Our worlds are similar, Beau. Writers. Photographers. Wanderlusts. We have a likeness about this wonderful world, one we find interesting and our sweet momentum will travel beyond, here and now. We'll go far together."

"Together. Our paths crossed for a reason, and our articles will outlast our days. God brought us together."

He raised her hand, up and down.

"When this war is over, Beau," she said, looking into the depth of night, "and the craziness of the battle ends, looking back will be different for all of us as friends. Though, some will regret they were born into a time of war, some will see it as a loss; some as a gain and others will see hope and find enough courage to start again."

"Be born again."

"Yeah. When the war is over, families will look around for friends and people who care about them, especially godly people."

He pulled her inside, and tugged on his jean pocket.

Beau found two drinks of port wine from the kitchen.

"How, Anna?" he asked, straddling his chair and leaning back. "How do you see life any differently than I do?"

She excitedly held his hand close to her heart, and said, "You see, we're forerunners, doers and thinkers, braving a new trail, the ones who lived it, the ones who make a living in dangerous situations, and we are writers who will gladly step into dark places and battle in the frontlines to get the truth to the readers. That's the treasure of a writer, to push the truth of history forward."

"We took chances. Risked our lives.

"We'll be admired and remembered, not for being the same. We'll be different because of hardships, the stories, the way we live, you were in Vietnam and I've wanted to know about you for years. We're the ones who will write our headlines and define our differences, wrongs and rights, and write about social injustices, uncover scandals, and what we witness will be printed for the ages, like the Civil War, the Greensboro Four, and other wars. Difference makers in society, bring the story to citizens.

"Baby Boomers are making the difference," said Beau, hand in the air. "We're a country of progression. Man, I love it! It's primitive and cool," he said, kissing her. "I can swing it, Babe."

"While the world wants to hide the '70s, Vietnam and Watergate, our job as writers and photographers, self-assignments, our homework, will be on the frontlines of America, telling the world how to stand for goodness and justice," said Anna, writing.

"We start today," said Beau, shadow boxing, "and sell stories to magazines, huh?"

"Heck yeah," she said. "That's the way we'll live our lives. I will commit to this project, if, and only if, you stay here in Fayetteville until we are finished, right?"

"Right on, Beau."

She stood, leaning against the center house beam for most of the night and spoke of protests, sit-ins and all the southern cities, like Montgomery, Memphis, Greensboro and others who stood for civil rights and told stories. Conflict and unresolved society issues had reached the hearts of millions of Americans. They made a plan to write stories, set up interviews, and encourage follow-ups. They were less different than Beau first thought. Anna talked late into the night, shared ideas and planned to meet people, good people who wanted to speak up and sound off about Vietnam.

To him, something was hidden in the darkness or at least inside his mind. He heard screams of soldiers and saw hurting faces, moaning and groaning, faces of pain had no voices. Life was gone for them and their stories needed to be printed. Something swiftly came to his head. Beau dodged it and never spoke much of the war to her.

"Bats. They're just bats, Beau. Relax."

"Bats flew into dark caves in Vietnam. I hate bats. I saw hundreds of bats the last time I saw Polly."

His mind was still in Vietnam.

Pain walked across his skin and then, suddenly, he blinked and swung and the bats were gone. Soldiers he knew and friends he'd made were still missing in Vietnam. He thought of himself as just a common man at war, still battling the past, fighting. He knew everyone was fighting something; he was wounded and felt guilty for what he had to do to survive in Vietnam. The clock reminded him of soldiers he'd known, some with round faces that succumbed in battle and died hard. Then, he smiled, and remembered Polly and Cadeo and Hien. He thought of his own hardships from the war. Letters filled his mailbox and the phone rang.

"Hello!" said Beau.

Someone introduced themselves on the other end.

"Times, huh? I already have a highly-intelligent chief war correspondent standing inside my kitchen. I'm sorry, Rat Writer, calling from the *Times* or *The Herald*. Anna Katsen has beaten you to the punch."

Beau hung up the phone and crushed his cigar.

"Is it puppy love, Beau? You're my man," smiling.

"Could be. You'll be the one who I trust with my past and ...my future."

"More magazines called here," said Beau, "more than I can shake a stick at. *The Charlotte Observer* and *The New York Times* called a few weeks ago digging for an interview. They wanted more inside stories, fire for the readers, Baby."

"Was that Mr. McClatchy on the phone?"

"How did you know that?"

"Word is out that Naomi is staying with Beau Le Mans in Fayetteville, West Virginia."

"How does Naomi know Mr. McClatchy?"

"She dated him. Some of his prints will choke a goat, though."

"My mind can't handle rewinding the war every day, Anna. It's the worst part of my life. I need my privacy in the mountains. That's the main reason I live here, climbing cliffs."

"We might need to travel, throw him off our trail. Mr. McClatchy will be here, since you answered the phone. He'll pay big, big dollars for a good story, one that'll jumpstart his journalism career again."

"Dang it, Anna!" He slammed the table.

"I'm sorry. I'll call my Pitt Panther Daddy. Tell him I'll be home soon."

"No, no, no. You can hide out in these hills and write stories here, Babe. Get away from that Pittsburg Daddy, right?" Beau stood. "We can go to Chicago, write sports for the Cubs and White Sox, huh?"

"Man, I gotta head West, Beau. I am sorry. I dig the big sky in West Texas. Naomi wants to chase the howl of the coyotes. We have a good amount to publish."

"It's not what we promised to write. You must stay and work together."

Again and again, he was reminded of the eerie howling voices: The ones that said, "Daddy, Daddy, Daddy," in Vietnam and how the dark, empty valley echoed throughout the jungle when he closed his eyes at night. Images of soldiers who were still missing in action and a sea of wounded soldiers, the dead rolled in the ocean, and the wounded pulled on his hands and clothes for help. He couldn't pull them all ashore. No one could rescue them. Some soldiers twisted in the mud, half vanished, sinking into the earth, stuck in the mud of rice paddies and being swept away by rapid water. Beau felt useless inside, as if he was too weak or careless to free them. Too many soldiers, still missing in action, and he heard the music of Taps and his eyes popped open. Even awake, he recited voices.

"Le Mans, help me, man? Help me! Help!"

Beau couldn't untie the war from his mind.

In his dream, still stuck, he was unable to be a hero and trees laughed at his failures. Raging faces and revengeful faces of Viet-Cong guerillas flashed inside his head, laughing and beating Henderson, Sam Law, Cadeo, Hien, and even pushing and ripping the dress from the arms of Polly.

"O' how the mirror borrows my past," he said aloud.

Anna held him as tight as she could, hands locked around her waist.

The horrible pain of his own beaten body, the lashes, wounds and the throbbing wouldn't vacate him. He recalled something else. Nothing was forgotten. The world marched without peace and happiness. Something more was needed. More like Eden. Beau wanted for the first time to tell her what he knew, the rest of the story crossed his mind about Vietnam and his dream about Eden. He needed Anna to write it. No one else. He questioned himself and retraced his own footsteps, recalling and circling back in his head, what he knew was the truth. They stood in the kitchen of his home. Beau second guessed his ideas about seeing his life printed on pages. Anna documented his stories for hours, writing, the both of them, and he saw a hundred typewriters, keys and ribbons flying late into night.

Beau hugged her back and kissed her. He was back.

"If I can think of more, I'll say it. Being a POW was real. When a farm tractor backfires or the mailman backfires I hit the deck."

"Tomorrow, we start again, say more, Beau. I have seven stories down and if one day I'm not here, you'll know I have enough to sell. Being a journalist is more than being in the right place, but being with the right person. I promise you that much about me. You're my right person."

"Am I, Anna? Are you with me just to get the Big Story?"

"Nope. I've fallen hard in love. You're Mister Right Now." She held him. "Of course you are Mr. Right, I mean, Beau. I'm joking."

He kissed her forehead and brushed her hand across his head.

"Mister Right Now, huh? Even when you've had too much in your glass?"

"We can share as much as you like."

His face was full of truth and his reflection was calm. Mellow man. She was what he needed to help resolve his own personal issues. He knew the U.S. government had left behind soldiers, missing men, those still stuck inside an endless jungle, just like Henderson and others. She documented his story from his time with "big boots on the ground" until he rotated back to his home state of West Virginia, mapping his past.

"These stories are what I saw, Anna. My broken life was real, real pain."

"No one else can be you, Beau Le Mans."

"There are more good men left in Vietnam, prisoners, brainwashed and broken men. They deserve to be home again where they belong. President Nixon had us in a firefight that could not be won. He sent us to Hell. We need to print pages that matter and mean something."

"Take your time. This is important stuff. One question: Have your thoughts changed since you came back home?"

"Vietnam was hopeless from day one. It's still hopeless and sad. I need to wash my face."

Beau left the room abruptly.

"Did you get his story, Anna?" said Naomi, who had heard their conversation from the top of the stairs. "We have enough to take it all the way to San Diego, don't we? My Dad's newspaper will love this beat, man. I'm digging this guy. What a story? Let's leave in the morning. Did he believe your dad is a lawyer?"

"Yeah, girl. He took the bait. Get back upstairs. This is the Holy Grail. Mission accomplished. Hurry, go, go."

"I'll be in my room if you need me. Route 66, here we come."

The cheeks of Anna were red and shiny, like the tomatoes Beau loved so much.

Beau saw his face in the bathroom mirror and the mirror became a television. He watched himself fight the enemy by day, huddle inside a tent and write stories at night. Pages and articles flew into the high winds, spinning from Vietnam until the pages reached America. The war wasn't over for him. He turned the knob on the mirror, like it was a TV dial, changing the channel, but the war did not disappear. He heard click, click, click, and like an empty rifle, and he was out of ammo. His face was lost when he opened the glass door and saw his prescription for PTSD. His battle was inside his mind, not in the mirror. The future would be no different for him, even a medicated future, he thought. Beau respected the words of Dr. Rogers, his counselor, a man who fought in Korean, and now, the top Veterans hospital doctor in the country. To be in the mountains or Texas, he thought, but not in California. Could he leave the battle behind or talk it out or feel better about himself or resolve the past by chatting over coffee and apple pie with Anna? More stories, untold pages, books and journals flipped inside of Beau. Other vets had to cope with the past and each man brought home memories and a broken heart, for the rest of their lives. He had spoken that much about the war since he was in Vietnam. Were they okay or like him, locked in memories? Beau was mindful of their value to him and their families and they needed closure. They needed the truth. Whatever happened to Henderson, Polly, Cadeo, and the sad day Hien lost his life and the death of Sam Law, all of it was noted. He had always wondered about his friends. Alive. Dead. Happy. Or were they lost in a world at war and drugged. Beau saw the many faces of Communism, faces red with hatred, and moaning faces and hanging heads: One was Ben "Caveman" Henderson, and he became curious again and saw his profile in the mirror which startled him. Le Mans jerked his head and gasped for air, leaving the bathroom dark, the way he'd found it.

He walked slowly back to the kitchen, head hanging.

Anna cleared her throat and said, "Do you want to take a drive, get some air?"

"Let's go. You drive the Jeep, though. I'm curious about something." His hard eyes saw her. "Can I really trust you, Anna?"

"Yeah, for sure, man." She told him. "What's up?"

"This "Man of War," Anna, is staying here, in the hills. The war took something from me and I'm not planning to leave the mountains to find anything new. I have the cafe and my good family. My life is here."

"What?" She shifted gears. "I thought we'd travel, Babe, see the country and write."

"I can't. They robbed my life, cut into my soul when I read lies and trash about Vietnam or what they think the war was like." He pointed. "Drive to the river, please."

"You can tell me, Beau," encouraged Anna. "Get it out and say something."

His voice was low when he answered her, as sweat beaded on his forehead.

"I killed to stay alive. It wasn't fair for anyone. Why did my buddies die? Why was I the bad hand of the butcher, killing for the puppet master President Nixon and his Black suits?"

"You signed up to serve your country. I'm sorry Nixon mastered such an animal raid. Him, and many others are war freaks, rushing into the politics that broke humanity."

"Stop. Here's where we met. The best day of my life."

"I love this view of the New River Gorge."

They sat by the river, skipping rocks, and lost in thought. He removed his shirt and she touched his skin.

"Scars are on my back, the ones you saw here. Stripes and marks. This is what a Man of War looks like. I'm no hero, Anna. No man with a bunch of war tats and ribbons is a hero. We are survivors, the lucky ones. When I tell my side of the war to students about some senseless political war in Vietnam, I show them my deep scars and one bullet wound. Vietnam was a place we should've never been and soldiers died for no reason. That's no Man of War, Anna," he said, throwing a rock into the water. "I was a marching puppet."

"There must be some reason why they call you Man of War. I'm sorry for making you upset and digging. Tell me." She nodded, waiting, red cheeks curling a long smile, "Can you talk about more, the truth?"

He built a small fire.

"Do me a favor, huh?" said Anna, breaking a branch. "Never ask me about my lovers again."

"How many men have you had, Anna?"

"Two."

"Hey, I'm trying to get to know you. Woman of love. The truth, right?"

"No. You want to judge my past. That's something to fight about now and load more ammo for later on when you're mad or drunk. I've seen my parents fight about flirting and when someone touched them and winked." She raised her hands.

"You must've asked my mother twenty questions about my ex-girlfriend in Wyoming County, didn't you? Spill the beans."

"Yeah. Yeah. Yeah. I was just trying to make conversation, follow your orders, Army Man. How often do you meet a war hero, anyway? I'm sorry, Beau. I'm not sure we can go anywhere together. Our personalities are too strong to travel in a car for hours."

He jumped inside the Jeep.

"Where are we going?" yelled Anna.

"Nowhere!" said Beau. "It's fine. Now you know what makes me mad as hell. Don't dig into my love life. Man, you're nosey."

"Take me home, Beau. Now!"

She stayed in her room with Naomi and Beau paced the floor. He never said he was sorry and neither did Anna. Naomi made Anna's dinner, not spilling any beans about her best friend, and the trio kept their distance.

The next day, hours passed at Beau's family restaurant as he worked his normal shift. He was on the grill and listened to football stories that he'd missed and picked up on local gossip from friends and took orders. Beau overheard where the Mountaineers football stars were headed and who had turned pro. Danny Buggs and Artie Owens would soon play on Sunday. He chimed in on the predictions of how Bobby Bowden would handle Pittsburgh and Boston, which became a debatable dinnertime topic at Cafe Le Mans.

"Here, Beau," said his mother, "go be at peace with those beautiful women. They're good for you."

"I should charge them for the dessert, right?"

"Nope. Beau, I raised you better than that. Go. You better not charge them a penny. That sounds like something your father would say, anyway."

"Leave me out of this fight," said Sherman.

"I'll be a good man about it," said Beau, who sat at the bar.

Beau's mother handed him a chocolate cake and Beau, being a thoughtful man, took Naomi and Anna each a slice. His father's shirt and bib were wet from cooking and preparing meals and he was exhausted.

"Hey, Beau?" said his dad, loosening his blue tie.

"Yes sir!" said Daddy Le Mans, as he held the cake in both hands and propped the door open with his foot.

"I've been here since 4am." He gripped his coffee cup. "Can you close the cafe for me tonight, son?"

"It's a hot weekend, old man." His face was red, and he was sweating bullets. "Hero's weekend," he said, as he tried to debate with a chicken dinner in his hand. "Yeah, what time, Dad?"

"See ya around ten o' clock, Beau."

"You got it, old man."

"Something I hate about this job is the long hours of cooking," his father said.

"It's a restaurant. But I do know what you mean, the hours." Beau handed him a glass of water. "Comes with the territory, but my poor mother never takes a break."

"My cooking gets you back inside her heart," said his mother. "A mom's job never stops. Don't you say a word, Sherman."

"I'm not being dirty minded, BettyAnne." Sherman told her.

"Go on, Beau," said his mother. "Take the food home to the girls."

Later, back on the front porch of Beau's home, coffee was served by Anna, and they watched the brilliant glow of pink and orange disappear into a dark galaxy. They had made up. The world had melted the sunset and bright stars arched a blanket over the High Country. Beau and Anna watched a star race across the sky over Fayette County. Beau pulled three chairs up to the banister where he tapped the armrest, and Anna and Naomi joined him.

"Nothing like milk and cake to make up with a lady, Beau," said Naomi.

For several hours stories and food were shared, and they laughed and flirted, the three of them were back to normal. Sometime after midnight Anna went to fix warm coffee. Naomi leaned and kissed Beau.

"What was that for, Naomi?" said Beau, eyes as big as a cupcake.

"Maybe I want to know you, Beau. I want all of you."

"You can't treat Anna that way."

"She is using you, Beau. I was against it from the start."

"Using me?" Beau turned his chair, "Why?"

"Articles. She has been planning this since her Junior year at WVU."

"I don't believe you."

"You will find out soon enough."

"Is she really going to screw me over?" He looked inside the window for Anna.

Naomi held his back pocket and nodded.

"I can treat you right, Beau." Naomi put her face on his stomach and giggled.

Beau walked away, stood, neck red, and his heart busted. He stepped in the doorway.

"Anna, do you need help?"

"No, just chat with Naomi. I'll be there in five minutes, okay."

"Yeah. Good idea." Beau sat beside Naomi. She rubbed his leg.

"Have you considered us? I'll be your dugout player and catcher, Beau."

"Has Anna planned this for years, indulging herself on my dime and playing a game with my heart. Is this summer Puppy Love some joke?"

"Yeah," said Naomi, running her hand up and down his jeans. "I'd keep you close and cuddle with you all night."

The door popped open.

"It's a hot cup of brew. Be careful," said Anna, kicking her feet up on the rail. "Thanks for the delicious cake and superb company. You're a true showman."

The night was dark and candles waved on the banister.

"You've treated both of us like queens, Beau," said Naomi, hand on his shoulder. "Yummy, I could stay here forever, Anna."

"Well, Darling Naomi, we can't," said Anna.

"Naomi said that you celebrated your Favorite Days of the month that reminded you of your parents and grandparents, little celebrations, Anna," he said, turning to her. "Well, well, I had to do something nice, being you're away from your family in Pittsburg and the only guest I've had in my home. Other than a few cousins who helped us move into town."

"Nice family, Beau," said Anna. "Mr. Le Mans wants to fish with you sometime."

"Oh, you talked fishing with my father?" Beau jumped out of his chair. "Oh, crap! I forgot to close down the cafe tonight. I need to call him."

"I took care of it, Beau-man," said Naomi. "I got your back. Sit down, Beau." Her hand patted the seat, and she grabbed his shirttail. "Don't worry. Your mother told me you'd forget, partly because of PTSD, and your sweet distraction toward two sweet ladies. She agreed to lock up the restaurant, if you got busy being a good host with us all night."

"When did you call, Naomi?" said Anna, thumb on her ear. "When did you become his secretary, girl?"

"Just trying to look after him since you were napping and forgot about it," said Naomi. "Who can forget about the host, Anna, and his generosity, huh?"

"I did, I guess," said Anna. "Was I out that long?"

"Thank God for my mother, Naomi, and Anna. I feel I'm surrounded by sweetness." He kissed Anna.

Naomi blew out the candle.

"Hey, wait," said Naomi, face against Beau's shoulder. "I didn't forget about you, Beau," whispering, "Kiss my cheek."

"I need a bathroom break," said Beau, stretching his legs.

"I forget everything," said Beau, opening the door. "Thanks, Naomi. You remembered my father and I assumed he's got it."

"Relax," said Naomi, slapping his butt as he walked by. "The restaurant is in good hands."

Beau slipped inside.

"What are you doing, Naomi?"

"Oh, Anna, get over yourself. This is a big game and we're in the ninth inning. Now, I want to play extra innings."

"It's not a game anymore. I care for him."

"Liar. You've lied to guys all your life. So, why now, huh? You said he can help your career and that's why we came here in the first place."

"This is no lie. I'm in love with him."

"He already knows it's a game." Naomi pulled her long necklace down her chest. "He likes my melons over your peaches, anyways."

"How does he know?"

"I told him you were playing, okay."

"You bitch!" Anna cocked her hand back. Naomi blocked it.

"I can have him, Anna, if I want him." She adjusted her shirt. "He wants this juicy fruit." Naomi met Beau in the doorway. "See you later, Beau. I'm in bed."

Beau sat beside Anna, eyes on Naomi.

"What was that about?"

"She wants you to pluck her fruit tonight, I guess."

"What?"

"Don't be stupid, Beau. You know what she is up to."

"Let's go inside."

Anna simmered down after they'd walked in the living room.

"Well, I'm glad you're here," kissing her hand. "New friends. Puppy Lovers. Well, I'll take dad fishing this weekend. Good idea. That's one thing about me; I keep my word and do my best for people. I don't play silly games and hurt people."

"Beau, I know what Naomi told you."

"You do?"

"I'm not playing some game with your heart. I care for you."

He crossed his legs, hand behind his head.

"Well, I don't know who is being truthful and who's the big fat liar, huh?"

"I'm being real with you, Beau."

"Time will tell, Anna. Only time will tell about you. Let's listen to music."

They sat on the floor and Anna opened a handful of new records.

"Do your parents give you the third degree about living with two women?"

He grinned, and said, "Dad and mother are happy for me."

"You're lying." She stopped reading the record and squinted her eyes.

"True. I am. The preacher reminds them every day 'Beau, he's living in sin with those two sorority harlots. How can you allow that to happen, Sherman?' he tells my dad."

"Harlots, huh? What does your mother think?" said Anna, head on a bean bag.

"She's just glad I'm not a POW. And, my mother is more mellow than my father. She tells the preacher to keep his trap shut. Don't judge."

"How do you feel about being with two gorgeous women?"

"I-I-I think it's good for my morale and ego. Make a good story."

She climbed atop him.

"Your morale?" reaching up his shirt. "Are you sure this is good for you?"

"My VA doc said it's good therapy for me." He rubbed a grin into his goatee. "This is good for both of us. You need this as much as I do after your boyfriend broke up with you for some hot pom-pom girl from Ripley on the WVU campus."

"That was cold of Naomi to tell you. I'll get her butt for that."

"Light a candle. Turn up the music."

"Okay. I'll wake her up." Anna cranked it up.

"Turn that down," said Beau, grabbing the knob. "You'll wake up my friend."

"Aren't we just the caring type now, huh?"

"Nope. I just respect others when they are resting."

"You want to squeeze her melons, don't you?"

His eyes popped out. "What? Why did you say that?"

"She has a good body, Beau, and works out like some Olympic athlete on LSD. Be honest, you see here as a hot body, right?"

"Play some music, Anna, will you?"

"Yeah, yeah, yeah. I'm not blind. Cool record collection."

"Thought about being a Disc Jockey, if the Army journalist job didn't pan out."

"I love music," said Anna, dancing.

"I used to DJ in my head as a POW. Music played in my mind and it kept me strumming my air guitar. It kept me alive, I guess. I take music with me, and songs settle me down."

"You have good taste in music. Does it get you in the mood?"

"Yeah. It works when it needs to."

A fine collection of music was amassed by Beau, from the time President Kennedy was inaugurated to the time Nixon claimed his victory, Beau had a passion to work in the music industry. He had boxes of vinyl, boxes of 8-tracks, and his father had collected autographs and records for him while he was at war. Anna spun from the wall to the center of the room and danced to Bad, Bad Leroy Brown, a popular Jim Croce song Casey Kasem promoted months earlier. Blanketed with fascination, Beau lifted the needle in mid-song, slapped on another label and played Nate King Cole's "Unforgettable" and sang the words to her as they swayed in front of an open window.

"Your mother said you had a few records. Beau, she failed to mention how you have a wonderful singing voice and can move."

"You're not here just to sing and entertain, are you?" holding his eyes on her. "What are you really doing here, anyway? Is your father in the legal business or in publishing?" He held out his hand for a dance. "With a year ahead of you to spend your family's hard earned money, why aren't you having crab cakes in Lewes, Delaware, or sipping wine in Hilton Head, why are you in Lansing, West Virginia, dancing inside a renovated farmhouse?"

"Okay, the truth," she stopped dancing, "I had to pee and we stopped at Cafe Le Mans," clearing her throat and coughing out a smile. "I'm here because my bladder was full, and that's the wonderful magic truth of my life."

He turned his head in disbelief and laughed

"You need to pee, huh? My grandfather used to say "anyone who clears their throat has a big, fat awful lie to boast about or they got a frog inside their mouth, Anna, which one do you have?"

"I had to pee," holding her flat stomach. "That's the truth."

Touching her chin, he said, "I don't see an amphibian on that coffee tongue, so you lied again. You were traveling, needed to pee, building your resume as an aspiring journalist, and a singer, and... then what?"

"You have a smart mouth, Beau Le Mans. As I was about to say, a nice looking guy was in his Army uniform and your father kept bragging about how his war hero son was home from Vietnam, half naked by the river, and how proud he was to have him working in his new cafe, far away from the war.

"You have my articles for years? Was that another lie? I hope you choke on the half-naked part."

"That was a plus, hillbilly." She poked his pocket. "Your sweet mother handed me a picture of you, and said "You might like Beau," whispering, "he's about your age. He climbs rocks and I don't know why. My son is just a few miles from here, Honey" and that's the way it happened. She handed me a picture of your green Jeep and I thought about how I'd like to drive it. Well, he's a big time Army hero and that's when Naomi said it might be a good idea to meet a photojournalist from the Army Times, plus I've studied your work in college."

"Well, do you?"

"Do I what?" she was unsure, brow tight.

He held her hands and whispered, "Well, do you like Beau, the photojournalist or is it a big game and another lie?"

"It's too early to tell and it's getting late, so we can talk about it tomorrow," smiling.

"Bet I can do something to sway your thinking." Beau opened the window, waving his unbuttoned shirt. "It's hot, Anna."

"It's too late to buy me a Favorite Day present," she said, eyes smiling and full of life.

He leaned in, kissing her, eyes closed.

"Beau, I lied to you. I'm involved in a relationship, to be married." She spoke real fast.

"Engaged! Naomi said you played games, but I didn't believe her." He stood, rubbing his red face. "What was that for?"

Footsteps echoed.

"What she means to say is," said Naomi, who leaned in the doorway, "I can't do this again, Beau-man, I'm engaged to Naomi's brother, who is an officer in the Navy."

"Naomi!" said Anna, waving her hand to halt her. She walked to the record player and flipped the switch to the off position. "Yes, Beau, I accepted this guy's ring. He lives in San Diego."

"Sailor? Boatman, huh?" Beau sat at the bar and poured himself a strong drink. "You are going to marry a big time Navy SEAL. All this was a big game to you!"

"I'm sorry," said Anna. "He's a SEAL, out to sea for another year."

"You're a twisted liar, Anna!" said Beau, glass empty. "The both of you."

"We lied. Beau, she's badly in love with my brother, and it hurts me to see her love you, caught up." Naomi winked at Anna. Then, she seductively walked over to Beau. "I'm just so surprised she hasn't cried on your shoulder or told you about my brother."

"I've been used. Played."

"Beau," touching his face, circling and whispering, "I'm single and fully rested. We could lie down and dance, or talk all night while Anna writes another long boring letter to my brother."

"What's his name?" Beau studied Anna's face, bent in frown.

"Eddie," said Anna, brightly.

"Robert," said Naomi, laughing. "Robbie, I mean, his name is Eddie Roberts. He's my half-brother, Rob, we call him."

"Well, congratulations, Mrs. Anna Eddie "Robbie" Roberts. You'll be married soon, darling. I hope he "robs" your little heart and sails away with it." Beau poured each lady a drink. "Here, it's a toast of tumblers to liars and lovers, babes to the old. Put both of you together and someday I might get the truth out of you, but I doubt it."

Beau decided to have his own idea.

"Naomi since Anna is to be engaged, we might talk and dance, huh?" said Beau, eyeing Anna for the truth, a lady he'd spent the last month with and thought he trusted her with his heart and life.

"Yeah, for sure. I'll take the arm of the famous Beau Le Mans, the Army hero," sipping her drink and suddenly she hugged her date.

"Let's go to the drive-in on Friday, Naomi. This should be fun."

Excited to see her flirt, he helped Naomi unroll posters into Anna's hands. Together they held Buddy Holly's picture, and quickly shuffled through a stack of Elvis 8-track cassettes.

"Buddy is a Texan," said Anna.

"Yeah, and it's so easy to fall in love," said Naomi. "I love Buddy Holly's glasses and his voice and style will catch on soon."

"He's from Lubbock," said Beau, firing up his cigar. "I'd love to live in Lubbock."

He stepped between the ladies, holding up Naomi's hand. She sighed.

"I want to buy you a cigar in Texas, Beau," said Naomi, arms around his neck.

"I'd like that very much," rubbing his hands. "You know where I'd like to go?"

"Where, Beau?" said Anna, stepping up close, gum popping in her mouth.

"Ladies, I want to smoke a cigar on top of a rock in the Palo Duro Canyon. That's my summer wish, to climb that rock," he said, hugging both ladies. He turned to Anna, who ignored him. Then, his eyes found Naomi. "So, Naomi, would you like to see Texas?"

He had his own game plan in mind. Beau was tired of being played. Naomi just loved men and being with a man drove her crazy.

"I'd love to see Texas." Naomi stood and spun around, and said, "Let go."

"I want to take you," he said excitedly. "I want to take us all the way to the Cadillac Ranch."

Naomi took his cigar, puffing, and sang, "The stars are bright, big and bright, deep in the heart of Texas. Let's go to Texas, then, Beau, I'm in and already packed."

He held Naomi tight and hugged her. But, Beau's big heart was still tethered to Anna. Behind her, in full view, Anna, and she wiped her eyes, crying and walked away, even as he held Naomi.

Facing the glossy window, Anna said, "I'll go to Texas with you, Beau. And kiss you at the Palo Duro Canyon when Naomi leaves you. Who needs to be lied to and tied down in the '70s, right, and miss out on great friendships?"

"You're right, but some of us, counting you, have other plans and games to play with a man's heart, Anna," said Beau. "To be married and live happily ever after in urban San Diego, California, loving a sailor man, huh?"

"I'm taking these sweet melons to bed," said Naomi, hand stretched out, "Beau are you in the fruit business?"

"Go on ahead, Naomi. I don't need to start another war."

He gently lifted Anna's hand from the records and waited to see her face.

"This isn't a game, Beau," she said, leaning on him, "and it's not puppy love."

"You don't have a golden band, so until I see a wedding ring, I'll say you are free in my book."

"But she might be married in her heart," said Naomi, walking down the stairs and she took his hand away from Anna. "She's already spoken for, hero." She slid the cigar into mouth. "I'm not tired yet."

Hopped on the table, and wrapped her legs around Beau. "Let's talk about something else. We could go to Seneca Rocks, rent a cabin and hike. We don't have to drive to Texas, do we?"

"We do," said Anna. "I want to see this canyon with Beau Le Mans."

The two of them played tug of war with Beau's heart. Was it another game, he thought? He stared longingly into Anna's eyes, gently pulling on her long ponytail.

"Well, Anna couldn't answer whether or not she loves Robbie, so I might have to leave my options open since she has declared her love for a sailor."

"O' Beau," said Naomi, rubbing Eskimo noses with the man, "she loves him as much as Jesus and John Wayne."

"Naomi, why don't you just fall on your back and make it easy for him."

"Well, these lips are in love with Beau, and you're telling the truth, sailor's mate." Beau walked over to the window and grinned at Anna. "Wait!" He tugged on his collar. "We were just dancing a moment ago, Anna?" His cowboy boots hit the hard wood in a snap, walking over to where Anna sat, and said, "She's not in love. She's hooked on a feeling and she wants to "Boogie Down," right, Anna?" Beau played right along.

Naomi gave Anna a big hug and whispered in her ear, "I hope I didn't say anything that wasn't true, honey."

"You've had enough to drink, girl." Anna told her. "Go to bed."

"You ladies stay up as long as you want," he saluted. "I'm in the shower."

Five records were stacked in Naomi's arms, and she jumped high into her bed and broke every one of them. Anna rolled her over, face up, eyes half closed.

"Look, Naomi, you're a drunk! You scared him off with all that fake flirting."

"I'm a smoker, I'm a cigar toker, and midnight joker," said Naomi, rolling over on her side.

The ladies crawled into bed, pink wrapped Naomi and baby blue was tied around Anna's waist. Beau held the door.

"Hey, I'm the midnight joker. Good night, Anna." Beau waved and sang, "I feel like making love."

"Good luck with that!" said Naomi, laughing.

Anna turned out the lights, and pushed him out the door.

CHAPTER SIX

Button for a Lady

Sunlight beamed into the front windows of a densely shaded Cafe Le Mans, hidden by stodgy oak trees and rugged rhododendrons in Fayetteville, West Virginia, and sometime after six in the morning the first customer settled down for breakfast. He ordered grilled ham, flanked beside fluffy scrambled eggs, and fried potatoes freckled with salt and pepper. Centered at the bar was fresh orange juice, and hot brewed coffee, dark and favored, was poured as often as he liked. If sugar was rocket fuel, he'd have enough for a Moon landing or two. The warmth of a Monday morning sunshine beamed a yellow ball glaze of life onto the fresh coat of new pearl white paint Beau had spent the spring sprucing up between fishing for trout, and rock climbing the New River Gorge.

Seated before Beau was his pastor friend and counselor, Carl Baker, who cleared his plate before he divulged a single sentence that could be recognizable as the English language and a man generally more understandable during his flashy, long winded sermons on Sundays. However, about the time the school year was over, his contract was near completion, Carl was referred to as the "Earthshaker and Soul Savior of Fayette County" to his congregation.

"Third plate, Reverend Baker?' said Beau, who topped off his coffee cup for the seventh round.

"May the Lord bless, and certainly, son," said Pastor Baker, wiping his mouth. He has no reason for preaching on gluttony and plumpness because he knew God had given him a larger appetite than most people. He was once a smaller man, but his body just grew around his style of eating. "Is this meal free, Beau? I'm accepting gratitude as a form of grace; it's one of the necessaries of life."

"Nope. I bet you had enough dough on the church plate at the last camp-meeting to buy the governor's house and half the Rhode Island Red hens in the hills, huh?"

Pastor Baker lifted his hand across the bar, wrinkled his face and brow, with a tsk tsk tsk sound from his lips, and said, "Don't you begrudge what the Lord gives a shepherd for shepherding his flock again, young man."

"Don't you short change the laborers in the field, either, Reverend."

The man of the cloth opened his greedy hand, dropped a handful of change, slowly quarter after quarter, some copper pennies fell, and the man dusted his hands over the counter and tilted his head.

"There, Beau, will that do?"

"No way. This doesn't look like more than ten percent of the cost of the meal, Pastor Baker. I expect your congregation to offer you a fair tithe on Sunday, huh?"

"What do you mean?"

A quart sized jar rattled when Beau released his hand, flipping the change inside, and twisted the Mason jar, and the First Lutheran Church of Fayetteville building banner fund had a giver. Beau dusted his hands.

"There, Reverend Baker, life runs in full circle, and you reap what you sow, right? That isn't shaken down and running over, now, is it?" Beau threw a towel over his shoulder, a lot like his father when it came to fairness, and slapped his shoulder at the register. "Now is it, sir?"

"No, Beau, it doesn't. Okay, you got me. It appears you did listen at the camp-meeting, huh?"

He untucked his wallet and it was empty.

"I'm a humble man, snappy," said Pastor Baker.

"Everyone knows you keep two wallets, Baker, one empty wallet for show and tell, and one fat wallet for things you covet."

Carl Baker untucked a crisp one-hundred-dollar bill from his fat wallet, and Beau was right. One wallet was thick, and Reverend Baker said, "Take your part for breakfast and a handsome tip, give the rest to the next person who cannot make that broken doorbell ring more than once and greet them with a big bear hug, Beau. I'll show you how the Lord provides for his saints and sinners."

"God loves a cheerful giver, Reverend Baker, see you at the next counseling session and say hello to that lady you're dating in Beckley."

The preacher's frequent smile elapsed and a petulant expression caused his eyes to be less illuminated except when he knew he was in the wrong, beat, and his hands raised in guilt and shame, the pastor backed the door in silence and adjusted his purple sport coat.

"Don't be late for your PTSD meeting. Beau, stop chasing those girls from Morgantown. They'll just get you in a world of trouble, soldier."

"I'm trying to convert them."

The air whistled when laughter burst from his lungs, and suddenly, the man returned for two more slices of cinnamon toast and a red apple.

The glass doors opened and two ladies slipped inside Cafe Le Mans.

"Hello, and good morning," said Reverend Baker, racing to meet them. "Fine, find morning, isn't it?"

Naomi grabbed the menu.

"Surprise, and good morning, Beau and Baker. It's such a lovely day. Chef Beau, where have you been hiding yourself over the past few days, huh?" She clutched his hand at the bar.

See ya, Beau," said Reverend Baker, eyes on the guests.

"Visited my parent's home." Beau confessed.

"I missed morning coffee with you," said Anna, pointing at Beau.

The doorbells sounded as if it was Christmas and two angels received her wings.

"Can I have a hug, Beau?" said Naomi. "I've been very worried about you."

"I like to "play" Chef. Been kind of busy, playing ladies." Elbows on the bar, face tired, Beau popped up in a new white chef's outfit, looking as if the material had just been picked up from the cleaners in Paris, France.

"Where were you last weekend, Beau?" said Anna, taking a seat in front of him.

"Old girlfriend, Beau?" said Naomi, spinning on the bat stool.

"Yeah. Maybe. Play dates and drive-ins, huh?" Anna told him.

"He's in love, love, love, Anna," said Naomi, drawing a heart on a napkin. "He's found a Lollipop for Friday. Might as well drive to Texas, girl. We blew our chance with Beau."

"You know how it goes, Anna, you have a Navy boyfriend, and had a soldier, right? You two enjoy the big house. Won't get by much with the new Lollipop."

Bells on the door sounded.

"Beau, pardon me," said Reverend Baker, who removed his hat. "Is it possible to pick up two apple pies tonight when you close the restaurant? Ladies, pardon me, I didn't mean to cross into your conversation."

"We're fine, Reverend Baker," said Naomi, spinning to see the man.

"You certainly are," said Reverend Baker, winking at the ladies. "And I speak the truth, if you need to be baptized, or married, I'm an expert."

"Reverend Baker, my friend," said Beau, clearing his throat, "these two sweet ladies have already been spoken for and confirmed, and they're fine without husbands, except for Anna, here. Naomi nor Anna haven't had the sniffles since Kennedy was in office, but Anna Katsen, here, is so excited for her new wedding, though. But, I'll have two almost heavenly apple pies ready for you at nine o' clock sharp, buddy."

"Offering my services as a community pastor, Beau," said Reverend Baker, waving. "Have a fine, fine day, ladies. That reminds me. I need to get to the produce stand." The godly man left still waving, window down, hitting the horn on his black 1967 Lincoln Continental. Polished rubber, pearl white finish, the car was as long as Noah's ark.

"Well, well, Beau," said Naomi, "Anna has decided to see the Cadillac Ranch in Amarillo. Sad to say, we will not be staying this summer as planned."

"Broken promises, huh? When are you leaving?" said Beau, looking at Anna's sad face.

"Gotta see fireworks in Amarillo on the July 4th," said Naomi, speaking for her. "After Texas, California, here we come! Muscle Beach, baby. That's my heaven."

"Are you leaving for good, Anna?" asked Beau.

"We never intended to stay this long, but things happened." Anna stood.

"You have your Wyoming County Lollipop to keep you warm," said Naomi. "Anna has Robbie, and we have a tight schedule to get to California. I'm so excited to see the beach for the first time."

"Is that true, Anna?" Beau stood beside her.

"Yeah. We're leaving."

"Got just a few weeks left." said Beau, face worried.

"Yep," said Anna, taking a deep breath. "Goes fast."

"Soon as the money is wired, Beau," said Naomi. "We're only days from being in your memory."

"Let's talk, Anna." Beau held the door.

"No."

"Why?" said Beau, reaching for Anna.

Naomi walked behind them.

"I can't allow myself to." Anna told him.

"See ya, Beau-Man, gotta plan a big trip," said Naomi, helping herself into the kitchen. "Love the root beer float, Beau-Man."

His friends left, jumping in the car, windows down, waving. Beau was broken and slapped the bar.

The double shift drained Beau as his mother and father worked with him from lunch up until seven o' clock, right before his mother baked the prize-winning Dutch apple pies for Reverend Baker. The restaurant was packed until about eight o' clock. Beau wrapped the pies on the front counter by the register and stepped into the kitchen to wash the last stack of dishes. The phone rang.

"Hello, Cafe Le Mans. Hey, Reverend Baker," said Beau, cord stretched in his office. "Yes, for sure. Got two warm apple pies by the register for you."

"Thank you, a bunch," said Reverend Baker. "I'll dance at your wedding, Beau. See you in ten minutes, my brother."

Seated inside the restaurant when Reverend Baker called were two outlaws, the Hatcher brothers, men who had slipped inside when Beau was in the office. The two guys were known to fight and steal to make a living. Their motto was, "Why make it, when you can take it, right?" Two men who were also suspected of murder.

"Todd, it looks like Beau Le Mans wants us to grab apple pies for the road, whatta ya say, brother?"

"Well, Timmy," said Todd, pacing toward the register. The man gently pushed up each sleeve and grinned. "Believe I'll take my pie here."

"Won't end well for you, boys, if you touch my food." Beau told them.

Timmy lunged his hand deep inside the warm pie, scooping a gooey handful of apples, and stuffed his toothless mouth. Both men stood around the pies, grinning, and Todd put two fingers into the second Dutch apple pie.

"Hey, get out!" yelled Beau, running from the kitchen to the bar. "You're the two dirty sons of bitches who killed my brother!"

He grabbed each man's wrist and hit Todd.

"Todd," Timmy said, leaning back and, shaking his head, "for some reason Beau thinks we harmed Wells Le Mans while he was off fighting Charlie? What do you think about that?"

"He punches like a little girl. Don't remember harming anyone of importance, do you, Timmy?" He held his face, lip bleeding.

"My brother's murder has been unsolved for years," said Beau. "You rats know something, huh?"

Each man chuckled and then spat apple pie into the floor. Red flashed in Beau's eyes, and without delay he ran as fast as he could, tackled Timmy Hatcher; one hard right hand busted his nose with a solid blow, cracking his forehead and dropping him flat on his back. Beau punched several more times; blood covered down his chin.

"Todd, get this man off me!" shouted Timmy, kicking. "Get him off of me, man!"

"I got him, brother." said Todd, the bigger one of the two. "I'll break him!"

Suddenly, brass knuckles belted Beau's neck; the fighter fell, dropping like a wet sack of potatoes. Beau rolled, face down, and motionless.

"Out cold. Beau-Man, way to knuckle up, brother," said Timmy, kicking Beau as he stood. "Take the money from the register. Let's go before somebody sees us."

Timmy Hatcher cleaned blood from his face with a towel and threw it at Beau. One claimed the money and the second stepped in the kitchen; two cases of soda were picked up.

"Pies are mine. Six bottles, mine as well, Todd. Killed Wells. Beat up Beau-Man. What a night to celebrate on the river, brother!"

"Do what you want," said Todd, pockets puffed with dollars, and soda in hand. "Ain't nobody gonna stop us if we wanna take something in Fayette County."

Pain thumped inside Beau's neck, which had been bleeding for about ten minutes. He muscled his way up, eyes blinking, and made his way to the bar when headlights beamed at him through the glass window and the horn blew.

"What in God's name have you been doing?" said Reverend Baker. "Cut yourself?"

Beau's eye was injured, dizzy and still bleeding. "I'll kill the Hatcher boys if it's the last thing I do, Reverend."

"They'll lock you up, Beau, ship you to Prunty town." He packed ice on Beau's head. "First, we have no proof of what happened to Wells. I heard the same rumors that you hear. Sin lives on every corner, son. They'll get caught. I know people, just maybe."

"The hell we don't have proof!" said Beau, moaning. "They murdered my brother when he made the night deposit. Timmy Hatcher just admitted they killed Wells."

"Your word won't stand for a second in a Fayette County courthouse, unless it was recorded by the police or witnesses heard something. They'll not admit it again."

"So, what do we do? I know they killed Wells?"

The preacher handed him water and sat beside him.

"I'm more familiar with saving souls than killing people," he said, looking Beau square in the eye. "Don't you do anything stupid, son. This ain't Vietnam; you just can't walk up and kill your enemies. The law protects them more than it does you, nowadays, it seems."

"You expect me to just let them get away with murder and assault, huh?"

"I'll do something, Beau, and let God do the fighting. I'll handle the Hatcher Brothers. I'll solve it. If that doesn't work, do what you have to do."

"Scripture says to leave room for God's wrath, Reverend." He pounded the bar several times, and said, "I'll do my part one night, too."

"That Baileysville Rough Rider brother, Wells, man, he was the fastest tailback in West Virginia in 1970. Listen, Beau, if you take revenge into your own hands, you'll go to prison, right away, son. Sometimes I wish we could take an eye for an eye, but that's out of reach."

Reverend Baker cleaned up the apple pie mess, mopped the dining area and talked to Beau, like his son. Another car pulled up in the parking lot. A figure materialized out of the car and a big man ran inside, a raincoat covering the person's head.

"I called your house," said his father. "Anna said you hadn't arrived home yet. What in the Sam Hill happened to you, Beau? You're bleeding, son."

"The Hatcher boys jumped Beau, Sherman," said Reverend Baker, seated, gripping a mop. "They admitted to Beau that they killed Wells, bragging."

Sherman sat beside Reverend Baker. With the ice removed, Beau's face had three bad cuts, bruised neck and ribs, and his eyes would soon be the color of coal.

"Knew it was them! That's all I needed," said Sherman. "Hot damn!" He stomped his way into the kitchen, "Lord, yes, yes, yes, answered prayers. We can finally put my son's murder to rest. I knew it, knew it, knew it, the Hatcher brothers are no good rats. Where are they now, Beau? I'll kill them both. He pulled a gun from his office."

"Back down, Sherm!" said Reverend Baker, grabbing his arm. "I can't allow this to happen. No guns." He stopped Sherman at the door, spinning his revolver.

"It's time for them to meet their Maker," said Sherman. "Good as dead."

"Dad!" said Beau. "We need to be crafty about all this."

"No, no, no, stop it, Beau and Sherman!" Reverend Baker locked the door. "There's a better way. I don't want to think about any premeditated murder. It'll destroy my career and your cafe."

"They destroyed my family," said Sherman, getting emotional. "Killed my son."

"Tell me anything that's fair in this world, Reverend?" Beau became loud. "They killed my brother and laughed about it."

"You'd feel the same, Baker, if it was your boy, right?" said Sherman, pleading his case. "But you can't do a thing about it. The police can't do anything about it, either."

"Guys, listen!" Reverend Baker raised his hands, "No. You're right. We can't make this go away, but God can pull things and surely do His part. He'll be honored in the process. Beau, hand me a couple of good pies and let's go home in one piece, see you two in the morning. Promise me, you won't do anything stupid, huh? Let me fix this mess, please."

Beau and Sherman sat and nodded, halfheartedly.

"Don't go telling a bunch of folks until Reverend Baker fixes this mess, okay?"

"Yeah, Dad. I got it."

"Men, I gotta get to Beckley. Let me think this over on the drive and I'll fix it when I get back tomorrow. Dang it, Beau, thank you for the pies."

"Here," said Reverend, "they'll need to be warmed."

"Thanks, Sherman. When you steal and kill, expect the same," said Reverend Baker, the man's face turned red. "The Hatchers have a death wish."

"Call me in the morning, Baker," said Sherman. "Beau, maybe you need to take Anna and Naomi up on their road trip to Texas, and stay out west before this gets out of hand, huh?"

"After I see my brother's killer jailed," said Beau.

"Tomorrow is your birthday, Sherman," said Reverend Baker, as the big man walked between the two men, arms around their necks. "And I expect you two gentlemen to be in my church bright and early for prayer on Sunday."

"Good idea," said Beau, who started his Jeep and watched the reverend drive away. "Dad, I'll pack for Texas when this is solved. Will you and mom be alright with the cafe, if I leave you shorthanded?"

"Yeah, Beau. We handled the cafe while you were in Vietnam. You need to cool off before you do something stupid and wind up in prison."

"Do you mind if we take the '66 Chevelle to Texas?"

"What? That fight must've knocked something loose in your head, boy."

Beau laughed and so did his father.

"Yeah. I can see you driving down Historic Route 66 with a blonde in the front seat and a brunette in the back seat.....I-I-I know what image that portraits in your mother's eyes, Beau."

"Bull-bologna, dad." He waved at him, rolling in the parking lot, "You might be a bit jealous, huh?"

"Hey, that '66 Chevelle is in mint condition," shaking his hand. "Keep it that way."

"I'll shine it up, send you a postcard from Texas."

"That's a deal, Beau. Take a good picture of it at the Cadillac Ranch."

CHAPTER SEVEN

Night of Surprises

Owls sounded in a symphony of cadence atop the mountains. Above them, in their own world, he counted seven aircraft across the dark canvas sky, blinking red in flight and a white line tailed each aircraft. Shooting stars blazed and stretched as the endless galaxy floor, which became a carnival of entertainment between earth and sky. The show only happened once, but Beau witnessed a rare masquerade of delight in Fayette County, West Virginia. What was once a dim and desolate home at night now glowed at the end of a country road, stunningly alive and alluring because of the sagacity of two women, who had made him shape a healthy grin on his face. Two ladies unselfishly agreed to care for Beau. After a week of healing and medication, Beau was eclipsed by the new arrangement of a magical residence, even reading the house number to make sure he was at the right place, home. Beau slowly paced into a world that had moved on without him, a privileged world of pleasure and appreciation for taste and style and pattern, wrapped in vivid designer curtains of floral colors, yet manly, comfortable Carolina furniture, and imported rugs, rugs too glorious to be marked with foot traffic. The new arrangement was meant for musical space, for song, for dance, and for movie auditions. The home's new aroma and vibe shouted elegance, along with ambiance and functionality. Aromatherapy lingered inside the window seals, and a small table waterfall brought the outdoors inside a grand living space. A kitchen table where he had once wolfed down corn flakes was now a journey of provisions, such for a larger crowd or a traditional gathering or sadly, a going away party, perhaps.

Who was coming and how many people? The mayor, the governor, or a king and queen, all would have felt right at home beside him and his friends from Morgantown. Not just from the glow of the residence but room-to-room, floor-to-floor, all were decorated for dining and entertainment. No more playing baseball inside, he thought. Modern designs hung in sure radiance and fashion that would last beyond his generation, causing him to greatly appreciate his guests, and his jaw-dropping response, soaking up the high-life like a puppet on stage when he flipped the lights on and off to make sure each room wasn't fantasy or a God-sent dream in the night. All of it was real and tangible.

No objection or resistance was given by Beau at his silent reception. Naomi waltzed in, dropping handfuls of petals on his pathway, and soft flowers preceded his steps on the hardwood floor. He mumbled and stuttered. Naomi stood close and gently covered his lips with her fingernail and discouraged his voice. They joined arms, silently strolling, while Beau followed her lead, faintly hilarious, taken on a tour, heads angled in awe, eyes popping, as she dragged him through the spectacle glitter of animation, still life pictures, landscapes, and a stunning capriccio of wheels and flowing waterfalls. Her brief journey with Beau had ended in the lavish great room, escorting him to the splendor, the most glorious part of the tour, where someone waited.

"Anna?" said Beau. "You did this for me, huh?"

"Yeah. Your mother said, you wouldn't mind some recon," said Anna, pleasantly. "The place could afford a young woman's touch, so to speak."

"Mighty women," said Naomi, adjusting her sparkling dress, hip and bosom. "The two of us had a few ideas we mixed together and this place was the perfect palette to express our artistic designs."

"Showroom style." Beau circled the room, noticing similar patterns and styles, backtracking until he returned to Anna's side. "Hope I can afford it."

"Your mother and father covered the cost," said Anna, arms stretched out. "You can hug them in the morning."

"Can I hug you now?" said Beau, finding her eyes.

"Start with me," said Naomi, standing in heels, arms out wide. "Oh, my feet hurt; I'll be in my room, babes, if you need me."

Naomi dimmed the lights to where Anna and Beau, standing alone, became dark figures in a grand room, and then she dashed upstairs in her bare feet. Naomi knew Beau was more attracted to Anna, more than puppy love, so she surrendered.

Beau was alone with Anna, something Anna had planned from early morning.

"You look remarkable in that sparking jade dress."

"Thanks. Something to drink, Beau?"

"Yeah. You know my favorite. What's the special occasion?"

"I wanted to do something that would make you remember me."

With a paroxysm of surprise, Beau closed the gap between them.

"Where are you going?"

Her eyes stared without a sparkle.

"We had a good time, Beau. Naomi and I are headed to Texas in the morning. Her father leased a large place somewhere in Robin's Egg, a town away from Bishop Hills. We will retreat and write as planned."

"Robin's Egg, Texas, huh? Heard of the place. So, in other words," he said, hands gripping the tall ladder back chair, "Reverend Baker would say this is our last supper together." Beau's quick humor broke the somber moment, bending smiles. "Amarillo, huh?"

"This summer has been magical, Beau." She said passionately. "I had no idea when we stopped in your quaint town to powder our noses, that I'd be so attached to you."

"Perfect timing, I suppose. Have you thought about us, I mean, beyond this summer, Christmas, vacationing together, and even more?"

"Yeah. You have your family here, the cafe, and let's not forget your prissy lady princess in Wyoming County, with Hollywood green eyes, and her figure makes me sick, so jealous." Turning to watch the rain shower on the widow, she walked away. "She's a keeper, Beau, with her seductive smile that goes on for days and gags me."

"I suppose we have got close. Lovers even?" He walked up behind her and touched her neck. "I've given you the space you needed over the past week, to plan for the sailor and a big wedding. Something you were struggling with, something you didn't want to talk about. I suppose it's your decision to marry the sailor or not, huh? I'm a soldier, on solid ground, and a land lover. Mountaineer."

"You're a lover, all right."

Beau sat inside the large, bay window and rubbed her shoulders as they watched a full strawberry moon relax above the mountains and drift away.

"Puppy love?" He whispered.

"Real to the puppy. Hmmm." She sighed and closed her eyes. "You sure know how to tempt a lady."

"We've had a remarkable friendship? Do you want a life together, start one?"

"It's not about what I want, this is about my fiancé. It's what my parents want."

"You say you believe in God, Anna, so you must believe the Lord intervened and stopped you in my town for a reason. How can you deny that part of your so-called summer fun?"

Anna walked to the next room. Beau followed her, handling a Charles Krug Cabernet, and promising thoughts made him chipper, so he poured her the glass first.

Her eyes sparkled.

"What would happen if you joined us in Texas, Beau?"

"I'd never leave your side. That's my word for you, here, and in Texas. I can come in the fall. We'll write."

"I'm not sure I can say yes until I speak with Naomi, having you join us in the apartment this fall."

"Well, I guess I'm going to Texas then." He laughed, glass to his lips.

"You're one cocky country boy, aren't you?"

He kissed her.

"Naomi whispered the plan when I walked in the front door. She's not a sailor's fan."

"You think you're cool, don't you?" she said, pushing his shoulder. "She doesn't mind being called the "biggest flirt" in town, you know."

"I've heard much worse from her."

She held her glass with both hands.

"This may not be the best plan in the world, Beau, but I do see your point about divine intervention. We're not in control of our lives, are we?"

"Nope, not really," said Beau, sitting beside her. "Vietnam might have taught me that much. So, if I told you "No," what would you do if I stayed here?"

"I'd be highly disappointed." She nodded. "I'd respect your decision, though. Follow your heart, and if I'm not in it, you stay here, and know I'd miss the love of my life. Let God control you. Pathways are just decisions we've decided to chase. You do have a choice. Naomi has given you a room in Robin's Egg, Texas, or will you stay in Fayetteville?"

Beau took a big gulp.

"The ball is in your court now, soldier, huh?"

"I'm not playing. My family is here. Brother's murder is unsolved."

"You won't, Beau. I mean, you won't follow me to Texas, will you?"

Beau stood up and held a picture of his Wyoming County beauty. Held a picture of his brother in his football uniform. Tears broke the corners of his eyes.

"I have better things to do than to be a tag along with someone until your Navy sailor comes to town and you run to San Diego. My heart strings have been played, Anna. "

"I can't help it." She held her face and pushed him away. "I love two good guys. I'm not sure what I'd do." Her head dropped.

"Anna. I don't play second fiddle and I don't like to play the fool."

She stomped upstairs and packed her bags.

"I'm going to your mother's house," said Anna. "I'll talk to her about all this."

Twenty minutes later, the ladies met Beau at the threshold. Naomi walked outside.

"You had the open door, Beau, and you closed it. Always remember that about me," said Anna, bags packed. "I care for you, but I'm leaving."

"Well, I expect it takes some time to appreciate a man who has treated you better than your own family. Why didn't you decide to marry the officer at the Naval Academy, on that weekend fling in Annapolis? You chase popular men, those in the paper and try to call it God's intervention, Anna."

"No. It isn't like that," she said, hand on the Monte Carlo, "and you know it, Beau." From inside the Monte Carlo, she shouted, "Don't expect a call from Texas."

"Stay, Anna," said Beau. "Let's eat and talk this over."

"I've lost my appetite!" said Anna. "We are over, Beau."

Beau slammed the house door, turned and eyed the long dinner table, and said, "It must have taken days for her to collect the recipes, baking and making this meal, all of it for me, a simple going away celebration. I blew it."

CHAPTER EIGHT

The Great Gus Silver

Dinner and desserts lined from one end of the table to the other, rolls and cornbread, turkey and dressing, mother's Dutch apple pie, and father's pickles, and every kind of bean a man could want. The oak table was decorated in linens and bows by Naomi and the curtains and large floor pillows were hand selected by Anna. He was too disappointed to eat alone. In the mirror, lost, his reflection gave way to the image of a British butler, dressed in black and white, tie in a knot, Winsor cut collar, the kind of a discreet servant would wear, and so he adjusted his tie and prepared to serve himself.

The doorbell rang.

Beau quickly swung open the door. A tall man stood in everyday jeans, hands down, and waited on the grand front porch.

"Pardon me, sir," he said, speaking politely as an educated man. "I'm Gus Silver."

"What's up, Gus? I'm Beau."

"My group is in a bit of a dilemma. We're lost. Cafe Le Mans is closed. They're hungry. Could we have some water for the kids and we will be on our way?"

Beau stared at the largest vehicle that had been parked in his driveway. The bus was painted with traditional school colors of red, white, and blue; horses ran down each side, themed in Old West and patriotic, and yet stars and stripes weaved into the painting.

"How many kids are on the bus, Gus?"

"Twenty."

"Twenty, huh?" He slapped the shoulder of his new friend. Beau paced around the long bus, like a game show host. Windows dropped, and he saw bubbly-freckled faces, head after head, popping out, like a nest of small turtles. Beau and Gus stood, counting heads and faces on one side, the same amount on the other. "I have a meal prepared, Gus, and it's still warm."

"God does answer prayer, Mr. Beau."

A loud roar came from the bus, the same friendly celebration echoed inside his head, smiling faces, images of "Welcome Home, Soldiers!" banners flashed, waving colorfully, the same when he rejoined his unit in Vietnam, and he was truly at home.

By this time, Gus paced to the bus door, the sprinkling rain had stopped, and the kids were loud and obnoxious. His crazy time in Basic Training at Fort Jackson, South Carolina ran through his mind, when he observed behavior of disrespect.

"I have a little treat for them," said Beau, stepping on the bus.

"Sure," said Gus. His hair was thick and long, and his nerves were shot, being the only adult on the activity bus. "See what you can do with these animals from Pittsburgh." This summer youth crew stuff is for the birds, Beau."

"Listen!" He yelled. "I'm Beau Le Mans, owner of the House of Food and Surprises." The kids gasped. Beau stood inside the vehicle, whistling and holding up both hands. "Eyes on me, soldiers! You in the back, talking, turn around, up here, mister! What's your name, anyway?"

"Name is Shumate, Marvin Shumate," said the stocky teenager, with a shaky voice, popping bubble gum on his lips when he walked, causing a riot with his peers.

"Okay, Mate, you're my leader tonight." The kid was cocky and sure of himself, which reminded him of his younger days, reckless and untamed. "You're in charge, Shumate."

"That's a bad choice," said Gus, anxiously. "Pick someone else, Mr. Le Mans."

All the kids laughed. Beau whispered something inside his ear, and Marvin became a drill sergeant. Shumate took charge and snapped the students up and into attention, forward march, marching the students into the dining area, and each one stopped behind a chair at the table. One empty glass, utensils, pearl white napkins, and then appeared Beau, a man unsure, but he did it, anyway. The cupboard had the exact number of plates and glasses that sparkled under a string of patriotic woven lights. Each one had their own seat.

"How was that marching, Beau?" said Marvin Shumate.

"Outstanding!" He returned. "You're a born leader, Shumate."

"Take seats," said Marvin.

Beau handed out the sides of creamy mashed potatoes, green beans, and golden buttery corn on the cob. He carried out the main course of fat turkey, handed out glazed country ham, smothered cheese over elbow macaroni, along with toasted bread rolls as big as young pumpkins. Marvin, Gus, and Beau served more than water that night. Glasses of carbonated drinks, purple punch and pink lemonade, and long curly straws touched hungry lips of red.

For dessert, coconut cream pie, Boston Creme pie, and Dutch apple pie, with whipped cream, and cherries, for those who desired tall toppings. Beau brought out the ice cream machine, with only three flavors: strawberry, chocolate, and soft-serve vanilla. Food fit for a King and a Queen, and a farmhouse of servants, for Beau, he had no idea how Naomi and Anna had gathered and prepared such a delicious feast for him. Some of it would not have made it overnight, if it wasn't for Gus and his bus full of happy and hungry guests, food would have been lost.

When the meal was gone and the dishes were cleaned, the time had concluded.

"How did you pull this off?" said Gus, shaking hands with Beau.

The smallest and youngest one of the bunch, tugging on Beau's shirt.

"Where are the surprises, Mr. Le Mans?"

"What's your name, son?" said Beau, who bent down and whispered his answer.

"David," said the boy, who stood with his arms at parade rest.

Beau stood in the threshold of the door to his surprise room.

"I have twenty surprises ready for you and your friends."

He had not misspoken, lined with the epiphany of truth, and meant to keep his word to Gus and his crew. Behind chairs, Shumate snapped the team into attention, marching them to the grand living room. Inside the room, his brother's toys and pictures of professional baseball players stood beside autographed basketballs, and posters of football players. Small planes, Army tanks, and aircraft, all polished, sat alongside leather footballs, and signed baseball cards by Mickey Mantle, Babe Ruth, Stan Musial, Yogi Berra, and others. Things he'd collected, and found, hundreds of items became surprises, lined in glass showcases and most hung in dusty frames by teams.

"Gus, with your permission," said Beau, "each young man can take one surprise."

"Permission granted," he said, and nodded.

"Why would you give away your collection?" said Gus.

"What is a collection, Gus, without friends? It should be shared with good boys?" said Beau, smiling. "I'm happy to do it." Beau announced, "There's only one rule, though."

"What rule?" said David, politely.

"The rule is, you have to tell me why you are picking out the one surprise. What is the reason or motive behind your choice?"

Gus and Beau invited each kid into his game room by themselves and seventeen kids were going to take Beau's valuable collection to the pawnshop. Gus wouldn't allow it to happen, returning each boy to the bus for being disrespectful and ungrateful for the gifts of a Vietnam War hero.

"Please accept my apology, Beau, for their lack of manners." Gus rubbed his head, face red, sweating as if he'd exercised. "I hoped there was at least one kid on my bus who can relate to the value of a man's prize possessives. I swear there has be a boy taught better."

Two more brothers walked through the door with autographed baseballs. They planned to trade the gifts for bicycles as soon as they got back home.

"Get out!" shouted Beau, lips tight. "Who's next?"

"Little David." Gus held the boy's shoulders.

"Well, send him in, Gus." Beau took a seat, smiled happily as the door opened, and was curious to hear what the polite kid, the new leader, had to say for himself. "What's on your mind, David? What gift would you like to pick?"

"Sir," said David, with his thin outreached hand. "First, Beau, Sergeant Le Mans, I'd like to thank you for serving in the Army. I know all about you. I know being a prisoner must've been tough in Vietnam. I'm sure all the guys already told you how they appreciate your wonderful feast tonight."

"No. You're the first to add a compliment, David," said Beau. "Thank you."

Tears rolled down the cheeks of the youngster, ten or so, in front of Beau and Gus, who looked at each other, faces puzzled. Gus shrugged his shoulders.

"What's wrong, David?" said Gus, hand on his back.

"I know who you are, Sergeant Le Mans," said David, wiping the tears from his eyes. "I should've said something sooner, maybe when I first got here, but I didn't."

"How do you know me, David?" said Beau, knitting his brow and leaning forward to hear what he had to say.

"You see, me and my grandfather followed the story of "The missing in action Army Journalist Beau Le Mans" in the jungle, and that was your story on television. I hated the mean guys with guns, and how they had soldiers chained in camps."

They sat at a small table. Beau scratched his head and was stunned at David's memory and interest in missing soldiers.

"You watched my story in Pittsburgh with your grandfather, huh?" said Beau, shaking his hand and hugging the small framed kid with teary eyes and sandy hair. "Your grandfather must be a good man."

The boy pulled out a military book of newspaper clippings, some were several years old and others were from the late '6os.

"Cafe Le Mans was closed. I knew it was you when we pulled into the driveway and you walked out with your dog to the bus." His face curled and tiny teeth shined. "But I almost didn't recognize you in the butler's tuxedo uniform."

Gus and Beau laughed when the boy snickered and his cheeks turned red.

"I'd sure like to meet your grandfather for making this binder of newspaper clippings for you." Beau reached his hand out. "Do you mind if I look through the pages while you pick out a surprise?"

"Sir, I don't want a gift. My grandfather found out we were stopping for dinner at the Cafe Le Mans in Fayetteville. He made me bring it so I could get your autograph. Would you mind signing this page, *Christmas in Chains*? My grandfather was in Pearl Harbor when the Japanese bombed his ship."

"I am sorry. Sure." A tear came to Beau's eye. "Better yet, take my Army hat. I'd be proud for you to have my hat, the one I wore in Vietnam. Give my number to your grandfather. It'd be my pleasure to write a story about him and his time in Hawaii."

Beau tucked the pages inside the album, and fat tears fell again. David slid on the Army hat and smiled.

"You're the best, Sergeant Le Mans," David stuttered and his small hands wiped his face. Beau slapped his hands, and a giant grin stretched across the boy's face. David saluted Beau and returned to the bus; arms tight around his album.

"Beau Le Mans, I cannot believe I had a chance to eat a meal with you, a real war hero." Gus walked to the front porch. "You're a true patriot. First class, buddy. Welcome home, soldier. We take trips like this one every summer, but this one has been the highlight of my career. The pinnacle was meeting

Dolly, down in Pigeon Forge. But you ran a close race, my friend."

"I liked to meet Dolly in Tennessee. Hey, Gus, the pleasure has been all mine."

The kids were piled up inside their seats, bellies full, half asleep. In a certain farewell, David waved at Beau and his German Shorthaired Pointer pup, Cooper, and the journalist gladly returned the salute, being in good company made his day. The red taillights on the bus disappeared into the silvery fog of the mountains. When, eight hours later, the warm sunlight beamed through the farmhouse window, Beau was excited to share the experience with Naomi and Anna. The kitchen was spotless and the feast was consumed, as if it were a new home on display. He had made his decision to apologize and start over.

At the kitchen table where Beau meditated in early mornings, he brewed coffee and crunched on biscotti, and noticed a piece of paper purposely tucked under his wiper blade on the Jeep. Perfume coated the folded letter, a bold reminder of a wonderful summer with Anna Katsen. Clipped at the foot of the note was a shiny Cafe Le Mans pin. With the letter in hand, he checked upstairs in Anna's room, Naomi's, but both were empty and the beds were made. An empty feeling crossed him, like when he left Polly at the cave. No, it was a true reality and he felt guilty. He called his parent's, and his mother spoke about how the ladies left before daylight. The Monte Carlo was nowhere in sight. From the porch, eyes down the driveway, his body dropped and he sat in dismay, holding the letter against his face, mapped in anxiety and dread.

***

Dear Beau,

These last few months with you have been out of this world. Your generous personality pulled me in, cruising in the Jeep, swimming in the river, hiking trails, climbing rocky cliffs, nights under the stars, and you're a bit of a parade, Beau. You have made happy memories and beautiful pictures, the ones I will take with me to Texas.

Last night I fell into a deep sleep, dreaming of a man who was wearing blue, not Army green; He was a sailor and not a soldier. I'm sorry to have to tell you this in a letter. My decision is to move on without you in my life; it's the most difficult heart-wrenching time I've ever dealt with. I don't know if we were right or wrong, or how I will feel next week or next month, but time apart will help me clear my head in Amarillo and find my heart again.

Naomi and I decided to leave early from your parents' home. In my dream, I kissed your sweet head for the last time. At that moment, I fell apart, rushed out, and penned this letter instead of telling you goodbye in person. I have decided to stay in Robin's Egg. The long distance helps us both forget about this summer, begin again, and start new lives as if this summer never happened.

Naomi said you are an amazing man. You are truly a man of character and to lose you, will be my loss and I know it. I have to try to move forward.

You will find love, so treat her well. Let this letter be our farewell speech. We made great memories, Beau. Never forget the night by the river in sleeping bags, and how it made you feel deep inside, carry it with you. I feel the same way.

Love Always,
Anna Katsen

***

He spent the entire day watching Anna change records and dance inside his shattered mind. In his record room was where she practiced ballet steps, slowly dancing, and a long kiss would soon follow; one lasting moment faded with each passing day, the good kind, the moments he held onto inside his broken heart. By midweek, he remembered her warm touch on the sandy riverbanks and under the starry nights, positioned, close and personal, until being awakened by a buck and a doe swimming across the New River. On the other hand, distancing herself became a reality, honoring her own plans with a sailor she'd dreamed of marrying when she watched the Navy Midshipmen outscore West Virginia as a kid, as Roger Staubach marched past the Mountaineer defense in the fall of 1963. Life had not changed for her.

Planning to march on his own journey, Beau gained the strength and courage to forget about the summer fling with Anna, and how she made him feel. What more could he become with encouragement, climbing rocky cliffs together and building each other up with sincere confidence? The time to let go, struck him, and the rope was cut.

He paced from the porch to the hayfield, walked with his dog around the property line, fed his horses, fell asleep under a tall row of seemingly endless persimmon trees, and his heart was defeated. At sundown, he built a fire and camped and counted stars to remember his wonderful night with Anna. Was she counting the same stars, he thought? Without a drop of desire in his tank, he recalled their first night alone at his home:

"I'm glad we are friends now," said Beau, words in a whisper.

"Me too. Do you like music?"

"Yeah. To break my thoughts from Vietnam, I'll play Duke Ellington, Louis Armstrong, and Billie Holiday. Hope you like New Orleans style jazz. I stack jazz high, and have over a hundred vinyl records beside the turntable, go, help yourself."

"Naomi hates jazz." She examined his collection. "But I love New Orleans jazz and how the smooth saxophone sings to my soul, tapping my foot, just frees my thoughts with a euphoric sensation, I softly fall asleep."

"We have a lot in common," said Beau, flipping the wool hat on her head. "You make Bruno Capelo look cool, man."

She gently placed a fedora on his head.

"The underlay matches your cool blue eyes, Beau."

"One of a kind, Doll Face, the smoothest wool you can find in the Great South, and it was made on Saint Charles Avenue, downtown New Orleans."

She snatched his golden sunglasses, too. In a seductive movement at his place, the lady slowly adjusted the lens and temple tips around her face, loosening her cinnamon hair, a colored style she favored, down to her shoulders.

"We'll be friends for a longtime," said Anna, finding her reflection in the wall mirror, "as long as I can wear your hats and adjust your tie in the morning." She sniffed his cologne.

"Make yourself at home," said Beau, who stood behind her. Their faces saw each other inside the frame of a wide mirror, and for the first time, he felt comfortable and relaxed beside a lady. "How long are you staying, by the way?"

"We just planned to powder our noses and leave. Now you, handsome you, made me want to stay." She pranced around the room and looked at his military medals and awards from the Army. "Then... we're headed to the Cadillac Ranch, near Robin's Egg, Texas."

Beau slipped behind her in an oval mirror, smiling as if a camera was pointed at them in a Valentine's Day kissing booth. She wore blue jeans, white shirt, smooth and tied around her hips. Her cheeks had small dimples. His attire was a baby blue shirt, half buttoned, draping over his shoulders, and he stood equally impressed, holding their pose. She jumped beside him, arms locked, and was riddled with genuine happiness.

"Robin's Egg, huh?"

"You should visit Robin's Egg sometime, Beau."

Five days had passed since Naomi and Anna had left West Virginia for Texas. He'd predicted they'd made it and hoped the phone would ring. His eyes closed, blanketed by a deep depression, harboring a burning sadness, yet silent, like he had never felt before. Other than being a prisoner, it was the lowest point of his life, wishing he was in Texas. *What will I do with myself,* he thought?

CHAPTER NINE

Crestfallen

Two more weeks had passed; the friendliness that richly hummed regularly inside of Beau Le Mans, known among friends, was gone, and his ways were of a crestfallen funeral director. The chipper, smiling-eyed journalist whom so many people loved and admired, was reserved and lived in regret. Folks drove miles and miles to meet and greet a war hero at Cafe Le Mans. They worried about his PTSD and sadness. Ten minutes into the conversation, Beau would have drifted off, pacing before them robotically and lifelessly, a shell of his former self, drifting into the past. To him, the mirror reflected a giant, shutdown fool, a quitter, stumbling over thoughts, letting her go, and a summer of memories and warm moments, the ones he wanted back. Was he the guy who jumped around from one thing to the next, he thought? Maybe Anna was right?

Customers gossiped to his father, Sherman, when Beau's downhearted disposition appeared so obvious at the restaurant, it brought discontentment. The slump reminded Beau's father of the dreadful time the barber had taken his handsome hair and turned his head, a boy of eight, into a slick Crenshaw Melon. That's when young Beau rubbed his head and felt he wanted to be a fighter, a soldier, mean and green from Baileysville. No different from Samson when he lost his long, wavy hair, and how the internal spirit and strength vanished from him according to Scripture.

Sherman summoned his wife to the kitchen.

"Is Beau's PTSD taking over his life?" asked Sherman, gripping his face. "I don't get that boy, dear. He's played the field and now it's time to work again."

"Leave Beau alone," she said, standing beside him at the sink. "He's lovesick, Sherman. Love sick, love sick, love sick, that's it. That mountaineer lady took his heart and soul and crushed it. Now what can he do? He's alone."

"We are losing good customers due to his pathetic behavior towards a girl he knew for two months," whispered Sherman, rolling his eyes. "He wasn't this shaken when he was stuck in the POW camp with a gun to his head, I bet."

"The problem is," she replied, lifting her hand, "did you remember what it was like to be in love, head over heels, stuttering to me, with roses and thorns inside your hands, sweetheart?"

"That's not fair, honey." He stopped washing dishes. "We'd known each other for three years."

"You don't get it, do you?" She crossed her arms. "It's not a term in office; it's about having the ultimate feeling for each other. Depth, Sherman, not length of time on the clock."

"I don't get him."

"It's not a lease. That rare, soul wrenching, connectivity feeling, and that's the missing link of love. You hear it every day on the radio, in love songs, heartfelt poetry, and cool lyrics. You were once the predator in love, right?"

He dried his hands. She bumped his shoulder, grinning.

"You think Anna is the 'other half of him,' the woman Beau can't live without?"

"I was lovesick over you when you flew with your father to Honduras, rode a horse to buy your coffee beans and set up a deal with farmers, to get three diners started."

He opened a sack of coffee, sniffed a handful of beans, and closed his eyes.

"My Le Mans Coffee Company has made us some big money. I remember that, and you're right. A guy must have someone to love and share his life with." he whispered. "They both had each other brewing, don't you think?"

"Yeah. I remember you being gone for a month, writing letters and calling long distances to tell me about your day. That's what love means, you care and you show that you care." She poured her coffee and added cream and sugar. "I knew exactly when you were the other half of my heart, Sherman. Here's your coffee, honey, warm to the touch, just like you love it, Sugar."

"Hmmm, *yeah*." grinning. "When did you know about us?"

"The dance. The kiss. That thing you did to get my attention." Knitting her brow, she puckered her lips and kissed him. "Don't you walk away from me, Sherman Le Mans!"

"I can still kiss you." She hugged him.

"Beau? Hey, Beau-Man." Sherman was in the doorway with lipstick on his face.

"Yeah, what, sir?" He stopped what he was doing to listen.

"You and I need to talk tonight after work, okay?"

"No. I'm busy, Pops." Beau bused a table and whispered to his father. "I don't want to talk about taking over Cafe Le Mans in Oak Hill or Sutton."

Sherman walked over to where Beau stood and blended beans in an old-fashioned hand grinder and watched his son.

"I can't hear you over the blender!" said Beau. The machine stopped.

"Your mother thinks you're lovesick over Anna. Is she right?" said Sherman. "You're too good for her, Beau. She cheated on the sailor, right? She lied and played you. Played us all."

"Maybe. Anna was too good for most men," said Beau, pouring water into the coffee maker. "She was a manipulative little brat, yet stunning."

"Beau, like it or not, we're grabbing a bite later and having a chit-chat, the old father-son talk, so plan for it, bud. We haven't had one since you left for Vietnam."

"I still remember the talk in 1968." Beau handed him a look-alike, jet-black Honduran coffee and a spoon. "Try my blend, old man. It was too long ago, and your speech wasn't that good to begin with."

"What? You know better." He held Beau's shoulder when he turned away, grinning. "That was a life-saving talk, Beau, and a good M-16 brought your butt home from Vietnam, didn't it, soldier?"

Beau's left eye closed. His shooting finger twitched when he thought about the Vietnam War. Clouds in his coffee reminded him of smoke, forty rounds, load and reload, and he spilled a few drops on the bar. The First Team found him floating and knocking on Heaven's door, dreaming in another world, Eden, perhaps.

"Son?" said his Dad, rushing to the bar. "Your hands are shaking."

Sherman grabbed his son's frozen arm, and pulled him out of his trace. Since being home, Beau had drifted off into the world he had left behind in Vietnam, a normal process for transitioning soldiers to normality. Some agreed to go back to Vietnam, fighters. But, Beau, he had other ideas since his brother was killed. He was locked to finding out who the killer was in Fayette County. Sherman carried him to a booth and alerted him of where he was and what had happened.

"Beau," said Sherman, talking in an Irish accent, "are you up for the Dublin Grill, you remember, Big Mike?"

His deep, thundering voice said, "Welcome to Dublin Grill, Le Mans! I believe it was for my going away party."

His father interrupted him.

"Yeah. It was your 18th birthday. And, now, for sure, we celebrate today," said his father, poking his arm. "Before you shipped out for the Army. I had to carry you to bed."

"I remember," said Beau, hand on his face.

"By some miracle you crawled your way upstairs, shoes untied, but still on your feet and you rested. When you got to the second floor you slurred "Airborne daddy on a one-way trip, Airborne...Airborne... Goodnight, Big Daddy!"

"I remember waking up, head pounding and starving. My stomach was sick."

The waitress from the Dublin Grill walked up to the Beau.

"Can I take your order?" she said. The pretty lady held his shoulder, blinking her soft green eyes at the former mean and green soldier, and leaned on him with both elbows, chewing gum.

He dropped his mouth, "I'll have ..."

"Don't mind him," said Sherman, watching her eyes scan Beau. "He's not used to carbonated beverages. He's more of a sparkling water kind of guy."

"Nope. Not this time, Army water. We'll have two pints of Dublin's finest stout, and make both as cold as Iceland, please."

"He was a POW," said Sherman, nodding. "Let's make food and drinks for Beau Le Mans. One shot for the great times; one to bring home missing soldiers."

"One for yesterday, the next for tomorrow," said the waitress, pouring and sliding the glasses between Beau and his father. She lifted the brim of Beau's baseball hat and flirted.

"What are we toasting tonight?" said Beau.

"They won't be toasting to Wells Le Mans," chuckled a guy at the end of the bar.

"Todd Hatcher, huh?" said Sherman, nostrils flared, sporting a half-cocked grin.

Beau jumped up.

"Hold on, Beau!" said Sherman. "Our time will come."

"We're funnin' you two slugs," said another man, face greasy, and half drunk.

"Timmy Hatcher, huh?" said Beau, gripping his glass. "This is a gold mine."

"Yeah, lucky me," said Timmy Hatcher. "We saw a blue '66 Chevelle parked outside, just had to join our friends for drinks, because..."

"Just because," said Todd Hatcher, lifting his glass. "We wanted to see if Wells Le Mans would join the party." He held a stone-cold pose with his fist. "But wait." He spoke slowly, "Oh, Wells, Wells, Wells, boy? Where are you, Wells?"

"Bet I choke him, Big Mike," said Beau, hands on the glass handle."

"Ain't heard anything from Wells in years," said Timmy Hatcher, brushing beer from his lips, bent in laughter behind his dirty hands.

Big Mike, the man who owned the Dublin Grill, heard the conversation from behind the bar, cleaning glasses, rushed in, and shook his fist in the faces of the Hatcher brothers. The two brothers were known to slip out the back when their tab was heavy or when a fight broke out.

"Ten steps to the door, Timmy," said Big Mike. "Grab the arm of your bigmouth brother, take him outside with you."

The brothers ignored Big Mike, clamming up. They hoped he'd walk away, but Big Mike, arms out, wasn't known to get lost. And he wasn't the type to let hotheads overtake his Irish establishment and harass the good citizens of Fayette County. The art of disrespect brewed the blood of Big Mike, and when he was ignored by the Hatcher brothers, he became more heated. That's when Big Mike reached under the bar, cocked the sawed off shotgun and aimed the firearm into the face of Timmy Hatcher.

"I told you to take Todd and get out of my face!" Big Mike's voice would've turned a grizzly bear back into the woods.

Timmy dropped ten dollars on the bar and flipped his finger up. He nodded to Todd who gulped the last sip, and eased out the back door. In the doorway, he shouted, "We didn't finish our conversation, Beau and Sherman, did we?"

"Boy, those pies tasted expensive, didn't they, Todd?" said Timmy.

"Gave me bad gas," said Todd, robbing his palms.

"You would've wanted to hear my part, Tommy," said Beau, standing.

The door slammed.

"None of my business, Sherman, but do you think these two boys committed murder?"

"Yeah, for sure," said Sherman. "Bet my life on it. They jumped Beau and admitted it, weeks ago."

"Me too. Sorry about those crooks, gentlemen," said Big Mike, "but I hate the ground those guys walk on. Called the cops on them a dozen times last year."

"Well, Big Mike," said Sherman, sliding a coaster under his glass, "You've heard the last of those two rats. They won't bother anyone tonight."

"Rats, like the Hatcher's, find the time to trash talk," said Big Mike. "You don't have to say it," who cleaned the bar and polished empty glasses, "but who was pinned with your brother's murder? Wells, he was here the night he was shot, Sherm. So were the Hatcher's."

A giant lump formed in Beau's throat, the kind of lump that took shape at funerals and when a man lost his child in the delivery room. The Army man drank and sat in silence.

"The murder is unsolved," said Beau, spinning around to Big Mike. "My brother was killed when I was a POW, and still no witnesses have stepped forward to claim a reward."

***

Beau faded back into his bloody days at the POW camp.

"Henderson?" said Le Mans, eyes glossy. "You got any brothers and sisters?"

"I'm a loner," said Henderson. "My father was a rounder, cards and women. Nobody ever said that I had a brother or any sister."

Beau remembered playing baseball in the front yard.

"Catch the ball like Yogi Berra, Wells."

Beau cocked his arm, and stepped toward home, kicking his leg high like a major league pitcher and threw it to Wells. His brother caught the ball like a pro.

"Dang it, Beau!" yelled Wells, knees in the dirt. "You throw like Whitey Ford."

"You keep it up, Wells, and you'll play minor league ball in Bluefield."

"You pitch and I'll catch for the Orioles, Beau." Wells told him, popping his mitt.

***

"To the best of my knowledge, Big Mike," said Sherman, he began awkwardly, and in a slow voice, "Wells broke down after he left here, and the Hatcher boys stopped to help him, at least that's how they told it to the deputy. I believe they robbed him and killed him."

"I swear," said Beau, hands tight. "I'll call the grave digger."

"Had to be a weapon matching the shooter's gun." Big Mike stopped and listened.

"Bet the police never searched Hatcher's car for a dang weapon, did they?" said Beau, twisting his seat.

"I heard they did," said Sherman, fingers raking his beard. "Found nothing."

Mike tapped Sherman's shoulder.

"Here's some money," said Sherman. "Good food, but the Hatcher's have cranked my stomach into knots."

"I liked Wells," said Big Mike, handing a drink and some to Beau. "You men eat here for free. Keep your money, Le Mans."

"We pay our way, Big Mike," said Beau. "My brother was a cool guy, stubborn as heck, but he was well-thought of in these parts."

The mental pabulum between the men about Wells and his baseball and football potential made for an evening of flipping toothpicks and good talk. They told tall-tales, and how Wells followed the great C. C. Ryder on his motorcycle trips, claiming Namath made the best film since "The Wild Angels" and how it topped theaters in 1966. Big Mike talked for an hour about how Wells Le Mans was the caliber of Jerry West, but his temper cost him a scholarship at West Virginia in the State playoffs in 1970.

"We have had a heck of a good time tonight, Big Mike," said Sherman, drying his lips, as he dropped a generous tip inside a Mason jar. "Gotta start early in the morning, scrambling eggs and making gravy biscuits for the monthly news reporters breakfast at the cafe."

"Been an absolute blast, Sherman," said Big Mike, who stood in the doorway. "Beau, we need to bird hunt that full-blooded pup of yours, soldier. Stop in anytime and let's talk about some pheasant fields."

"You're talking to the right man, Big Mike," said Beau, hand out. "I'm a crazy bird hunter, dog man."

"I had a cousin die over 'Nam," said Big Mike, hat off, and resting his back.

"We'll have to do this again, Mike," said Beau, saluting the Warrant Officer, who had served in the Korean War. "Help me get dad inside the car."

"If I had a dollar for every time I had to carry a man," said Big Mike, grunting.

Sherman belted in the passenger seat. Beau pulled out on the highway.

"I love the way this car handles," said Beau, who spotted his father falling asleep against the window.

"Hey, Pops?"

"Just let Sherman sleep it off, Beau." A man rose up from the floor in the backseat.

"Timmy Hatcher, huh?" His eyes split time on the road and in the rearview mirror.

"Thought I smelled something."

Timmy rammed the pistol into his neck.

"Me and my .38 Special, do whatever we want, Beau." Timmy bumped the barrel a few times. "Drive this damn car to the Cafe Le Mans, crack open the safe in Sherman's office and, uh, there better not be any funny business or Sherman dies, just like Wells Le Mans bit the dust with this gun, accidentally, of course."

Beau slammed his brakes. Timmy busted his head, when he mouthed off. Sherman had passed out in the passenger's seat. Beau had no witnesses to Timmy's confession to murder; the shaking of an earthquake could not turn Sherman back to his memory of the drive to the restaurant. A black 4x4 truck followed them.

"Timmy," said Beau, "rumor is, Todd can out shoot you with eyes closed."

"Todd Hatcher couldn't hit a big red barn the night we fought Wells. I had to handle the business, hit him, and shoot Wells on my own terms, doing it my way."

"So, ... you are the dirty bastards who killed my brother." Beau, red faced, eyes of a warrior, slammed his foot on the throttle, hitting high speeds."

"Damn you, Beau, slow the car down! Hey, I'll shoot you!"

"You'll die, too, when we hit the trees!"

Less than a mile away from Cafe Le Mans, Beau slid off the pavement, turning into the gravel parking lot. Timmy cussed him with every breath. Beau parked the Chevelle, and the black parked, and Todd Hatcher jumped out. Timmy slammed the door on the Chevelle; Todd rushed over to the driver's side and hit Beau with his fist.

"Did you kill Sherman, Timmy?" said Todd, sweating, and looking inside the car.

"Not yet," said Timmy, pushing Beau. "Sherman passed out."

"Good!" said Todd. "Fat Sherman won't get in our way. No witnesses tonight."

After Beau opened the front door, he walked by the front counter, and flipped an emergency switch, one that rang the police station and Reverend Baker's home, who lived in a parsonage, less than a mile away. Beau knew one of them would be alerted to the cafe at midnight. Most people knew the restaurant closed at nine o' clock sharp.

"Walk to the big safe, war hero." Timmy slammed Beau in the back of the neck.

"War hero, get us some money!" shouted Todd, chuckling and kicking Beau.

Nerves simmered, legs ticking like a second hand on a clock, and Timmy nervously changed hands with the gun several times. Halfheartedly, Beau manipulated the safe like a baby with a new toy, killing time and hoping his father or Reverend Baker ran inside. Down in the floor, he failed several times, and on his third attempt, he groaned and wheeled the door open.

"Look at that dough, would ya?" said Timmy, sweat on his face. "Hand me the bread, Beau. Out of the way! Cover me, Todd."

Todd walked to the kitchen, snooping for food. Timmy turned his eyes away from Beau. That's when rage popped inside the soldier's head, fist tight, first strike, and Beau kicked his ribs three times.

"I'll break every bone in your body!" yelled Beau, hands hammering Timmy's head.

"Todd!" yelled Timmy. "Help me!"

Beau was taught in the Army to impact pressure points, landing punches in the chin and abdomen. The act of self-defense worked, but Timmy escaped before Beau could slam his knee out of socket.

"Fight like a man, Hatcher!" shouted Beau, locking his neck and arms.

"Tommy!" said Timmy, face against the wall.

"I got him!" shouted Todd, arms cocked, hammering Beau.

The three men saw the diner lights flip on, and the room glowed. Without a moment to spare, the man rushed across the cafe, caught Timmy blindsided, and knocked his gun out of reach.

"I-I-I-I-I hate you, Hatchers!" yelled Sherman.

"Waited a long time for this," said Beau, uppercutting Tommy's jaw.

"Pow!" One man was dead. "Pow!" A second man was shot in the chest. "Pow!" Three shots were fired by the time Beau and Sherman saw the shooter.

"Hit the outside lights, Beau," said Sherman. "Timmy's dead."

"Todd's dead, too," said Beau, checking his pulse.

Beau rushed to the outside door.

"Reverend Baker, it's bad," said Beau, who watched the pastor's body slide down to the entrance of Cafe Le Mans.

The sheriff rushed inside behind Beau.

"Beau, I settled the score for Wells," Reverend Baker whispered. "I loved that boy." Reverend Baker spoke low for a minute. "That's for you and Sherman, too." He closed his eyes, said, "God forgive me."

Blue lights blanketed Cafe Le Mans. One important thing happened that night, the sheriff asked Reverend Baker why he'd shot the Hatcher brothers. They believed his word, just as if it was one of his earthshaking Sunday sermons. Beau told the sheriff how Timmy had taken him hostage at the Dublin Grill. Sherman went into shock, when the ambulance arrived, and the stone faces of three dead men resting in peace, blanketed on the floor, had caused it. Hard knots formed on Beau's head and a red towel enveloped his forehead, but, for the most part, his injuries were minor.

The next morning Sherman and Beau gave additional statements to the Fayette County police department, and no one was charged. The cafe was closed until the police marked and collected needed evidence. On behalf of Wells, Sherman agreed to keep the restaurant going on the same schedule. His wife needed time to process the loss of their friend and the family pastor, Reverend Baker, who was buried in the Lutheran Cemetery, less than a week from the horrific night at the cafe.

After fishing, dinner was a common occurrence at Sherman's house on Friday night. Beau and his father spent the evening thankful and supportive to each other, watching the Braves play baseball.

"Dad, I have a question: Why did Reverend Baker risk his life for us?"

"Cancer."

"What does cancer have to do with it?"

"He felt lying down his life was easier than the burn of chemo and radiation treatments, I guess. The doctor gave him a short time, just three months. He died for us."

"I feel guilty for giving him such a hard time about his second and third plates," said Beau, hands on his head, leaning back in the booth.

"Beau, he knew you were just pulling his leg. Give people a little time to impress upon you their thoughts and differences. Abe Lincoln told how he didn't like a particular man, so he planned to spend more time with him and get to know him better," said Sherman, getting up from the booth.

PART III

272

CHAPTER TEN

↔

Robin's Egg, Texas
Labor Day, 1974

His right forearm was inked with fat letters - **Infantry**, left with his brother's name, and the most difficult memory to swallow, one Beau's stomach turned over and over, when he drove into Texas, more than the war in Vietnam, his brother. He thought of Ben "Caveman" Henderson and Sam "Law" Lawrence, and stories that each man told about how he was proud of his hometown - that is why he made the drive to Robin's Egg.

There was a second reason he came to Texas. Love. No sign of Anna and Naomi at their apartment when he arrived in Robin's Egg, his first stop, so he had one more destination. Rusted cars and trucks, all needed work, abandoned, hoods up, lined ranches when he arrived at the farmhouse on a hot Robin's Egg morning. He tapped the screen door, like he was checking the ripeness of a watermelon. Two cats scurried across the front porch when the wind picked up in North Texas and he'd startled them. Just like an alarm in the morning, a friendly Lab dog barked when the screen door rattled, and the pet walked to the door and licked his hands. The soldier scanned the neighborhood for someone working outside. Aside from birds and chickens in the front yard, nothing more than cows and horses moved on a dusty ranch, one in the Panhandle of Texas, anyway.

"Anyone home? Hello?" said Beau. "Paradise found, and he stood on the other side of war, just like Caveman talked about." I can see why Ben liked it here, he thought.

When his voice sounded, a young boy looked at him who had a curious stare. His hand was on the dog's collar and the lad disappeared into the back of the farmhouse, and maybe he was a scout like his father was, years ago.

"Hello, young man." His voice sounded low and pleasant. "Anyone home?"

A sweet lady's voice sounded, and the radio died.

"Just a minute."

Beau could not see her face, from the bottom floor.

"Yes, ma'am, it's Beau Le Mans."

She stood at the top of the stairs, adjusted her clothes, and said, "If you are selling anything from Montgomery Wards or Sears, just turn around and go back to where you came from in Amarillo. I don't have any extra money."

"No. I'm here to see you, in private." His teeth shone and hair parted short and neat as if he'd been to church. "Never been a good salesman, anyway."

"Taxes were paid last April." She walked slowly to the door.

"Not a tax man." Beau found her eyes smiling back at him. "Not the milkman, if you still need to guess, lady, I can go all day with the same answer?"

The boy reappeared at the end of a dim hallway, being pulled around by the jet-black dog who had licked Beau's hand. The lady stopped and stared at Beau. Face serious and cautious and then she walked slowly down the steps in a honey red holiday dress. Beau's dark sunglasses fell against his chest. His dad's voice sounded in his head: "Son, you better watch your step. Anything red, be it a stove or a lady, is subject to burn you."

"I'm sorry. Do I know you, sir?" said the lady who held the door. "Wasn't expecting anyone today."

They saw each other through the screen door, and her face curved happily.

"No, we've never met. What happened to your eye, Little Red Riding Hood?"

"Oh, my ex-husband. We're still working things out."

"You mean, punching it out, huh? He doesn't seem friendly."

"Not all the time. But it's nothing."

Beau walked inside the door and reached for her face.

"A shiner looks like something." He leaned in, and said, "I was a good friend of your husband."

"Do you know Roland?"

"Nope. I don't know Roland. But I was a friend of Ben Henderson."

"Oh, you knew my first husband, Ben Henderson. Roland was the next man on my short-timer's list." Her hands waved over to a nice sofa. Beau was being licked by the dog again. "So, uh, that makes me a low-down, dirty divorcee, doesn't it?"

"Not to me."

The dog jumped on Beau's hip.

"Take that darn dog outback, Benny," said his mother. "He's romantic."

"Let's go, Wolf. Come on, boy." Benny pulled the dog outside.

"Well, I'm here because I made a promise to Ben Henderson." In Beau's hand was an envelope.

"What was the promise?" She held her chest.

"The promise was from soldier-to-soldier and happened in the midst of war," said Beau, hand on his chest. "I said I'd give you something from Ben Henderson, if I ever made it to Robin's Egg, Texas. I'm here for the first time."

Beau scanned the wall and recognized pictures of Little Benny as a baby being held by his father Ben Henderson. The hot room had a round mirror, a small black and white television, a few paintings of Jesus, and a large rug where the dog had returned to sleep.

"Well, uh, Ben and I split before he left for the war."

He nodded and brushed his mustache.

"We fought together in the jungle. Had lots of crazy laughs together, too." Beau handed her the picture given to him by Ben Henderson under the bridge. "He was the toughest POW I served with in the Army."

"Did you see him die?"

"No. He went missing."

She took a seat on her small, green sofa and held the picture, crying. Beau moved beside her, letting her have a moment. He walked around and spotted albums on a record player and more were stacked on a bookcase. Photos of Benny were atop the television.

Brushing her thin tanned face, she asked, "What part of Texas are you from, Le Mans?"

"Not from Texas," he said, hands atop his knees. "Call me, Beau. I drove from West Virginia to see you."

"Wow. Virginia?"

"Nope. West "By God" Virginia. Not Virginia. After high school, I joined the Army in 1968. My grandfather left my father a string of cafes in West Virginia." Looking around the room, he added "It's a long way to Amarillo, and up to Robin's Egg."

"For God's sake, what are you doing in Robin's Egg, Texas? What's the special occasion, Beau? I know you didn't come all this way to hand me a picture. You could have mailed it, right?"

"No. Sorry it took a few years. I promised Ben. I had to deliver this picture in person back to you, the rightful owner." Beau turned around and faced her. "He said he loved you and Benny, more than anything in the world."

She wiped her eyes and hugged Beau, kissing his cheeks, and he waited in shock.

"He was the most stubborn, hard-headed, S.O.B., good-for-nothing, two-timing lying cheater I knew. Missed me, huh? He wasn't missing me when he went behind my back and slept with that floozy Susie who worked at the Sundown Drive-Inn in Amarillo. I caught them in our bed."

"He told me he screwed up and you divorced him."

"Shouldn't be putting our business out on the street, but I'm sure he told you about his late-camping trips to the Palo Duro Canyon."

"Some."

"She was a red lipstick slut, and had a dozen just like him on her tail. Little Benny was just a year old or so when we divorced. Then, Ben got mad and joined the Army. I never saw him again. He's Missing in Action. He left his insurance to his parents. Not a penny of the government's money made it into my purse. Is that love, Beau?"

"I'm sorry he left you high and dry."

She cleaned her face, eyes to her necklace and looked at Beau, crying in a mess.

"You knew that stubborn goat well. He didn't mention being in love with any lady, only you."

"He had his own way with women, didn't he? O' boy, he had a string of babies."

She walked toward the kitchen, and said, "Yeah. How about some Texas sweet tea, Mr. Beau Le Mans from West Virginia? Hope you love sweet tea; all we got in Robin's Egg."

"Yeah, for sure," he said, touching the dimple amid his chin.

"Well, where is my manners?" She poured sweet tea into tall glasses. "I'm Jeanette Renee. Pardon my red dress and tears, Beau. It's for a job interview this afternoon."

"I wondered when you might offer your name." He sipped his tea. "Good tea. I'm sure you'll land that job." He adjusted his collar, "You sure make that dress beautiful."

Lifting her arms and fanning her powered face, she opened the back door to the kitchen for a cool breeze. "We have no air conditioning, can you believe how hot it is? This job would buy us some cool air and fill the Frigidaire. Little Benny, he tossed and turned all night last night with the windows open. Must've been a blazing hundred degrees last night."

"Let me look in town, see if I can locate an AC unit, huh? How about that?"

"Oh, no, no, no." She stared at him, nodding and waving her tissue.

"I insist."

"Well," said Jeanette, smiling, "Benny would love it, though."

"When I last saw Big Ben, well, his face just melted when he talked about you in Robin's Egg, Texas, seeing you and Benny on his next leave."

"He remembered his ex-bride, huh?" She touched her eyes. "The Starr Pharmacy has cool air and keeps my makeup from running, so all the women want to work there." Grinning, she added, "But I can't ask you to do that, Beau."

"I think I saw a place with units on sale, Jeanette."

"Yeah, Ben Henderson, could fix anything," said Jeanette, fanning her face. "Can you tell me what happened to him?"

"We escaped the prison together. Ran the river and trenches until the bitter end. We'd made it, just the three of us. Freedom. Sam Lawrence, Ben Henderson, and myself escaped. It's the least I could do, install a cool unit, you know, to show you how good of friends we were in Vietnam and what he meant to me as a friend."

"I'm not asking you to, Beau, but, boy, it'd be nice to have AC in the room upstairs."

"You will have cool air tonight. I'll make it like an iceberg."

She opened the living room door.

"God bless you. Hmmm, will an AC unit fit in that beautiful 1966 Chevelle?"

"I'll have it delivered."

"Nonsense." said Jeanette, hand on her hips. "Let's swap vehicles for the day. You can drive my truck and I'll take your Chevelle, right?"

He finished his glass of tea.

"Do you always think ahead, like this?"

"Yeah. Quick on my feet." She laughed, arm on the door frame.

"I'll install two AC units, one upstairs and one downstairs, hmm, if you will have dinner with me tonight, Jeanette Renee?"

Pacing toward him with a large pitcher, she touched his cheek, humming, "Well, Mister Beau Le Mans, that's a deal I won't pass up. Cool air and a cool guy." Adjusting her dress, head tilted in the mirror. "Where's the key to that Chevelle, Mr. Beau? I've never driven a Chevelle before and I've always wanted to."

"Here, Jeanette. Try to keep it under a hundred. I know how Texans like to drive fast, take a rocket to the moon and back."

"That Chevy will help me look first class, Beau." She turned the keys on her fingers. "I'll tell you how it runs when I get back, in record speed, I bet."

Pointing at the boy who stood watching from the hallway.

"What about Little Benny, where will he stay while you're gone?"

"His Granny lives in Bishop's Hill, not two miles from her, and she watches him while I look for a job. Benny, let's go, little man."

"I'm ready." He walked out and had the face of a young Ben Henderson. Their looks were uncanny. The boy didn't say a word.

Walking up next to her, opening the car door, he said, "We'll have dinner, say seven o'clock, huh, and I saw a good steak place in town, will that work?"

"Yeah, dude. No one cool has asked me out in ages." She slowly turned to him and slid her hand down her pearl necklace, said, "Heck, and maybe, it will be a new job celebration."

"Yeah. Hope so. We might be out past Benny's bedtime, so, well, you may need to rely on his grandmother until after midnight."

"Don't make promises you can't keep, Le Mans. You must be planning on a nightcap, aren't you?" said Jeanette, eyes steady.

A smile ran across Beau's face and he held the lucky button on his shirt.

"We'll see. I'll pick you up at home, and I'll be on time."

She cranked the motor and Benny jumped inside the fancy car.

"You better be, Beau, but I might surprise you with a new job."

"I hope so."

"Wait and see, country boy." She tipped her dark sunglasses.

CHAPTER ELEVEN

↔

Twenty Years Later,
Take a Look at My Life, 1994

He lit a match to fire up an old-fashioned oil lantern on his Texas patio, traditional and rustic. Beau dropped the long stick into an empty tray when his wiry face reflected the glow of pure blue and aged eyes on the glass vase. He watched the wavy dark smoke cloud roll and fade away above his head, and Cafe Le Mans, the place he sold, and the loss of his dog and parents over the past two years crossed his mind. Beau adjusted the small dial and looked at the lady journalist who had visited his ranch from West Virginia, where she examined a handful of Vietnam maps. Other places tumbled through Beau's head, sporting younger clothes. He never saw himself as an aged man, but the years flew by, like a jet plane over an Amarillo sky.

"Katie Collins, you're here to interview me about Vietnam, huh?"

"Yeah, if you will cooperate."

He laughed madly. "I'm not sure I'm a good fit for this project."

"Don't try to back out now. I'm here and you're here. My time is two weeks, and you better not clam up on me, Dr. Beau Le Mans. I need a session of total recall from you."

"I'm not backing out. Okay, shoot, let's get this show started. War and women, huh? I did things, the things I needed to do in Vietnam, just to stay alive."

Katie leaned back and crossed her legs.

"I need to know about the fighting in Vietnam and if you had a love interest while you were there. My research includes your love interest as much as it does your time at war. It's about "How Soldiers Impacted Women of Vietnam," okay?"

"Yeah. Strange topic." He adjusted his shirt and tied his loose shoe.

"It's not strange. Women had relationships with American soldiers and that is part of my cultural assignment for next semester."

Beau snapped his head up.

"What does my love life have to do with the war?"

"My research is entitled 'The Cultural Impact Vietnamese Women Had On American Soldiers While Serving In Vietnam,' so can you help or not?"

"Yes, for sure. It's my pleasure. And you're a feisty lady." His face was colored in a wide grin.

She stared at the page and back at Beau, and waited for an answer.

"Well, good. It looks like I'm off to the races, huh? My paper includes interviews and a mountain of research."

He paced nervously around the room.

"This paper will have a strong presentation for you." He nodded several times. "You're welcome to write whatever you like," he said, crossing his arms. "Polly was the only lady who had any impact on my life in Vietnam. Katie, she was sadly killed, though."

"I'm sorry, but sir, Dr. Le Mans, please don't jump ahead. Okay?"

"Yeah, sure. I'll snap to it."

The year and the town he last saw Polly was clear in his memory and he showed her on the table map, talking about a specific timeline as a POW.

"Polly was a wonderful lady. She knew love and so did I. Life was random and adventurous in my early twenties, sowing my wild oats, but she wasn't one of them in a POW camp. We never dated, but she has always meant something to me. After the war, I finished my education at Texas Tech University, trying to make something of myself in Lubbock, and forget my time in the war. I visited Vietnam after the war in 1979."

"They say war is something that can never be erased from a soldier's mind. Do you agree or disagree?"

With the palms of his hands, Beau pressed his face and slowly descended his hands, forehead to neck, leaning into the past.

"I agree. Not sure if being something is a good thing, sometimes. However, being a good professor makes me proud, time in service, tough times, were times that shaped my soul and broke an arrogant young man. To break a horse, makes it a better horse, but the horse still remembers his times jumping and bucking his way around the barn."

"Professor Le Mans, hey?" said Katie, tapping her pen. "Would you tell the story from the beginning, exactly as it happened? In all due respect, put down the Ed Roth rat rod magazine and don't leave out a single moment. Two weeks, that's all I've got over Christmas break to make you a better horse."

Beau laughed no differently if he'd been seated beside Johnny Carson.

"You have my attention, little lady."

"With all due respect, I say, sir, your story reflects my grad school grade, sir."

Laughing, and a bit distracted about where to start, Beau rolled his finger over the mug handle, dragging the warm glass over the table of his Robin's Egg Ranch, Texas home and he told how he bought the place from Jeanette, Ben Henderson's first and ex-wife, years earlier. He watched the sun melt away into the December horizon and in deep thought, Professor Le Mans brushed his mustache and rubbed his wiry beard, over and over until he stopped and stared at her. He pondered answers to questions he thought a man, one who lived a private life, should not have to deal with once he'd moved beyond a certain age in life.

"I'm not sure a college-aged lady from WVU can handle my stories, the trenches of war and the cracks in bad relationships. The death of someone I cared about, Polly, cuts like a shape, jagged knife."

"Try me, professor. I've flown a long way." She stretched her grin. "And we don't miss much in Morgantown. Same as Robin's Egg, I suppose. What was her full name again?"

"I only knew her as Polly. Vietnam. Here was the location of the camp. No, the war does not leave a man and neither does his heart accept farewell. You could type a chapter about Polly's nature and beauty. Can't believe I never got her last name. Vo, that was her married name."

"I bet Polly was something else if you're still speaking about her twenty-five years later."

"She was the best person I never had the pleasure of fully knowing. I was curious and the world was different, way different for us both, years ago. War made us different, and without it, we would've shared the same things. The chemistry was there, but we never had a chance to talk and mesh our lives, the way couples wanted. Candlelight and a late wine."

"I know, sir, and I could finish the good thoughts in my mind."

Notebooks lined the kitchen table and her word processor snapped under her fingers. The kitchen reminded him of the eleven years he spent at TTU, framing degree after degree for his office.

"You'll want to take good notes, gal, I mean, Katie. I only have a short time to tell this wonderful story." He stared across the long range of his land, where the wild wind pushed tumbleweeds through the thick mesquite trees to the endless posts and fences, electric fences that surrounded the farm and touched other cattle farms, even larger tracts. Dust lifted into the high clouds, horses raced across the land, and a herd of cattle divided the other half of the ranch. A mule was in the middle. Cactus and mesquite trees tried to outgrow each other on the ranch. "The world is a cold, cold place, gal. Thank God for good people, especially you, who can hone my spider's web of a life into a suitable Vietnam story." He raised his mug.

"I have figured you out, sir."

"What? Figured me out, huh, in just a few hours, Collins?"

"Yeah. You're not much different than other young men, soldiers on the hunt for another beautiful lady to brag about with the guys. A score, a good one, a little snatch on the side, you know, and tell a good story over beer and pretzels, right?"

"Wrong. I don't care for pretzels." He told her.

"At the end, we'll see if I surprise you," whispering, pushing her glasses, "and we'll see who was right about the ladies and the pursuit of happiness."

"Yeah. I think we both might embarrass each other. Do they say "snatch" on campus, Katie?"

"They say worse. And, I hope we do, Dr. Le Mans." She insisted, adjusting her shirt, prim and proper, attentive to his movements, facial expressions and the cocky pitch of his words. She noticed him and documented his behavior, jotting down his look and story, down to his buttons, and how to push them to land a good story, too.

"We were talking about Polly." She told him, arm out.

"Polly is a popular and plain... but a very pretty name. People make a name attractive or not." He nodded and remembered her face. "You want to hear about the '60s and '70s, Vietnam stories, and how I got to Texas, right? I live for my research, little lady, pick your poison, right? My glory days and the dirt of my life, it has been about Vietnam, some in the papers."

The camera clicked, rolling tape, and Katie's hand panned the frame at him purposefully.

"I think the world wants to hear me from Robin's Egg, the whole story, from POW soldier to Tech professor."

"Start with your reason for joining the Army, sir."

"You're a peculiar lady, I'll give you that much." He lifted up and respected her time. "Let's start with my love life, I mean, begin with the impact of Vietnamese women on American soldiers. I only had one experience in that area."

She eyed her watch. "To be honest, I'd rather write about your relationships over boot camp. I need more than a sentence or two about love. Most young men have no game, anyways. And, you didn't even get her last name, Player."

"You are a bit salty." Dr. Le Mans bent over. He belted out a laugh that the lost horses from a hundred years earlier could've heard outside Amarillo.

"I'm sorry, Dr. Le Mans. I shouldn't have said it that way."

"You're a bit of a smartass college writer, aren't you?"

"That's what real men like, right, sir?" She tapped her lips with the pen. "A big challenge."

"Not all of them. But, some do like social pressure. "Hello, haven't I seen you in art class before, Susie Q?" She mimicked a guy's voice. "That's about a useless pick up line. Men, they're so predictable and sad."

"Who taught you to be sassy, huh?"

Katie crossed her legs and said, "You also dated Anna Katsen, the lady who was at Woodstock, right?"

"Yes, I did. We met her in 1974. She stopped by Cafe Le Mans, in Fayette County, West Virginia, which was a fine cafe and had a good powder room. We lived near the New River Gorge Bridge."

"I love that bridge."

"We were attracted to each other on the first day. I lost track of her. Married a sailor, or a dog catcher, I think. Anna loved a Frogman, she said. Last track I had of Anna, yeah, it was mid-1974. She stopped in Robin's Egg, Texas, and wrote the first article about the Cadillac Ranch and the Ant Farm guys. I followed her here, asked around town, but she'd left before I arrived. Then, I matriculated to Texas Tech. There was talk about her and her friend, Naomi, taking off to San Diego. Mrs. Jeanette knew her for only a month or so. Anna and Naomi had rented a place from Jeanette's father, an apartment. If you want to see the ranch, can we take a short break?"

"No." She popped her neck. "Maybe on another day. Let's try your fireplace, right now. I need to keep typing and making notes."

"Good. Let's get this story down."

"On second thought," said Katie, stretching her arms, "let's have an intermission." Katie closed her notebook.

They told stories for an hour and flipped through old photographs, a bit sidetracked, and relaxing, but much of what was discussed covered his time during the Vietnam Era, so it was okay. After a short trip from the kitchen, he paired a bottle of chardonnay with slices of creamy goat cheese, a pod of sweet, seedless grapes, alongside oranges, red strawberries, blueberries, drizzling honey, and the star of the plate was a chocolate covered pear.

"Now I know the horses didn't teach you how to place a charcuterie board, now did they, Dr. Le Mans?"

"Anna Katsen taught me more than I'll ever admit about a charcuterie board."

"She seems like a sweet person."

"Manipulative and evasive. Sweet, it's on the list somewhere. Our friendship sadly faded in the summer of 1974. I had more to give. The last I heard, she was an Adjunct Professor at Fairmont State, or was it Glenville State?" He chewed a blueberry. "She was a berry."

"Nope. Neither. You're wrong. Dr. Anna Katsen was recruited by WVU, and has taught journalism and communication in Morgantown for the last decade."

"What a berry? Well, good for her little, sweet self." Dr. Le Mans crossed his arms, and his legs followed, and his lips puckered in jealousy and surprise.

"She's one of the best in the nation," said Katie, hand aimed at him.

"That's not what I heard. Back to your research, Katie," said Dr. Le Mans, eyes cut in a grudge, "well, West Virginia has sent several students to my ranch in the past ten years, you're the first female student I've proctored in Texas."

"Ladies are more inquisitive than guys. College guys are more like green horses than steady mules. Men stick to the facts, screw things up and write bad notes, not from the heart. I want the emotional truth and the good stuff, Dr. Le Mans. I write stories that make people realize they're still human, lively stories, and from the soul, but, um, upbeat and care."

"The war was not upbeat." His glasses dropped down on his nose. "The war and Anna took my heart away. I've been more reserved in my relationships because of her."

"Lost your touch, huh? It happens to men you age. Don't you bottle up on me. We need the whole enchilada. Spill the beans, professor."

"Don't print that I lost my touch with women, okay?"

"I won't say a thing."

"It's not true."

"I understand denial."

He paced around the room with a handful of berries and chewed.

"Denial? We've had too much war and not enough love in this world. Communism and oil, that's all we fight about these days. Real estate. Power struggles. Star Wars. Global warming. And who is going to break down a wall and build a better mousetrap, huh? Everyone has a better mousetrap, you know that, Katie?"

"Yeah. My trap includes your cheese and wine. Keep talking, Doc."

Despite Katie's laughter, the image of his love life with Anna was clear in her mind and what he told was documented and remembered. Katie's soft voice, lingering perfume, sparkling jewelry, made Beau Le Mans covet his youth, longing to be young and passionate once more, just another day with Polly or Anna. His heart had been a tug of war for each one. How was Anna doing? Was Polly alive? Did she live through Communism? His thoughts left the battlefield and his first love, a Vietnamese lady, still softly drifted, a picture perfect memory rolled inside his head. He thought about calling Anna, to see if she had thoughts about him? The closeness of friends, the ones he had never forgotten or spoken about in years, warmed his heart, years earlier and still did. Ben Henderson. Polly. Cadeo. Hien. Sam Law. Anna. Naomi. He'd never had close friends in Texas, like the ones he had during the early 1970s, as a young man in Vietnam and West Virginia. Friends were rare jewels and special berries. He wondered why he never married and had children. His professorship owned his time and borrowed time from his days.

He sat, dipping the chocolate pear into the honey and his eyes danced. He had abandoned the thought of marriage and had made a comfortable, yet private, life for himself in Robin's Egg. He poured himself a glass of wine and was satisfied with his privacy.

"If there was a rare jewel," said Dr. Le Mans, head tilted, "though, I saw it in the heart of Anna Katsen after the war. We needed each other. She would never admit it." said Dr. Le Mans, who chewed fruit and adjusted his watch.

"Yeah. True. You never completely know what a person thinks about you until later in life and you've missed out," said Katie, hands together. "That's what I want to hear from you, sir. That's it."

"What?"

"You can trust me with your intimate thoughts and the time you spent together with Polly and Anna. Even though you have hit a dry season."

"Dry season?" said Dr. Le Mans, leaning forward. "O' girl, I had my time as a romantic man, traveling. Women have made me coffee and eggs in the morning. Don't limit me to a few ball seasons." He sat, eyes cocky. "Dry season, my... The truth is, I was in my mid-twenties, a lean rock-climbing machine, part-time writer, full-time dreamer, and had a death wish on the cliffs of West Virginia, I guess. My thoughts were not all saintly when we met. We lived and touched the sky."

"I heard there was talk about you being nude in the New River, right?"

"Nude. I cooled off that way. Her pursuant of me at the New River, saint and a sinner and she kept a camera and notebook, years ago. She knew what she wanted. Journalists are curious and selfish people. She knew what I wanted to do with my life. Anna was twenty-two, a few years younger, and we both were adventurous and unrighteous that summer."

"My age, huh?"

"Yep. The sky was broken up by pockets of cotton clouds, a soft baby blue sky hung above the towering rocky cliffs at the New River Gorge Bridge in the springtime of 1974, and a blazing evening sun dropped fast behind the high Blue Ridge

Mountains over the top of the gorge when I saw Anna and Naomi pull up in a spotless blue Monte Carlo. Yeah, I scanned the skyline westward in my birthday suit. No different than the day before, the same ball of fire and ambition burned inside our hearts the more time we spent together, further the war was away. She and Polly had that kind of power over me. No other lady has captured my emotions in that manner. Two women from different parts of the world, different lives, and they tugged on both sides of my heart."

"Your love life didn't start until you were in your mid-twenties, interesting, huh? What would Freud say about that, sir?"

"Freud? Hey, don't start that psychoanalysis Freudian bull crap. I had my share of dates and darlings, morning sweet rolls and hot cakes. I tend to cook and you have to ..." he thought, grinning, "have to know your sweet rolls to qualify as a bachelor."

She popped a grape into her curious mouth.

"Why so late in life, though, Studly?"

"Life, it's not always a cookie cutter romance. Clocks don't tick the same for everyone, my dear." He stood. "If that was the case, your university wouldn't keep sending so many journalism students to my ranch for research and thesis development, well, if I wasn't an interesting Romeo and a war hero, you'd have little to write about in Morgantown, right?"

"We sure enjoy the entertainment and humor."

She slowly removed her wire glasses and dropped her long hair, and said, "No. Romeo poisoned himself, Professor Le Mans. That's not the best analogy. Believe me," said Katie, who stood starry eyed. "There's no more Romeo's left in this loveless world, are there?"

"Sure, they are. Your Romeo is somewhere between Robin's Egg and Morgantown." He cleaned his glasses. "Plus, you'll be in your mid-twenties soon, so don't psychoanalyze my life with your double major, little lady. It's far from the people who gather around the New River Gorge Bridge and grist mills of the mountains. Best people I've ever met come from the mountains. I haven't lost my touch."

"Yeah, sure. The New River Gorge is in its twentieth year of service as a highway, a bit of a tourist attraction for the Mountain State. You were the first person to cross the bridge, right?" Her head tilted just like all the other cub journalists and scholars taught by Nancy Reagan's speech to curl determined eyes democratically, and position hands, cheek to chin.

"Yeah. That's a fact, Katie. I was the first to write about the New River Gorge Bridge and walk the bridge."

The reflection of himself in the tinted sliding glass door reminded him of his age and so much he'd forgotten years and memories, both kept deep inside himself. He wasn't always young and artless. Age became his worst enemy. Once young and full of life, his eyes were stalled after she returned from the kitchen, kicking up her feet and she made herself comfortable, head back and feet atop pillows. In his heart, Dr. Le Mans was not disappointed in his escape from the mountains of West Virginia to his Robin's Egg Ranch, shaping his career and trading hobbies for speaking venues. Pages and pages were written by the time the moon made a silvery face in the sky and his mind was sharpened when she asked questions about Vietnam and his love life with Polly. Memories spun like strings of yarn, unraveling his part of the past, and without a blemish, he was sent to his days as a prisoner and the years that followed in the Appalachian Mountains.

***

The swift wind whipped through the deep, rugged gorge. Miles of nature kept him hooked to the rocky face of West Virginia, and more than anything else, he remembered dangling from the high cliffs above the northward flowing New River Gorge (one of the oldest rivers in the world, he told her), where he'd camped dozens of times since 1957. His pastime was the great outdoors, where God painted beautiful flowers on the canvas of the earth, humanities best, to the Gorge, such as Anna and Naomi.

Katie saw the photographs and made them the topic of conversation. Geography and geology were like old friends to him, hiking and rock climbing robbed him of his extra time before and even after the Army, too. "To go full tilt in my twenties," he called it, "meant climbing to clear my head, to see mountaintops, to soak up the picturesque view, to hang from the highest cliffs, and mainly, to flush Vietnam far from my head. If I had to pick a favorite place of peace in the world, the country roads beneath the New River Gorge, it would be my favorite spot and my favorite memories, too. Coal country, the place I grew up, is my life after the war. It's my home."

Burning within him was an unstoppable desire to explore the Grand Canyon, scale the Rockies, hike the Arches of Utah, and explore the ghost towns of the Old West. All of it was on his bucket list; he'd conquered half.

Hundreds of photos, stacked as high as a can of Cafe Bustelo Coffee, lined his desk from where he'd climbed the Red River Gorge in Kentucky to the time he'd roped off the coast of Maine, where he'd fallen asleep at sundown, and stayed the night against the smooth pink granite cliffs of Acadia National Park. At the pinnacle, he often killed his flashlight when climbing, and hoped for an open window to the Seventh Heaven at Cadillac Mountain. Rock climbing and repelling canyons were the reasons he'd joined the U.S. Army, for adventure, to see the world, he told the truth, and to serve his country. He did it, too. War was hell for him, and much more than he'd expected, staying with him night and day, far beyond the landscape of Vietnam.

Katie readied her pen after a short break of television.

"Tell me about the battles of Vietnam, sir."

"On 10 April 1974, Easter Sunday, I gladly left Vĩnh Long, Vietnam; it was the most exciting day of my life. I slept the entire night in peace. Several of my Army buddies were less fortunate. The next day I landed in Hayward, California, a cool town, too." The first meal of many meals without the thunder of bombs and firefights. "That's where I was amused by the dance of a candy striper. Then, well, I out-processed from Uncle Sam's Army at Fort Eustis, Virginia, headed for the hills, of which, as you know, I did stay several years in the mountains. Then, after Anna broke my heart, all my undergrad, graduate, and doctoral studies happened in Lubbock, Texas."

Jotting down each sentence as fast as he spoke, Katie was locked to his every word, from war to love to education, writing as he remembered.

"I understand you considered Beckley College and Marshall University after leaving Vietnam. Is that correct, sir?"

He stood, held out his hand.

"Nope. Neither. Hey, your stomach rumbled, Katie. I heard it, dear. Free that hunger. You flew here on your stipend and work-study money, didn't you?"

"Yeah." She gathered her things. "I have to watch my money, mom said."

"From here on out, all expenses belong to me. Please see it as a gift, and having to deal with that know-it-all, Professor Anna Katsen. Make it my treat to you. The next time you see her, please, please, tell her how wonderful and sweet I am and how well I live." They walked with arms locked. "There's a little place I'd like to show you, here, good food, in my adopted town."

He spoke about Vietnam on their way to dinner at Bishop Hill's Mexican Restaurant, outside Amarillo, Texas. He loved the smell of a Mexican grill, and honey drizzled sopapilla was what he ordered. She picked a dining area next to the warm fireplace to document his story. The Texas air was brisk and cool, and the wind had died down. Turning their seats toward the west, where a head of Texas Longhorns moved across the landscape, like something out of a western film, she mentioned the contrast of the flat land versus the mountains of West Virginia. The building was lined with stone walls, a three-story building, with views of the countryside from the knoll of a cleared hillside, which she said, "Was a far cry from Dorsey Knob, in Monongalia County, West Virginia."

Pouring wine was a thin Mexican lady with hair dark as coal, big white teeth shone and as friendly as a homeless puppy. Katie loved her Spanish accent and spoke some.

"Perfecto." said Katie, hand stopping the lady from pouring. She quickly raised her glass to Professor Le Mans. "Instead, sir, let's toast to your doctorate and to the many faces of democracy, Amigo."

"I say, let's toast to the Mountaineers, past and future, and to the fans who cheer them each week." He said, tapping glasses with a cheerful voice.

"To West Virginia, and to Dr. Beau Le Mans."

"And to you, Ms. Katie Collins. One glass for the Blue and one glass for the Gold in Morgantown."

They emptied their glasses, smacked their lips, faces full of joy. When her glass hit the table first, she said, "Now, well, what page was I on, slow poke." She adjusted her glasses, still laughing at him. "My head is spinning."

"Yes. That's why I hope to retire in Texas. When the stars spin, it brings me back to earth and reminds me that I'm a down-to-earth kind of guy."

Staring into his relaxed and happy face, she sighed, and said, "Did you have the desire to write after you left the *Army Times?*"

His father's voice echoed in his head.

"Son, war never leaves a man, it's always brewing inside your mind, and so is your ability to write. You were born to tell stories and write."

He poured himself a second glass for his father's encouragement, a Korean War veteran, followed with another for his mother. Other than a tour in the Army, his father lived and died in West Virginia, and his mother was known to stay at home.

"Doctor Le Mans, are you okay?" said Katie.

"When I came back home, I spent my time rock climbing the New River Gorge. I have dozens of good stories for you. They've never been read by anyone but me. My father and sweet mother encouraged my work in literature, and said I should publish my war stories and love stories, too. Anna was an encouragement, but she lied and broke her promise. She left."

"Why didn't you write and publish all your stories?"

His head fell back and his eyes closed slowly.

"To be honest, I didn't think anyone cared about romance and war. The war made sour faces for readers and many good stories never made headlines. More stories, the truth is starting to be printed more than expected. It takes courage to mask pain."

She grabbed his hand.

"Would you consider letting me publish this story beyond graduate school?"

"Not in a million years." Flagging the waitress, he added, "Heck, no."

She stood quickly and grabbed his things.

"I see, I've wasted my damn time with you, sir. My advisor said you were a good man, a man worth a visit. I see she was wrong."

She tucked her personal items into her bag, left ten dollars for the waitress, and walked away.

He blocked her path to the door.

"Who's your advisor?"

"Dr. Anna Katsen!"

"Anna Katsen, huh? I'm not surprised. Well, she played somebody and worked her way to the top, didn't she? She's a good liar. I could not trust her in the 70s and I bet she hasn't changed her selfish ways."

"Her classes have a waiting list, Dr. Le Mans, do yours?"

He bit his lip.

"Anna flew you here to see me, why?"

Beau touched her shoulder.

"Hey, Dr. Le Mans," said a broad Mexican gentleman, draped in a blue bandana atop his head, "leave the lady alone, man. We have zero tolerance."

The man took a swing at Dr. Le Mans.

The professor ducked and sent a rocket of an uppercut to his chin. The man dropped back to the seat he had left and his head slammed into the table.

Dr. Le Mans followed Katie outside.

"Tell Dr. Anna Katsen, I'm not sure what she's brewing in her deceptive mind. But, if she wants good information, write something to make herself look better on the hill in Morgantown, go somewhere else."

Blocking his steps, a Mexican lady faced Professor Le Mans, lip curled, and she said, "You don't cause trouble in my business, homes. Leave and don't come back!"

Dr. Le Mans watched Katie spin out in her rental car and drive away. He had time to think about what he'd said as he walked two miles back to his home. He wondered what Anna Katsen wanted and why Katie was at his home questioning him.

After the military, Beau wanted to be a long haul truck driver, and see all fifty states, but he spent his time submitting to magazines and getting threats from Black Suits for his Vietnam stories. Cafe Le Mans had exhausted him, and that was when he first met Anna Katsen, in 1974. Adapting to civilian life was difficult, but he had the urge in his mid-twenties to do so much more with his life them write about geology and climb rocks. However, that particular year changed America, the Watergate scandal happened, the impact of the oil crisis, muscle cars were souped up, and the fight for fuel slowed travel and made people crazy at gas stations. Mohammad Ali and George Foreman made headlines in boxing, and professional wrestling started in West Virginia.

Much had taken place since Beau Le Mans spent a few years in the Army. For him, there was a stint at SMU, the craft of writing, an old craft influenced by Thomas Wolfe and F. Scott Fitzgerald kept him typing his stories, stories that went unpublished. After his death threats, the keys on his typewriter were cold and dusty underneath his fingertips, and became a paper weight machine after he was blackballed about Vietnam, so he spun one story about coal deposits in the rivers of the Mountain State. Beau was inspired by articles written about the military and had hardly found the truth in the newspapers, but maybe it was time to print what he knew - the truth and the way he lived it in Vietnam.

***

The screen door clapped against the frame and the bell rang. Daylight eased its way under a long stack of rolling clouds, which stretched like cotton candy at a circus from Amarillo to his Robin's Egg Ranch. Knocking on the door, the student and writer, Katie Collins, the lady had more to say. The professor stopped in front of a mirror to comb his hair and paced across his ranch home. He pulled the curtains to one side, glad it wasn't the man from the Mexican restaurant and recognized the female, long hair through the dusty window and he wanted to clear the air between them.

"What are you doing here so early?" He unchained the door, and said, "Get in here, Katie. People should be sleeping in a rainstorm like this, lady."

"Good morning, Professor Le Mans. Do you have some hot coffee, because it's time to write your story? I am sorry about last night. I should respect your private life."

Rubbing his eyes, he said, "Well, well, well, I thought you'd gone home, back to the Appalachian Mountains, and made up some strange Vietnam story about me. You had the chance to write a new thesis about The Impact of the War on Bosnia, or something else, huh?"

"I'm sorry, okay? Let's start again."

The lady stood inside the foyer in her favorite yellow and navy sweater; the long sleeves swallowed her tiny arms, and Katie had a binder to detail his stories.

"No. I spoke to my advisor. I begged and pleaded with Dr. Katsen to release me from the project. She dared me to let you off the hook, so I cannot fly home until it's finished and I'm satisfied with the depth of your story."

"That sounds like Anna." He took her wet coat. "Fair enough. Let's get started."

"Yeah." She stomped and kicked, knocking water off her boots.

"O, what did the little hag tell you about me, anyway?" Angling his head toward Katie, to see if anyone had followed her. "Come in, come in, get yourself dried off."

"You were angry because she dumped you."

"Dumped me?" His hands gripped and wrinkled the coat when he hooked it.

"I know that part, but she also told me to write or fail the class. Failure and a long Christmas break sounds like it might be the best, though." Shrugging her shoulders, she said, "I have no choice, Doc. Let's research and write."

"I wouldn't let you fail... so get the questions ready. Take a seat, please. I'm sorry about last night. I do have a private life."

"Agreed. Deal." She dropped into her world of writing and loved his big ranch sofa. "My time is truth and honesty from here on out. Doctor Katsen said you'd help one of your own - a lady Mountaineer."

Laughing and handing her a towel to dry her wet face, Dr. Le Mans took her bag and felt comfortable with her eagerness to know his history.

"How can I say no to you? But, Katie, I haven't seen or heard from Anna in years. It's been a peaceful twenty-some years since she lied to me. Our last conversation was about her plans to have a big wedding. She was nowhere to be found in Amarillo, Robin's Egg, and I know nothing about her now. She never tried to call my parent's cafe or even send a Christmas card."

"She's not that bad, is she?" Katie opened her binder.

"Our relationship was final when she left me for a sailor."

"Don't you mean, dumped you for the sailor?"

"Nope. I wouldn't chase her and she got mad. To have me drive cross-country and then she disappeared, was the worst part." He turned to Katie, and said, "I have plenty of room if you decide to stay at my Robin's Egg Ranch, leave the hotel world of continental breakfast for a more civil and comfortable setting." Pointing out the window, Dr. Le Mans said, "Horses and cattle are all I have left to keep me company. Some coffee and a good fireplace to read by, Katie?"

"Yeah, please. I'll take your offer on the room and some good coffee, sir. Dr. Katsen said you'd be a nice guy if I could get a cup of Cafe Bustelo out of you."

"She lied." He grinned.

"Got my coffee, Doc," Katie said, laughing, "so we'll see. And I have a dry room."

"I can interview with you until lunch, then I'm off to Lubbock."

"What's in Lubbock, Doc?"

He pushed biscotti in her direction. She wrapped her cold hands around the cup of coffee and closed her eyes when the coffee warmed her face.

"Classes. I have business to tend to while you wrap up a few chapters about me."

"Can I go with you, milk some chapters out of you while we ride to Lubbock? I'd like to see Lubbock and tour Texas Tech while I'm here."

"I'm not sure. We better get to know each other first, before we ride around Texas."

"Please, sir, huh?"

"Okay. I'll go for it. No arguing, though. Grab a thermos in the cabinet, Katie. You might write better under a second cup. You'll get to see where I work and I have a list of my own for next semester, students who love my courses."

Not to waste a drop of his coffee, she capped her thermos and stared out the window at the long backyard. Not a toy or a children's book was inside the home. He was private.

"Do you have any pets?"

"No pets. No children. We need to go. I have lazy cows and wild horses."

"Maybe you could teach me how to ride a horse?"

"When we're done. You have less than a week left to write your story and another to review. Life for me will be back to normal when I take you to the airport. We'll just stick to writing and see what happens, okay? No horses yet. Turn in the rental car and save yourself a few dollars."

"I see you are tight with a dollar, Doc."

Tilting his head, Dr. Le Mans said, "Yeah. My father taught me to keep a dollar and you'll have a dollar when you need it.

Don't spend money on things you want or you will have to sell things you need to cover your mistakes."

"Good advice."

She started with questions about his parents and grandparents, personal questions about the Army and veterans he knew, what he saw in Vietnam, and did he harm anyone in the war?

"It's time for me to go to Lubbock now."

"On the trip, you can tell me about this lady, Polly."

"Polly, huh? Why does everyone want to learn more about my Vietnamese beauty, Polly, than the war?" He hopped in the truck. "I have only spoken about Polly a few times in my life. Everyone loves a good love story."

"I'm not just anyone, sir. I'm a Mountaineer."

"You are, Katie, for sure, and you'll be a great investigative journalist, too."

"Let's start with how I met Dr. Anna Katsen."

"This might piss her off, Doc, when she reads it. I love it. This is good stuff."

He hit the gas, and turned onto the interstate and grinned.

"I sure hope it pisses her off when she hears my opinion of her."

CHAPTER TWELVE

↔

Birds of a Feather

They arrived at his office, where stories and books about Vietnam lined his desk and dozens more were tucked in bookshelves that filled the wall space. For some reason, pictures were not being withheld from newspapers and journalists covered articles about the war, stories emerged, some over two decades old, and broken battles still rang in the hearts of most war veterans. The world hummed about shady politics.

After seeing the world through his articles, she talked about why he returned to West Virginia after Vietnam. Dr. Le Mans turned a few stories of his own with her webbing his memory, and a cool desire sparked - Peace, Love, and War; his mind was filled with expressions and he kept to himself, a man with his own opinions about the past and reasons for what happened in Vietnam. It was time to speak, he thought, and little by little, he unfolded pages, a loss of his private life was behind him.

After the war, he climbed the sandstone and shale cliffs of the New River Gorge, and even had a nickname for the place "Mountains of Serenity." The lonely eagle faced him, eye-to-eye, both in admiration. With pages filled, he remembered the summer of 1974 when he first met Anna Katsen and Naomi Lewes in Fayette County.

Katie wrote as he recalled part of his life with Anna Katsen. Dr. Le Mans told how he was in love with Anna Katsen from day one.

"That's impressive how you hung off of cliffs like some monkey in the jungle," said Anna. She pushed her long hair away from her eyes, curled a smirk, and caught his attention. He wasn't blind and she was not naive.

***

"It's much harder than it looks, doll," said Beau, grunting as he continued his climb near the new construction of the New River Gorge Bridge. Beau saw the license plate of a Monte Carlo, tagged Pennsylvania. "Rock climbing is better than the streets in Pittsburgh, that's for sure."

"Pottstown, man," said the female driver. "Anna rode from Pittsburgh. We have the best beverages and the coolest hippies around. All of us were at Woodstock, three days of peace and music, dude." A second lady hung her thick head of hair out the passenger's seat and whistled. "Don't disrespect the Keystoners." A lady swung open the car door and tied a bandana.

"You need to move out of my route," said Beau.

"The man at the restaurant said we could find a professional climber," said the lady with a soft sweet voice, blocking the sun with her hands to better see him. "Half nude climber."

"Oh, don't believe the cafe owner for a minute!" said Beau, who widened his snow- white smile. "You didn't eat his cooking, did you?"

"Yeah, why?" The lady moved closer to his ropes.

The climber made it to the top.

"He likes to poison hippies from Pottstown and Pitt Panthers," said Beau, laughing, "Just for the fun of it, especially students from Pitt."

"I live in Morgantown. A Mountaineer grad and majored in journalism." The lady touched her soft cinnamon hair. "The man gave me a discount because I'm a wild Mountaineer."

"Are you just another West Virginia party animal, are you?" said Beau, hand on his goatee.

"Can you go back to Vietnam, if you can't be pleasant and cordial with us, dude?" She tightened her paisley bandana and pulled it down, trying to look like a bandit robbing a bank.

"Don't ever throw rocks or point that middle finger at a climber again. That finger might go off and kill someone, lady. That goes for both of you, wild Lady Mountaineers."

"Your father is a number one liar!" said the lady on the ground, wiping the sweat and dust from her face.

He turned to the ladies, feet hit the ground and he walked out of his gear.

"What did the man at Cafe Le Mans tell you, anyway?" He threw ropes over his shoulder, then tossed his gear into the back of his CJ-5 Jeep.

"He said, you'd teach us how to climb, man. Let's get the heck out of here, Anna. He's a G.I. jerk." The lady draped her legs out of the driver's seat of the Monte Carlo, popped her gum, and eyed Beau.

"Sorry. My reputation isn't as good as I thought," said Beau. "My rock climbing season is almost over, and I'm headed west," he said, taking a drink of water from his canteen. "Find someone else to bother at the river, go jerk someone else's chain in the Gorge. There are two or three climbers who might help you. Or they may not care, private folks."

"Let's go, Naomi." said Anna, winking at the climber and facing her friend. "Let's go back to the cafe and rob it."

"Robbers? Yeah," said Beau. "You look like cheerleaders, not robbers." Beau told them, laughing into his ropes.

The lady stopped, turned and stared at the climber, three feet away.

"On second thought," she said, walking over to the Jeep. "I'm checking out this new Jeep. I like the color green, naturally, a vehicle that matches my eyes."

"Maybe we got off on the wrong foot," said Beau, grinning. The climber stuck out his hand to the ladies. "What's your name again? I was up so high; I couldn't hear you." Plucking her hands from her pockets, pacing over toward the tailgate of the Jeep, and she grinned and ran her hands over the paint of the vehicle. "You can buy us dinner to make up for being rude."

"Ha-ha-ha." said the climber. "I don't buy strangers pork chops and baked beans at Cafe Le Mans."

The climber was highly impressed when she walked around his 4x4 CJ-5 Jeep, and mentioned how she'd love to drive a military style Jeep: One favored by an Army photojournalist.

***

Katie propped up her legs in his office, and his candor stretched into the past.

"That wasn't what I heard. That beautiful blonde, Anna Katsen, she had you in her trance, didn't she, Doc?" said Katie, glancing up at him after she'd taken notes.

"Yeah. I was interested, and not because she was a blonde. I had choices and later found her to be highly intelligent, even civil and cultured. She was someone I could not trust with my war stories, or my heart. I wore my Army patch on my coat and my heart on my sleeve in 1974."

"That's why Doctor Katsen is the head of the Department of Journalism in Morgantown. Former President Reagan trusts her journalism. She has connections in D.C."

***

His mind faded back to Anna Katsen, and the time she stayed with him.

His good heart wouldn't allow times like that to leave him. After watching the work crew ease across the new section of the New River Gorge Bridge, Anna nervously glanced from the riverbank. Each day smaller sections of steel were linked, and by May 1974, the idea of a bridge had taken shape into what was printed in the newspaper by Beau Le Mans, and yeah, it was him who covered the entire story of the bridge construction. More steel and concrete were planned, large rigging units held partial steel structures of the bridge on cables and expanded the bridge, unit by unit, until it reached 3030 feet long, to intersect 876 feet above the New River. Anna requested to pull off the road and admire the cool bridge construction, adoring that part of West Virginia.

"This is the only way to appreciate the skyline of the Gorge," said Anna.

In a slow and gentle movement, Anna eased her finger, just as though she was painting some imaginary line across the sky, mountain to mountain, arching her hand to form what would be named the New River Gorge Bridge. Suddenly, her eyes caught a patch of flowers along a hiking path, off the beaten trail, halfway up the winding road, where Beau parked his Jeep.

"Would you show me what a Prairie Trillium looks like, Beau?"

Darting down the hiking trail, said Beau, "My mother often spoke of the flower, but she was the outdoor type like me."

"Do you see one?"

"They are often confused with the Chickweed and Star of Bethlehem," said Beau, dropping to one knee. "Here's one, see the three leaves and golden stem. Bees love this flower in the spring, so be careful. It's delicate."

"It's soft and tender to the touch."

"There's a mountain bear."

She grabbed his arm, scanning the woods and yelled, "Where's the bear?"

Laughing and smiling, he was close enough to smell her perfume, as the flip of her long hair brazed his face. "No, not a black bear." Still laughing, he rubbed his chin. "But you were scared, weren't you, Anna?"

"You said there's a mountain bear!"

"Prairie Trillium has the nickname Mountain Bear. You'll see them in the rich soil, growing near an old stump, in moist areas and along the hillside or covering a partially shaded area."

"You made me jump out of the skin, Beau." She mocked him, and said, 'There's a mountain bear,' pushing his arm. "Don't do that again, rock climber."

"You're a scaredy cat, aren't you, Anna?"

"No, but I just like to be prepared and ready to fight a bear."

Beau made his way up the winding hairpin turns to the top of the New River Gorge Bridge again, where they sat on another rocky cliff and watched the slow flowing river churn over rocks like the river had done for thousands of years. He pointed to where the span of what was to connect Highway 19, mountain to mountain, to improve transit time for freight haulers and school buses and for thousands of vehicles predicted to cross the bridge each day. They watched the workers until the sun melted to the west as if a large candle faded away. She turned on the Jeep lights and watched the night take over the day.

***

Dr. Le Mans kicked his feet on his office desk.

"So, she stayed with you the whole summer, Doc?"

"No. Only eight weeks or so. Let's see the Red Raider cafeteria."

They talked about campus life and the nice bookstore.

"Here's a good thin crust pizza," said Katie.

"Talking about Anna might spoil my pepperoni pizza."

She stuffed pizza into her mouth and chewed. Dr. Le Mans bought her a TTU shirt in the bookstore and it was time to head back to Robin's Egg. She climbed in the truck.

"Did you and her, you know, get intimate? Kiss, kiss, and smooch, smooch." She closed her eyes and kissed the pizza. "Kiss, kiss, kiss. O' pizza."

"Just eat your dang food, Katie." He shook his head, clapping on pizza and cleaning his mouth with soda. "Don't choke."

"No way!" Katie chewed her pizza, smiling. "It's time to hear about Polly girl."

Beau remembered Polly like it was yesterday.

"Polly, huh? You're right, I didn't even know her last name."

"Did you know Dr. Katsen spent three years of her research and hundreds of hours in her spare time researching stories about the thousands and thousands of babies who were born in Vietnam, half American, and half Vietnamese? Their fathers were soldiers. Love or not, children were born."

"Thousands, huh? I didn't realize so many children were fatherless."

"Over 100,000 babies were born by Vietnamese women. Some were given to orphanages; most kids were blackballed and refused to be educated. Children, all fatherless, you are right. The sad part, half American, and half Vietnamese, those times meant abuse to children, even babies."

"I cannot understand hatred toward babies, little ones who are not able to help themselves. I fear they were bullied as they got older, too."

"Some took their own lives. Others were killed."

"Thousands of fatherless babies were raised in orphanages, huh?"

"Yeah." She rubbed her eyes. "Very sad times."

"They did not know their parents. It was retaliation against American forces, men like me, I guess."

"Yeah. Many of the Vietnamese leaders thought sleeping with an American soldier was an act of betrayal against their own country. Women were beaten."

"Jealousy and rageful. It was a time of war and Communism. I can relate."

Two hands grabbed the steering wheel, as Dr. Le Mans turned north on Highway 27.

"What do you want to know about Polly, Katie?"

She jotted her thoughts and turned the page.

"How did you and Polly meet?" Her eyes watched his face brighten.

"Soft music played on the radio, strings, not keys, and red lights hung overhead inside the small Vietnamese diner. Polly had Vietnamese Fish Cakes. I had ordered the spicy Vermicelli noodle soup, hue style, and I remember the soup was very hot."

She slapped his shoulder.

"Stop. Dr. Le Mans, come on, seriously, how did Polly get inside the head of a POW? Was it lust, or another dry season?"

"I have not lost my touch. I wish life would've been dates and hot soup. I've never had a dry season, by the way. Life was far from sailboats and sunbathing in Vietnam. No walks on the beach existed. But, you're right. We did meet at a POW camp. The first time I met Polly was with Henderson, Sam Law, Hien, and Cadeo."

"Let me guess," said Katie, one foot on the dashboard, and a notebook on her knees, "she had dark hair, thin paper lips and a cool figure. Was she your Delta Dawn, huh?"

"Delta Dawn, what's that flower you have on?" he sang. "To me, Polly was more than a groovy figure. She was one of the few women among the American and Vietnamese fighters who cooked at a POW camp. I read very few camps had women cooks. A prisoner watched for the cook, smelled food in the air, and their nose chased the aroma coming from a steel wok. A lady more human and more spiritual than anyone I've ever met strolled into my life. I could have given her the world, but the war had us chained and separated."

"How could you tell the soul of Polly because of the limited time you had with her in the camp?"

"I daydreamed. God intervened."

"God? I bet he did, Dr. Le Mans," said Katie, scribbling. "What made Polly different from other ladies you had met?" Her eyes saw his face bite on the question and then his mouth opened, no voice, and then his lips closed. Sitting up tall, she said, "Is it because you were a desperado? There were no other women around the POW camp, correct? Were you a lonely man?"

"No. This was different. Two souls met. It was meant for us to have that short time together. God prepared it long before we saw each other. I was stronger with God during the war. I'd like to see her again, if she's alive, and talk and have soup."

"You mean, kiss, kiss, kiss, and lock the doors?" said Katie, humming Delta Dawn.

"You are a hot shot writer, aren't you?"

"I need the molten lava, my friend. I want the goods."

"Okay. That's fair. I never had the chance to know her, kiss, kiss, kiss, the way I wanted to in Vietnam. We were caught amid the circumstances of two countries at war. The land was bloody and unfair. I'm pretty sure she was killed after we escaped. She betrayed her husband and let us out while he was drunk and nude with another lady."

"But while you were there, she did care for you, right? Made you feel special, okay? If she really cared about you, she did think of you and acted a certain way to help you. She risked her life for you, Doc."

"She saved my life. I can never repay her for that. Is it trivial and childish to wish and hope to see someone again, even as a man who relives the past in his forties and teaches the history of journalism?" He felt his thin beard and his eyes held on the road.

"It's not wrong to walk the road into the past. Some people never reveal their hopes and dreams to others, in this way, like this, sir. I respect your emotions and time. We're almost in Amarillo. Robin's Egg is the next turn. That was a two hour drive. I got a solid charter out of you."

"Yeah, the drive clears my head. Are you game for a cup of soup or coffee, huh?"

"O, I love soup and crackers." She rubbed her hands together. "That's a deal. I love Barringer Stew."

"I know just the place, down the road." Beau snapped his fingers. "They have the best stew in the Panhandle of Texas."

"I could see myself in Texas, sir, living here." Katie lifted her glasses and smiled.

"You would fit right in the Lone Star State, Katie. You are lively and young."

***

The next morning was dusty and hot by the coral fence.

"Nice day, isn't it, soldier?" The man adjusted his camouflage hat and walked up behind Dr. Beau Le Mans. "Looks a little like my ranch. You have three more barns and lots of horses and hay, my friend."

"Yeah. Who are you?" said Dr. Le Mans who scanned the man, feet to face. "How did you know I was a soldier?"

"Vietnam, baby!" yelled the man, excitedly. "I was right there, man, fighting," said the man. "By the way, did you know Private Lawrence, a soldier from Virginia?"

"Yeah." Dr. Le Mans remembered Sam Law wanted to attend Holy Cross and Notre Dame.

"Did you know a soldier from this town, called "Caveman," a big, rough guy," asked Doc. "Broke his leg and left for dead, I believe?"

"No, man. Different road."

Dr. Le Mans became curious of this guy and knew this man fought, shoulder to shoulder, and hit the front lines in Vietnam, where and why?

"Lawrence was K.I.A. Henderson was reported M.I.A and....." He pitched his coffee on the ground and walked near the man. "Were you a medic or gunner? I feel I might know you from somewhere in Vietnam, years ago, Infantry, perhaps, huh?"

"Not me." The man pushed off from the fence. "We never met. Good to meet you, man. Carry on, Senator's son."

The strange man jumped inside his truck and spun out.

"Wait! Wait!" Dr. Le Mans held out his hand. "Hold up!" The man's truck was gone. To be called a "Senator's Son" meant to be the son of a millionaire, a white collar man, non-working class citizen who saw little to no combat and may not have even served in the war, but only read about the war in the newspapers. Dr. Le Mans witnessed a long cloud of dust in the distance and leaned on the fence, leg bent, deep in thought.

He saw the man flash a Peace Sign with his hand. Dr. Le Mans walked back to his house, mind wondering about the strange man.

"What's wrong, Dr. Le Mans?" said Katie. "Pardon me, sir, but you look like you've seen a ghost."

"Nope. There was a strange man in camo who approached me at the cattle fence. I just can't recall where I met him in Vietnam or in Amarillo."

"Sir, everyone from Amarillo to Lubbock, well, people read your war articles and know your face from Vietnam. It's nothing. Dozens of reporters and television personalities have sat inside your home in the past four years."

She tossed the keys to Dr. Le Mans, and said, "I love Robin's Egg. Take me for eggs and bacon. They better have good coffee. How 'bout it, sir?"

"Well, it's nothing, you're right," he said, pulling on his goatee. "Nothing shocks me in this world, especially the strangeness of strangers and their grievance for the war and soldiers who fought in it. I must've written something where he recognized me."

She slammed the truck door, arm hung outside the truck.

"People love to stir the pot with smart remarks when your name pops up in the newspapers each week. Just let it go, sir, and don't let him spoil our breakfast together."

"Dang, I'm hungry," said Dr. Le Mans, adjusting his seat. He turned down the street to the Starr Cafe, but still couldn't place or predict how he knew the stranger, or if he ever did. "Let's go. I bet the cafe has breakfast plates as big as Potter County."

Her hands pressed her lips, and Katie's eyes were filled with anticipation. They sat in the corner at the cafe, spoke of their empty stomachs, and waited for breakfast.

"Look," said Katie, eyes toward Dr. Le Mans. "Over there is a man in a camouflage hat. Is that the soldier? He just pushed the waiter. What arrogance?"

"Yeah. Yeah. That's him." He stood. "That's the man that approached me this morning at the ranch. I'm going over there."

"Wait. Let's see what happens?"

"I forget names, but I hardly ever forget faces, especially rude guys."

The waiter walked to Dr. Le Mans and Katie.

"Who is the man in the camo hat?" said Katie, who cleaned the table with a napkin to keep from staring at the soldier.

"He's a jerk," said the waiter.

"What if I pretend I'm with the paper, a reporter, and interview him, right?" said Katie, opening her notebook, tapping the table.

"No need for that," said Dr. Le Mans, relaxing. "He's leaving. No worries."

Inside Katie's hand were a notebook and a camera.

"I got a picture of the camo man, anyways."

"Back to our coffee. He left the building." Dr. Le Mans removed his hat. "Maybe you should have interviewed, got his name. He was messed up in the war, I guess. All of us are messed up in different ways."

"Robert Louis Stevenson wrote how a menace is an 'unscrupulous man of action' and I believe him if we consider what we hear and see from some people." Katie had written down what the man was wearing and what he'd said to Dr. Beau Le Mans. Though she might use his behavior as part of her research, adding to her section on PTSD.

"He's in the parking lot beside his truck, Katie. I can't take this anymore. I need know where this man knows me from and what he wants." Dr. Le Mans walked across the room as if a fire was blazing in the parking lot. He and the man disappeared for several minutes.

The clock on the wall was stuck at 10am, but it seemed like the professor was gone for an hour. Suddenly, Dr. Le Mans popped back inside the restaurant, hood over his head and rain dotted his jacket.

"What did he say, Dr. Le Mans?" She patted the seat beside her. "Your eggs are cold. Come on, I'm curious. I have to be nosy. What happened out there?"

"I walked around the corner and lost him." He stirred his hot coffee. "I searched everywhere, but no man in camo was on the street or in the parking lot. His truck was gone when I came back."

"Dr. Le Mans, I usually keep things like this to myself," she said, looking down at her coffee, "but do you believe in God or coincidence or chance?"

"Yeah, of course. God has everything planned, the way we walk, the way we talk, our height, our character, but it's up to us to decide how we use these things in life."

She opened a pack of sugar.

"What do you mean?"

"Do you think it was by some odd chance we're here talking about some man who we thought was a stranger and who may be perfectly normal once we get to know him and talk to him over a meal for a while?"

"I think God knows what we need and when we need it. We don't surprise God, and the Lord upstairs had a desire to be in our lives today. We may think something is strange, but God knows it's his plan to provide for us and accompany us through this journey we call life. It might be different to us, but the Lord is still with us and wants us to make the right choices."

She rubbed her full belly.

"That was the best conversation I've had about God and the most delicious breakfast I've ever tasted. Thank you, sir."

"This cafe makes their own coffee and the beans are roasted in Robin's Egg. Potatoes and beans are harvested in Lubbock County. Let's go, we will ride the horses before dark."

Katie snapped the hood of her coat over her head. They jumped inside the truck.

"The rain missed us. Now we are talking, Doc. You can tell more about Polly, right?"

"What is it with jealous American women, who have a desire to know about beautiful Asian women and their bedroom secrets with men, huh?"

"Jealous?" She turned off the truck's radio. "What? Curious, but not jealous."

"I need to change the subject before we have another war." He coughed into his hand. "That BLT tasted great, didn't?"

"Bedroom secrets of Asian women, right? Just drive, Doctor Lover." She bit her lip and twisted her long hair. "We'll talk later, sir. No wonder Dr. Katsen laughs when she tells stories about you to her students."

"Wait! She teaches her class about me, huh?" A cocky grin cut his face and his shoulders jumped. "Interesting. She still cares. I love it."

"She says it's nothing worth remembering."

"What? She still fills the room with candor, I see. Don't serve bologna for her sake."

"She spoke about missing the serenity of Robin's Egg." Katie grinned, and said, "Secrets of Asian women, you wish, huh?" She hit his shoulder as if they'd been friends for years, and her questions about war and relationships had not ended after an evening of horseback riding. Katie promised to return before Christmas.

CHAPTER THIRTEEN

Mending Fences

The precious days of life were given thousands of years ago, and for Beau, who studied history, hiked the landscape of Palo Duro Canyon, meaning "hardwood," was where he snapped photos and recalled lost loves, pondered the war, and studied answers to thought provoking questions. Beau hashed out his problems riding horses and mending fences in Potter County, and wondered about the ages that had done the same thing.

He'd have it no other way, the mental stressors and the psychological issues that came with education, war and the economy, then and now, were said to be remedied, at least partially, when a man flexed his muscles and labored for hours each week. Some thoughts stretched back to his time in the coal country, where his forefathers lived and labored in West Virginia and Virginia. So, for Beau Le Mans, laboring the mind and the muscles meant pushing himself from sunrise to sunset, caught in a world of workmanship and hobbies, where the outdoors was his regiment and remedy.

Back at home in Robin's Egg, Dr. Beau Le Mans added a new line of fence to his corral for seven new Shetland ponies he had delivered, a few weeks before Katie arrived for Christmas. She aimed to stay the length of her planned research.

"I got some ocean front property in Robin's Egg, Texas," said Beau, singing and sweating, "and from my ranch, I can see the sea..." He heard footsteps.

A man walked up behind him.

"What do you know about the sea?" said the stranger. "Are you a sailor or soldier, huh? I thought you were a good soldier, man. Earned medals and ribbons from Vietnam and wrote about the mission, made money, right?"

"How can I help you, fellow? You were the man in Lubbock, and now you have followed me to my ranch at Robin's Egg?"

The man shook a few fence posts and tested the strength of his work.

"I told you," he said, smirking and smiling, "if I ever got home I'd buy you the biggest steak dinner in Texas, didn't I? But I've changed my mind. You, of all people, should be the one buying the meal, professor."

"Ben Henderson! O, my God, you made it buddy. You've been Missing in Action for twenty years, man. Jesus, you've got a stern personality, my friend. Why didn't you say something in Lubbock or before?"

Beau reached out his hand. Henderson refused, hands stuffed inside his Army jacket and lifted his chin. The man had changed drastically in a few decades; Beau had no idea who it was beside him. His mind had gone cold, but not his memory.

"You dang right it's, "Caveman" Henderson, to you. Don't act like we're best friends or something, you freaking coward." He pointed into the face of Le Mans.

"Wait, man! What are you talking about, Ben?"

"Le Mans, you left me with a broken leg. You left my butt to die in Vietnam, didn't ya? I see you got home and everyone celebrated the day you landed, I read about it."

"You got it wrong, man. Hell, no!" Le Mans bent his hand off his chest. "If that's what you heard, somebody lied to you, buddy!"

"We ain't battle buddies!" yelled Henderson. "We ain't friends. Not for a long time. I saw you leave, to take care of yourself. You didn't bring back soldiers for recon, did you? Did you even circle back? Left me to rot in a nasty creek bed." Henderson spat and bit a stick of straw, backing up.

"Do you really think we left you to die, man, huh? We circled back with helicopters and men on the ground for days, weeks even?" Le Mans threw his tools in the back of the truck. "You're singing the wrong dang song, Caveman."

"Yeah. It's obvious when the Vietnamese pulled me for miles on a broken leg, hopeless. And look, I found you at my ex-wife's ranch. You double crossed me, and Communism won out, didn't it?"

"No sense in arguing over this, man. Get off my property, Henderson. Dozens of soldiers looked for you, on the ground and from the air. We came up empty handed. We found others, but didn't find you."

"You didn't look very hard enough." Henderson leaned on the tailgate.

"We looked for you for weeks. And wondered what happened to you."

A strong wind picked up and dusted the two men, as Le Mans packed the hole and tested the fence. Henderson rushed beside Le Mans, faced him, and stopped his work.

"I'll tell you what happened, hillbilly, The Buddha, the lion's roar. That was what saved my life, not a cross. And I fought for Vietnam, brother, and handled my business over to them and that's what saved my soul. Not the First Team! No Uncle Sam, only me. I played the game and lived with Charlie. I made my life happen and I aim to tell my big story. Make millions, like you."

"We searched for 27 days, Henderson."

"I'm curious. How did you, a poor coal mining hillbilly, get Jeanette's home and all this in Robin's Egg? I told you my wife lived here, and now here you are, owner of the largest horse ranch in Robin's Egg, and a big time professor at a major university. Did Uncle Sam set you up? They filled your bank and pockets? Mighty strange, Le Mans. Mighty damn strange."

"By the way, Henderson, I saw your ex-wife leave Robin's Egg with your son, Little Benny, the month Reagan took office. She was so happy with her third husband. They moved to Raton, New Mexico. Said she wanted to live among the brown bears and teach Little Benny how to fish and hunt. You can find her working at the El Raton Theatre, I bet."

A truck rushed down the road, turning at some speed, raising lengthy dust clouds. Henderson thought Le Mans was distracted. The man, full of rage, bottled up for too long, swung for the head of his friend. With quick reflexes, Le Mans ducked, eyes elated and tackled him.

"Wanted to fight you, Le Mans, since we were prisoners, man," grunting.

The two grown men rolled down the hill, faces flushed, bodies turning over field grass and weeds and dirt. In a flat of sand, they stopped and exchanged punches.

"You were afraid!" said Le Mans. "Like you are now, man." Le Mans struck him several times, body and head shots, elbow to the forehead.

"You're a lightweight, been one all your life, Le Mans." Henderson belted him in the jaw.

"I'll knock your lights out!" Le Mans head butted him.

The driver of the truck slammed the brakes. He'd recognized Le Mans, and saw he was in bad trouble. Ranchers and farmers carried shotguns, and looked after each other and their land in Potter County.

"Le Mans! Beau Le Mans!" yelled the driver, sliding down the hill.

"Mickey Starr, break this mule down!" said Beau. "He's insane!"

"Get up! Break it up!" said Mickey, popping Henderson in the neck with the butt of his shotgun. "Hardheads."

Ben Henderson fell on his face. Le Mans rested in the dust and caught his breath. Mickey pulled him up and both men leaned on a big rock.

"What got into that man, Doc?"

Le Mans and Mickey Starr climbed the hill and poured water on their hands.

"We were prisoners together," breathing heavily. "The man thinks the Army left him high and dry in the jungle. So, when the Army did not find him, he joined the Viet-Cong, and fought against the U.S. Forces. In a rage, he hunted me down. He thinks Uncle Sammy gave me money for this farm."

They both held their chest and laughed.

"Believe me, Le Mans, the government doesn't give money for nothing."

"They take it, though."

"Yeah, for sure. He looks with a Communist eye. Revenge," said Mickey. "In Korea, if a soldier wasn't at the rally point, we circled the landscape in Korea, and Recon, to search again, was not different in Vietnam, I bet. He's been brainwashed, my friend."

Mickey sat on the tailgate and looked over the hill at Henderson, out cold.

"We were the last of our platoon. Our promise was to look after each other. His leg was broken and I went on for help. When I returned for him, Henderson was gone."

"He wants to pin you for it, huh?" Mickey dusted off his friend's back.

"Yeah. Now what?" said Le Mans, resting. "I wonder how long this psycho has been looking for me?"

"For years, I bet." Mickey turned up the water and washed his face.

"Henderson was in Lubbock the other day, and found me at Texas Tech. His looks had changed so much, Mick, I didn't recognize his face." Beau wiped dirt from his hair. "How much time do we have before he wakes up?"

"Not long. Maybe an hour." said Mickey Starr, grinning. "I'll drive down and pick him up, take him to the cornfield at the Cadillac Ranch. He'll learn to hunt you."

"Yeah. Would Diego and his motorcycle gang like to help?"

"Good idea." Mickey rubbed mustache, chuckling.

"He owes me one. Better get started. Diego can tie him to a 1949 Cadillac, for me," said Beau, lifting the big man inside the truck bed.

Mickey Starr held his cowboy hat and laughed.

"After Diego's message, Henderson won't come back to Robin's Egg for a long, long time. He'll wish he was back in Vietnam sucking on bananas."

"O' he'll be back. The man's crazy. Henderson has a death wish, Mickey." He slammed the tailgate. "Men of his type don't give up until he tastes death. Twenty years, Henderson has had it out for me."

"He'll stop fighting." Mickey Starr snapped his dog tags from his neck and read the tags. "Dog tags say he's a Baptist. Some people are full of crap, you know it, Doc? He's far from a Baptist."

"He's a Buddhist!" Beau held the tags.

"A what?" Mickey held his glasses over the tags.

"Yeah. When we were in the Army together, Samuel Lawrence, God rest his soul, was a Catholic from Virginia; Henderson claimed he was Buddhist; and I was the only Baptist of the bunch."

"Well, Henderson is on a trail to even the score."

Mickey Starr dialed Diego from his truck cell phone. Hung up.

"He'll die before he loses." Le Mans told him.

"Doc, let's get your ranch ready for a big battle. My time in the Korean War says we might have more company."

"My bones hurt, but I haven't forgotten my time in the Army, Mickey Starr."

Le Mans grinned, wiped the blood and dust off his face.

"I'll talk to Diego, and we'll do our own Recon on the ranch."

"Think you're right, Mick," he said, his eyes in agreement. "The man is the type who will keep coming back until he's satisfied with how he's beat up on others. He told me how he used to bully the weak and small in high school. And, from what

I see, the fight in him will not stop until someone is underground."

Dr. Beau Le Mans gazed across his ranch and turned around.

"Yeah." said Doc, dusting his hands. "Or he's underground. Mick, there's a young lady, a college journalist at the house from WVU. She's halfway into her research project, so we need to be careful."

"How long is she staying?"

"Five more days or so."

"Get her out and fast. I'll take Henderson to Diego's garage. Be careful."

"I'll meet you at my house at sunset."

"Good deal." Mickey Starr opened the truck door and leaned out. "This man may have others working for him."

"Nope. Alone," said Doc, face in a frown. "He lives in a lonely, private world, Doc. One-man show. I've seen his type in Savannah. No witnesses. No worries."

"One monkey can't stop the show, Mickey. We do what we have to do to protect our own friends and family. To me, he's neither one."

Mickey Starr served in the Army, fought in Korea, and stayed in his Amarillo ranch house for half the year and spent the other half in Savannah, Georgia. The Starr Family owned the largest fishing company in America. Mickey roped Henderson as good as any sailor or cowhand could do. Both men knew trouble, and Henderson was capable of anything, and the deadliest man Doc knew, stood for Communism.

CHAPTER FOURTEEN

Face of an Angel

"Oh, my God, Dr. Le Mans, what happened to your face?" said Katie, who stood when Dr. Le Mans walked through the living room, blood on his face and hands. Katie followed him into the big bathroom where he scrubbed away dried blood from the fight with Henderson.

"Did a horse throw you, sir?" said Katie, hand on his face.

"Nope."

"You might need stitches, Doc."

He flinched when the cold pack was applied.

"You might live."

"Katie, dear?" holding her hand. "Well, you might need to leave Robin's Egg."

"Why, sir?"

"Things might get a little dangerous around here. We can continue this research on another trip. There's a man, a soldier, seeking revenge. He thinks I left him behind with a broken leg in Vietnam."

"Henderson?" I dreamed he'd come for you.

"It happened this morning."

"The man in the camo outfit, right? Let's call the police, put a stop to this assault." She held the phone.

"Put the phone down. It doesn't work that way between soldiers. There's a code."

"A code? Sure it does. Assault. Police. Jail time. He broke whatever code you had."

"You're right." Doc sat at the bar. "Who would believe a story about a man who came home from Vietnam to resolve a grudge during the war, one that's two decades old?"

"Hatred has no time limit, Doc."

Katie walked into the living room. Doc poured coffee.

"His idea of hatred is domination and power." He told her. "He has nothing else going for him."

"Do you think the police would want to investigate a story like this?"

"Nope."

"The authorities have donuts to fry. And, well, no real crime has been committed."

"A big hit to the head is not a real crime for a man who spent time in a POW camp." Le Mans leaned back and closed his eyes, and said, "Mickey Starr and I will be watching the ranch house for a few weeks, working out our plan. We're only a few days from Christmas and fireworks at New Year's Eve, anyways."

"Will this man come back for you again?" hands on her face.

"You bet your lunch money on it. Are you flying back home?"

"No way. I am staying." Katie stood at the window, curtain bent and she saw only cows and horses moving in the field. "What kind of research journalist would leave in the middle of a great story, huh? Didn't you say in your last book, 'Face the Story,' or was that just a bunch of educational jargon that gets you through a salty day and sales pages?"

"You did read my book. Yeah. Stay and face the story. That's the way to write it. I can't believe you track my work." Doc sipped coffee. "You don't just write it; you listen and live it, don't you, Collins?"

"Yes, sir. That's what we'll do, sir."

"What?"

"Live it. Recon and Resolve."

"Just keep your typing fingers far from firearms, please."

She gently opened the desk drawer, popped a full clip into a 9mm, and swung her arms around until the bead landed on a ten-point Mule Deer on the wall, one he'd taken in Idaho.

"How's that for Hammer Time, Doc?"

"Heck, gal, you're staying here in Robin's Egg."

***

Four days had passed, like ice melting on a winter day. Robin's Egg had Christmas lights on every dusty corner, glowing with sparkling reds, brilliant blues, like the sea, greens that matched and twisted around garland, and peppermint candy hung down the halls from all four Christmas trees that Katie had decorated for Dr. Beau Le Mans. She loved the time of Christmas. He'd hung old family photos, ornaments, and candy canes that reminded him of the best snowy winters in his life, times in the West Virginia Mountains.

"Sir, who is the young couple in the candy-cane frame?" said Katie.

"That good looking man is yours truly, and that's the only photo in the world left of me with Anna Katsen. I put the picture out to see if you knew her face, years ago."

"Yeah. Look at you. Two happy people, full of life. You were a beautiful couple, weren't you?"

Tapping the picture, face bright, Doc remembered himself before he was an educated fool and caught up in a world of journalism and research, a way of life that caused him to spend many years alone on Thanksgiving and Christmas. Was it worth it, he thought? To give up the pursuit of Anna Katsen, to educate himself with journal articles and see his name on books, making a career for himself in his chosen field. Was it worth all those years?

"She was the one, the most beautiful lady I've ever seen. Katie, this man has traveled to many places in the world, spent holidays in Spain, and Rio, so I can say that about Anna with great confidence. We're not really foes."

Katie sat; legs crossed. Doc snatched the picture from her hands, grinning.

"Look at you and her. Do you ever drift back to the days with Dr. Katsen, sir?"

"Yeah. I get mad at myself for giving up so easily. The 'what if' questions haunt every man. Anna, Dr. Katsen, and I stayed the summer together in Fayette County, and boy, was it a hot summer. Then, she took off to this town. And, well, I chased her. But, well, she had moved on, had other plans with other people and chased a Naval officer to California. My advice, be honest with yourself, especially when it's about someone you care about or someone you love very much."

He poured himself a drink. She waved him off.

"O' my Lord, I can't believe you and Dr. Katsen shacked up together? What a secret story, huh? I love it."

"We shared a house, a large Edwardian home, outside Fayetteville. Anna and her sorority sister, Naomi Lewes stayed upstairs. No, we didn't shack up together. I remember she loved music and we danced to every song in my collection."

"Naomi Lewes?"

"Yes, she was Anna's best friend from WVU."

"So, you lived with two women, right?"

"No. Yeah. Wait! Wait! Wait! My floor was downstairs. Well, I guess I did."

"Was it like the behind the door, private show, like Three's Company, with Jack Tripper and Chrissy Snow and Janet Wood? Come on, drop me some secrets, Doc."

"Yeah, in some ways, I guess it was. My grandfather had given me a farmhouse in Fayette County, near what would later become the New River Gorge Bridge, back in West Virginia. I acquired the place when I was a teenager, long before my time in Vietnam. Anna was addicted to my mother and father's homemade style cooking. They were the best cooks in the world, though. Much better than what I can do."

Katie leaned forward and smiled. "Tell me, please. What was her favorite meal?"

"Chicken masala!"

"What's in it?" She readied her pen.

He walked over to the refrigerator.

"Since it's time for a meal, I'll make you famous Chicken Masala by Le Mans, just like it was prepared by my father at Cafe Le Mans in West Virginia. Man, I sure miss my parents. Good folks. Sherman and BettyAnne. Wells was my brother's name. We were best friends growing up."

"Tell me what's in chicken masala, I may not like Italian chicken."

"I use sweet and savory sauce, white button mushrooms, spread over a boneless chicken breast, a straight-up drinkable

Marsala wine, and it's Italian-American, by the way. I use thin angel hair pasta. It's to die for, little lady. I hope you like it."

"I'm already sold. Please hurry. Make me hungry, Doc." She ran into the kitchen and slid across the floor in her socks. "You're starving me to death and we haven't even started yet. Pasta and buttered bread are my specialty."

"You can't get my style of chicken masala in Morgantown."

"Yeah, but I won't be in Morgantown forever. Aced my courses. I have a plan."

"What about graduate school at Texas Tech?"

"I'll take it one semester at a time."

Katie decorated the kitchen table. Doc Le Mans handled the chicken and garlic mashed potatoes. Candles on the table were lit, the big bread basket was full, and she'd chilled the drinks. While the meal was cooking, Doc checked the windows and doors, not forgetting about Ben Henderson and his attempt to take revenge.

The meal was blessed by Doc Le Mans. The steamy aroma of the chicken punched Katie in the nose, as she sampled, and sipped drinkable Marsala wine.

"I'd like you to take the big bite, see if you enjoy the gravy and mushrooms, like Dr. Katsen did the last time I cooked for her."

She rolled the angel hair pasta over her fork, and the spoon was used to pour gravy over the chicken and pasta. Ice cold soda and warm bread rounded out the meal. The grand fireplace burned pleasantly amid December.

She took a tiny bite. "I love, love, love your mushrooms, sir."

"Stop nibbling and take a real bite of the chicken, lady." Doc laughed. "Dunk that chicken into the gravy and sweep the crunchy bread across the garlic mashed potatoes. Here, we're not dining at a fancy Pittsburgh culinary school. This is Texas, gal. Dunk it."

"Hee-Haw. Okay, cowboy." said Katie, dunking her chicken and sweeping the bread into the gravy. "Here's my first real bite of Chicken Masala by Beau Le Mans, just like your parents made at Cafe Le Mans, years ago."

"Give me the goods. What do you think of my cooking?"

"This is a taste of heaven, sir. Dr. Katsen should have married you just for this secret family recipe, right?"

"I wished she would have."

He layered his bread with gravy, mushrooms, and soft garlic potatoes. He chased the bite, cleaned his palate with soda and sweet tea. He had to have two or more beverages with each meal.

"You nudge the bread against the chicken and savor the flavor of the sides, soak up gravy and just take one big bite of chicken. If you find a mushroom hiding his face inside the sauce, it's a bonus bite in my book."

Laughing with bread in her mouth, Katie followed his method and loved him for it.

"Did your parents teach you that dipping method as a teenager?"

"A special person, one I miss, taught me how to swoop the masala with a pinch of broken bread and, well, believe it or not, every time I pass an Italian restaurant, I think of the summer of 1974, and Anna Katsen, or Dr. Katsen. I believe that's what you call her."

Doc Le Mans leaned back into a sweet memory, head tilted, heard music playing, and he listened, still grinning as he pictured Anna having dinner with him, happy campers.

"Did you know, sir, that Dr. Katsen never married the Navy sailor?"

"I have not heard from your professor in years." He looked at her. "Wait, there was a good turn out to a journalism conference, six years ago at Wake Forest University, and we briefly spoke afterward. I praised her on his presentation and asked her for her autograph. She laughed at me. We hugged for a long time, Katie."

"You didn't?" She held her belly and wiped his face. "An autograph? That was cool?"

"I did. She spoke on "How American Soldiers Impacted Cultural Trends Since Vietnam" and I was impressed at the depth of her research. She interviewed hundreds of mothers in Vietnam."

Turning her head, Katie leaned toward the door.

"What is it?" asked Doc, who pushed himself to his feet.

"Outside." Her hand pointed at the door. "Did you hear that?"

"Yeah." He eased his way to the door, pulled the weapon from the drawer.

"Someone is out there." Katie whispered.

Doctor Le Mans found his position and unlocked the deadbolt and scanned. He jumped; gun in the face of the man.

"Henderson!" shouted Katie.

"Nope," said Doc Le Mans, arms and shoulders dropped. "That's my neighbor Mickey Starr, Katie. He's a fisherman."

"Who else were you expecting, Rudolf the Red-nosed Reindeer and Santa?"

"Well, well, Mr. Santa Claus," said Doc, "You almost got yourself..." In Doc's belt, was where his 9mm rested, safety on.

Katie was introduced to Mickey Starr. Doc carried his bag full of gifts.

"Hope you're hungry, Mr. Starr," said Katie.

"Can't a man be friendly, and bring Christmas gifts anymore without being shot down, huh?" Mickey unloaded a shopping bag of gifts. "I have to go out of town, Doc, family emergency in Savannah, but I wanted to leave you and Katie with some good Starr hospitality."

They sat at the kitchen table.

"Hope it's not a life or death emergency, right?" Katie held her gift.

"My grandson, Tipp, broke his arm in a fishing accident, offshore angling. Gotta get back home. Fly out of Amarillo in the morning." He raised his hands, and looked at Doc. "I have Diego and his men on the ridge, twelve of them are camping out until New Year's Eve. If a rabbit moves in the field, they'll find his long ears and fire on the hare."

"Mr. Starr," said Katie, "no disrespect to your friends, but I know what happens when a bunch of fraternity gets together, so I fear it's not much different for a Texas motorcycle gang, right?"

Katie crunched ice and waited for his answer.

"I'll get you some more sweet tea." Doc told her.

"Campfire. Men. Food. Drinks." said Mickey Starr. "I-I-I'm not going to lie to you, men have to hydrate themselves, if you know what I mean, Katie."

"I've been to a backyard brawl against the Pitt Panthers. I sort of have an idea."

"Mick, you take care of Tipp, bring him and Volt Hendricks back with you in January."

"Love Volt Hendricks!" said Katie, hand on her chest. "Midnight Whistler is my favorite song."

"I have two trail horses they can ride in the Palo Duro Canyon."

"I realize Christmas is just two days away," said Mickey, hands out. "But, but, but I want you to open your gifts, right now."

"Tonight?" said Katie. "You don't have to tell me twice, Mr. Starr."

Mickey Starr pushed a small envelope into the hands of Doctor Le Mans, hand bouncing.

"What's this, Mick?" said Doc, who twisted his mustache.

"Open it." Mickey grinned.

Beau Le Mans took a knife from the table and cut the edge of the letter.

"Oh, um, well," said Doc, "where did you get a picture of Polly from Vietnam?"

"It fell out of Ben Henderson's pocket when Diego and his boys dropped him in a cornfield. Diego forgot to give it to me until today. I thought you might know the lady from Vietnam, Doc."

Katie leaned over Doc's shoulder, just enough to see the photograph.

"Polly? How beautiful she is. Look at her smile." She pointed, "That's Polly, huh? Whoa. Her hair makes me jealous."

"That's Polly. Been a long time." Doc stood, poured a glass of wine. "Thank you. Do you have more gifts, Mickey?" Doc felt the long box. "You shouldn't have. Carolina blue is my favorite color of tie. Navy blue is not."

"Oh, Mickey," said Katie, holding up a blanket. "Where did you get a Navajo alpaca wool blanket?" She stood. "This thing is taller than I am, sir. Feel of this material, Doc."

"Three shades of blue." Doc wrapped the blanket around her shoulders. "For me, the turquoise shade makes this blanket a keeper. Hey, Katie, if you don't want this thing, well, I'll..."

"This blanket goes back to West Virginia with me, gentlemen."

Mickey Starr reached inside his coat pocket. "I also forgot this one little gift."

"Oh, that is a nice Honduran leather wallet, Mickey. Thank you, buddy." said Doc.

"I got Tipp the same wallet on my last trip." Mickey told him, coat in his arms. "You two are in good hands. I'll be gone for several weeks, maybe a month."

"Mr. Starr, sir," said Katie, "my time in Robin's Egg comes to a close soon. I guess this is Merry Christmas and Happy New Year and goodbye, all in one big hug."

"Always a pleasure to meet a friend of Doc's, little lady. And, well, I was thinking, Tipp, he's about your age and he graduated from the University of Georgia. If you see yourself in Savannah, we have the best sunshine and seafood this side of the Outer Banks."

Wrapped in her Navajo blanket, she leaned and hugged him again.

"Savannah sounds good compared to the snowy Morgantown mountains that I'll be in soon," said Katie, arms inside her blanket. "I might have to call you next summer and plan a trip to Tybee Island."

Katie returned to the kitchen and finished her meal. Doc and Mickey stood outside.

"Look, Doc, you can see Diego's campfire from here. There's nothing to worry about. I'm sure the restored 1966 Chevelle will be showroom ready when I return." Mickey slapped his arm.

"Hey, I'm more worried about Katie than the muscle car. Her time is almost up, so she will be leaving for West Virginia soon.

Ben Henderson has come a long way across the world to finish what he thinks is his revenge on me."

"He didn't like it much when Diego and his men dropped him off at the Cadillac Ranch," said Mickey, grinning and coughing, "roughed him up for jumping you, too. He'll be back, Doc. Be safe and stay armed. I know you have the next few weeks off from Texas Tech, but remember to watch your back. Get that Recon mind back about you, the one you left in Vietnam, and the one I left in Korea."

"War never leaves a man, especially when you're being hunted."

"Doc, I got to run and pack for Georgia. Take care of yourself and Merry Christmas."

"Mickey," said Doc, right hand out, "thank you for the picture of Polly. I'm not sure how this picture made it across the world, but I'll keep it in good hands. Good memories."

"I know you will, soldier."

"You keep well, Mickey Starr." Doc told him. "Hey, be sure and tell Tipp, I said to put a Band-Aid on that broken arm and get his butt out to my Robin's Egg Ranch."

"I'll do it, my friend." Mickey waved. "Ho - Ho - Ho!" shouted Mickey Starr, "And Merry Christmas to all!"

CHAPTER FIFTEEN

New Year's Eve

The days between Christmas and New Years ticked slowly because Doc roamed around his ranch, and Katie felt robbed of her time to question him about Vietnam. Each day she penned more new discoveries of his personal thoughts about what he said and did as a prisoner of war and her interest, emotions shared, and to recall his past intrigued him. He was in his late forties by that time in his life, still stout and broad, managing himself well, but Doc was preoccupied. In that short span of time, Doc expressed his friendship and trust to the aspiring journalist and would soon remember her benevolent smile. Additionally Doc soon realized that Diego and the members of the motorcycle gang had met their obligation with Mickey Starr, and Diego would exit Robin's Egg Ranch on the first day of the year. Only two dozen hours existed on the wall clock until Katie flew out of Amarillo, Texas to Pittsburgh, Pennsylvania, ending her research on the 2nd of January 1995. The most important aspect of getting to know Doc Le Mans was how easily he opened up, revealed himself and spoke freely about his emotional time as a POW. Friendships were rare as gold in Texas, especially to Doc Le Mans. He dreaded the part of letting go and parting ways with her, not knowing if he'd ever see or hear from her again.

Katie walked around the room, grinning and humming, and almost dancing when she realized what she'd typed on the last page of her independent project.

"Sir, my work here is done," said Katie, stuffing a notebook inside her book bag. "I think we should do something on my last night."

"Like what?"

"Do you mind if we head into town and join the revelers?"

Thunder sounded from Harley hogs outside. They walked over to the doorway where a dozen bikers had fired up their motorcycles, and Diego parked and waved at Doc Le Mans.

"Hey, Doc." Diego, dressed in black, removed his gloves. "My men are getting restless on New Year's Eve, if you know what I mean. They're thirsty for fun. We've been here half of the month of December and have not seen anything but a rabbit and whitetail deer."

The motorcycles were loud and his men were ready for fun and drinks.

"Funny you should mention it," said Doc Le Mans, who looked at Diego and back at Katie and saw the bikers bent in laughter, singing Rudolph the Red-Nosed Reindeer. "We were thinking of going into town, Diego. Would you and your gang join us at Garrett's Place in Amarillo?"

Diego looked at his men and back at Doc Le Mans.

"What's the problem, Diego?" said Doc Le Mans, hands in his pockets and he zipped up his leather jacket.

"Not sure my men have the Benjamins to hang at Garrett's Place with you and Katie for food and drinks, Doc." Diego propped his foot atop the steps. "It's a little pricey, don't you think, amigo?"

Katie looked at Doc and saw him grin and as if he'd won the lottery.

"Do you know who just bought Garrett's Place?" said Doc Le Mans, pointing down the road.

"No clue, boss." Diego opened his jacket pocket and handed the man ten thousand for two weeks of Recon at his Robin's Egg Ranch.

"Hey, you are the man, Doc Le Mans," said Diego, stuffing his leather jacket.

"Mr. Mickey Starr owns Garrett's Place, and he said, 'If Diego and his men get hungry or want to break something, just send them to Garrett's Place, and it won't cost them a penny' and that was Mickey's very words."

Doc Le Mans winked at Katie and she hugged him.

"I've known some fine men in my life, but never have I known anyone finer than you and Mickey Starr," said Diego, waving the leader over to shake hands with Doc Le Mans. "Ricco, over here."

The men shook hands and wished each other a Happy New Year.

"Yessir, Diego," said Ricco, taking his hat off as he got close. Diego's men could chew a rubber tire on a rainy day, but they honored Doc Le Mans and Mickey Starr with the highest respect in Potter County. "You needed me, sir?"

"Yeah." Diego smiled and pointed at Katie and Doc Le Mans. "Because of these two great people and Mickey Starr, we are headed to Garrett's Place!"

"Dang it, Diego. Not much dinero, boss." Ricco flapped his hat in his hand. "We have collected our money, all of us, and we have enough firearms to start another war, but only a few dollars in our pockets for Garrett's Place."

"Nada. Zero. This man, your boss, Doc Le Mans has worked it out with Mickey Starr about food and drinks. Nada, Ricco. We need nothing when we ride with Doc Le Mans and Mickey Starr."

Diego handed Ricco his part of the take.

"Holy Mother of Mary!" said Ricco, leaning backwards inside the doorway.

"And don't you forget Bad Katie Collins," she said, who tied a navy and gold sarape sash around her neck. We're going to have a blast; it's New Year's Eve!" shouted Katie.

"We'll follow you, Doc Le Mans," said Diego, "Lead the way, amigo."

"See you in ten minutes," said Doc Le Mans.

Everything about Katie was young and vibrant and her hair was long and the color was cinnamon. She turned on the radio and danced to "Telephone Man" by Michael Jackson.

"Doc Le Mans, sir, do you mind if I make a phone call. It's important."

"Help yourself, dear." Doc Le Mans tied his dark boots and pulled his belt tight. He had on jeans and a white dress shirt with a black vest. She disappeared into the kitchen and did not return for several minutes.

Doc Le Mans zipped Katie's sparkling purple dress, and after a few minutes in the mirror, she sang and hummed her way around the living room, still dancing. Doc Le Mans offered to lead her to his 1966 Chevelle, and she accepted. Only one photo was taken by Katie before Mickey Starr left for Georgia, and this was the second.

***

Garrett's Place, New Year's Eve, 1994

They sat at a large table beside the window, and half of Diego's men had not denied themselves, caught amid food and drinks. Others paced and enjoyed the dance floor and lights and what the night had to offer. There were as many ladies as they were men, bunched together when fast songs played, and the celebrators cranked up the atmosphere. When the waitress left the table, Katie sat beside her friend after she returned from the restroom.

"We have only two hours until the New Year!" shouted the disc jockey.

"I have a surprise for you, Doc Le Mans," said Katie, smiling and holding his hands. She tipped the disc jockey to play a slow song and he did. "It's part of my research."

"I'm not much for surprises," the professor said. He crossed his legs and waited.

The lights dimmed and the music slowed down.

"Would you dance with me, sir?' she said, hands opened.

"I haven't danced in years," Doc Le Mans said. "I don't get out much, Katie."

"Something tells me, you will do just fine."

They danced through the first two verses and the chorus.

"Is this the surprise, Katie?" he whispered. "A dance?"

"Katie, could I cut in," said a lady.

"No, Doc." said Katie, letting go. "She is your surprise."

"What?" said Doc Le Mans. "I'm not sure I know what's going on..."

The lady stepped inside his arms for a dance; her hands fit perfectly inside the palms of Doc Le Mans. The room was dark in certain places, faces unknown.

"So, Beau Le Mans, I hope you remember me." She wept.

"Polly?" His hands slipped around her face. He lifted her off the ground. "Oh, my God. I don't believe this."

"Le Mans, I never stopped looking for you. Never." Tears rolled down Polly's cheeks as Beau Le Mans kissed her lips, hugging his old friend and kissing her again.

"How did you get to America?" said Le Mans, wiping tears from her cheeks. "Polly, this is the best surprise a man could ever have. I hoped and prayed you had made it out of that camp. I am so, so sorry. I meant to come back for you, but...but I was shot. They sent me back to America. How did you find me?"

Her small hands held the face of Beau Le Mans and she kissed him, passionately.

"A little Katie bird found me, and with the help of Dr. Anna Katsen and her connections in Washington, D.C., things changed for the better. They asked if I would ever consider seeing you again, and I cried before I could answer them. Your friends are so sweet to fly me to Amarillo, Texas."

"This is not a surprise, Polly," said Le Mans. "This is a true miracle."

Doc Le Mans walked her to the table, and Katie stood beside Dr. Anna Katsen at the bar. Smiles and tears broke loose, as they toasted from across the room. Katie and Anna walked to the table.

"The reason they were able to bring me to America," said Polly, "is because of our daughter, Bian."

Polly handed him a picture.

"Daughter? Do we have a daughter together?" Doc Le Mans held his own face.

"From the cave?" said Polly, touching her tears. "One morning."

"The cave." He told her.

"Yes, Beau Le Mans, from the cave. My friends, Dr. Katsen and Katie were pivotal in their research and helped make this meeting possible. Of course, we must do a DNA test to prove it, but we can become a family. She has your eyes."

Le Mans kissed her forehead and lips several times.

"I never married, Polly. But I have a question for you. This picture was found in the pocket of Ben Henderson a few weeks ago. I thought he was M.I.A, but he is here, back in Texas. Did he make contact with you when he had a broken leg, a long, long time ago?"

She held her face and cried.

"I did see him, Le Mans," said the Vietnamese lady with a broken voice. "He was captured and beaten. I know he signed papers to fight for the Viet-Cong. He was in my village for three years. He told me that you killed my husband, down in the creek. So, I know he stole things from me. I was never his lady, Le Mans, I swear."

People moved to the bar when the song changed.

Beau heard a man yelling in the doorway.

"She's a liar, Le Mans!" said Ben Henderson, face red. "She was my girl for three years, and she loved this Texan very much, hillbilly. She loved me, not you!"

Polly screamed and ran to Dr. Anna Katsen and Katie; two ladies seated with others at the bar, while Le Mans and Henderson faced off.

"I tolerated you in the Army," said Le Mans, sniffing, "But I don't have to smell you or look at you anymore."

Henderson kicked Le Mans in the chest and he hit the floor. Henderson tackled him where he landed and pulled a knife to his neck.

"You don't want to do that, Caveman."

"Rank and mouth don't help you outside the Army, Le Mans."

He cut the right arm of Le Mans, bleeding from the swing of the blade. Le Mans blocked the next thrust toward his heart and penned him to the ground. Henderson was a big man in the Army, kicking loose, and an even bigger man at Garrett's Place. Le Mans blocked and punched. They both landed blows.

"You want me to take care of him, Doc," said Diego, hand on his throat.

"No." said Le Mans. "This man is mine."

"You better get someone to fight your battles for you, Le Mans," said Henderson, who swung a chair at Le Mans.

"Step up and finish it, Henderson."

Henderson jumped right toward Le Mans and kicked the knife with his hands. Henderson's arm was broken with a hard kick. Le Mans must have struck him a dozen times before Diego and his men pulled him off.

"Call the police!" someone shouted.

Le Mans checked the blood on his sleeve and wrapped his arms around Polly, Anna, and Katie, and hugged them all in one large concentric circle of care and love. His dream, the ladies that made him whole, and what he'd spoken to God about for years, all of them rested inside his arms.

The police took Henderson away. The crowd had calmed down.

"I'm not even sure how you pulled this off, Anna, after all these years," said Doc Le Mans, "but, to me, this is a New Year's Eve miracle."

They watched as Henderson was stuffed inside a police car, lights flashing.

"He'll be jailed for his crime," the arresting officer told them.

The four friends found seats at a table.

"This is a part of my research, Beau, and I'm sorry that I could not have reunited you two sooner, even fourteen years ago, when they voted to pass the AmerAsia Immigration Act."

"It's thirty seconds until the New Year!" shouted the disc jockey. "Get your cool champagne glasses ready for a Big New Year's toast!"

"I can't believe we are all together in the same place," said Le Mans, grinning happily.

"It's a wonderful surprise, isn't it, Doc Le Mans?" said Katie, with arms around him. "These two ladies love you and have traveled a long way to see you."

The crowd counted after KISS played on television.

"Anna," said Le Mans, whispering, "You could have flown us to New York City to see KISS."

"I don't have Mickey Starr's money, Beau." She kissed him.

All eyes turned to the grand television aired from New York City, with the famous host, Dick Clark.

"Ten, nine, eight, seven, six, five, four, three, two, one - Happy New Year! Happy New Year everyone!" shouted the DJ.

So, in Amarillo, being on Central Time, the crowd celebrated twice, and partied both times. Le Mans kissed Polly and Anna at the same. Third, it was sweet Katie Collins. They hugged in a giant circle and celebrated new and old friendships. And toasted, like they'd known each other since high school.

"Who will be around tomorrow?" said Doc Le Mans, searching their faces.

"Does Amarillo have a cave, Beau?" said Polly, drink in her hand.

When she broke the tense evening of Beau's older lovers, eyeing each other, the four of them placed their arms around the table.

"I'm sorry. It wasn't the Ritz, was it, Polly?" said Beau Le Mans, toasting her.

Dr. Anna Katsen firmly grabbed Beau's hand.

"Beau, I'm so sorry to cut the visit short. Katie and I have an early jet to Pittsburgh," said Dr. Katsen, who bent a frown. "But I wanted to be here, we all knew it would be something very, very special."

"It's something of a miracle, isn't it?" said Doc Le Mans, hand together.

"Yes. We all wanted to see this wonderful reunion, Beau. You and Polly, old friends, lovers ever," hand raised, "finally reunited. It is a big miracle."

"How many years has it been, Polly?" said Katie, leaning.

"Too long," said Polly. "Plus, our daughter, Bian, will be in Amarillo in the morning. We can all meet each other for the first time at breakfast."

Katie and Dr. Anna Katsen held their glasses.

"This is more than research, even though this part fulfilled my dream, a longtime burning flame, still aflame. Let's make a toast to our new circle of friendships, and may we never part ways because of time or distance." Dr. Anna Katsen welcomed each person into her arms, eyes wet and hugs tight. "We are better when we're together. All of us have been alone too long and now we have someone to call anytime on holidays and birthdays."

"Dr. Katsen," said Polly, and her soft broken English accent was no different than when Le Mans had heard it for the first time in the late 60s.

"Yes."

"From the bottom of my heart, I want to thank you in front of everyone for bringing me here from Vietnam. I'm so nervous to be here. My arms are shaking, and, and I do not know what to say to all of this - this wonderful, welcome home friendship. You people are too kind. It's not always that way in my country."

"O' honey," said Dr. Katsen, "this was a project from the U.S. The team in Washington D.C. are the ones who pulled this altogether, but knowing Sergeant Beau Le Mans, here, had fathered a daughter, makes it a special event and a true miracle. Family. I had to see this reunion and be a pivotal part of it. I made my way to Amarillo, so you could know the man I once loved after the war."

"I loved him first," said Polly.

"So, you did," said Dr. Katsen, grinning and taking a sip.

Katie was taking notes and snapping pictures. She had no questions for the couple, and sometimes hugs and tears meant more than broken words and a page of notes. The crowd at Garrett's Place had thinned out after midnight. Doc Le Mans held seats for each lady, head high and holding each one was among the greatest joys of his life.

"When I first saw Le Mans," said Polly, "he had blood about his hands and face. He was a little reluctant to speak to me, but he did. He's a flirt."

"What did he say?" said Katie, biting her pen.

"You're a purdy little lady," he told me. "What's your name, Doll Face?"

"That's the hillbilly in me," said Doc Le Mans, holding Polly's hands.

"That's the funniest thing I've ever heard," said Katie, hands over her mouth.

"He said to me, 'Do I have company?' in his country accent," said Anna. "Of course, Beau was nude when we first met, Polly."

"You three are killing me," said Doc Le Mans, hand on his gut, laughing.

"I'll never forget his crazy accent as long as I live. He made me laugh so hard with his smile and dirty grin." Polly told them, leaning on Le Mans and hugging him. "He's sweet."

"Dirty grin?" said Le Mans. "I had not bathed in a month."

"He looks good and smells clean tonight," said Dr. Katsen, winking at him.

"Yes, dirty, dirty grin and bad, bad mind." Polly shook her hand at Le Mans. "You know you had dirty thoughts, Beau. All American soldiers had the same thoughts back in Vietnam. If they got lucky, it was something to talk about."

"No different than the men I know in college," said Katie. "And women."

"It looks like he got lucky, didn't he?" said Dr. Katsen. "You can laugh at that joke, Polly and Beau. I'm a humorous professor."

The table of friends belted out laughs and shared big smiles.

"It was lucky that I made friends with a great lady, Anna." Polly told her.

"We are friends, aren't we?" said Dr. Katsen.

"That was my luck and thank you, all of you." said Le Mans, cupping the hand of Anna and Polly. "When will I see Bian, Polly? I'd love to meet her."

"She wants to see some strange Cadillacs in the dirt tomorrow. It's somewhere in a cornfield on Route 66. I don't understand the wealth and prosperity in America. Now who would take the beauty of ten running cars and bury them in the ground?" said Polly, hands up. "I don't get it."

"They call it "art" in this country," said Katie, raising her glass. "It's the world of art and design.

"We could see the Cadillac Ranch now, right?" said Le Mans, eyes wide for an answer.

"No. I'm truly sorry, Beau and Polly," said Dr. Katsen. "I have friends and family to meet in Pittsburgh. My prior obligations… and I can't break them. But this, you two, the love you had, it is why I flew to Amarillo, for you both."

"Well, ladies, at least let me drive you back to the hotel or hug you both at the airport in the morning, huh?" said Doc Le Mans.

"Nope. This is the best celebration anyone could dream of, Dr. Le Mans," said Katie, who started to cry and she put her head on the shoulder of her professor. "It has been a miracle. I sure better get a top score on this project."

"I know it was only for a day, Beau, but it was worth it," said Anna, now crying along with her student. "You see reunions like this with the military and on television, but to be a part of one, to feel good inside your heart, it's much different. I feel blessed."

"It's much better for me," said Polly, and the wetness of her eyes was genuine. "I did not think it was real when the letter came from America. So much has gone wrong with my life." She wiped her face. "I consider this meeting an answer to my prayers, and to see the four of us, your kind faces, is a dream. I know love lives in your eyes. I see it in good people." She extended her hands. Everyone held her hands. "You are good people. Once I heard the government passed the AmerAsia Immigration Act, I still felt hopeless, until I heard the voice of Dr. Katsen on the phone. Now I know people care. Americans made it right."

"To meet you, Polly," said Anna, "has been one of my great pleasures in my life. Words cannot express how bringing you and Bian to Amarillo has meant to me." Anna kissed and pressed his face.

"Me too." Doc Le Mans told her.

"Beau, I've wanted to tell you in person how I respect your work in journalism. I'm not sure how you have time to keep packing journal articles and peer-reviewed research. Some of the best work I have seen. I hate to admit it, because it's good stuff."

He kissed her forehead.

"I'm married to the ranch and my work, I guess," said Le Mans, laughing.

"I will not be here," said Dr. Katsen, sipping her water, "but the plan is for you to meet Bian and Polly in the morning. Please take some good pictures."

"Bian takes good photos." Polly held Beau's hands. "She will finally get to meet you, Beau Le Mans. Her father."

"I'll bring some paint," said Doc Le Mans, snapping his fingers. "We will paint out names on the cars at the Cadillac Ranch."

Katie and Anna stood, and many close hugs were given, and their hearts were filled with joy and sadness. They held each other and watched the couple who met in Vietnam talk about their first meeting.

"Anna, I don't know how I can thank you for making all this happen. And Katie, you are welcome to my Robin's Egg ranch anytime. The door is open to you as well, Anna," said Doc Le Mans.

"Thank you, Beau. The worst part about meeting friends is someone has to say goodbye," said Dr. Katsen, tears in her eyes and on her fingernails.

"You're a wonderful man, Doc Le Mans." Katie held his hands and kissed him. "I'm sure there's room for me in Texas. I loved riding trail horses in the Palo Duro Canyon. You are grumpy in the morning, Doc, but I will trade horse rides for good stories." Turning to Anna, she added, "And he made Chicken Masala, Dr. Katsen."

"What? He did," said Anna, smiling in her eyes. "I've not had that dish in years. The mushrooms are to die for. That's a pleasant meal at night with candles and wine."

"You are right, it's time to call it a night," said Doc Le Mans. "Give me kisses and hugs and this is good-bye, Anna and Katie."

"Happy New Year, Beau," said Anna, "and this is the first time we have ever said that to each other."

"I remember our Chinese New Year, Le Mans," said Polly, hands on her face. "It was the Year of the Earth Rooster, and not a good year."

"We could talk all night and we need to rest," said Dr. Katsen, who stood beside Katie.

In a flurry of tears and waves good-bye, Dr. Anna Katsen and Katie Collins flagged a cab at midnight. Doc Le Mans blew a kiss and stood alone on the curb, and didn't say anything to Polly. They watched each disappear in the silvery fog just as it happened before. Then, he followed the cab to the Starr Hotel where they sat in the lobby, still whispering as if they were back in the POW camp.

"Polly, I still can't believe you are here. You're as lovely as you were when we first met, and the war seems like a lifetime ago. We all lost something, didn't we, Polly?"

"Yeah. I have found you again and gained a daughter from the terrible war. Thought of you thousands of times, Beau Le Mans. Many days I imagined how you would propose and we'd be married in America. My eyes have turned to stores with beautiful wedding dresses and I became jealous. Finally, the two of us are together, here. I love it."

"What about Bian? I missed the chance to tuck her in at night and read her books. Please forgive me for not being there for you and her. Is she married?"

"She's married, Beau. No children. Yes, you did miss all those beautiful days and Father's Day. I had no one to share them with when I raised her, in the best way I knew how. Her husband will meet us in the morning at the Cadillac Ranch."

"Why did she not come tonight? I'm sure Dr. Katsen invited her and she was the main reason you flew this far," taking her hands, "for us to meet each other, right?"

"You're an American. My people are Vietnamese. She had a hard life in our country being both. Bian fought and defended herself more than she deserved from men and women and kids her own age. She has been brave and through all of this... the cultural changes, the hardships of life and war." Tears rolled down Polly's face and Beau held her on the lobby sofa. He felt her cold hands, and saw the redness on her pale cheeks. "I lied to you, Beau."

"No, no, no. What's wrong?"

"We have come a long way, struggling, poverty, living in lack and want, and for what? Was this just to see you? Can meeting you put my life back together? Put our lives together, huh? Is this a fraud?"

"This is not fraud. We are still friends. I don't know, Polly. We can try, the three of us. I have a big home for you and Bian and her husband, if he likes. Will you come home, live here?"

She sat tall, found a deep breath, and dropped her head.

"This is all so overwhelming and sudden. I cannot move. I was so excited to hear your name and have this chance to see you. The closer the time got to seeing you, the angrier Bian and her husband became with the thought of this... and Americans... this war-baby situation."

"She's more than that, to me, Polly. I'd love to meet her. Hold her."

He kissed her hands and face. They stood. Le Mans kindly cleaned her eyes.

"I will call Bian tonight, talk to her and see if she'll do me this one favor. Beau, she came to Amarillo. I-I-I hope she will know the wonderful man that I know you are. You are a professor and writer, and you have a nice ranch. It is what we have dreamed about. Could you pick us up in the morning at 10 o' clock?"

"Yes, yes, yes, for sure. Oh, Polly, you don't know how much all of this means to me. To see her eyes and hold my own flesh and blood, my daughter, our baby girl, and to have her sweet face with you. I have often wondered what became of you and now, my prayers are answered. Yes, I will see the three of you in the morning."

It was a sleepless night for Doctor Beau Le Mans, up early, coffee on the stove, long before the crow of the cock and sunrise. When sunlight found the home, atop the trees above a blanket of snow covered the land, hundreds of birds: Northern Cardinals, Blue Jays, American Pipits, Pine Siskins, and Robins.

At first light, a small, timid Robin flew to the banister on the front porch, three feet away and Beau fed the small creature a piece of his Danish at his ranch in Robin's Egg . Being able to share that chilly Sunday morning with Bian at the Cadillac Ranch, and he imagined holding her for the first time, as they stood, and witnessed a snow-covered cornfield, would be another miracle along Route 66.

***

Beau Le Mans parked his Suburban in front of the Starr Hotel, just as he'd planned, twenty minutes before the agreed time. He'd practiced in the mirror while shaving what he'd say to his daughter, but now he struggled to recall his speech. What were the first words? He had never been around children and always wanted to have a daughter to hold and someone that knew the same love he shared for her. The time had come to meet Bian.

He walked to the office counter.

"Sir, I'm here to meet two Vietnamese women, a mother and daughter, and a young man about twenty something. Have you seen them?"

"Not in a while. They had breakfast over there. It was early, five or so. My shift just started," said the man in a thick Mexican accent. "But, wait, yes, I did call a cab for the sweet mother, a Vietnamese lady." He looked at the clock. "They left, went to the airport." The man turned around and shuffled some papers, said, "Blanco, white. Wait, she gave me a white envelope, and said to give this to Dr. Beau Le Mans."

"I'm Dr. Le Mans."

The man handed him the paper.

***

Dear Beau,

Bian and I talked most of the night about our options, about hopes and dreams and what it would be like to settle down with you in Texas. She cried as much as I did. We held each other through the night. Our hearts have been broken for many years, too many times, and you have to know that. It all changed when I received a telephone call from Dr. Anna Katsen, and I knew it was true because she described how you were such a lovely and caring person. She said she was in love with you after you returned home from Vietnam.

My son-in-law did not want to meet you. He lost his father and uncle in the war against Americans. Instead, the three of us decided to fly back to Vietnam, not meeting with you again. By the time you read this letter, we will be in California and on our way back home.

I am not mad that we met. My love for you will always be true. Bian may understand our relationship one of these days, but at this time, she is not ready for a father. I must stick by my sweet daughter's decision. My heart would be broken to lose her after what she has been through over the years and what I have endured to help her be brave and walk with confidence that she is loved by us.

Dr. Katsen was right, you are a lovely and kind man. It is my promise to you that we will one day see each other again. Let me see if I can change things while I am at home. I am sorry to leave in this sad way.

Love,
Polly

CHAPTER SIXTEEN

Long Point Trail

Six months had passed since the New Year's Eve celebration at Garrett's Place, and the year 1995, being a warm spring, Beau spent much of his time hiking trails. He had championed the past decade on trails and cliffs, and on his long breaks as a professor, Beau Le Mans traveled to Oregon, hiked a hundred miles across Montana, camped for 37 days in Alaska, and flew to Georgia, where he climbed Stone Mountain, as if it was a set of steps on his front porch. Such trips were meant for adventure and to clear his head from a year's worth of journalism and teaching, it was how he pondered past memories with Polly and Anna.

After a few phone calls, he'd planned to hike Twin Falls State Park in Wyoming County, West Virginia, a place he had not hiked since his youth. With a curious change of events, he'd made his way north to Long Point Trail, something he'd missed, and overlooked the magnificent view of the New River Gorge Bridge. He'd loved both places after returning home from Vietnam. In the early '70s, he had watched steel bolted and arched to form the New River Gorge Bridge. His family served construction workers and engineers at Cafe Le Mans, but after their passing, Beau had decided to part with the three locations and sell off the real estate and rent out his home in Lansing, West Virginia.

A million dollars would not buy his Fayette County home. Beau didn't have the heart to part with the home his grandfather had built after WWI, still sitting off the beaten path 80 years after its construction. The farmhouse was fully furnished, a good place with plenty of room for a large family. By 1996, the family who had rented it for a decade, felt that North Carolina had a stronger market and so they moved to Hickory for a new start in the booming furniture industry. They moved out, and Doctor Beau Le Mans moved in.

Beau had spent a week hunting for a good record player, a colorful Beatles jukebox, and a larger, more economical refrigerator for the kitchen, a much-needed upgrade. The rest of the furniture fit his taste. Music and writing, typing the traditional style, hunt and peck, and it was the way Beau had preferred to spend the rest of the summer.

Aside from the war and clothing, the '60 and '70s still played in his head, from old songs to the hippie culture, and it was where he became a writer of purposeful words and good stories. On that particular June day, coffee in hand before the rooster crowed, Beau climbed from the valley floor to the New River Gorge Canyon Rim, just as he did on the morning after he returned home from Vietnam. The next day, with the eagerness of Katie's update on her second year of graduate school in journalism, Doc Le Mans had arranged a meeting, a long anticipated conversation.

One lovely lady sat, wide sun chaser hat, and was reading; she held *Leaves of Grass*.

"Hey, look at you digging Whitman, see you like this trail as much as I do, Katie."

"Well, well, well, you made it from Texas," said Katie, hugging Doctor Le Mans, "And I want to add that I'm considering a doctoral program at TTU. I owe that to you, sir."

"O', I'm proud of you, Katie," said Doc Le Mans, "the way you kept me on my toes about war stories and relationships. That's wonderful news."

Someone walked up behind Doc Le Mans.

"Beau Le Mans? Doctor Beau Le Mans," said Anna, closing her book, grinning. "What in the world are you doing here?"

"Wait! Only one person knew I'd be here at my Lansing home, Katie?"

"Hello. Goodbye." Katie said. "I'm headed to the New River Visitor's Center," said Katie. "Then, I'm headed home."

"Anna, Katie said you'd been coming here every summer since 1974."

They hugged Beau Le Mans. One in reception and the other was a farewell.

"I clear my head just like you do in Robin's Egg, Texas, I guess. How did it go with Polly and Bian, your new family, Beau? I bet it was a wonderful reunion."

Beau studied the morning clouds for a moment.

"I never got the chance to see Bian. Polly left early for Vietnam the next morning."

"Dang it. But, Beau, I set that meeting up a year in advance," Anna said, leaning back, "to bring your three together. What happened?"

"They decided to not see me. Bian wanted to leave. Because I was an American soldier, her husband wanted to retaliate." Beau pressed his hands together. "I was broken-hearted for a long time, months even. I hiked and climbed the Palo Duro Canyon, heard thundering hooves of the ghost horses running at sundown. I finally had to let them go from my heart."

"I am so sorry, Beau. I meant to do something good."

"You did something good, but they did not. It's the monkey and fish story."

"The monkey and the fish?"

"Yeah. The monkey sees the fish as drowning and he decides to save the small fish, so he pulls him on the bank and hugs him. The monkey celebrates. However, the fish needs water and not air. The fish starts to die. They are meant to live in two different worlds, like people. Sometimes, Anna, people are doing fine where they are and don't want to do better or change. We try to help them, but they're not comfortable in another world."

"I see. I felt it was the right thing."

"It was good, a true blessing from God. Polly and Bian could not cope with that kind of sudden change - to be Americans, and they have a right to immigrate here."

"Seems like we all have ghosts, long stories, and secrets from our past, and there's things we can't handle," said Anna, eyes wide. "Things we are not ready for."

Facing Anna, Beau hung his legs over the rocky cliff, and Anna did the same.

"I'll admit it. I called Katie and had to see you, Anna. I was ready for a change."

"She told me, Beau. I wanted to see you." She bumped his shoulder, and said, "It's just like old times. The green Jeep, Chevelle, Monte Carlo, and I can't let those days go by without smiling and seeing your eyes when that Jeep jumped out of gear."

"I had a dream about us. Here." Beau touched her hands. "You wanted to see me, huh? In the river nude, I bet."

She blurted out a laugh and squeezed his hands.

"Yeah. But, not in that cold, muddy river."

He remembered her sweet perfume, years ago. "And, to you, congratulations on your status as Program Chair at WVU."

"Thank you so much. Hey, you have established yourself in the Top Five Shooting Stars in Southwest as professor of Journalism and Communication, right? People speak of your lectures and research at conferences, and yours truly, your biggest fan, netted a copy of your latest book, Dr. Beau Le Mans."

"Can I have your autograph?"

"No. There's something that... Well, what you said pissed me off, years ago?"

"Something I said?"

"Anna, I was motivated by something you said in 1974. Your words cut me, but changed my life."

Anna found his eyes. "You remembered something I said in the '70s?"

"Made me mad as hell and turned me into a new man." Beau puckered his lips. "You taught me something about myself."

"Good Lord, what did I say? Hurry, I'm curious."

"Your words lead me to Texas Tech, so I started college and kept going." He threw a rock over the rocky cliff.

"The richness and heart you poured into journalism, Beau, could only have happened with someone who had lots of time on his hands."

"You mean a man who was alone, Anna?"

"You know how I love the Steelers. You are the Terry Bradshaw of journalism, Beau." She pulled the book he wrote close to her chest.

"You must've seen something in my writing that influenced you to speak frankly about what I'd be good at, back in '74."

"All a fire needs is one good spark, Beau. Way back when, I saw something inside you, a good-hearted man, a good thing, not many people have an eye for it, and I knew others could learn from your style of journalism and your kindness. Plus, I didn't want you to work in a diner as a cook when God had bigger plans for you after he got you home from Vietnam."

"That's the truth I have been looking for from you. Accomplishments. Degrees. We did it." Beau sniffed. "We took separate roads, but we did it. None of it matters, the way you want to matter in life, if you don't have someone to share your successes with over dinner and a movie."

"We had different paths."

"A good Army friend of mine from North Carolina told me his idea about being alone. He went to Germany after Vietnam, stationed at Heidelberg, where he stayed in beautiful villas, canoed the Rhine, and hiked the Alps."

"That must've been something special."

"Special?" His cheeks balled. "The soldier told me how he'd spent four years lost inside a German and Austrian world, a land of paradise, touring the cold land all alone."

"We are housed in the imprisonment of our desires, Beau. When it's hot, we wish it were cool. When it is winter, we wish it to be summer. You write about the confessions of soldiers inside a warzone, desires and regrets, and lifelong struggles of unhappiness because of dissatisfaction, or the way something went great or didn't go your way. It's all a laundry list of predilections and cravings, isn't it? Think about the discontentment and counseling sessions because of loneliness. God didn't mean for men and women to be alone."

He stood and removed bark from a tree branch and watched an eagle glide across the long valley. "Yeah. I think we all have hopes and dreams. We need solidarity as much as we need companionship. The hope for better days, and better times, flap our wings, learn to fly, but we can't glide into expectation forever. At some point, whether we like it or not, we land in an open field of reality and hit another wind of change and we're far away from where we first started. My time alone is over."

"My pride and selfishness has cost me lots of lonely weekends, too, Beau."

"Yeah. When we are lonely, we desire someone to take it all away; a companion, but not just anyone can be good company. It has to be someone special. That's the marvel of life. God does not want us to journey solo."

"I know what you mean. Friends. We are best of friends." She waved him to join her, down on the rocks, and hugged him.

"As much as I enjoyed helping Polly, I'd like to see if there might be some better days and better times with us, Anna. I have no feelings for Polly, in the way you might think I do. That was a long, long time ago, and an open door that the world tried to close, but too many people were hurt by the war in Vietnam. I have devoted my life to writing and studying about the impact of war on a culture."

He pulled her close, head on his shoulder and she sighed.

"For years I thought about us and hoped you'd write or call, Beau. I struggled with pride and selfishness, but knew you were the one. I never liked being alone." She searched his face for the same answer. "But when we ran into each other at Wake Forest

University, and in five minutes, your face warmed my heart. I held onto those feelings, good memories, and held them in a good place for a long time. I hoped you would come to the meetings at Duke, but you did not show. It feels good to be here with you again, Beau. I've waited a long time to hold you."

"It doesn't look like either one of us has stopped looking for each other."

She chuckled. Beau thought of them holding hands, feet kicking an old porch swing and admiring the earth tones of autumn in Fayette County, the same picture he'd kept from years earlier.

"Do you mean grow old together, Anna, sip coffee, forget where we put our glasses, and change each other's socks in the morning?"

"I love you, Beau Le Mans."

"Anna, God how I love you. I've waited a long, long time to love you the way you need to be cared for and change your dirty socks, gal."

"But, Beau, I can't do love right now."

Beau twisted to face her.

"What? You could share our daughter, Katie, with me couldn't you, Anna?"

Her pale face blushed. His eyes were locked on her.

Guilt ran across her eyes, and she said, "How'd you find out Katie was your daughter?"

"Anna, no one knows as much about their professor as Katie did about you. On her two different visits to Robin's Egg, the second time was the most obvious to me. The part that gave it away was when she said, 'I've never seen this picture in our album before, sir.' and that's the way she said it. So, those words, too much information, and her facial features reminded me of you. Even her voice sounds a bit like yours when she gets mad."

"I've wanted to bring Katie to Texas many times and open Christmas gifts with you."

"You should have."

"She does favor us. I am sorry, Beau. I should have said something, years ago."

"I missed her childhood, Anna."

"You missed child support, too. I never called you out for a penny, Beau. Not one penny."

"She might be a sailor's daughter, huh? Who knows? Maybe he has some child support and doctoral money for her, right?"

"No. She is yours, Beau. You got lucky twice, that's what you got."

"At least twice."

She grinned and he wiped his forehead.

"Close one."

"Close two, Beau."

"I would not have dodged my job as a father, if that what you think, Anna."

He adjusted his legs.

"I never said that, Mr. Le Mans."

"Did you realize Katie has restless leg syndrome just like I do? Another thing, Katie's right hand tapped the recliner when she was thinking and writing. Have you noticed that about our daughter and yourself?"

"No. I've grown used to her quirkiness, I guess. But she's a lot like you, Beau."

"Does she know I'm her father?"

"Yeah. She's known since high school."

"How'd you say it? Here's some mashed potatoes and O' Doctor Beau Le Mans at Texas Tech, that's your father. Good potatoes, Katie, aren't they?"

"No, no, no. It was her senior year of high school, all her friends danced with their fathers, but she was alone. I danced with her. She was very unhappy. That's when I told her the truth."

He stood and offered his hand.

"Would you like to see the old house in Lansing, just down the road?"

"I'd love to be your uninvited guest again, Doctor Beau Le Mans."

She followed him home. He fixed her some lemonade, while he had coffee and Dutch apple pie. Walking through each room of his farm house, Anna felt as though she'd never left. Time had given each one of them freedom, solidarity, so to speak. They'd used up years of ego and pride on each one's calendar. They'd spent most of those years tied to teaching college. Despite being in journalism and communication, they had not written to each other or called in over twenty years. Neither of them knew why, and that's why Beau invited her to his home. Both had unanswered questions and unsettled thoughts.

The same oak dinner table where they laughed and played cards, now worn by time and family meals, was before them, a relic from their past held coffee and conversations.

"Anna, we are so close to becoming a family." He held her shoulders, and sighed behind her. "What do you think about living here, or in Morgantown, or in Robin's Egg, Texas? We could make this thing official and chase the same desires, and answer this long overdue question between us. We could bury all this denial and bitterness we've been harboring for too many years."

She pushed his hand down gently.

"Let's have dinner and just enjoy the place. Where did you get that jukebox? I love it. Let me buy from you." She opened her handbag.

"Stop. Put your money away. You can't just throw money at things, and solve it."

"I was just being polite. I've always loved the nostalgia of your taste in music. Does it work? I don't just throw money at things, Beau."

"Okay, okay. Try it."

"Let me see if you know this song," said Anna, pulling her long, wavy cinnamon hair and pushing the buttons on the colorful jukebox that lit up the room like a carnival show.

"If it's from the 70s, I know it, Anna."

He crossed his legs, and waited for the voice inside the speakers. Three beats.

"Neil Young!" said Beau, snapping his fingers. "Nailed it."

"Old Man, 1972, that's one of my favorites," she said, snapping his fingers, "living in a West Virginia paradise, makes me think of two. It makes me think of you. He wrote that on his ranch in California, and toured the United Kingdom with that big hit."

"I love that song, it makes me think of you."

After the song ended, Anna danced her way over to where he sat and fell into his big arms. He embraced her and said, "I like your version better. My hand wrote a little poem when Katie said you had decided to drive to Fayetteville."

Her jaw dropped and her eyes bugged. "What? Poem? Well, um, didn't know you were a journalist and poet, Doctor Le Mans. Poetry. Read it aloud."

"If you stick around a while, you may discover I'm fluent in French and Afrikaans. I have had many years to paint as well as learn other romantic languages."

"Well, Mr. Edgar Allan Poet, let's hear your poem."

His notebook was full of short stories and poems, so he found the last page, the one he'd written specially for her when Katie said she'd be in Fayette County with her mother. The notebook was curled inside his aged and callused hands from being a rancher as well as a writer and he grinned.

Against the war I had to battle,
against the places I had to be,
against the miles of country roads,
and on every cloud and mountain I find a sweet memory.

Against the sands of Padre Island,
I etched your name,
against all odds, I felt the voice of a bride,
And I saw myself as the groom; you took my name.

And in an instant our lives were changed.
Against the roaring of the tide, the heart I drew was washed away.
Against all doubt and dismay,
On every sea and river, I find a sweet memory.
Tomorrow, my dear, is another day.

***

She dropped her glasses, took the poem into her hands, and read it aloud again. "I can tell this poem is from your heart, Beau. Are you trying to persuade me?"

"I'm trying to seduce you, gal." His elbow rested on the table and he grinned.

She punched him.

"Seduce me with a jukebox and some poetry, huh?"

"My persuasion started at the New River a long, long time ago, my dear. I'm trying to love you. I am trying to love you, Anna."

She laughed at him.

"You're a crazy romantic. One kiss for the poem. That was sweet, Beau. How many days did it take you to write that poem?"

"Oh, you thought I wrote that for you? I found that on the inside of a payphone booth, down in ole South Padre Island, Texas."

She tackled him on the bean bag. He tickled her.

"Are you lying to me, Beau? Inside an old telephone booth, huh? Is that where you get your inspiration?"

"Yeah. You'll never know, will you? Wish I could write like that. You'll find the best poetry and rap songs inside bathroom stalls and telephone booths, Dr. Katsen."

"You're pulling my leg, aren't you?"

The second time he read the poem in French, and years of study unfolded, pictures of the country, followed by his family albums.

"I'm impressed, Doctor Beau Le Mans. You have been busy."

Katie left after the New River Gorge visit. Unexpectedly, after 14 days together, Anna and Beau had traveled to Burnsville, Summersville, Twin Falls, Baileysville, Hanover,

R.D. Bailey Lake, spent three days at the Botanical Area of Cranberry Glades, and stayed the night at Snowshoe Resort.

When summer finally closed, Anna Katsen packed her bags for home, and it was a long and sad ride back to Morgantown, West Virginia. Tearful goodbyes and giant hugs were felt. Packed and headed in the other direction, Doctor Beau Le Mans traveled to his ranch in Robin's Egg, Texas. Inside his mailbox was a letter inviting him to Vietnam. Beau flew to Vietnam, and finally met Bian for three days, a special treat on her birthday.

"Bian, I'm moving, and here is my new address." He told his daughter.

"What?" said Bian, paper in her hand and hugging her father. "That is a long way from Texas, I bet."

"This is something new for me, and it will kick my cultural butt," said Beau. "At Garrett's Place, your mother was saying how you ride a bike and love cycling."

"Dad, I've watched cycling since I was eight," said Bian.

For the first time, Beau felt like he had a family and took his role as father.

"Could I fly you to France next month for the Tour?"

"I will be there," said Bian, jumping into his arms.

"I'll wire you the funds when I get settled in France."

"You are so very kind, Beau," said Polly, crying. "I'm sorry for leaving so early in Amarillo, Texas. That was wrong of me and my daughter to skip out on you."

He kissed her forehead.

"Don't worry about it. With the New Year's Eve celebration and the fight with Ben Henderson, I was not a good role model to be a father that night. I do understand family now and would like to spend time with my daughters, Bian and Katie."

He explained to Polly how he'd found out about being Katie's father and Polly became furious. She accused him of hopping on every boat that floated.

The airport was crowded when they dropped him off.

"Goodbye, Beau Le Mans, and I love you."

"You are always loved, Polly. See you in a few weeks, Bian. I love you both."

CHAPTER SEVENTEEN

1996

Chamonix and The Rose

In two days his large nine-hundred-acre ranch was listed and sold in Robin's Egg, Texas. Mickey Starr couldn't pass on a ranch adjacent to his real estate and doubled his ranch. The large check cleared the bank. Three days later Beau Le Mans had a sizable offer on his fifty-four acre farm in Fayette County, West Virginia, but he pulled his land off the market and decided not to list his West Virginia home. In a sudden decision, Doc Le Mans had taken a sabbatical from his teaching position at Texas Tech University. His first call was to Katie, and his new daughter reluctantly agreed to join him in France. His new gun dog, Roar Cooper, a ticked, liver, and roan German Shorthaired Pointer that followed him everywhere, like Velcro, the hound took up homesteading. The dog loved the mountains of France, spending most of the day chasing birds across the front porch of his new residence.

Wherever Beau traveled, he took his three worlds with him, the past, the pleasures of the present, and tomorrow's hope. Soon Bian and Katie, half-sisters, from other parts of the world, with birthdays less than three years apart would be living together for the first time. In the meantime, Beau bought ropes, and when he felt strong to climb, he did. He was happy to find a new four bedroom home, high in Chamonix-Mont Blanc, in Eastern France, not too far from the Le Mans Estate. He intended to rent a chalet in Les Rez de Chamonix, but the deal fell apart.

The sisters landed at de Gaulle Airport in Paris two hours apart. The two of them, Bian and Katie, hugged and cried and didn't know what to say or do, at first. They each were told to bring a surprise gift for each other, and they each purchased something special for their father, the fine doctor who was familiar with the height and climate of cool mountains.

"How did you ever find this place, Mr. Le Mans," said Bian, bowing to him.

"Call me, Dad, please. It wasn't easy, Bian."

"Yessir," said Katie," falling onto the sofa, "and thank you for inviting me to this wonderful part of France. It's a paradise."

"What are we going to do here for a month, Pops?" said Katie, laughing. "I will fall asleep; it is so peaceful and beautiful here in the mountains."

"In just a few days the Tour de France will race across the country and riders will climb The Alps and shoot through Chamonix Valley at high speed. I've waited all my life to have a family. Now, you two have made me speechless. It's special to have you close and watch the race."

Each sister found a luxurious room that pleased them. They stood beside each other for the first time and studied the grandness of snow-capped mountains from the living room window at the end of June 1996.

"Father, we rarely see snow in Vietnam," said Bian. "This is a snow-lovers paradise, Dad."

"We're hungry and happy, Pops." said Katie, with a voice that reminded him of her mother, years earlier.

"Let's go get some French food," said Beau.

Within a week, Katie fell in love with Le Monchu, a little place on The Arve River, and Bian, her taste buds leaned on the Le Panier, a sandwich she favored at the Le Cap Horn, made her tilt her head back and lick her lips. To have his daughters by his side fueled his appetite to please them and made each lady jovial. Neither of his daughters had landed positions in the workforce that they could not do without, so they stayed through the fall, loving the snowy winter, and by the spring of 1997, Beau knew his daughters loved him as much as he loved them. Beau took them to concerts, supplied a generous wardrobe, and they could not only speak some French, but they had kept singing and music lessons each week. In a short time, Chamonix had taken them to a world that was almost fantasy for young aspiring ladies.

One evening in April of 1997, Katie had selected Albert 1ER, a place steeped in wonderful history, serving delectable dishes, and fine wines from the vast region. About the time the standing ovation happened for the piano player, Beau clutched his side.

"What's wrong, Dad?" said Bian, holding his arms.

"I injured myself climbing yesterday," said Beau, catching his breath. "I've pulled a muscle or something bad. It's nothing. But we need to go."

"Are you sure?" said Katie, who held his hand.

Before the piano player turned the page for the next song, Doctor Beau Le Mans had fallen and collapsed. By 7 o' clock he was admitted to the Hopitaux du Mont-Blanc, amid Chamonix.

Later, he was transferred to Praz-Coutant, a hospital specializing in treatment. Katie and Bian waited in a nearby room.

"Doctor Le Mans," said the doctor, "How long have you known about your bladder cancer?"

"Four weeks, Doc."

"Can I invite your daughters inside and deliver the news, Doctor Le Mans?"

"Wish it was good news, Doc. Fought in Vietnam, traveled to a dozen countries, and as soon as I started to enjoy life in a beautiful place, bad news breaks my heart. Doctor Austine, let me be the one to share the news with girls. Can I do that?"

"Yeah. Fair enough," said Doctor Austine. "The doctor held his hand. "You are among the best cancer doctors in the world, I've heard."

"Doctor Le Mans, are you medical or academic?"

"Education. Journalism. Plus, I've been doing some research on my condition."

"Pardon me, but you need to stay here for treatment, not travel back to America. Use our library, the one in town for your best research and articles. That's my two cents."

"I will start next week."

The doctor crossed his arms.

"You should start treatment in the morning."

Beau pressed the button that raised him up, and waited.

"Serious, huh?"

"Very."

"Bad news. I can take treatment here. That's the good part."

Doctor Austine opened the room's door and waved Beau's daughters inside. Beau and Doctor Austine explained the type of cancer he had and the care he needed to battle the disease.

"How long does he have, sir?" said Katie.

"Well, ma'am," said Doctor Austine, clipboard under his arm, "there's a few factors to consider: medication, chemo, radiation, and how his body reacts to all of it. This disease can be beat. I've seen it happen."

"Cancer, what's it good for?" said Beau. "Nothing." His voice was low. "Just like war, what's it good for?"

Tears flooded the eyes of Katie and Bian, and Beau just closed his eyes and listened. The three of them wept. Each hand was held by his daughters and for the first time, the man was not alone. Chamonix was full of surprises. When Katie and Bian went back to his home in Chamonix, inside Beau's notebook was full of poems and songs he'd written to each daughter before they arrived. They read them aloud and just held each other on the big sofa.

"I barely know him," said Bian, eyes wet and sincere. "What do we do, Katie?"

"I'm not sure we can do anything. If you pray, let's pray together."

"Does he have any family that we can call?" Bian held a book.

"He had a brother, Wells, who was killed in West Virginia. No sisters. His parents passed away. He never married. We are the only blood relatives he has left."

"I will stay as long as I can for him," said Bian. "My place is here, not in Vietnam."

Adjusting the pillows, Katie sat up, and said, "I met him a few years ago in Texas. He has been good to me, even before he knew I was his daughter. Dad has not had anyone close to him in years. He lived alone in Texas, had a ranch, and talked to his horses and cattle. He does have a good friend in Georgia, Mickey

Starr, a wealthy fisherman. He has his new puppy, Roar. I can call Mickey Starr and Tipp Starr and give them the bad news about his cancer."

Bian paced around the room, arms folded, and said, "Call Mister Mickey."

"I will."

"We can both get to know him better, and take turns visiting him in the hospital. I'd like to hear his stories about growing up in Virginia," said Bian who abruptly sat at the kitchen bar. "He seems like a very nice man."

"It's West "By God" Virginia, not Virginia," said Katie, eyes confirmed. I understand he is one of the best men my mother knows," said Katie, pouring some coffee. She stood in the kitchen by the window, soaking up the view of the tall mountains. "The 1997 Tour De France starts tomorrow, maybe we can watch it together on television, huh? Dad loves cycling."

"We could stand by the road when the riders race through Chamonix?"

Bian clutched her sister's hands, and said, "Yeah. Dad has waited all his life to see this big race in person. We can watch the race together. He'll love to have us with him to see the riders."

Katie found Mickey's number in a notebook.

"While we wait, I'll call Mickey." Katie sat and cried.

In two days, Mickey Starr arrived in France. Beau was grateful to see his friend. They watched the race together, and on the fourth day of the race, Beau was released from the hospital. On the day the race finally reached Chamonix, the valley was full, thousands of people from all over the world had flown in for the Tour. Mickey Starr escorted Katie and Bian to watch the cyclist race through the good town. Beau was too sick from the chemo to watch the race he'd always wanted to see in person. The door was left halfway open for Beau's half grown dog, Roar Cooper, to help himself to the great outdoors. The breeze was cool on the mountain top and the dog chased birds and barked.

"Hello, is anyone home?" A man yelled from the doorway.

"Yeah! Mister Mailman." said Beau, behind the wall in the kitchen. "I'll be right there, man. Just making myself a sandwich." Beau stepped into the open room and the man saw him.

"Well, well, Doctor Beau Le Mans."

"Ben Henderson. I hoped you'd died."

"Diego and his boys can't hurt me. The fight at Garrett's Place just got me excited to see you again. You think I'm going down without settling this old fight, hillbilly."

Beau caught his breath and sat down on a stool.

"Hey, Caveman, let's just call it even. I have cancer, can't keep fighting this way."

"That's a damn lie. We know you're loaded from the real estate you just sold to Mickey Starr and Tipp Starr."

"I am sick, Ben! It's the truth, man. Cancer. Look at the bruises on my arms from needles and chemo." Beau held out both arms and flipped his hands.

"You're afraid, Le Mans, like you were as a young punk kid in Vietnam."

"I remember nights when you cried yourself to sleep, Henderson. Cried like a baby!"

Ben walked around the room, picking up the ceramic vases and touching the French artwork that hung up on the wall and helped himself to the refrigerator for a bottle of wine. He found a seat and made himself a sandwich, watching Beau rest, head down.

"You never heard me cry. That must've been Sam Law or Hien."

"What kind of gun is that in your hand? Do you plan to kill me, Ben? What good will that do, man? I'll be a dead man in a few months, anyway."

Ben walked over to Beau, stood four feet away, and his cold face broke into a large smirk. He held Beau's medication, read aloud the daily dose, and threw it across the room.

"It may save you some chemo sessions. Let me put you down, Le Mans, like an old hound dog. Look around the room, flowers and family, you're going to be dead soon. When you get visitors during the week, you are going to die, man. Cancer, it's got your name on it, Le Mans. You ain't "The Beau-Man" anymore. You're done, soldier. Mission accomplished."

The door slammed. "No, you're done!"

"Bian, this man is crazy!" said Le Mans, arm out.

"This must be Christmas," said Henderson, chuckling, "two of my favorite people are here, celebrating his real estate deal in France. Your mother told me, years ago, Beau Le Mans was your father. He had no idea I watched over you for three years and paid your way."

"I hate you for raping my mother. You're trash!"

"You had a big mouth in Vietnam, Bian. Distance has not changed you."

She walked slowly toward him with a new confidence that Beau Le Mans had never seen. Shyness had been left behind. Her eyes never left Ben Henderosn's face, stopping and waiting about eight feet away. The way she'd defended herself in high school, perhaps.

"Wait, Bian!" said Le Mans, hands up high. "He's crazy. I know him. He'll kill you."

"I'm crazy, Ben. You better watch out for me," said Bian. "He doesn't scare me. I'm tired of him beating up on me and my mother."

"Stay back, Bian." said Ben, voice low and his hand waved at her. "I've waited a long, long time to settle my score with Le Mans, not you. We have old business to settle, doll, don't we, Le Mans?"

"I don't get scared." She took a step closer. "Shoot me. Take your best shot."

Henderson moved around in front of the door.

"Okay. No witnesses." He eased up the gun.

"Caveman!" yelled Beau, throwing a mug at Ben Henderson.

When Ben flinched, and turned, Bian kicked his hands. The gun fired and flew into the doorway. Ben raced to pick up the firearm and so did Bian.

"Too late, Henderson," said Mickey Starr, "I saw you come up the hill. No one wears camo in France on race day. This is the man who fired the gun, Mr. Policeman. Attempted murder from Ben Henderson."

"On the floor!" said the police. "You're under arrest."

They rushed Ben Henderson into the police car.

"Mickey, you should've seen Bian. She is my hero."

"Are you okay, father?" said Bian, touching his face.

"Yeah. I'm fine," said Le Mans, wiping blood from his arm. "He had no aim in Vietnam. You're brave. Polly was brave when we escaped the POW camp. You are just as brave as your mother, Bian."

Katie drove up the hill after the cyclists passed through Chamonix, and Bian told her what had happened with

Henderson and how she and Mickey Starr saved their father from being shot to death.

***

Katie's Notebook, September 1999

Two years twisted by in France, and I documented dad's condition. I'd like to say that was the last time we saw Ben Henderson, but it wasn't. It was a moment that made my hand take over the family writing and photography. In February of 1999, Henderson broke into our home in France, and without blinking, Bian shot him in the chest on Saint Valentine's Day.

The police questioned Bian, but she was released from jail the next day. We were all there, and told the same story, the same way it happened. Bian did not shed a tear. No one was charged.

***

The following year was 2000, the Tour de France returned to Chamonix in July, and Bian, Dad, and I, all of us cheered until we lost our voices, so loud the television station taped our excitement and caught our America flag on camera. For good luck we rubbed our father's bald head in front of the camera. He'd lost all his handsome hair. We caught one of the water bottles from the cyclist, and lo and behold, another bottle slid under my father's seat. Lance Armstrong, the rider my father had followed for years, had dropped out, days earlier. To this day, we have no idea the name of the cyclist who threw the bottle.

Dad decided to leave the home we had become so fond of for two years in Chamonix, after the Tour de France concluded, and he said "This home has served its purpose, ladies." The doctor's said his cancer had spread, and since there was nothing the doctors could do in France, we all three moved back to Fayette County, West Virginia. Bian fell in love with the New River Gorge valley and loved Twin Falls, down in Wyoming County. Dad wasn't sure how long he had to live, but he was not ready to give up his life yet.

"Katie?" said Dad, resting in bed. "Could you come here?"

I left the living room for his bed and rushed in each time he needed something. I dared him to ring that dang bell again. One more time and I would've thrown him and the bell from the bridge.

"Is everything alright?" I asked him. "Are you comfortable?"

He quickly sat up, and I placed pillows behind him, remote in hand, fluffing goose down pillows just the way he liked them.

"Could you open my jewelry box?" He pointed to a box in the corner of the room with one hand while holding his Army hat with the other, the way he held it at all times. "Reach me the dog tags that have the name Samuel Lawrence etched on them. I'll take my dog tags, as well."

He had not worn his dog tags in over twenty-five years.

"Here. What are you doing with another soldier's dog tags?"

That's when he told Bian and I the story of how Samuel "Sam Law" Lawrence, Ben "Caveman" Henderson, and my father escaped the POW camp, with the help of Polly and Cadeo. Bian had heard the story from her mother a dozen times, but, with a wet face, I jotted down his every word. He wanted to record him and play it to his grandkids in the future. I couldn't do it.

"Yeah. I'm fine, Katie. I made a promise to myself, well, years ago, that I'd hand these dog tags and a Cherokee Purple tomato to the parents of Sam Law, my great friend in Vietnam. I have not done that yet, and it couldn't be too far of a drive to Winchester, Virginia from Fayette County."

Someone stepped on the front porch and Roar Cooper barked.

"Hello, Beau Le Mans. Welcome back to West Virginia, buddy."

Dad got out of bed when he heard a familiar voice from Georgia.

"Dang it, Mickey Starr!" said Dad, cane in his hand and glasses covering bright blue eyes. "I'll be a monkey's uncle. What the heck are you doing in the hills of West Virginia? Why aren't you catching some seafood in Savannah with Tipp?"

"Friends are more important than fish," said Mickey, laughing. The man removed his hat and gray hair popped out like a clown at the West Virginia State Fair, and he entertained us for the next hour. We had not seen Mickey Starr since France, two years earlier.

"Dad was talking about visiting the family of an old Army buddy, Sam Law, who had lost his life in Vietnam from a sniper, a guy from Winchester, Virginia," I said. "But I have a few things to do and can't take him, Mickey."

"Hey, my calendar is clear for the next two weeks, Doctor Le Mans. Whatever you need, Beau, I'm here for you, my friend. Let's go to Virginia."

Bian and I served lunch in the living room, and we talked about riding horses in Texas and how France was much like the Rockies. Dad told Mickey where they could catch a few trout on the banks of the New River. They took their fishing gear with them.

"So," said Mickey, "well, Beau, when are we leaving for Winchester?"

"We could leave bright and early in the morning," said my father.

"I'm already packed, Beau. If you want," Mickey looked around the room, "I can leave today, right now, buddy."

I poured Dad a glass of water. Mickey offered him some Turkey Tail, a mushroom from the Northwestern part of Washington. The man from Georgia had a few connections from a Chinese medicine man in Savannah and felt it might help fight the cancer.

"Let's go, Mickey. I feel good, brother." He looked around the room for a consensus, and faces acknowledged his happiness to go to Winchester. "I promised myself to return my friend's dog tags and a tomato after I found his body in Vietnam. I need to keep my word to God."

"I'll pack you an overnight bag," said Bian.

"Got my Army Dress Blues, please, Bian."

"You could grab a hotel tonight in Winchester," I said, "and find Lawrence's home on Friday morning. You could wear your uniform, if you like, Dad."

They stayed the night in Mount Jackson, outside the vineyard of Andy Oliver, saw a hundred geese, and stayed at Weston Laramie's bed and breakfast. Mickey called every four or five hours to let us know if Dad was strong enough to meet the parents and deliver the dog tags and tomato of Sam Law, and he was doing well, full of energy for a cool September day in the brisk Shenandoah Valley.

After two hours of driving around Winchester, Mickey Starr must have knocked on twenty doors, until finally he met someone who knew Samuel Lawrence.

Mickey stayed in his truck. Dad slowly bent down, dirt layered both hands, and he did it for Sam Law, a soldier who never had the chance to kiss the Virginia soil of his family home. Dad took a deep breath, tomato in hand, knocked, and stood in his Dress Blues, a decorated soldier. The medication caused him to lose his appetite, so his Army uniform fit perfectly.

"Yessir, how can we help you, soldier," said the lady who answered the door.

"I'm Sgt. Beau Le Mans, ma'am, I served with your son, Samuel."

A thin nosey man stepped inside the screen door, pushing his gray hair over his ear and he must have been eighty years old.

"Is this some kind of joke, young man?" said the old man in the doorway. "Why would the U.S. Army send a man holding a tomato to our home after more than twenty-five years, huh?"

Mickey said Dad held the door, but he could not hear what was being spoken between him and Mr. Lawrence, so he quickly walked toward the home and lent his ear to the conversation.

"Pardon me," said Mickey, "Sgt. Le Mans, here, is a modest man, he is a world famous journalist and teaches at Texas Tech University. I know you may be surprised to see him in uniform, but Mr. and Mrs. Lawrence; he has cancer and wanted to give you something that belonged to your son. Also, Samuel wanted you to taste a Cherokee Purple tomato."

Mickey Starr shrugged his shoulders.

"Strange folks. But, well, come inside," said Mr. Lawrence. "Take a seat."

They sat in the small living room of a white two-story farm home. Dusty pictures of Samuel Lawrence were on the wall, and more pictures from his Army days down to his first school year. His favorite of them was the picture of Sam in kindergarten. A single Catholic statue stood alone on the only shelf in the room. A Notre Dame colored football was on the shelf by the television.

"Here," said Sgt. Le Mans. "Samuel's dog tags. Tomato."

"Samuel, Samuel, Samuel, please come home!" said Mrs. Lawrence.

His mother, Ruth, fell into a thousand pieces when she read his name on the dog tags. Sam's father cried on her shoulder, and they cupped the dog tags and chains inside their shaking arms. Dad had spent hours that week shining the dog tags, pondering his speech, talking to himself, and had brought the dog tags back to their original stainless steel color.

"Sam was a strong Catholic; the faith we shared together saved us and gave us hope to escape the POW camp." My father told them.

"They said Sam was killed in a POW camp, Sgt. Le Mans, right?" said Mr. Lawrence, hand together.

Mrs. Lawrence held Sam's picture and cried on the floor.

"No sir, Mr. Lawrence. Ben Henderson, Sam, and myself, the three of us broke free from the POW camp and escaped. Sam, your brave son, led the way and we got out. Thanks to your son, we walked for miles, cutting our way through the jungle and we were almost home free."

"What happened to my son?" said Mrs. Lawrence, face wet. "Tell me."

"Sammy, he was gone all the time and lived in the mountains as a boy," said Mr. Lawrence, crying. "He was a good hunter and led us through the woods each fall."

His mother dried her eyes.

"What happened to Samuel?" asked Mrs. Lawrence.

"What else did my Sammy do, sir, tell us?" said the old man.

Mickey said that was when Dad started coughing and needed some water for his throat. "We had stayed the first night away from the POW camp, Sam, being the great leader, took the front and marched us out of the jungle to a small village, a hot zone."

My father started to cry.

"You alright, Beau," said Mickey, hand on his shoulder. "Drink water."

"Yeah. Samuel Lawrence was my best friend. Heck of a soldier." said Sgt. Le Mans.

"What happened, sir?" said Mr. Lawrence, down on the floor, shaking my father's hands. "Please go on. We need the truth."

"Sam had courage, and spoke of going to Holy Cross College, then Notre Dame. He boldly stepped out into a clearing, and that's when the Viet-Cong sniper spotted him."

Mrs. Lawrence fell on her face and started to scream, "I hate guns. I hate war! I hate soldiers and the government, and lying President Nixon, he's the devil for killing my son."

Mr. Lawrence walked to the front door and pointed outside.

"Gentlemen," said Mr. Lawrence, "We appreciate you stopping, but this is too much for us. The story, his death, and it's a hard time reliving it again. Your sad story was enough to tell his friends at church. We don't need any more sad stories about my son. You men need to leave, and leave my home now. Get out!"

"Let's go, Beau," said Mickey, pushing his friend outside.

My father grabbed the doorframe and held it.

"I kept my word to Sam Law, sir," said Beau, walking off the porch. "And to God."

"Go! Leave my property! God help you both!" yelled Mr. Lawrence, waving his cane, pushing my father off the porch. The old man threw his cane and breathed heavily.

Mickey Starr said he pushed Dad and that's when he lost his balance on the steps and fell into the front yard. Mr. Lawrence threw the tomato and hit Mickey Starr, bleeding tomato juice down the back of his white shirt.

"Are you crazy, old man?" said Mickey Starr, pulling him up. "This man has cancer. Touch him again and I'll flatten you, Lawrence! This was his dyeing request."

"My son didn't have a dyeing request, did he, Sgt. Le Mans?" said Mr. Lawrence. "Got off my property!"

Mr. Lawrence, gray headed, skin with aged spots, was up in years. Mickey Starr, a man of sixty, tanned skin from fishing, had helped my father to the truck. Mickey drove to Mount Jackson before either of them spoke the first word about the rudeness of Samuel Lawrence, Sr. and his wife, Ruth. That was a sad afternoon, one that broke Dad's heart. He'd waited a long time to give Sam Law's dog tags to his next of kin and it ended in a disaster, not at all how he'd pictured the morning in his head.

"I've made peace with the dog tags, Mickey."

"You have done the right thing, Beau. As grumpy as he was, I'm not sure the milkman wasn't Sam's father."

The men cackled.

"He's got a good arm, though. He could pitch for the Rangers, like Nolan Ryan."

An interstate sign pointed them to Andy Oliver Vineyards, where they met Weston Laramie again, and Mickey felt the need to make amends himself and bought ten cases of his best port.

Night fell fast on our farm in Lansing, West Virginia, in early fall. Dad was asleep by the time Mickey reached Lookout Mountain, a small place in Fayette County, Dad favored in the evening. Mickey's truck pulled up, lights on, and Bian helped Dad to his favorite recliner.

"How was the trip?" said Bian, face curious.

"Not good. We got kicked out and hit by a purple tomato." said Dad. "Stubborn mules. Both of them. Good arm, though."

We all sat in the living room and had popcorn and soda.

"Beau," said Mickey, elbows on his knees, "said what he needed to say, in my opinion. He told old man Lawrence what happened to his son, Sam Law, and how he was killed, that's when Sam's mother broke into tears and started screaming at us."

"That's when the old man got short tempered," said Dad, "told us to leave, get out, and he pushed me out the door and into the grass."

"Should've flattened that old goat for touching you," said Mickey, leaning.

I remember my father, and some nights stood out more than others. Once, out of the blue, Dad asked to turn off the television. I felt what others must have seen when they first met my father, and in that room, everyone saw it too, a sort of hero, a magical man in good spirit, and one of those sweet revelations in life happened. Beau Le Mans was a rare Mountaineer. We all hoped and believed in the Turkey Tail vitamins that Mickey Starr's Chinese friend had recommended. He laughed and sang and told funny stories.

"I've only been in love twice in my life," my father told us, head bobbing. "The first time was with your mother, Bian, and Polly was an angel when I served in the Army." He rubbed his throat and held back the tears.

Mickey passed him a linen napkin, of which, being my father, he made it into a pirate's hat, made a tie, turned it into a long beard, wrapped the cloth around his head like some Compton gangster, and the last thing he made, a long rose. We laughed, the four of us, caught in amusement, and our bellies hurt from the look on my father's face. Bian snapped picture after picture for our family album. He requested the door be open a bit in the evening time for his bird dog, Roar Cooper, ears flipped up, who listened for owls, inside the doorway.

"My next love was... Anna Katsen." He held the rose in both hands. "I always hoped she felt the same. I love her with all my heart. She has a heart of gold. I hope you know that about your mother, Katie."

I saw my mother pet the dog and step inside the house. Her finger covered her lips. My father did not see my mother and kept talking.

"How much do you love my mother, Dad?" I asked him.

She dropped his head and cried.

"I love you, Beau. I always have," said my mother, who heard the truth of his love for her. She petted the dog in the dark, stood inside the doorway, and saw him craft a lovely rose.

"Oh, Anna," said Dad, face full of tears. "I meant what I said. And, lady, look at you, like sunshine on a rainy day. Beautiful as ever."

My mother wept and kissed him many times. They were the other half of each other.

"I got the keys to that old Chevelle," said Dad, grinning.

"Keep wishing, Beau." She told him, eating my popcorn.

Dad, in his creative mind, turned that crimson linen into a long, round rose again, and even better the second time. Being that he still loved my mother very much, he handed her the stunning rose.

All of us stayed up late telling stories: Mickey, Bian, Dad, Mom, and their fascinating stories held our attention, a world of laughter. That night was loaded with jokes and kindness was held between friends. Dad hugged everyone's neck and called his own bedtime. He was wired that way.

"My gut hurts," said Dad. "Too much fun. Let's do this again tomorrow night. Au Revoir. Goodbye until we meet again. Au Revoir, everyone." Dad told us all, still laughing, half bent, holding the cane.

"Au revoir. Au revoir." I told him, smiling.

Ironically, the next day was Bridge Day in West Virginia at the New River Gorge Bridge, it happened on the second Saturday of October.

I typed a letter about my father, and mailed it to *The Charleston-Gazette*. I had no idea the number of friends he'd made over his lifetime. My story had reached the media as far west as Arizona and as far north as Montana. Get Well cards and letters came from people whose hearts he'd touched in his days as a journalist and as a gifted public speaker, from small towns to big cities, from the mail carrier to senators and fellow colleagues. Each one shared a sincere word of hope and prayers. One lady wrote how Beau Le Mans traded her his high-dollar bolo tie because she fell in love with his Texas horn bolo design at a restaurant in the wonderful town of Bossier City, Louisiana.

The following day, Bian, who wasn't good at goodbyes, flew back home to Vietnam, and did not want to be around when her father passed away. Mickey Starr drove back to Savannah, where he ordered enough Turkey Tail for a small Army. In a strange turn of events, an experience of sorts, something that Mickey Starr has laughed about when medical doctors said they could do nothing more for my father. After months of taking the Turkey Tail mushroom from the woods of Washington and Oregon, the cancer my father, Beau Le Mans, had for years, started to go into remission. The hair on his arms and pits returned, and the hair on his head grew in as if he had the hair plugs advertised on television. His energy level returned to normal. Prayers were answered and he walked trails, just as he did before his sickness. Yet, he did not return to Texas Tech University, but signed up for his retirement. Words flowed, pages were filled, and my father published his tenth book about what really happened in Vietnam.

When the novel hit the Best-sellers list, he jumped out of his socks and celebrated.

"Someone in a dark suit is at the door, Dad," I told him.

"That doesn't surprise me." He went to the door in a rage and met him in the yard.

"Can I help you?"

The man removed his glasses.

"I thought we had a deal, Le Mans." He snuffed out his cigarette on our door post.

"That was twenty-five years, man. I've got freedom of speech, Jack. I write and say whatever I want to say. Do something about it?"

Our dog bit the fire out of his legs.

"We'll see, Le Mans. You'll see, you don't embarrass a former president."

"He embarrassed himself."

The man drove away and his hand emerged from the car window.

"Let's call Mickey Starr, have him pull some rank in D.C." I told him.

My father made a call to Mickey Starr. I'm not sure who Mickey Starr called, but the man in the dark suit never returned to Fayette County, West Virginia. However, we stayed in Lansing, the night the ball dropped on New Year's Eve, 1999. It was two hours until midnight when a black car pulled into the driveway.

"Are you expecting anyone, Dad?"

"Nope. Not again."

The man approached in a dark suit, shoes shined, shirt white, and he held something inside the bend in his arm. I found the peep hole in the door.

"You're not going to believe this, Dad? Here comes another black suit."

The man stood, back to the door, and he had something in his hand.

"I'll take care of this jack-wagon, Katie."

My father opened the door in a heated rush, and put a gun to the man's neck.

"Thought we told you to never come back here, huh?"

The man quickly spun around and the gun flew into the bushes when the man kicked my father. Both men flip-flopped to the ground.

"I told you, Le Mans. I'm a good fighter, hillbilly. I told you, a long time ago."

The cold face of my Dad broke into a giant smile when he knew the man's face.

"Cadeo! I love Cadeo." My father jumped to his feet. "I love this man. Katie, Cadeo, is here in the mountains. I have loved him all my life. This guy saved my life because he was the saving grace with Polly."

"This place, hard to find, Le Mans, very hard to find. Big mountains. Safer than Vietnam."

They walked inside, talked and told stories for a long time. His arm, tucked and deformed, was no different than it was at the POW camp. His hair was gray and a mustache and goatee covered his chin.

"How did you find me?" said my father, lifting him off the ground.

"I saw Polly and Bian last year. They gave me money to surprise you. No taxi drivers wanted to come from Charleston to Fayette County. Five of them said 'no way, man,' and were mean men, Le Mans. Not nice men like you, hillbilly. My pockets were fat, not no more."

"O' God, Cadeo, I thought you were shot the day we escaped the POW camp. I heard guns fired. What happened?"

I took notes and pictures as Cadeo and my father spoke about the time of the escape at Briarpatch and what happened when they were prisoners.

"The gun was fired in the air, shot out of anger for the bad situation and how the Americans escaped." Cadeo held his deformed arm with his good hand and he'd gained weight. "Polly and I went back inside the POW camp, and we planned it that way when we returned from the cave. They left us alone. I was turned loose. No longer was I a prisoner when you left. I wondered if you made it or not. Found freedom, saw the eagle fly in West "By God" Virginia. It's a long, long, long way to West "By God" Virginia from Vietnam, Le Mans. Bus. Train. Car. Plane. A long, long, way."

My father's face beamed with happiness, even smiling in his eyes, and his heart glowed in the way he treated Cadeo, catering to him like a brother.

"In the POW camp, Katie, your father was a jokester, pranking and laughing all the time. So, on the plane I heard a joke, do you mind me saying it?"

"Yes, please," said my father. "I want to hear a good one."

My father leaned in and listened.

"Three moles decided to go on vacation. They walked from Branson to Disneyland, and moles are blind, and used their noses a lot. The Papa mole ran into a wall and could not see, so he said, 'I believe we are at a pancake house, with a thousand pancakes.' The Mama mole slammed into Papa mole, not being able to see, and said, 'I believe we are at a pancake syrup factory. I smell sugar and a thousand different syrups at a hotel.' And they shuffled around and Baby mole slammed into the back of Papa mole, and sniffed, 'We are not in any of those places. All I can smell is mole tail, mole tail, mole tail.' "

Cadeo laughed so hard his shirt button popped and his black coat came open. My father was so happy to see Cadeo that they almost forgot what day and time it was.

"It's time for the big ball to drop, Cadeo."

I filled glasses and we counted down until the ball in NYC fell and the world celebrated a new century together. In Fayette County, fireworks sounded and soared across the open sky and Cadeo had never seen anything like it, and he pounded and beat up our pots and pans. To this day, our cookware has dents and bent handles.

"Almost forgot, Le Mans," said Cadeo, who picked up something off the ground. "I have something for you, a gift. I dropped it when I kicked your gun. I found it in the tree."

"For me?" My father held a cardboard box.

"He has carried that gift around the world." I told Dad.

"I hope to make it here by Christmas, but it did not work that way."

"Go, go, go ahead and open it, Le Mans. Katie, I'm sorry. I have no gift for you."

My father slowly removed the red, white, and blue wrapping paper.

"You being here, Cadeo, is a gift enough." He said. "O' my Lord, Cadeo, where did you get my camera from the war? How did you find it?"

"Is this the camera you took in Vietnam, Dad?" I asked.

Tears rolled down his face, and my father remembered the day he lost his camera and the Viet-Cong took him and kicked him until his eyes were too swollen to see where he'd dropped the camera.

"Yeah, this is the camera."

"What is the lettering?" I asked.

"Nikon, the favorite among photojournalists in Vietnam." My father held the camera, and imagined his time in the Army, boots on the ground, and the day he'd lost it in the mud. "Some guys favored Leica, but I was not a fan. I had a short telephoto lens that day."

Cadeo reached in his black sport coat, inside his hand was another gift.

"How in the world did you find my camera and lens, you are a true saint, Cadeo?"

"Dad, this is amazing stuff."

"I never wanted to go back to the POW camps in 1975, when the war was over, Le Mans." Cadeo got emotional. "I remember you said you lost your camera and lens the day you were taken by the Viet-Cong. I had passed my driving test and I had some courage. I went to the first POW camp, and in 1985, I learned to drive better. Good driver, too. It was still dark when I first arrived. I told myself 'Here comes the sun' and soon I could see a reflection in the mud. I turned over the dirt and it was a lens and beside it was your camera. Later, I drove on to Briarpatch POW camp and saw where Hien died. I lit candles in a good Christian way, said prayers for him, and did not stay long. Here, I have another gift."

"What is it?" My father took the box. "Is this the key to the POW camp?"

"Yeah, Le Mans. Old keys."

They just held each other's shoulder.

While they talked about the keys, I spun and snapped photos with his Army camera.

"The keys and the camera. How?"

"God led me to them. I prayed like you told me, Le Mans."

"Vietnam gets a lot of rain and flooding," my father explained. "Miracle."

I watched Dad hug his Vietnamese friend, Cadeo, and inside his long sleeves and hands, tears. He grinned and his eyes, still wet, caused his voice to break. They became friends all over again.

Later, I loaded the camera, still operational, as if it were new, and snapped a picture of our family friend, Cadeo, beside Sgt. Beau Le Mans, father of two, and the best man I ever knew. That picture is on my desk, a treasure I keep from a world broken by war and politics. Cadeo returned to Vietnam a month later. When I look at people like Polly, Cadeo, Bian, and my father, Doctor Beau Le Mans, and my mother, Doctor Anna Katsen, good people, I see a world of hope down every trail I take in life. I'm glad they met.

On a beautiful autumnal day in 2001, something happened in Wyoming County.

"Do you, Anna Katsen, take Beau Le Mans, as your lawful wedded husband?" said Pastor Weston Laramie.

"I do." said Anna.

"Do you, Beau, take Anna, as you your lawful wedded wife, to have and to hold from this day forward?" said Laramie.

"I found this berry, and I'll make her mine, I do, Anna, I loved you first," said Beau.

Their honeymoon was at Twin Falls State Park, located in Wyoming County.

The Register-Herald
Beckley, West Virginia
4 July 1974

"It's war, and a horrible place for war. War has no winners, only fighters, the dead, and the living, the ones to tell their story after it's all over, and in our hearts, the battle never really ends. Keep yourself alive, they say. Good people are thrown amid politics and the decision of sin, and Vietnam was the worst battle since Hitler ruled the Jews. Leaders with the room and funds to acquire more resources and prove a point against the other side, adding power, the power of young men. It's about power and the loss of love. Until we find love, war is all we have to cheer about and that's no way to live and love."

—Sgt. Beau Le Mans

My Dad, a good spiritual man, Doctor Beau Le Mans, was right about the cold struggle of dominance and power. He told how soldiers who fought and walked away from war, those who lived, battled inside, for their country. War shattered all men, forward afoot, with no way to erase yesterday's battle, a tug of war, heart and mind, broken feelings, from men who prayed and looked for an open door. We can be a loving shoulder and a kind heart, mending and holding in a circle of good company, avoiding war, if we meet all cultures with the same spiritual benevolence shared by the Lord, the true Open Door.

This aforementioned letter was found in my father's Army jacket in 1974, a love letter he left to be read aloud for the world.

—Katie Collins Le Mans, PhD

About the Author

Photo credit: Debra Lester. Thanksgiving 2021, Tybee Island, GA.

PETE was born and raised in West Virginia, alumni of Baileysville High School (Home of the Rough Riders), in Wyoming County; and holds degrees from Concord University, Liberty University, and a Doctorate from Tennessee Temple University. Pete is a U.S. Army veteran and an award-winning painter and international artist.

SOUTHERN FICTION NOVELS: *The Tobacco Barn* (2019), Amazon Top #600, August 2019, *When Geese Fly South* (2021).

WESTERN NOVELS: *Saddles of Barringer* (2021), *Sunday Rain* (2023). In 2023, Pete was inducted into the Western Writers Hall of Fame, Buffalo Center of the West, McCracken Library, Cody, Wyoming.

MEMBERSHIPS: Western Writers of America, Hemingway Society; F. Scott Fitzgerald Society, Thomas Wolfe Society.

Also by Pete Lester:

Made in the USA
Columbia, SC
06 June 2025

59035190R00237